# SWIMMING

## *in the* MOON

Also by Pamela Schoenewaldt

*When We Were Strangers*

# PRAISE FOR
# Pamela Schoenewaldt

"A beautifully rendered and poignant family drama that teems with the life of early twentieth-century America. . . . Schoenewaldt has given us a whole universe between the covers of this book."

—DANA SACHS,

author of *The Secret of the Nightingale Palace* on *Swimming in the Moon*

"Lush with historical detail. . . . Pamela Schoenewaldt delivers another novel full of richly realized characters who transport us to the immigrant neighborhoods of early twentieth-century America."

—JESSICA BROCKMOLE,

author of *Letters from Skye* on *Swimming in the Moon*

"What's at the heart of this beautiful book is not the romance between Lucia and Henryk . . . or even Lucia's passion for social justice and her work for the unions; it's the relationship between mother and daughter."

—PATRICIA HARMAN,

author of *The Midwife of Hope River* on *Swimming in the Moon*

"As a reader and frequent reviewer I long for this kind of lovely prose. A cut above."

—CAROLLY ERICKSON,

author of *The Hidden Diary of Marie Antoinette* on *When We Were Strangers*

"Readable and engaging. . . . This is a story that is not finished simply because the reader has reached the last page—a memorable novel."

—NANCY E. TURNER,

author of *These Is My Words* on *When We Were Strangers*

"Schoenewaldt's heartbreaking debut is the late 19th century immigrant coming-of-age story of poor, plain Irma Vitale. . . . Irma's adventures and redeeming evolution make this a serious book club contender."

—*PUBLISHERS WEEKLY*,

on *When We Were Strangers*

# SWIMMING

## *in the* MOON

## Pamela Schoenewaldt

*wm*

WILLIAM MORROW
*An Imprint of* HarperCollins*Publishers*

P.S.™ is a trademark of HarperCollins Publishers.

HarperCollins books may be purchased for educational, business, or sales promotional use. For information please write: Special Markets Department, HarperCollins Publishers, 10 East 53rd Street, New York, NY 10022.

FIRST EDITION

*Designed by Diahann Sturge*

Library of Congress Cataloging-in-Publication Data has been applied for.

ISBN 978-0-06-220223-9

13 14 15 16 17    OV/RRD    10 9 8 7 6 5 4 3 2 1

*To the memory of my father,*
*Erwin Schoenewaldt, who lived the joy*
*and the dignity of work*

# Contents

One     SINGING TO VESUVIUS   1

Two     FEVER AND CHILLS   14

Three     FALLING ANGEL   31

Four     DIPPING CHOCOLATE   46

Five     TAPPING AT THE WINDOW   58

Six     FROZEN WAVES   80

Seven     NAPLES NIGHTINGALE   98

Eight     AT THE HAYMARKET   117

Nine     YOLANDA   135

Ten     UNACCEPTABLE GESTURES   144

Eleven     PARADISE LOST   165

Twelve     USEFUL WORK   184

Thirteen     "WHAT'S WRONG WITH ME?"   199

Fourteen     READING THE NAMES   211

Fifteen     WE ARE THOUSANDS   226

Sixteen     RAIN ON THE LAKE   244

Seventeen     GERM PLASMA   259

Eighteen     DUSK BY ERIE   277

Nineteen     CORSETS IN KALAMAZOO   292

Twenty     IN THE PARLOR   306

Twenty-one     SANTA LUCIA   317

Epilogue   336

Acknowledgments   339

## Chapter 1

## SINGING TO VESUVIUS

*I spend hours* in trains now or shivering in borrowed Model Ts, bouncing down rutted roads between towns strewn like rocks across frozen fields. I wash in sinks and eat at roadside stands or from china plates, served by ladies with more wealth hung on their bodies than I'll ever hold. I speak in parlors and parks, taverns, churches, and drafty union halls in the great Midwest. I can't go home to Cleveland yet. "Believe me. You *can* win," I tell those whose bodies are deformed by long hours in factories and mills. My voice grows ragged and rough, harsh as a crow's. Who would guess my mother was the Naples Nightingale?

I ask for water, clear my throat, and say: "This is 1913. Your lives *can* change. Think of your children." Workers stare, disbelieving. When their doubts claw me, I hear my mother whisper: "Lucia, even crows must breathe." So I take a breath, plant my feet as singers do, and go on. When women kiss and thank me and men's work-roughed hands press mine, then the torments of this path, the jail slabs where I've slept, the betrayal of friends, and the ache for those abused when I'd sworn they'd be safe, all these things have their purpose.

If our maps show rivers, lakes, or canals, I ask to see them, even when the shallows reek and oil slicks the water. I stand on shorelines and feel my body easing after so many hours of work. Inside laced shoes, my feet are bare again. I'm wading in the Bay of Naples, that warm scoop of blue held in a green embrace, watching the bright bob of fishing boats and hearing peddlers' cries. It's my last summer in Italy, and I'm still Lucia Esposito, passing out of childhood and content enough with my life. Mamma and I are servants to Contessa Elisabetta Monforte in her rosy villa that juts into the bay. I was born in the kitchen and never in my fourteen years slept anywhere but on a narrow cot with Mamma.

Where else would I go? Lemon, orange, fig, and golden plum trees filled the orchard. Lilacs and bougainvillea climbed our walls. On Sunday afternoons, our half-days off, we took bread and wine to the great flat rock turned like a stage to the cone of Vesuvius. If Nannina, the cook, was in good humor, we'd have chunks of cheese and earthen bowls of pasta with beans. Tomatoes and sweet peppers that birds had nibbled were ours. Ripe lemons dropped from trees; we scooped them in our skirts.

"I saw lemons at the fruit market," says a young man from the union hall.

"Were they as big as two fists, with dimpled skin?" I ask. "Heavy as melons and nearly as sweet? Were the skins warm from the sun and the flesh inside cool as a sea breeze?"

"No," he admits, "nothing like that."

It would be hot on those afternoons along the bay, but not the heavy, coal-thick heat of American cities. Summer in Naples brought a soft, wrapping warmth. Our linen shifts, thin with age and damp with sweat, pressed like veils against our bodies. Mamma was beautiful at twenty-eight, with gentle curves, creamy skin, almond eyes, and waves of tumbling glossy black hair. Young men with baskets of mussels cut from the cliffs of Posillipo rowed by our rock, calling: "Come out with us, Teresa. You can bring your sister if you want."

She ignored them or answered back so brusquely that once I asked if it was a mussel diver who had pushed her into the seaweed when she was just fourteen and made her pregnant with me. "No, it was someone from a costume ball. The bastard wore a mask."

"Sing to me," I'd beg in times like these, when anger darkened her face and her body shook. Then she'd turn toward Vesuvius, the brooding mound she loved so much, and sing "Maria Marì," "Santa Lucia," or "Sì, mi chiamano Mimì" from *La Bohème,* her favorite opera. She'd soften as she sang, letting me unpin her hair, wind it into braids and loops or loosen it across her back. In my earliest memory, I'm plunging my small hands into that silky mass and drawing them up like dolphins from the dark waves.

On those Sunday afternoons, children played on jetties, fishermen mended their nets, and lovers nestled between rocks. All were enchanted by her voice soaring and dipping like a seabird, weightless as wind. I leaned against her shoulder. She held me close, our skin melted together, and she was all that I needed.

I never saw signs that her mind was so fragile, or else I read them wrong. Her sudden rages, the precious porcelain figurines that slipped from her hands by seeming accident to smash on marble floors, the count's threats to send us both away, and tense conferences between Contessa Elisabetta and Paolo, the majordomo, were the familiar texture of my days. What did I know of other mothers? Only now, looking back, do these signs speak to me as clearly as black woolen clouds over cornfields tell of coming rain.

If I thought of my future in those days, I imagined us both in service to an aging countess. "Lucia, if you read and do sums, you could manage a great house when you're grown," Paolo said once when we were alone. A wide smile cracked the solemn face he wore in public rooms, and I was thrilled. But what would Mamma do without me? No, I'd stay in the villa forever.

What would I do without the rock of Paolo's steady watching out for us? Once I mused aloud how sweet our lives would be if he were my father. Mamma and I were dusting the sitting room perfumed with lilacs that framed the high windows. Her face turned wistful, then darkened like the moon masked by clouds. "Well he's not your father," she snapped, dusting a porcelain shepherd girl so roughly that it toppled. I lunged across the carpet to catch it.

"But *all* men can't be so bad—" Her glare withered my words. When I reset the little shepherd girl, her silly painted face seemed to mock me, saying: "*I* have a good father."

"Leave me alone! Go help Nannina," Mamma snapped. So I was banished to the kitchen again and set to scrubbing crusted pots.

"What now?" Nannina demanded. I confessed my grating fear: that Mamma saw *him,* the masked bastard, whenever she looked at me. How could I dig him out of me? Hot tears dug holes in the billowing suds.

"Here," said Nannina, handing me a slice of yesterday's bread softened with ricotta. "First, lots of people don't know their fathers, more than you think. And second, that man made you. Do you want to be not born?"

"No, but sometimes she's so—"

"*Difficult.* I know. But she loves you. She loves only you. Remember that."

"*Unstable,*" I'd overheard the count complain to Paolo. I pictured Mamma standing on a tottering rock in rough waters, unstable.

With nightfall, her anger faded. As she brushed and braided my hair for sleep, I tried, as I often did, to have her ease her mood with stories. "Tell me about your father, Mamma."

"He was a—choirmaster." And another fantasy began. Her father was a handsome fisherman, no, no, a cameo carver, a fencing master, an actor from Paris, a German prince. Once, after wine at a street fair: a magical fish-god. Now she muttered: "Here's the truth: he left us and then my mother and brothers died of cholera. I found work with the countess and had you." She never spoke of him again and I understood that we had no family but ourselves. We lived in the villa by Paolo and Countess Elisabetta's good graces. "Close your eyes," she said softly, "and I'll sing you to sleep."

Early the next morning as we swept the terrazzo, she suddenly stopped and hugged me fiercely. "My little Santa Lucia. Nothing bad will ever happen to us. Nothing!"

"No, Mamma, of course not."

Just as suddenly, she set to work again, declaring it was my turn to spin a story. I made us mermaids in a watery villa where the sea washed all dust and dirt away, brought us food, and polished our coral dishes. We slept on seaweed beds that needed no ironed linen sheets. "We can read all day," I continued dreamily. Mamma's creamy brow creased as if this were the strangest fantasy of all.

Looking back, I find it odd that I never thought of leaving Naples. In 1905 ships sailed constantly for America. Peddlers, day laborers, fishermen, even water boys had someone "over there." Paolo and Nannina, our gardener, Luigi, and Alma the laundress all had photographs of family and friends in America. Old Bernardo's marionette shows about his brother's adventures in New York featured splendid painted backdrops of the Statue of Liberty and magnificent palaces on Fifth Avenue. Yet none of these wonders seemed reason enough to leave Naples.

No, our path to exile began with an octopus the summer I was fourteen. Most summers Count Filippo fled the city heat for his hilltop villa in Capri, his pleasure palace where, Nannina muttered scornfully, "*certain women* entertain him." That year malaria trapped him with us, restless and querulous. Early one steaming morning in August, he demanded a lunch of pasta with octopus sauce, mozzarella, tomatoes from the slopes of Vesuvius, and lemon gelato from Caffè Gambrinus.

"Dr. Galuppi said to eat lightly," Countess Elisabetta warned.

"I'll eat what I damn please," he roared. So Nannina sent us shopping with orders to hurry home; the sauce took time to prepare. At the fish market Mamma bargained skillfully for a fat octopus and slapped it dead. The Big Olive Man filled our jar, and then we bought tomatoes, bread, and milky balls of mozzarella. Now we carried the heavy basket together.

At the café we waited for gelato behind women talking excitedly about Milan's great conductor, Maestro Arturo Toscanini, who was arriving soon at the San Carlo opera house. Mamma bent forward to listen, attentive as a bird. I tugged at her arm. "Look, Mamma, it's the nice clerk scooping gelato. Maybe he'll give us a taste."

"Have you heard," said the tall woman, "how handsome Maestro Toscanini is, and how 'gifted'—and not just in music?" She tipped a hat brim toward her friend's ear, whispering. The tinkling crystal of their laughter filled the café.

"Let's go to the opera house," Mamma announced, yanking me out of line. "I'll sing 'Sì, mi chiamano Mimì' and be discovered like Enrico Caruso." She pulled me along Via Roma.

The basket beat my thighs. Her flushed face filled me with dread and I gripped her arm. "No, Mamma, we have to go home. Count Filippo will be angry if we're late."

"The man was *born* angry. He was angry at seagulls this morning. If Toscanini likes my voice, we'll be rich. You'll have tutors. We'll go to great cities." She was panting now, damp curls pressed to her face. "We'll have servants and eat off china plates. This is my chance to be a diva. I might not get another."

"But the octopus sauce—"

She stopped, grabbed my shoulders, and shook me so hard that my head hurt. "*Basta* with the octopus sauce! Do you want to scrub floors all your life?" Near the opera house, an excited crowd spread like a skirt from the main door. "When Toscanini steps out of the carriage, stop him so he hears me sing."

Blood pounded in my head. "How can I stop him?" Knowing nothing about opera, I knew this: servant girls must not bother gentlemen.

"Grab his coattails. There's the coach! Hurry." In the end I never touched him. Frozen with the certainty of disaster, I watched my mother plunge into the crowd, blocking the maestro's path as three little girls brought him roses. She took a breath, settled her feet, opened her mouth, and sang. Terrified as I was, I knew her voice had never been so beautiful, so high and strong and pure. The crowd hushed. Some might have thought she was part of the city's welcome. Arturo Toscanini was indeed handsome, with a white brimmed hat, black eyebrows that swooped over his piercing eyes like a hawk's wings, a fine mustache, and an elegant dove-gray suit. When he cocked his head to listen, I held my breath. Perhaps she *would* be discovered. Then she reached for his jacket.

"No, Mamma, don't touch him!" I called out, but she had already grasped his lapels, as if she were Mimì and he the lover Rodolfo. Toscanini leaped back, snapping his fingers.

*He's calling the guards,* I thought in horror. Yes, red-cloaked officers were pushing toward her while Mamma's voice made glorious waves of sound. I ricocheted between terror and pride: *Mamma, stop, run away!* I thought, and then: *Maestro, make her a diva!*

"The trouble with Naples," Toscanini told a covey of young men, "is that even women of the street sing like angels. Listen to that agility, that timbre. Yet she's obviously a servant or worse and too old for training. I can't use her, but if any of you would like a private serenade, I'm sure it could be arranged." Then he was gone, lithe as a cat slipping into the opera house with a swish of gray tails.

I dropped the basket and raced to Mamma. Her face bloomed with rage. She raised clenched fists, screaming after him: "You bastard! You whore of the rich with your lovers and silk shirts. You came from nowhere and now you won't help an honest woman." When she lunged for the door, I was left grasping her shawl.

The guards seized her. "Let me go! Count Filippo Monforte won't have his servants mistreated," Mamma screeched.

The guards called for a coach and pushed us in. "The basket!" I protested, watching, agonized, as young boys clawed at our basket, fighting for spoils. One waved the octopus. I closed my eyes. What would the count do to us now? In the hot, crowded coach I struggled for breath, wishing yet again that my mother could be reasonable and serene like the countess, who enjoyed elegant chambers that other women cleaned. Yes, the count was a crude and surly husband, but he was often gone. She had leisure to read, visit friends, and stroll by the bay. A rich woman had props that no servant possessed. Of course she'd be more stable, less difficult and vulnerable to the rages that Nannina called my mother's demons.

"If you weren't from a noble household," one guard was barking, "you and your sister would be singing in jail."

"My daughter," said Mamma between gritted teeth. Wedged between guards, she clenched and unclenched her fists, furiously repeating: "Woman of the street! 'If any of you would like a private serenade, I'm sure it could be arranged.' Bastard!" I shrank from the beautiful face, made grotesque by anger.

At the villa, guards marched us up the marble staircase and delivered us to Paolo, relating Mamma's crimes: laying hands on Maestro Toscanini, threatening him and mortifying the city of Naples, where he was an honored guest. If not for Count Monforte's generous patronage of the opera house, we would surely be in jail. "If this woman is *ever* seen near the San Carlo again, if she troubles Maestro Toscanini in *any* way, she'll be locked up. You understand?"

"There will be no trouble, you may assure the maestro," Paolo said with such magisterial certainty that the guards stepped back as if a lord had rebuked them.

When they left, Mamma sank into the French settee before realizing her error: the fine furniture was not for us. She stood again, weaving slightly. I hurried to her side.

"Teresa," Paolo said curtly. "I'll have to tell Count Filippo about this. Of course he'll be angry. He might even send you away. Think of Lucia."

"I *was* thinking of Lucia. If I sang for Toscanini, she wouldn't be scrubbing pots."

"And the octopus? Count Filippo's lunch?"

"At the San Carlo," I stammered.

"I see." Paolo's voice was cold as the ice blocks he ordered. "Well then, Lucia, *you* tell Nannina why she can't satisfy Count Filippo."

I dragged myself to the kitchen, where Nannina slapped me for the money squandered and her own mother's basket lost. "What can I cook for him now? *What?* Tell me!"

"Broth and rice as the doctor ordered," said a soft voice behind me, the Countess Elisabetta. "And that's enough, Nannina. None of this was Lucia's idea. But the count wants to see her." Fear stiffened my legs. A hand on my back pushed me gently along. "Remember that he's sick. I've given him laudanum. He'll be sleeping soon."

Count Filippo's room was a long hall away, but his voice already pounded in my ear as I walked stiffly forward. "*And* I let you keep your little *bastardina*." The voice rose: "Is that right, Teresa? This is how you repay me? Attacking the Maestro Toscanini?"

I was in the doorway now. My mother's back, stiff as a marble column, gave me courage. "She didn't attack him, sir," I said boldly. "She only sang from *La Bohème*."

"You!" He pointed at me, his fleshy, blotched face damp with sweat. "Always reading! What servant girl, what *bastardina*, needs to read? You should be cleaning this cesspool." He flung his hand around the room. Sunlight glistened on the china and wood I dusted daily. He yawned. "Get out, both of you. I'm surrounded by imbeciles. The laughingstock of Naples."

"All Teresa did was sing," said the countess, who had just arrived. "The maestro called her an angel. Who else has a servant like that? You should rest now, Filippo."

"Where's my octopus?"

"I asked her not to get it. Dr. Galuppi said to eat lightly." We slipped out the door as the countess eased the fuming count back under his sheets.

In the windowless chamber off the kitchen where servants ate, I gripped my stool, which seemed to dip and sway as if at sea. If we were turned out with Count Filippo's word against us, what noble house or even decent merchant would hire us? Tradesmen's servants slept in stairways, eating scraps. But Mamma heaved with rage, tearing at her bread, cursing our life. Better a count's servants than any other fate open to us. Couldn't she see that?

"Are you crazy, Teresa?" Nannina demanded. "All the great divas of Europe want Maestro Toscanini. *Madonna mia*, why would he pick you?"

"I don't know," said Mamma in a voice suddenly dry and brittle as eggshells. Her wide, dark eyes raked the room. "Does he know we live here?"

I put my arm around her heaving shoulders. "No, Mamma. He doesn't. He's probably forgotten all about us. There's an opera tonight, remember? He's busy."

"He heard me say 'Count Monforte.' "

"No, he was already in the opera house by then."

"The guards will tell him."

"Maestro Toscanini doesn't speak to guards," Nannina snapped.

Paolo called for us. The matter of Toscanini, piled on other troubles, had given the countess another headache. The count's debts and many dalliances tormented her. He constantly reminded her that *his* money had restored her family's crumbling villa, that all *she* brought to the marriage was a noble title. After each tirade she suffered throbbing pains that only gentle singing eased. Each time my mother's misdeeds threatened our place, I reminded myself that Countess Elisabetta needed her servant's voice.

When the headaches came, she took to the sitting room, put a silk cushion over her eyes to block out light, and had the windows opened to the gentle wash of waves. Then Mamma sang softly: arias she heard from street singers, popular songs, French and Spanish airs she mimicked perfectly. I'd unwind Countess Elisabetta's honey-brown hair, brush it gently, and rub lavender oil into her temples.

These were our golden hours, sweet relief from the cramping pain of work: scrubbing pots and marble floors, polishing silver, cleaning fireplaces, oiling woodwork, blacking shoes, and hanging suspended on ropes to wash crusted salt spray from the high windows. With relief came the pure pleasure of ease in that lovely room. Breezes found it on the warmest day. Damask curtains pulsed gently as if Mamma's voice moved them. Even waves on the rocks below seemed to follow the rhythm of her song.

I see the room now. Tiny rainbows from a crystal chandelier dance over us. Polished silver glows. Sunlight glints softly on marble busts. Nannina's flowers bloom in painted vases. The Persian carpet we beat in the courtyard is soft as moss under my feet, richly colored as a summer garden.

"Read to me now, Lucia," the countess would say as the pain eased. Then I'd open a leather-bound volume of her favorite poet, Giacomo Leopardi. When I stumbled, she'd say, "Read slowly. Think of each word." I would and she'd smile. These moments are wrapped in my heart forever. Yes, I was a servant and the count called me *bastardina*, but those afternoons I swam in beauty and the joy of being needed for more than the strength of my arms.

"If we'd had a child like you," the countess once said when we were alone, "perhaps the count would be different." What if I *had* been hers, I wondered. Then hot guilt seized me for abandoning my mother, even in dreams. "Lucia Esposito," I repeated silently. "That's who I am. Lucia Esposito, Lucia Esposito, daughter of Teresa Esposito."

Laudanum lulled the count to sleep and the countess dismissed us when the headache passed. She would review accounts with Paolo and then retire. He met her in the hallway. I noticed, but put no meaning to how slowly they walked to her chambers and how close together.

Mamma and I went to our cot, sweating in the summer night. "Woman of the street," she muttered. "He meant *whore*."

"He also called you an angel. And we're safe now. You just shouldn't trouble him again."

"I'm not like you. I don't read books," she said bitterly. "All I can do is sing. You're Countess Elisabetta's little pet, but what about *me*? Maybe she'll find another singing servant and send me away. I'll never be a diva. I'll never be anything." She turned to the wall, shoulders heaving.

I lay rigid, shamed and helpless. In the heavy darkness, I imagined myself vanished, like a reflection in wet marble, gone when the marble dries. Would Mamma be happier then? The darkness blurred with tears. Our damp shoulders nearly touched, yet our pains were oceans apart. When the great pendulum clock tolled midnight, Mamma slipped barefoot from the room. Was she taking one of her nighttime walks? I listened with dread for the low groan of the great front door. Silence. When she finally returned, a cool hand touched mine.

"Where did you go?" I whispered.

"For laudanum. Do you want some?"

"No."

"Of course not. You're a child. You don't worry about anything." She gathered me in her arms, stroking my hair. "I'm so sorry, Lucia," she whispered. "You know I love you. It's like—when fog covers Vesuvius, it's still there, but you can't see it. Remember that with me. I'll always love you. Always!" she said, her breath hot on my neck. "Now sleep." I did, although in my jagged dreams a sea-monster count hounded us into a watery maze.

## Chapter 2

## FEVER AND CHILLS

*Malarial fever brought* Count Filippo near delirium by morning. He thrashed on his massive rosewood bed, cursing the African heat and demanding more breezes. For hours I beat the sodden air with ostrich feathers bound to a bamboo rod. Every muscle burned. If this was punishment for the octopus, it was more than enough.

"Take me to Capri," he demanded. "Where are you, Bettina, Rosalia, and Isabella, my ripe peach?" At each name, the countess winced.

Paolo had asked Dr. Galuppi to bring a vial of his best Peruvian quinine, told Nannina to prepare for the doctor's notorious sweet tooth, and relieved the countess of her sickroom duties. "Keep fanning until the fever turns to chills," Paolo whispered to me. I pictured Roman galley slaves chained to bamboo rods.

At last the doctor came, administered the quinine, and wedged himself into a brocade chair. "Now if your woman will bring me— Ah, yes." Mamma had come with a decanter of Scottish whiskey, our best Venetian goblets, and a plate of rum-soaked babas. I gripped my bamboo rod as he touched the curve of Mamma's bodice, the thick rope of her braid, her slender waist, and her cheeks, white with rage.

"More wind . . . harder," the count snapped when Mamma left. Sweat soaked his linen nightshirt. I had already changed the bedsheets. Yet he swore I let him "wallow like a pauper in filth." We couldn't wash, dry, and iron linens fast enough for the sweat, vomit, and soil of his illness. No amount of rosemary and lavender oil could sweeten that room.

Dr. Galuppi tucked a bit of snuff in his ample nose and watched me fan the count, round eyes roaming my body until, tiring of this, he took out a medical text and read while the count grunted himself into fitful sleep.

As Paolo had predicted, fever passed swiftly into chills. The count woke with a start and demanded that I cease my infernal fanning and bring blankets, furs, and a fire in the brazier.

"Do it, girl," the doctor said, barely looking up. With the fire lit, sweat poured down our faces, but he kept avidly reading, sometimes sketching strange machines in a leather notebook.

"Close the windows and lie with me. Rosalia, keep me warm!" the count moaned. Slowly the quinine did its work. The tremors ceased and he entered a lull between fever and chills.

"Good, now try *my* tonic," Galuppi announced, closing his book and pouring two liberal glasses of whiskey. He motioned me to a chair in the corner. "Sit there. We may need you."

I took my seat, and in the manner of gentlemen, they promptly ignored me, as if I were one more marble bust along the wall. Which was the worst of a servant's lot, I often wondered: the ceaseless work, pain in every joint, raw, cracked skin, and long hours, or the airy dismissal into nothing, to be called back to life with a flick of the hand? When the count waved at the fur mountain over him, I was to understand: take this away. "A man can go mad in the company of servants," he muttered.

"Certainly, certainly. Everyone's talking about the scene between that woman of yours and Maestro Toscanini. Clearly she's a hysteric of the most troublesome kind. However, she's a great favorite of your wife, I believe." The count nodded, sighed, and pressed his head into the mounded pillows.

"I have made a careful study of hysteria," the doctor continued, tapping his book. "The condition is often curable by means of intriguing mechanisms, sadly underused in Italy. With these mechanisms our Anglo-Saxon brethren have excised madness from diverse subjects, or at the least made them more malleable."

I must have appeared to be attending to the gentlemen's talk, for the count lifted a fleshy hand from the coverlet, indicating me. "You. Leave us. Close the door."

"Yes, sir."

In the dim cool of the corridor, I breathed deeply, free from the sickroom stench. Nannina and Mamma were helping the exhausted laundress. Paolo and the countess must have been reviewing the household accounts again, for I heard murmuring in her study. Barefoot, I crept back toward the count's chamber.

"Copious injections of ram's blood . . . patients as tranquil as sheep," I heard through the door. The count must have spoken. "Of course, some casualties. There's much to be learned." The rosewood bed creaked. In a rustle of sheets, surely I mistook the next report. Was it possible that doctors closed inmates in coffins pierced with holes, lowered them into water until the bubbles ceased, then hauled up the coffins and tried to revive the near-drowned victims? "Confronting death calms the lunatic." Some muttering followed, which I couldn't understand, and then: "Whirling chair . . . electric shocks to the female organs sometimes efficacious." I leaned against a marble column, sickened. The doctor's voice again: "You must eat lightly now, Count. I'll ring for the girl." Panicked,

I scurried to the kitchen to rinse my face, steady myself, and seem to be returning for my orders.

"Count Filippo is sleeping quietly," Paolo announced after our servants' dinner. "You're free until morning. I will attend to the count." But I noticed that he didn't turn left to the sickroom but right, to the private rooms of the countess.

"She isn't feeling well?" I asked.

Mamma and Nannina exchanged glances. Nannina's brow arched. "I suppose they're reviewing accounts."

Mamma stood up. "Lucia, let's go swimming. Come, there's a full moon." Soon we were running down to the rocks, hair flying behind us. I remember that night as pure joy. Still in our sweat-stiffened linens, we swam through a milk-white path laid out by the moon that seemed to stretch across the bay to Vesuvius. Warm waves washed our loosening bodies apart and then together. We caught the iridescent waters in our hands as the sickroom smells and weariness drained away. We were mermaids, princesses, sisters.

"We're almost free," I said into the star-sparkled heavens. "Either the count dies, or he gets better and goes back to Capri until the wintertime."

"And when he goes, the doctor goes," Mamma added dreamily. "If he doesn't, I'll poison his whiskey." Floating on the gently heaving water, we both laughed. My hand caught hers in the water. *I'll treasure this night forever,* I thought, and I did. It buoyed me through rough waters. It's here with me now, so far away from Naples. Too soon, bell towers rang for midnight as we dried ourselves, wrung out our shifts, and hurried barefoot to the villa. It would be our last night on our cot.

When I brought Count Filippo his breakfast, he seemed much improved, his color returned and brow clear of sweat. A morning breeze had freshened the room. Perhaps shamed by the basins of foul waste

I'd taken out in the days of his sickness, he was even cordial, using my name, thanking me for his tray and asking to see the countess "when it is quite convenient."

"He's better," I reported happily to Nannina.

"Good, but if you don't have to be nursemaids today, it's time to scrub the stairs," she observed.

I groaned. Cleaning the great marble staircase was the job I hated most. Mamma and I worked together, polishing each step with pumice stone, and then scrubbing with soap that burned the eyes. Our knees, shoulders, elbows, and hands ached. Usually she sang or we told stories as distraction from the pain. That day she was silent. We seemed to be scrubbing the Alps. Then suddenly, wonderfully, I was released.

Paolo called down the wet stairway that the Duchess Annamaria was receiving that morning and the countess wanted me to go with her, carrying Nannina's almond cake and helping servants at the palace, but first I must braid my hair neatly and put on my best dress. Mamma's dark eyes squeezed to slits as I hurried to change. I remember with bitter regret her hunched shoulders and flame-red hands as I passed her soon after, easing carefully down the wet steps, attentive to the cake on our silver tray and my clean, starched apron, as if I were the mistress and she the serving girl.

"I'll be back soon, Mamma," I promised. She didn't answer, and ever since, the sting of lye soap has recalled for me the sting of wrenching guilt when I tripped off like a little lady, leaving her to scrub the steps. What defense do I have but youth? As I walked along the elegant Riviera di Chiaia with the countess in her splendid rose morning dress, my spirits lifted and the old fantasy returned: I was the treasured daughter of a countess. Tutors would come to me. I would be presented in society, never insulted, never called *bastardina*. The count, my father, would have Paolo's face and manner, wise, kind, and comforting.

We reached the palace. "Bring the cake to the kitchen," the countess said, "and help with the sewing for now." And so my fantasy ended. In the servants' hall I was given bread, cheese, and a chair by a lighted window. After lunch, for entertainment with coffee, I was called to the drawing room. I'd never seen such a dazzle of jewels and lace, beautiful women chattering like birds, noblewomen and ambassadors' wives. I was to read Dante aloud, thus refuting a claim made by a viscountess that lower classes were incapable of comprehending the Poet. I was given a text, and the countess showed me where to begin.

I read slowly, attentive to meter, as she'd taught me. The chattering slowly ceased. Painted lips opened slightly, as if one of their fluffy lapdogs had commenced a recitation. Joy and pride infused me in that shimmering room as the divine words flowed from my mouth. The maid discreetly set a water goblet at my side, and I, Lucia Esposito, drank from crystal among noblewomen.

Prettily sent away after reading, I dropped stitch after stitch, reimagining my triumph until the housekeeper said: "Go home now, girl. Your mistress says she won't need you this afternoon." So I was a nameless "girl" again. I dawdled back to the villa, wandering through a park along the bay, watching rich children with their hoops and young dandies on bicycles. How often would I curse my ambling feet that afternoon!

Nannina was chopping onions when I returned, and Paolo was in his windowless, ledger-lined office. "Teresa's ironing," he said over his shoulder. "Go help her." I never reached the laundry. A strange whirling sound came from the terrazzo. Looking down, I gasped. The count and Dr. Galuppi sat watching a spectacle: a huge, hairy man, a hulking gorilla, turned a giant wheel that drove a spinning chair. A woman was strapped in this chair, black hair like a whipping tail behind her, the face blurred. I peered more closely. Mamma! Now I was running, flying downstairs. *The bastards, the bastards, the bastards!*

Once on the terrazzo, I saw that her face was sickly white, mouth stretched out in wordless howl, her apron stained with vomit. When I screamed, *"Stop! Let her go!"* my voice vaulted back from the walls, the orchard, and the bay. I screamed myself hollow, stunned by the sound. Both gentlemen stared. A servant dared shout at them? The gorilla man stopped dead. As the whirling chair slowed, clattering to stillness, my mother flopped forward like a rag doll, black hair matting her face.

"Ugo, bring the girl here," the doctor snapped. Rushing to help Mamma, I was scooped up and delivered to the doctor. Despite his fleshy frame, the grip on my arms was crushing. "Start the chair again! Don't move, girl, or we'll spin her another hour, and you as well for your insolence."

"Never mind, I've seen the chair," said Count Filippo like a child bored with an old toy. He cut himself thick slices of prosciutto with a long, ivory-handled knife and refilled his goblet as Mamma retched. My stomach heaved with hers. At a sign from the doctor, Ugo untied her; she tumbled to the ground.

"Mamma!"

"Be quiet, girl, or we *will* spin her again!" Galuppi said. "Ugo, bring the Taming Box." Then to the count: "I copied this design from an American journal." Eagerly, the count examined a padded black box designed to fit over a human head. Galuppi demonstrated the gag, blindfold, earplugs, airholes, and chair whose seat was a chamber pot. Mamma hadn't moved. When I tested the doctor's grip, it tightened as he continued placidly: "Immobilized, cut off from external senses, alone with his—or her—madness, the tranquilizing effect can be profound. Even for extreme cases"—he nodded toward the hulking Ugo—"the mere threat of it induces obedience. Thus the device both cures and pacifies the most difficult inmates."

The count looked in wonder at the box. "Fascinating. How long are the patients contained?"

Mamma heaved. I tried again to yank free, but a jerk of my arm sent tearing pains to the shoulder. "Twelve, twenty-four, even thirty-six hours for extreme cases." In their excitement, neither noticed Mamma rising slowly to her haunches, one hand parting a curtain of hair. Nor did they see Paolo hurrying toward us. "You heard the girl scream," Galuppi continued. "Was that a normal sound, a sane human voice? I tell you, my friend, hysteria can lurk in the young. It travels through blood; like mother, like daughter. Ugo, prepare the girl." I was lifted in massive arms, helpless as a rag.

Mamma tried to stand; her legs crumpled. Paolo had reached the count. "We've had no trouble with Lucia, sir," he panted. "She's quite obedient."

Sweat beaded the count's brow. "Nonetheless, Dr. Galuppi will examine her. You may watch, Paolo."

The doctor's fleshy hand palpated my skull. "The science of phrenology is exquisite." He stopped at my temples. "Here, for instance, we find stubborn willfulness."

"We do not find her so, sir," Paolo declared.

Galuppi smiled. "I advise the Taming Box to inoculate against hysteria."

As Count Filippo watched me struggle, his nostrils flared. None of the men saw Mamma moving stealthily to the table. *No, Mamma, don't. Yes! Save me.* The box was coming closer, the manacles readied for me.

In a flash swift as a tiger's leap, Mamma lunged forward, seized the decanter, and threw it at the count. It shattered on his bulging brow. Sometimes in dreams I see my last memory of him: blood streaming down the starched white shirt. My mother snatched the ivory-handled knife, light on her feet as a street fighter, facing now Ugo, now the count and doctor. Where did she learn this? When she lunged at Ugo, he jumped. The great hands opened. My trap sprung, I ducked away.

"Go, Lucia! Run!" Paolo hissed.

Mamma was nailed to the earth. I jerked her free. "Come!" The knife clattered on stone and she moved stiffly as a doll across the wide terrazzo.

"Paolo, stop them!" I heard behind us.

We reached the street. Mamma was stumbling, still dizzy, as Paolo appeared, grasped her arm, and helped me pull her between water carts and peddlers. She stopped to vomit; he let her gulp water at a fountain and then hurried us through the wide avenues before plunging into the warren of dark, narrow streets winding through the Spanish Quarters, where we could slow to a walk. "Bastards!" Mamma panted. "I'll kill them both."

"Teresa, you understand who you are and who he is? A word from Count Filippo and you'll be locked in a prison forever. The countess couldn't help you. It might even give him pleasure to have her see you locked away."

I imagined Mamma crouched on straw, chained. "He went for Lucia," she said flatly. "You saw him. The pig."

"And he had Mamma in that chair," I added. "He tortured her."

"I only threw—"

Paolo held up his hand. "Teresa! Lucia! There was blood, a decanter thrown at your master's skull, a knife drawn. No judge in Naples would excuse this. Come with me. Hurry." We followed, my head pounding. So suddenly we had become criminals, exiles from our sunny villa.

These were the dark quarters of the very poor. Doorways bulged with men and women catching faint light for their trades. Children's black feet had gone without shoes all summer. Their skin wept with sores. Even in servant dress, we seemed out of place. Three boys ceased a game with pebbles, silently drawing closer, mouths open like young dogs surrounding a weaker prey. Was this a bitter fairy tale? Would we be abandoned without a trail of crumbs to find our way home? And where *was* our home now?

Paolo barked crisp words and the boys drew back. He stopped us. "Listen, Terea," he said slowly, as if to a child. "You can't stay in Naples. At the *least* you'll be delivered to Galuppi for his experiments. It will be of absolutely no consequence to him or Count Filippo whether you survive. Or you'll end your days in prison as a warning to other servants. There is no place safe for you in the city."

My mother's face crumpled. Her lips moved without sound. I spoke for her: "Paoo, you saw what he did. Can't you talk to the countess, like other times? Can't you explain?"

"Lucia, this isn't 'other times.' Your mother attacked a nobleman. I told you, the countess can't save you anymore. You must save yourselves."

"Where can we go, what can we do?" Every other fear I'd faced, hard waves heaving me against rocks, rats in the garden, or rough men on the street, was nothing to this. The world was a black, swirling pit about to consume us.

Paolo wiped his brow with a handkerchief that blazed white in the dim street. "You have to go to another city far away. Rome is too close. Perhaps Milan or Venice."

Mamma looked dazed. "I was born here. How can I leave?"

"We'll go to America," I announced. Both of them stared at me, and even I was stunned. Where had the word *America* come from, like a shaft of icy wind on a steaming summer day? Yet certainty hot through me, more strongly than ever in my life: "They wouldn't look for us in America. They won't think to do that."

Mamma shook the thought away. "How? We can't pay the passage, and I want to stay in Italy."

But Paolo was already considering. "America, yes. You could borrow enough for the tickets and provisions from Countess Elsabetta and then pay her back when you find work. My cousin Rosanna has a board-inghouse in Cleveland." He turned to me. "Now Lucia, you could stay. You only witnessed the crime. We might convince Count Filippo to keep you if Teresa goes. Or the countess could find you a post in another city. I always said you could rise in a great house."

For an instant Mamma's fate dimmed in the glare of my possible future: me in leather shoes and a fine, lace-trimmed housekeeper's dress, gliding down perfectly clean marble stairs that I never scrubbed, wearing white gloves to check for dust. Then I saw Mamma, her face etched with fear. I saw her on her knees as I'd passed her with the countess. I saw her sickened from the torture chair, yet gathering strength to save me.

Paolo shook my shoulder. "Lucia, decide." Mamma was staring at me, immobile.

"We'll go together."

"You're sure?"

"Yes, I'm sure."

"You understand that means *two* fares to repay."

"I'll work in a factory," Mamma announced. "Lucia can go to school."

School? This was a new thought. To sit at a desk, reading. To write instead of scrubbing floors. All the fairy tales of America, the streets paved in gold and opportunities dangling like ripe fruit, were nothing beside a pen in my hand, the raw chafe of my knees and winter cracking of my fingers slowly healing as I turned my life to books.

"You'll need documents to emigrate," Paolo was saying. "But if the count suspects you're leaving, he has powerful friends to block you."

Mamma wilted. "So—we can't go?"

Paolo wiped his long face. "Papers can be forged. Authorities can be paid." He was moving again, and we hurried after him. "Meanwhile you'll stay with my cousin Ciro." We threaded farther. Some streets were beaten dirt, others paved in basalt, black as the smoke-soaked buildings above them. We stopped at what seemed an alcove scooped from stone, a mattress maker's shop. Paolo spoke in dialect to a lean, stooped man with his own long cheeks, transferring a small purse with a gesture subtle as a handshake.

"This is Ciro," he told us briefly. "He'll keep you until your papers are ready and make sure nobody tells the police. I'll come back and take you to the ship."

"We won't see the countess again?"

"Lucia, try to understand: Count Filippo will ask if she's seen you. Do you want her to lie? Do you want to risk being seized by the police? I'll say I chased after you and lost you in the city."

Memories of the villa tumbled through my mind: afternoon light pouring into the sitting room, the garden and orchard, the sea, Vesuvius, our rock where Mamma sang, Nannina's kitchen and gruff kindness. Most of all, Countess Elisabetta's gliding presence and many interventions for our sake, her calm voice and white hands on mine, teaching me to write and to read aloud, her patience when I stumbled. I'd never see her again, never hear that gentle voice? Now America seemed like exile.

"If you write to her, I'm sure she'll write back."

"She will?" Nobody had ever written to me. A *countess* might write "Dear Lucia"?

"Of course she'll write, but think, now. I'll bring your clothes. What else do you want from the villa?"

"My Leopardi book, it's under the bed," I ventured, ashamed to add another task.

"I'll bring it. I'll arrange everything. But you must stay hidden."

Ciro hurried us inside. His home was a *basso,* two rooms, one behind the other. Only the first, his workshop, had a window to the street. Bales of wool and rolls of stiff cloth filled the hot, tiny space, leaving only a clearing for the stove, small table, and three stools. Ciro's wife wordlessly handed us hunks of bread. We ate nestled against a wool bale. Surely we were safe here, deep in the entrails of the city. Who would think to look in a mattress maker's shop?

"Nannina's sister went to America," Mamma reminded me. "She used to be a chambermaid. Now she makes silk flowers in her own shop. Finish your bread, Lucia. Don't leave any for rats."

I wanted to talk about the villa and all that we'd miss, but Mamma's frozen face said to ask no questions. So in the stifling late-afternoon heat, I watched snowy threads of wool and cotton float by. Ciro and his wife, working not three paces from us, were wrapped in fog.

"Mamma, what's Cleveland like?" I ventured finally, when our silence grew unbearable. *Cleveland*—even the word tasted foreign in my mouth.

"It must be a city like Naples. Don't think about it."

How could I *not* think about a change so sudden and huge that I'd made in our lives? But I was young, and dreams bore me onward like a ship. Everything was easy in America, many said. Perhaps they were right, I thought drowsily. In the hot, close air, pressed into the wool bales, I slept.

When darkness came, Ciro called us to the doorway. Languid breezes stirred. Men were coming home with peddlers' sacks and wooden carts. Waves of smells lapped past us: beans and pasta boiling, chamber pots, garlic, rosemary, onions and fish, hot oil, wine and cut lemons, the tang of wet stone, and everywhere the sweat of those who worked hard in the sun and slept in their clothes.

Soon the street was lined with stools, old chairs, and mounds of rags for nesting babies. Ciro's wife had made pasta with lentils, onions, and chunks of lamb, evidently bought with Paolo's purse, and many turned curiously to sniff. She passed a plate of *struffoli*, little balls of sweet fried dough in sugar syrup. Old men played cards on boards held between their knees. Shouts and talk ran up and down the street.

"We could live here," Mamma whispered dreamily. "We don't have to go to America."

"The count would find us. He'd give you to the doctor."

She closed her eyes. "I suppose so. Everything will be different in America. New songs—"

"Yes, of course." She would shed her old demons like snakeskin. I'd go to school. We'd be happy forever.

The music grew louder, thicker, fueled by more voices. Mandolins, tambourines, and a guitar appeared. A song began, "Te voglio bene assai." When Mamma joined the chorus, weaker voices fell silent around the trio: a man, Mamma, and another woman, their voices leaping back from the walls, soaring over a bed of clapping, strings, and flutes. Children danced between us. As stars slowly filled the slice of sky overhead, other songs ran up and down the street like rag balls kicked by boys: ballads, love songs and mockeries of love, sea chants, and aches for the beauty of Naples.

In the loudest songs, under clapping and tambourines, I even dared to sing. Mamma always said my voice was like a crow's. "You're not even trying!" she accused me, no matter how I strained to catch the notes or hear when I'd fallen flat. But nobody noticed now or complained about my voice.

Wine was passed in jugs. Slowly, singing faded into patches of talk.

Many spoke of America. One man had just returned from Pittsburgh, where iron was melted like butter in cauldrons as big as a *basso*. "Flesh can melt there too," he said, showing his calf with skin gouged out nearly to the bone. "I came home before I lost my strong arms as well."

A young woman pulled him close. "And now you'll never leave again, Totò."

"Don't worry. That man was born unlucky," Ciro whispered to us. "Not everybody gets hurt, even in the mills."

"What's America like?" I asked.

Totò waved at the street. "Nothing like this."

"Did you learn English?" I asked eagerly.

"How? I lived in a boardinghouse with Italians, worked twelve hours, ate, slept, and worked again. Every fourteen days, they worked us two straight shifts. A man could die then and never know it. Why learn English? You're just pieces of their machine."

"Breathe," Mamma muttered. I did, slowly calming myself. Our life would be nothing like Totò's. I'd go to school; my mother would never work in a steel mill. As the moon rose overhead, weary breezes climbing up from the sea brought hints of cool. Dingy cats roused themselves to wander, wary of any touch. One by one, children curled in their mothers' laps like sleeping kittens were scooped up and taken inside. Up and down the street sounded the refrain, *"Buona notte, sogni d'oro,"* good night, golden dreams.

Ciro had made us a bed in loose wool. As guests, we had the front room; his family crowded into the breathless cave behind us. "You hear him coughing?" Mamma whispered. "He'll die early. Mattress makers always do." We listened to the coughs, cats and children crying, and distant scratch of rats. Wine and heat had made me groggy, but I'd never spent a night so far from the sea. New fears lapped over me, and I tugged at Mamma's sleeve: "Will Count Filippo blame the countess if he can't find us? What if she gets her headaches and we're not there? Are you listening?"

"Stop worrying. She's rich. And the headaches might stop if I'm not making problems for her."

"Totò said everything's different in America. Suppose we don't like it?"

"Do you *want* everything the same?" she demanded fiercely. "Should we be servants again? Should we go back to the doctor?"

"No," I whispered. Guilt squeezed my chest and I brushed fluffs of wool from her sweaty face. "No counts, no doctors. We'll be free."

"Yes, free. Try to sleep now."

But I couldn't. My mind rolled back. Had our troubles truly started with the octopus and Maestro Toscanini? Or earlier, when I cried too much as a baby? The count was cruel, but was there something in us that provoked him? Would bad luck cross the ocean with us? Were there doctors like Galuppi in America? "Stop moving," Mamma said. "You worry too much." Pushing down a rise of wool between us, she sang "Santa Lucia," each verse more slowly until she'd sung us both to sleep on our slick of sweat in a gently heaving woolen sea.

I woke coughing in the morning. It was the wool, Ciro explained. Since I couldn't go outside and risk being seen, I sat by the window, wheezing, inventing number problems for myself or reciting poetry I'd learned from the countess.

"Amazing," said Ciro politely, "all those pretty words in your head."

Paolo came in the afternoon, elated. The duchess had arranged our documents; a ship was leaving in the morning. "Count Filippo is furious he can't find you. He says that servants attacking their masters was how the French Revolution began."

"The police are looking for us?" I asked anxiously.

"Yes, but not at the port. He knows you don't have money for passage or family to help. Tonight we'll give him laudanum to sleep late. I'll come before dawn. Be ready."

How could I sleep? I sat in Ciro's doorway, breathing my last Naples air. In early-morning darkness we slipped through the quarter's silent streets. Our trunk had been stowed. Paolo gave us third-class tickets and a purse from the countess to begin life in America. We must stay in the crowd of passengers, ready to board at noon.

"Don't worry," I said. "We'll pay back the countess as soon as we're settled."

Paolo's clean, groomed hand patted my shoulder. "I see our Lucia's growing up." He took out a carefully written card. "Here's my cousin Rosanna's address in Cleveland. I sent her a telegram to expect you and you should send another from New York."

Morning light caught the long face I'd seen every day of my life. Now I'd leave that grave and kindly presence, the nearest I'd had to a father. He was clear water untroubled by Mamma's moods, a shielding rock against the count's cruelties, a mirror to my deep affection for the countess. He never once mocked my struggles to read or called me *bastardina*. Now when I threw myself in his arms, he took out a crisp linen handkerchief to wipe my eyes and his.

"Do well in America, Lucia. Be good and study hard. Write to the countess. Take care of your mother." He smiled and kissed us both. "Teresa, watch your temper and try to be happy. It's a new start for you." Then he was gone and our life by the Bay of Naples was over, like a song cut off too soon.

## Chapter 3

## FALLING ANGEL

*We were Teresa* and Lucia Esposito on the ship from Naples, on Ellis Island, and into Pennsylvania. And then we were not. I'd been seasick and sleepless for our passage and struggled to look healthy for the immigration officers. At last on the train for Cleveland, I slumped against a window, drowsing as rolling green fields ran past us like a vast sea.

Mamma had been anxious ever since we left New York, troubled by the broad swaths of forests. "It's so empty here!" she fretted. "Nobody told me." She held our envelope of documents, turning it over and around on her lap, running the dull edge along her palm with such force that I roused myself to trap her hand in mine.

"We'll be in Cleveland soon. Everything will be good there."

We were slicing through a forest. She stared at the blur of trees crowding along the tracks and announced: "I know where the trouble started."

"What trouble?"

"It's because of my grandfather," she said so loudly that even Americans turned to stare. "That's why there was always something wrong with me."

"There's nothing wrong with you," I said fiercely, forgetting to whisper.

She shook her hand free. "My grandfather Domenico was exposed, put up for adoption. That's why our name is Esposito. You didn't know?"

"Of course not. You never told me."

"I'm telling you now. His mother didn't want him. Maybe he was too much trouble. When he was five she took him to an orphanage to give away to anyone who needed a boy with a beautiful voice. A priest picked him for the chapel choir and named him Domenico Esposito. Aren't you ashamed now to be Lucia Esposito?"

"It's just a name, Mamma. Everybody needs a name."

Mamma clutched our documents. "We'll have bad luck in America. Galuppi said I was a hysteric. Something bad will happen to us. I know it." She held her head, staring across a long green valley.

"No, Mamma, no." When did the train grow so cold and the wheels begin rattling so loudly?

A squat man with a wide mouth sat across from us, dressed like an American and reading an American newspaper. He folded it carefully and addressed Mamma in an accent so familiar he might have lived beside our villa. "*Signora*, calm yourself. You don't need to be an Esposito. I myself was born Tommaso Russo. Now I'm Thomas Ross. You can be who you want to be in America." Schools wouldn't need my Italian papers, he explained. They'd take me with any name. Factories would hire or not hire Mamma for the work that she could do. Many immigrants changed their names or made them more American.

"Why did you change yours?" I asked. "What's wrong with Russo?"

"I live in Harrisburg and bake for immigrants. I make their focaccia, Irish soda bread, brown bread, rye, pumpernickel, sourdough, challah, babka, and stollen. I cut up loaves and hand the pieces around so people can try all the breads of America. So I gave myself an American name." Mamma turned her documents over and over. The baker smiled placidly.

"You were just in Italy?" I asked to fill the silence.

"I went home to see my family. I go every three years." So easily then, one could move back and forth across this great distance, living in two lands, like a tree rooted on both banks of a river. We could do the same if police weren't watching for us in Naples. "Here's Harrisburg," he said cheerfully, gathering his bags. "And there they are!" A family dressed in American clothes stood waving, all short and smiling like Tommaso/ Thomas, who hurried off the train to meet his wife and children.

"Mamma," I said as he left, "*we* could change our names too."

She nodded, her eyes glittering. "Yes, let's. Who should we be?" Her voice turned shrill with pleasure. "Russo's too common. Verdi, Garibaldi, or Leopardi like your poet friend."

"Vesuvius," I ventured, and she laughed so loudly that people turned again to stare.

"Caruso. Da Vinci."

"Didn't Toscanini say you sang like angel? We need a good angel in America. We could be Teresa and Lucia D'Angelo."

"D'Angelo, D'Angelo, D'Angelo." She leaned back, half closing her eyes as she did when spinning stories. "So . . . I was married. My husband, Pietro D'Angelo, worked inside the cathedral in Naples, painting a fresco high up in the nave. It would show Our Lord and His angels welcoming the Blessed Virgin into Paradise. One day the scaffolding cracked. My husband fell and died, crushed on the marble floor."

"It's bad luck when an angel falls," I added to her tale.

"Yes, Pietro's soul would curse all who worshipped there because the scaffolding was rotten. So the priest gave me money to erase the curse. We used it to come to America." She smiled. "It *could* be a true story."

"Let's make it true," I said.

Together, like bad children, we ripped the documents to pieces. We were crossing a bridge over a broad river: the Susquehanna, I realized later. Dividing the bits, we pushed them out the window, watching them flutter, spin, and flash white against the sky.

"There," said Mamma happily. "Now we're new." I pictured *Lucia D'Angelo* in looping black script. I imagined presenting myself to strangers: "I am Lucia D'Angelo." In tunnels, I peered at my reflected face. Here was Lucia D'Angelo. She would speak English perfectly, go to school, and wear American clothes. Perhaps her voice would change and she could even sing. At least when she spoke, people would stop and listen as they did when Mamma sang. *Hysteric, difficult, unstable, bastardina,* all the old, bad words of our old life were left behind in the green river valley.

"Lucia D'Angelo, sleep now," my mother said gently. We had been up long before dawn to see the Liberty Lady. As we rattled west, I dreamed of Pietro D'Angelo, the marvelously gifted artist who leans too far from the scaffold while painting angels. A foot reaches frantically for purchase in air and too-mortal D'Angelo falls, arms flailing. Priests run to catch him, black robes streaming. Too late for his poor twisted body splayed on the marble floor. "He died for holy work," the priests say. "His soul will be lifted into glory." At the requiem, Mamma sings "Ave Maria." The priests give us money out of love and pity. My dream melted into sleep so sound that we were entering Cleveland's Union Depot before I woke. Mamma had already gathered our bags.

On the platform, a tall woman with Paolo's long, scooped cheeks and square shoulders surveyed passengers spilling off the train.

"Rosanna?" I hazarded and was immediately corrected: "*Roseanne.* It's more American."

Her high-necked blouse blazed white against the smoky green of a long woolen skirt. "Made right here in Cleveland," Roseanne boasted, stroking the fabric. "No finer quality in America." She had wide painted lips and bulging eyes. "The train was very late," she scolded, "but I waited as a favor to Paolo so you wouldn't be taking the streetcar alone. And I bought your first tickets."

"A favor to Paolo," Mamma muttered as Roseanne helped us carry our bags to the streetcar, hoist them up, and claim a brass pole. In Naples I'd only ridden streetcars with the countess. Otherwise I walked. Everyone rode here, clerks and suited ladies, workers and immigrants like us.

"Standing is better," Roseanne advised as we rattled away. "You never know who just used those seats. Maybe Greeks or Bohemians. Slavs, people with fleas," she shouted in our ears and then related her story: she'd come from Pozzuoli on the Bay of Naples seven years ago with her husband, a stonemason who made enough to buy her a boardinghouse before he died of influenza. Her talk was pocked by English words and hard to follow: "Now be careful here because of the . . . And don't ever . . . because Americans will think you're . . ." She spoke in solid certainties, her words like stakes driven into stone. I studied her wide-brimmed hat studded with silk flowers. "Made in Cleveland too," she said proudly, stroking the brim. "Italian women did the flower work. It pays well for those with the knack. Almost as well as dipping chocolate."

"I'll dip," Mamma announced. "I don't have a knack for flowers."

"So," said Roseanne, as a half dozen weaving men from a tavern helped one another into the streetcar, "you left Naples suddenly, did you? Paolo wrote about you in his letters, but he never mentioned that you'd be emigrating. When I got his telegram I had an empty room that two Polacks wanted but I told them I had Italians coming, sent by my cousin."

"Thank you, Roseanne," I said quickly. "That was generous."

"It was Lucia's idea to come," Mamma announced suddenly, pressing her foot against mine. "She begged and begged, so I said we'd try America. Countess Elisabetta was very upset. We came as a birthday present to Lucia." I stared at Mamma.

"I see." Roseanne studied our bags. "Well, a friend of mine works for Stingler's Chocolates. She can help you get a job." As we rattled toward Woodland Avenue, Roseanne pointed proudly to a tangle of wires overhead. "Electricity and telephones." The air smelled acrid and slightly smoky.

"Is there a fire?" I asked.

"No, just lots of factories. There's one for lightbulbs and further on we have Packard Motor Car and Mr. J. P. Morgan's steel company. We have suit and dress factories; shoe, hat, button, and belt makers; and smaller shops doing piecework for the garment houses. Cleveland dresses America," she announced proudly. "Over there is Stingler's, where Teresa can work." She pointed toward the Holy Rosary Church, Central High School for me, and Hiram House, where we'd take English lessons. So our new life was laid out for us, like a puzzle missing only two pieces. Already I felt cramped.

"I don't need English, I'll just work," Mamma announced.

"Well, Lucia has to learn. Anyway, this is Friday night. Tomorrow we'll get you proper clothes. Church on Sunday and I'll show you around Cleveland. Monday you go to Stingler's Chocolates. As a favor to Paolo, I'll take Lucia to school. You have documents?"

"They were stolen on the train," Mamma said blandly.

"I see. Doesn't matter. Anyway, Lucia, you won't have to stay in school long. Most Italian girls start working when they're sixteen, some younger. They help their mammas with room and board."

I bit my lip. A man on the ship had proudly shown his son's diploma from an American high school. "*High* school," the name had danced in my mind. Lucia in *high* school. "Don't girls want to finish school?"

"What for? You don't need a diploma for factory work. Anyway, here's our stop." We hauled our belongings to a gray wooden house with wooden steps. "I know it's strange, so much wood. I guess they don't need houses to last."

Once inside, Roseanne dealt out her rules like playing cards. "There's one bathtub, and you two take your baths on Tuesdays. Boarders here the longest get Saturdays. Next longest, Fridays, and so on. Do your own wash or pay the Irish woman. Hang your clothes in the yard. In winter, they freeze dry. It's true, you'll see. Breakfast at six, dinner at eight. Factory shifts end at seven; you'll have time to get home. Latecomers don't eat. Your room has no view, but you'll be glad of that in winter. Front rooms get more light but they cost more and they're colder in winter from Canadian air off Erie."

"What's Erie?" I asked.

"A lake bigger than the Bay of Naples. When it freezes, you can drive a team of horses over on the ice. Well, here's your room." It was narrow and dark as Ciro's *basso*, with a bed only slightly wider than ours in Naples. A small window faced the next house, barely a stride away. "I could loan you a table for schoolwork," Roseanne offered.

"Could we see a front room?" Mamma asked.

"Sure. When there's a vacancy, you can move." We were hustled down the hall where Roseanne threw open a door and announced, "This is Irena. She's Polish, about sixteen years old. She makes buttons." Irena had a wide, pale face, blond braids curled around her head, and the bluest eyes I'd ever seen, as blue as our bay. She was sitting on her bed, curved against cushions, never ceasing her work. "Go see what she does, but you can't talk to her. All she knows is Polish and a little English."

Mamma didn't move, but when I drew closer to the bed, Irena looked up and smiled. I'd never had a friend my age; her smile warmed me like a woolen shawl. She shook my hand briefly before plucking a tiny square of blue cloth from a stack, stretching it over a button form, forcing both into a mold, folding in the raw cloth edges, and affixing a button back. I looked around the room. Sacks filled the floor: cloth to be cut, button backs, and finished buttons in various sizes and colors. But the work would be constantly the same. No silver polishing or floor washing could be so tedious.

"How long does she do this?" I asked Roseanne.

"All day to make her quota. A Russian comes for the finished buttons and brings her new supplies. She can't sit at a proper chair in a factory because of a streetcar accident, so she does home work. She pays more for the front room since she needs light to work. When her brother and his wife come from Poland, she'll live with them." Cloth squares were mounded by a calendar with dark lines drawn across each day.

"They're coming soon?"

"They'd better. She's behind in her rent. She might have to pawn some things." What things? A crucifix and two prints of huts on green fields hung on the wall were the sole adornments in this prison of buttons. "Well, let her work. Come downstairs. I saved your dinner, just this once."

We wished Irena good night and backed from the room. My limbs felt weighted, as if masses of buttons dragged me down. "She doesn't have friends?"

"You mean other Poles? How? She doesn't go out, and what would they talk about? Buttons? Here, you must be hungry. *Buon appetito.*"

We ate minestrone and spongy American bread. Then we helped wash dishes, since the kitchen girl had gone to bed. Finally Mamma and I climbed the creaking stairs to our room. A crack of light shone under Irena's door and I heard tiny pings of buttons dropping in a sack.

"At last, a bed that doesn't rock," Mamma said as she stripped to her chemise. She sighed herself to sleep while I lay staring at the dim window. When I turned to curl against her as we'd always slept before, she moved away. "In America," she mumbled, "people sleep alone." *In America, In America,* the words rose like seagulls against the sky. What else was new here? And what of my old life? Was the countess standing by the high window now? Could she hear waves and feel the warm sea breeze? Did she think of me? Had Paolo already hired new servants, easier to manage?

*In the morning* I hurried downstairs to look out the parlor window. American boys in woven caps and knickers hurried by. There were women in bright dresses, carts, and even an automobile. The sky was a flat, blank white. "Try to get used to it," Roseanne said. "That's the best way. You don't want to be like Neapolitans, always going on about blue sea, our special sun, our mussels, our mozzarella, our special tomatoes. *Basta!* This is Cleveland! Let's go shopping." I studied the white lid of sky as Roseanne hurried us along. *Was* there blue overhead? Yes, a sliver, but I didn't mention it. What else could I not speak of here?

We got secondhand American dresses, coats, and shoes at the Newcomer's Aid Society so we wouldn't look like greenhorns. Now we'd blend in and be treated better. Languages flew around us like angry birds. I couldn't pull English from the flurry. Why hadn't I studied on the ship? Between bouts of sickness, I'd seen clusters of people repeating strange words. How many did I know in Italian? Thousands after fourteen years. Would it take me another fourteen for English? Even

Roseanne, I noticed, spoke haltingly to Americans and veered toward Italians as small boats seek calm waters. Why hadn't I realized how useless my tongue would be in a new country?

"Come on," Roseanne said, "you need school supplies." At a marvelous store called a "five-and-dime" I selected a pencil, notebook, rubber eraser, pen, and ink bottle. I would have explored all the treasures there if Roseanne hadn't hauled me to the street and pointed: "There's the Lyceum Theater. Bigger than the San Carlo in Naples."

Mamma's eyes blazed. She walked slowly past the grand palazzo as I watched anxiously. If she accosted its maestro, she'd be taken as a lunatic foreigner.

My breath came easier when Mamma looked away. "Now we'll get a streetcar to Erie, the great lake," Roseanne announced. We took a northbound car to the edge of the city, where from the muddy shore a gray plate of water stretched out to a gray fringe of sky. Waves lapped listlessly at our feet, pushing up a slurry of old shoes, driftwood, scraps of nets, and canvas shreds. Rangy dogs fought over a dead gull. Nobody spoke. "This isn't the prettiest part," Roseanne admitted. "It's nicer with a blue sky, or when the trees turn color. There's a place over there"—she pointed—"where you can swim and sit on rocks, like in the bay."

"No volcano," Mamma observed.

"Which is good, right? Who needs volcanoes? They're nothing but trouble."

I took my mother's arm as we made our way home. That night I wrote my first letter to Countess Elisabetta, saying that Cleveland was beautiful, with a gorgeous lake. Roseanne was very kind and sent Paolo her love. We would work hard and repay our passage soon. We would be happy here.

And if we weren't? Suppose Mamma couldn't find peace at work or rages overtook her and there was no calming, distant volcano? Suppose

I couldn't learn English and therefore failed in school? Suppose Mamma was injured like Totò? Clouds of worries filled the little room; I dug out my book of Leopardi and eased myself to sleep.

On Sunday, we washed our clothes and polished our shoes. Roseanne watched us work, constantly giving advice. "You should be *Theresa*, with an *h*, and Lucia can be *Lucy*, to blend in better." We'd shed our last name. Wasn't that enough?

"I don't want to blend in," Mamma said, giving the washing machine lever a jerk.

"You will, sooner or later. And Lucia, you'll need a *fella*. That's American for 'a young man of your own.' If he's got a good enough job, you can stop working and have babies. Then Teresa can live with you." I bent over my shoe, buffing it hard, feeling laced in by her plans. I had no idea how to talk to "fellas."

"Tell me about chocolate dipping," Mamma demanded.

"Well, Mr. Stingler pays well enough if you're good at making swirls, but he likes his favorites."

"He doesn't have to like me, just pay me and keep his hands to himself. *I* don't want a fella. I'm widowed, you know. My husband, Giacomo, trained horses at the royal stables. He was breaking a wild Arabian for the king when he got thrown and broke his neck and died." I stared. What about Pietro? Roseanne knew that we'd worked at the villa for years and there was no husband, no Pietro or Giacomo. Did past lives not matter in America?

Roseanne pushed back a curl. "I see. I'm sorry, Teresa."

"Mamma has a beautiful voice," I interjected to pull our talk from fallen, imagined husbands.

"Stingler will like that. Good singers make the work go faster. Be sure you tell him you can sing."

"I won't be on my knees, that's what's important."

The next day she left for work before seven with a light step and shoulders squared. Since we'd come to Cleveland, Mamma had not once raised her voice. Perhaps an angel did watch over us.

So it was with hope and good humor that I went with Roseanne to Central High School to be enrolled as Lucia D'Angelo in the ninth grade. A stubby clerk took me to a classroom hung with maps and set with rows of wooden desks. He handed me a document with English words all over, pointed me to the teacher, and left. The students stared, giggling a little when my shoes creaked. At least I was dressed as they were. *Please, let me blend in.*

The teacher came gliding across the room, reaching for my document. Rigid as a soldier, I handed it to her. She had gray-blue eyes and a lace collar so high and stiff that it seemed her head swiveled on a white shaft. A brown-haired girl named Yolanda was summoned to translate the melodious voice. Her dress was like mine, but fitted better and was embellished with ribbons. "Her name is Miss Robinson and she is happy to have you. She's sure you'll work hard and learn English. If you speak Italian in this room or the halls of this school"—Yolanda indicated a slender wooden pointer—"she reminds you. Now go to your desk. We do history next."

There was no danger of my speaking at all. The history lesson was a torrent of words I didn't know. Drops of sweat ran down my face. Mortified, I wiped them away. When Yolanda turned to smile, I took heart and listened harder until, like rocks exposed by a retreating tide, I recognized the words *revolution, declaration, independence,* and *general.* Miss Robinson showed us a picture of General Washington standing in a tiny boat during a windy winter crossing. "Sit down, you idiot," any Naples fisherman would have told him.

Finally I heard "mathematics" and was happy. Numbers were a familiar face in a crowd of strangers. When Miss Robinson put multiplication problems on the chalkboard, I wrote the answers quickly in my copybook. She smiled and said, "Excellent, Lucia." Ah, she means *eccellente*. I basked in golden light, glancing in astonishment at yawning classmates. Were they bored? Had they ever spent mornings scrubbing on their knees?

After my lunch of pasta and beans came "recess," a raucous swirl of students in the courtyard. I stood against a wall, watching them until my new friend found me. "I'll take you to English class at Hiram House this afternoon," Yolanda promised. "Then school will go better. But," she added happily, "you can start working soon enough." I'd worked my whole life, I might have responded. As soon as I could walk, I dusted, stirred pots, folded laundry, and beat rugs with little sticks. Perhaps I washed two steps to Mamma's twenty, but I had no memories of "before working." Yes, I told Yolanda, I wanted English classes.

We reached Hiram House by straight, wide streets meeting at perfect angles. Cleveland seemed a child's city, ordered and easy to learn, but without the sweet tang of the sea. Not to seem like the Neapolitans Roseanne scorned, I didn't mention blue skies or sea breezes. Factory chimneys shot up thick plumes of smoke that left their smells behind. Yolanda sniffed out scents for me: iron and steel works, slaughterhouses, glassworks, automobile factories, and factories for "machines that make machines." Big-windowed garment workshops stood wedged between factories. "The windows are closed so soot won't stain the cloth."

Busy as it was with work, the city seemed dead. We passed no puppet shows or street singers, singing peddlers, fortune-tellers, gypsy dancers, or acrobats. Yolanda shrugged when I mentioned this. "It's America," she said. "You have fun inside."

Finally we reached Hiram House, a somber brick building with turrets and a wide porch. "Come on," Yolanda said, "the class just started." My English teacher was a bright-cheeked young woman who wrote in sweeping letters: *Miss Miller* and then *Welcome Newcomers!* She made us understand that both children and wary, stiff adults must stand by our chairs for a game called Simon Says.

"Repeat: 'Simon Says.'" We repeated. This much I could do, but how could we play in a language we didn't know? Easily, I discovered. Miss Miller's mobile face, boundless energy, and large gestures slipped meaning under words for Italians, Hungarians, Poles, Greeks, and Czechs. Some students knew more English than others and pulled the rest along. At Pentecost, our priest once told us, the Holy Spirit spoke to a crowd, each in his own tongue. Miss Miller had that power.

"Simon says, stand up. Simon says, touch your nose. Simon says, raise your hand. Touch your chest. I'm sorry, Niko and Ruth. Sit down, please."

We played short rounds so many could win. We shaped our mouths to hers. Miss Miller's good humor made even grown men laugh. I was understanding English! Pride shot through me, as when Mamma first took her hands from beneath my belly and I swam alone to the far flat rock, or when the countess opened a book, pointed to a line, and said, "Start here and read."

A girl my age wrote our new words on the board: *arm, foot, head, leg, chest, his, her, your.* Soon, I vowed, I would be that girl, writing. "Now, Lucia, you'll play with Henryk." She pointed to a tall, slim boy near my age with wide dark eyes. I'd noticed him in the schoolyard standing with a crowd of laughing boys.

"Simon says, stand up, Henryk," I managed. Astonishing: he stood. My first English sentence! My first words to an American boy! He smiled and brushed back a flop of hair. I'd play this game forever. "Tell Henryk to raise his hand." I did. He did. "And touch his head."

"Simon says, touch your head." Again the magic: his hand on the glossy hair. "Now, Henryk, tell Lucia to lift her arm."

"Lucia, Simon says lift your arm." I did. At Miss Miller's orders, he had me touch my shoulder, heart, and hand. "Good, now have Lucia sit and stand again." When we had done this, Miss Miller clapped and the class obediently followed. The girl wrote "clap" and we repeated this word too.

"Excellent, Lucia and Henryk. Now, shake hands." When she mimed this with the writing girl, I drew back. Henryk hesitated as well, looking down. In a stride, Miss Miller was next to him, offering her own hand and repeating firmly: "Shake hands." He did. "Excellent. And now with Lucia." He glanced at one of the boys, then reached toward me. I took the warm, firm grasp and quickly released. "See? It's no tragedy." *Tragedia,* she must mean. *Non è una tragedia.* "Please sit down." We did. I risked a glance at Henryk, who returned a furtive smile.

After our lesson, the class shattered like quicksilver. I was engulfed by Italians. Henryk was swarmed by boys who spoke languages I'd soon learn to spool apart: Polish and Yiddish. One looked sharply at me and whispered to Henryk: *"shiksa."*

"Yolanda, what does that mean?"

"Who knows? But it doesn't matter. English is what you need. Are you coming to class tomorrow?" Yes, I said. I'd come every day.

# Chapter 4

## DIPPING CHOCOLATE

*I raced home* and was there by seven, before Mamma arrived in good humor from Stingler's. "Only eleven hours and not once on my knees! You pick up a caramel core, dip it in the vat, twist, drain, and put it on the rack. That's all. Look." She held up a little bag of chocolates rejected for their mangled shape but delicious. "Other girls are sick of them. I sang, and everybody said it made the time go faster."

With the dignity of her new work and praise from the other dippers, she'd never been so ebullient. We passed a happy evening. If I couldn't persuade Mamma to attend English classes, she at least agreed that Simon Says was a good game. We played in the parlor with Italian and the English words I'd learned. To Roseanne's astonishment I lured Irena from her room, and she was happy to play with us.

"Yolanda will show me a garment shop," I told Mamma that night. "I want to see how clothes get made." The next day after school we went to Bank Street and stood on wooden crates to peer through a dusty window of the Printz-Biederman Company. Rows of women sat shoulder to shoulder, bent over machines, motionless except for their arms and hands. "That's my cousin Giovanna, sewing cuffs," said Yolanda, rapping on the glass and pointing to a girl who shared her wide mouth and slight build. Giovanna's eyes turned up briefly before dropping back to work. "She's afraid of needles. One girl got blood poisoning from a needle stick and lost her finger." I closed my hands tightly. "See how fast she works? They're paid by the piece." Stitch, turn the cuff, another line, and snip. Repeat for the next cuff. The finished shirt was laid on a pile with the right hand as the left one reached for the next. "Buttonhole girls earn a little more."

The work was slightly more varied than Irena's but still stunning in its monotony. All over the city, in hundreds of shops and factories, did girls barely older than I do this all day? Service work was hard, but at least the chime of a new hour rarely found me at the same task. There were always the great windows out to sea and hope of a swim in warm, moon-struck waters.

"The girls can talk, you see," Yolanda rattled on, "if the supervisor's not around. And sometimes there's a good singer like your mother." I saw lips moving, some smiles, perhaps a joke, and the different styles and colors of the women's own clothing. But still they seemed like machines themselves, as if at night they simply froze in darkness until the morning shift.

"What do they earn?"

"Older girls make ten dollars. Younger ones get less."

"Why, if they do the same work?"

"Because they do. And there's always fines. And rent for the machines, and then they have to buy needles and thread."

As if we'd paid Paolo for the use of his buckets and brushes. "That's not fair. You shouldn't have to pay to work."

Yolanda looked at me curiously. "If your mother doesn't get sick or hurt, you could finish high school, I guess. Then if you have good English, you could clerk in a downtown store and make more money."

"Italian girls do that?"

She considered. "Well, most shopgirls are Irish or Swedish or German. But you could be the first Italian. Let's go, before the boss sees us."

*I must finish school,* I determined secretly, *and at least be a shopgirl.* We had twenty words for a spelling test in school and forty for Hiram House. With others I'd pick up, I could learn a hundred this week. But what if Mamma tired of dipping, if she got sick or hurt or argued with Mr. Stingler and lost her job? My English would fade away over a sewing machine.

"I have to make dinner," Yolanda announced. She plucked at my charity dress. "If you take it in here and here and add some ribbons, it would look nicer, you know." Then she was gone, hurrying back to her flat.

*I never did* alter my dress. Not that I didn't envy Yolanda's effortless style, her deft use of ribbons, feathers, and dried flowers to make hair ornaments and hats. She said it was easy. I never found it so. I did study my face and body in a tall mirror at the boardinghouse. My body was changing and my face too, as if I were clay being molded by America. I was changing inside as well. In that first autumn, I got "the curse," as Mamma glumly declared when my monthly blood began. "Be careful, don't let what happened to me happen to you. Nothing's the same afterward."

Was *I* the curse? "It's not like that, Lucia," said Roseanne. But nobody said what *it* was like.

"Just be careful," Mamma said briskly. "You don't want trouble in America."

I tried to keep hold of Naples. I reread letters from the countess about street festivals, a new opera or scandal, and the count's increasing debts. There were always best wishes from Nannina and Paolo. They seemed so distant. I lay in bed imagining the villa. Was the bust of Julius Caesar on the right or left of the window? In what month did the setting sun spark more rainbows from the crystal chandelier? When, exactly, did the lilacs bloom? I missed the creamy tang of fresh mozzarella and rich, intense bite of tomatoes from the slopes of Vesuvius. *Come back,* I begged my memories. *Don't leave me in America with trouble.*

Mamma still sang her street songs and arias for me at night. But she had discovered the old player piano in Roseanne's parlor and eagerly memorized lyrics of popular tunes I sounded out for her. "If it wasn't for the piano," she said, "I couldn't keep going." And then quite calmly: "If Stingler ever says I can't sing, I'll drown him in a chocolate vat."

"Mamma, don't talk like that!" I saw the crystal decanter flying, the count's face streaming blood, our flight through the dark streets, and exile in America. Where could we go if her temper flared again and we had no Paolo to arrange our escape?

"It's just thoughts, Lucia," she said, and yawned. "Go to sleep." But thoughts can become acts: a sudden push, a body sinks in chocolate, police are called. *Just thoughts, just thoughts,* I repeated into the darkness. *Ignore them. Think other thoughts.*

When Hiram House announced a talent show for Christmas, I begged Mamma to sing "Santa Lucia" or "Maria Marì." I was sure people would be amazed. "Listen," they'd say, "she sings like an angel!"

"I'm too old," she said flatly. "Remember Toscanini?" Like a horse balking at a weakened bridge, she wouldn't budge, either to sing alone or to join the women's choir. "But *you* do something, Lucia," she said, "and I'll watch. Just don't sing."

I knew enough English now to ask Miss Miller after class if I could recite a Leopardi poem. Standing straight with my hands at my sides as Contessa Elisabetta taught me, I began "L'infinito":

> Sempre caro mi fu quest'ermo colle
> E questa siepe che da tanta parte
> Dell'ultimo orizzonte il guardo esclude.

A gray-haired Italian in a tweed suit stopped to listen, his lips moving with mine. Speaking slowly, eyes closed, he translated for Miss Miller: "Always dear to me was this lonely knoll and these woods that here and there concealed the horizon from my sight."

"Thank you, Umberto," she said. "But it's rather melancholy, don't you think? How about 'The Village Blacksmith' by Henry Wadsworth Longfellow, our great American poet?"

"Leopardi was very great."

"Of course, Lucia, but could you *try* the Longfellow?" She flashed the smile that had coaxed a room full of immigrants to their feet for Simon Says.

"Yes, Miss Miller."

Beaming, she produced a small volume of Longfellow's poetry. Umberto sat with me, carefully translating lines I repeated in English:

> Under a spreading chestnut tree
> The village smithy stands;
> The smith, a mighty man is he,
> With large and sinewy hands.

"Listen, Lucia," he whispered as Miss Miller watched Polish girls practicing a dance, "the Printz-Biederman Company gives a handsome book of English speeches to the newcomer with the best recitation. The Leopardi was lovely, but try for the prize."

I went home beating out lines to the thump of my shoes on slate sidewalk in the meter that Miss Miller favored: "Ta-*dum*, ta-*dum*, ta-*dum*." That night I read to Irena as she worked, repeating new words and rereading lines to learn the string of sounds. If I spoke more slowly, we discovered, she could make buttons to my time. Irena worked and I recited, until with a broad smile she dropped the last of the day's buttons in her "finished" sack, tied it with a cord, and held her hands over the gas lamp, rubbing them slowly and flexing her fingers against the cramping pain. I stood to go.

"Lucia," she said, "you stay a time here?" The countess in her sitting room could not have been more gracious in smoothing the bedsheets for me. We shared a little English now. Irena pointed on a calendar to when her brother Casimir would be coming, five months and thousands of buttons away. She brought out a Bible in Polish and opened it carefully to a page of handwritten names and dates. Using button backs, the words we shared, and much pointing between buttons and names, she assembled her family tree.

"Here my parents." She turned the buttons over. Dead, I understood. "Three sisters." Dead. She mimed how they died: fever. "Two brothers. Poland." Here was Casimir, the one she loved most, coming to Cleveland. She pointed to her ring finger. "Married, to Anna from our village." I brought paper and a pencil from my room and with clever drawings she showed that Casimir was a fine butcher, Anna made delicious sausages, and they would both work in a cousin's butcher shop. She could live with them and never make buttons again. "Look. Wedding present for Anna." She showed me a richly embroidered jacket.

"You *made* this?"

She nodded shyly.

"Beautiful. Anna will love it."

Irena beamed, but then she muttered something about the button dealer. With mimes and drawing, I gathered there were many girls doing home work who didn't have her problems of cramps and back spasms. "I must trust in the Lord." She pushed me a pile of buttons. "Now your family."

How to explain that a masked man had pushed my mother into seaweed and got her pregnant with me? Instead, I put down buttons for my great-grandfather Domenico, who sang for the church; for my mother's father, whose work was unknown; and for my own imagined father, the artist Pietro D'Angelo, who fell from scaffolding to his death. Yes, I lied to her. I didn't want to be a bastard in America.

A warm hand touched my cheek. "I fall from streetcar. But live. Poor Lucia. Alone with the mamma."

When I finally left my friend's room, Roseanne pulled me aside. "How did you make her talk? She *never* talks."

"I asked questions. We used English and drawings—and buttons." Roseanne's eyes widened as if I'd acquired astonishing powers.

That night I prayed for Casimir to come and bundle Irena into a warm, familiar Polish world. I prayed for Mamma to find peace, for the count to treat the countess well, or at least return to Capri, and for myself to graduate from high school. Sleepless, I followed wildly running ceiling cracks that recalled the swirling foam of tide pools. Outside, a slow clop of horses pulled me back to Cleveland and my poem: "The-smith-a-*migh*-ty-*man*-is-*he*-with-*large*-and-*sin*-ewy-*hands*."

The next day, Mamma came home in a foul humor. The chocolate vats were too hot for swirls to form properly, so Little Stingler, the owner's son, wouldn't pay for half the day's production. He also fired a girl for "insolence."

"Insolence about what?"

"Never mind. And we can't sing. Little Stingler thinks we're singing about him. The old man isn't so bad, but the young one's a bastard. A Sicilian girl who sits by the door whistles when he's coming."

"Well, *were* you singing about him?"

"Of course. He doesn't understand Italian. If I don't do *something* to get even, I'll think bad thoughts and then one day—"

"You better keep that job," Roseanne warned. "If you make trouble they put you on the blacklist and nobody hires you. Then how do you pay rent?"

I looked anxiously at Mamma, who seemed unconcerned. Something clattered in the kitchen. Seizing my chance, I speared more meat for Irena. "One piece each," Roseanne warned. "That's the rule."

"But she's so thin."

"And it's tough as shoe leather anyway," Mamma added.

"You think stew meat grows on trees? You know what it costs these days?" Thus began another litany of the price of beef, potatoes, dried beans, lard, onions, and turnips. If prices kept rising, what could poor folks eat? Cats and dogs like the heathen Chinese?

"So, where can I buy good marzipan and salami?" Mamma interrupted.

This was a clever ploy: Roseanne loved giving advice. "Go to Catalano's on Woodland Avenue. It's like you're home again."

After dinner I took Mamma aside as she headed for the piano. "We have to pay back the countess. We can't buy imported food."

"Don't we deserve it, after the pig swill we eat here?"

"Shh, Mamma, she'll hear you. We *can't* be buying more food."

"You think I *like* dipping chocolate all day? My back hurts, my shoulders hurt, and you're at school learning poetry." Her nostrils flared. "I want something special that isn't chocolate. Don't you?"

I did, actually. I longed for Nannina's cooking and home tastes. "Well, we could get a couple things."

"Exactly. The countess has plenty of money. She can wait a little longer."

That Sunday was astonishingly mild. "See? We'll have a good day," Mamma said, taking my arm as we stepped out of the boardinghouse. "We'll eat by the water like we used to. Don't worry. I'll make enough money and maybe you'll work a little. Breathe. There's not so much factory smell here." I gulped in the bright air, scrubbed clean by night winds. Quick walking was a pleasure.

In Catalano's store, everything American melted away. We spoke our own dialect, jostling and bargaining as if we were home again. I tried to hold back, saving pennies for the countess, but in the end we bought wine and bread, smoked mozzarella, salami, a paper cone of salted fava beans, marzipan, and two ricotta pastries. Then we took a streetcar to Lake Erie, found flat rocks to sit on, and opened our packages.

"Mamma," I asked as I cut the bread and salami, "are you sorry we came to America?"

"Not yet. And anyway, we had to. Let's eat." She shook herself as if casting off cobwebs and for the first time asked about school. I eagerly described our lessons until we finished eating and then I braided and unbraided her hair as she sang a street song, an aria, and an American song before pulling her braids away.

"Now stand up," she said briskly, "and tell me your poem." I gave her every line, proud that I'd learned them all by heart. "Ta-*dum*, ta-*dum*, ta-*dum*," she mimicked. "That's not poetry. That's a clock. Even your precious Leopardi isn't a clock."

"Let me tell you what the words mean. A blacksmith is a *fabbro*, so the poem is about—"

"The *sound* is the problem, the way you speak. Toscanini would hate it." Not him again, spoiling our time together.

"Mamma, the maestro won't come to a talent show."

A shadow crossed her face. She shook it away and put me on the flat rock as if it were a stage. Firm hands adjusted my chin, neck, chest, and back. "Now the first lines." She stood in front of me as I spoke. "No, *tell me* the story. Look in my eyes. Take deeper breaths, so you speak longer with each one. It's better that way." She listened to the poem again and again, lifting a hand when I could breathe.

"Mamma, it's only a talent show."

"Good. Then people will say, 'Lucia D'Angelo is the best talent.'"

"But how do you know all this?"

"I don't. I only know what's better than ta-*dum,* ta-*dum,* ta-*dum*. Again, from the beginning." I did. She listened intently, slowing me on a line, shaking her head if the "ta-*dum*" came back. "Again." And now the full smile, her hand patting my face. "Good, Lucia, very good." My chest swelled with pleasure.

Soon after, a scuttling wind reminded us that we still had the week's laundry to do. We packed our basket and scrambled onto the next streetcar before realizing that we'd taken the wrong line, going away from home. I asked a young girl who looked Italian for help.

"You have to change at University Circle. Don't you know that? Are you greenhorns?" She told us how many stops until our change and flounced away.

"Little bitch," Mamma snapped. Getting off at the fifth stop, I nearly dropped our basket. Young people barely older than I were strolling past with books. Couples sat talking on benches, as if this were their work for the afternoon. I stared like a beggar outside a bakery. A professor spoke with two women, *spoke with them,* discussing a point.

"See," I said. "Western Reserve University. Miss Miller told us about it."

Mamma studied the scene. "They're blond, and they don't look Italian. See how they walk, like rich people? You wouldn't like it here," Her work-roughened hand patted mine. But that night I unfolded my memory like a letter, studying it again. Yes, they were American and rich, but inside, inside, were they so different from me? They had finished high school; that was their first step.

The next Saturday I climbed onstage at the talent show and recited my poem. "Look at each group in the audience until someone blinks. That's what street singers do," Mamma had reminded me. I remembered each word and place for breath. I looked out at the faces until one in each group blinked. Even Irena had come, taking a break from her buttons. She smiled steadily at me as if each word were a gift.

I won the recitation prize and a gold-stamped book from Mr. Printz of the Printz-Biederman Company. Great things in America seemed possible that night: learning English perfectly, graduating from high school, even going to college. Look at Mr. Printz, who came to America with nearly nothing, Miss Miller had said, and made a fortune selling coats and dresses.

Two Hungarians played a violin duet; Polish girls danced, and Bulgarian brothers did acrobatics. Henryk passed balls to a friend who juggled with no particular skill but great good humor, both taking such extravagant bows for the modest performance that everyone laughed. At the end of the evening, when Miss Miller asked if anyone else wished to perform, Mamma suddenly stood by her chair, opened her mouth, and began "Maria Marì."

Silence spread across the room. Even those who didn't know the words sat transfixed. American women setting out cookies and cider stood still to listen. A lamp shone over Mamma's head. She moved toward the light until her shoulders dripped with gold. Italians closed their eyes, smiling. Pride filled me like a bucket overflowing.

After the last notes glided away, it was Henryk who began clapping first. Then Umberto and I, Irena, Yolanda, Miss Miller, Mr. Printz, and soon the whole room filled with beating, whistling, and stamping of feet.

I hugged her. "You were wonderful, Mamma. Everyone loved you."

"And *he* wasn't there."

Was she at last joking about the maestro? "No," I said carefully, "he wasn't. And look at my book. Isn't it lovely?"

"Yes, but don't start reading tonight. It's late."

We walked slowly, for Irena was tired. Others going home greeted Mamma as if she were a diva. *"Brava!"* they cried, or words in their own language.

"They're just greenhorns," she said, but her face was flushed.

## Chapter 5

### TAPPING AT THE WINDOW

*After her success* at Hiram House, Mamma began racing through dinner to sit at the player piano and sing. Roseanne was pleased. Enjoying the free entertainment, her two Hungarians went less often to Lula's, a lively tavern nearby; they saved money and paid rent regularly. Donato, who clerked at a men's hat and glove store, enjoyed the evenings too and ceased looking for new lodgings. Even Irena came downstairs to finish the last of her buttons for the day.

But singing wedged me away from my mother. Music filled the hours I needed for homework. Our bedroom was cold and dim, so I studied in the dining room, fingers pressed into my ears. "You're becoming a hermit," Roseanne declared. Mamma was offended and mystified that I ignored her for a puddle of books. "You're at school all day. Isn't that enough?" If Irena braced a chair with cushions and we made buttons in the dining room after I'd finished my homework, Mamma grumbled that I liked buttons more than music.

Our debt to Countess Elisabetta came between us too. She'd given us twenty-four dollars for the passage and another thirty we'd used for clothes, shoes, and school supplies. At first Mamma had grudgingly saved fifty cents a week in our little bank. Now, with piano rolls from Brainard's music store at thirty cents each, our savings were leaching away. Her shoes needed half soles. I needed a doctor when hot olive oil wouldn't cure my earache. Mamma craved Italian sweets and salt-cured olives from Catalano's. How could I object when she worked so hard to keep me in school? But we weren't repaying the loan. After three weeks of putting nothing in the bank, we had a furious argument in our room, fought in whispers since Donato slept next door.

"Why *must* we pay back the countess?" Mamma demanded. "She doesn't need it, and we slaved for years cleaning that old palazzo. How often did we scrub those steps?"

"But when we had to leave Naples—"

"That wasn't our fault."

"She helped us," I persisted. "She got our documents. Didn't you say that when I was born, the count didn't want me? She let me stay. She taught me to read."

"Right, she taught *you*. *You* were the little pet, remember?"

"But she protected *us*."

"I cured her headaches *and* cleaned her house. So she got her pay." My mother turned to the wall, humming loudly.

Furious, I dragged my chair to the drafty window, glaring out into the night. Yet it was true that the countess favored me, sometimes calling me from work to read to her. She gave me easy tasks on hot days. She took me walking by the sea after the count's rages and worst abuses. "My little shadow," she called me. It's true I was bound to her for reasons that Mamma couldn't share. This debt tormented me, even if a pair

of fine Venetian goblets in our rosewood cabinet cost more than the pal-
try sum we owed. *Our* rosewood cabinet? Mamma was right; nothing in
the villa was ours.

We barely spoke the next day. I tried to see our past through her
eyes, remembering that dark memories gnawed at her. Yet nothing prepared me for what she revealed a few nights later. Again we were whispering, and her words cut like tiny knives: "You cried all the time when
you were a baby. I couldn't make you stop. The count said, 'Give it away
if it won't stop screaming.' But when *she* picked you up, with her soft
hands and French perfume, you smiled. She called me to see. I'd been
scrubbing floors. When could I play with you?"

I had to ask: "Mamma, did *you* ever want to give me away, to have me
exposed in an orphanage?"

She flicked at the peeling wallpaper. "Not to an orphanage, but when
you were four months old, a friend of the countess came from Rome.
She had no children and wanted you. She said she'd give me thirty-
five lire and a new dress. She'd call you Flavia, like her dead sister. You
smiled. She had an ugly voice and a pinched, rich woman's face, but you
smiled at her."

The dark square of our window tunneled out to another life. I was
no longer Lucia of Naples but Flavia of Rome, a rich woman's daughter.
Sold for thirty-five lire. "I said I needed a day to think about it," the
piercing whisper continued.

"What did you— How did you think about it?" I lay rigid, barely
breathing, as if her choice hadn't happened yet and some stray move-
ment now would hurl me to Rome.

A warm hand touched my face. "You cried all night and the count
came twice to scream at me. In the morning, I washed and dressed you,
but when I heard that lady at the door, I couldn't bear to think of you living with that voice and nasty face. Who did she think she was with her

thirty-five lire and new dress? I put a pin in your diaper so you'd scream when she held you. When you did scream, I said she couldn't have you. I ran with you to the kitchen and took out the pin. You were *mine*," she finished fiercely. "I held you all that night and you didn't cry." She held me tightly again.

"Mamma, did you ever—were you ever—"

"No!" she said, driving her fingers in my hair. "I was *never* sorry about that pin. Never, never! Don't think that." How could I not? I had been dangled over a precipice. Yes, I'd been retrieved, but I *had* been dangled.

"Lucia, I was your age, almost a child. I'd had hard times all my life."

That was true, true. How could I manage my life now with a screaming baby? Could I blame her? Judge her? She worked early and late to keep me in school. We were woven together as tightly as the braid of her thick black hair. Yet years later, memories of that pin still jab me. Despite every voice that tells me yes, I wonder: have I been as faithful to her as she was to me?

"As for the debt," she said briskly, "you can agree or not, but I won't pay back the countess now." She yawned, turned over, and went to sleep.

*Debt. Think of the debt. Not—the other. She* didn't *give me away. She kept me. Think of the debt.* If we didn't repay it, I'd be ashamed. I couldn't write to the countess and if I didn't write, how would I receive her comforting letters of praise and encouragement? Who could help me with this trouble? Roseanne would discount any debt that put our rent at risk. Irena, so honest and frugal, would not understand Mamma's need for small indulgences. Yolanda? With twin brothers, a sister, parents, and a crippled aunt crowded together and constantly fighting, she yearned for escape. "If you have any extra money," she'd say, "buy a new dress so fellas will notice you and take you out at night."

In the end, I went to Miss Miller, who patiently helped me express my troubles in English. "It seems to me, Lucia," she said, "that if you earned some money of your own, *you* could pay back this debt."

"But if I work in a factory—"

"Not factory work. You can write Italian?" I nodded. "Some immigrants can't, and they want to send letters home. So they come here on Sundays and dictate to scribes. We keep the price low, but you do make something. Would you like to scribe?"

Yes, I said happily. That Sunday I sat with a long line of scribes writing in Russian, Yiddish, Polish, Czech, Slovenian, Hungarian, Italian, and German. Soon I was looking forward to each week's drama of other lives.

I wrote of jobs found, shops bought or enlarged, moves to new and better flats, marriages and engagements, the triumphs of children. I announced money being sent home for a family's passage to America or to buy land or houses in Italy. Sometimes I wrote anguished excuses: the promised funds weren't coming because of a job lost, sickness, injury, or death. "I had almost paid for my sewing machine," said one woman, "but it burned in a fire so I have to start over."

"Dearest Mamma," a hoarse voice would manage, and I knew to put down my pen and wait. I saw men and women convulse in sobs for the death of a child, crippling accidents to the breadwinner, or hoarded savings gone. A young widower awkwardly held a tiny baby; his wife had died in childbirth. How to speak of that tangle of blessing and loss? He couldn't care for the babe alone, but how could he give their son away or find a new wife with his heart so full of Maria? He doubled over my desk, stammering excuses to those behind him in line. Strangers reached to touch him. "Take your time," they said. "Don't think about us."

I saw subterfuge as well. A young woman described a happy married life when everyone knew her handsome husband had run off with an American shopgirl.

"Papa, I'm working at the mill," said a young man horribly crippled in the limestone quarries. In fact, all his children worked now; the littlest shined shoes.

"Next month I'll send a fine dowry to my beloved little sister," a notorious gambler had me write as those behind him coughed and glared.

My pay was low, but with many letters, I could soon begin sending my own money to the countess. "Do you feel better now?" Miss Miller asked. I told her yes, much better. In my third week, I noticed Henryk among the scribes.

His line moved more slowly than mine, but with jostling good humor. Buying vegetables for Roseanne at his father's shop, I'd noticed his easy manners with those who defended their pennies by insulting his goods. "My poor honest onions," he'd lament and make the women laugh.

We began walking home together, sharing stories we'd written. "I know your gambler," Henryk said. "He wanted to bet me which potato would roll off a cart first." We talked about how many people would read our letters "back there," how they'd become like holy relics.

"But they aren't our words," I mused. "We're just scribing."

"What would you write if they *were* your words?" No one had ever asked me such a question. With a patient smile he snapped off a maple twig and studied it as we walked.

"Maybe I'd write about them, how their lives could be better." I paused. "And you?"

"Well—" he began, but then we were both caught by a pigeon strutting past us with a slice of bread hung around its neck, calmly pecking at his dinner. "Dear Papa Pigeon," Henryk began. "America is wonderful. You can even eat your jacket."

"I have a bread house with a nice cheese floor," I added. We laughed until a passing bearded man frowned at us.

"Ah, we should be serious," Henryk said. "Tell me about Naples." How to explain the sea and its smells, the villa, and life on the streets, so different from Cleveland? I tried. He nodded. "Poland was different too. Even the onions were different."

"In Naples," I said, boldly, "I never talked to a boy my age unless he was selling me something."

He smiled. "Here is a very nice twig at a good price. Peeled by hand." I took the twig but couldn't think what to say. The evening air turned hot and close; even the twig felt warm. When I spied Donato coming home, I took a hurried leave of Henryk and bolted up the stairs.

Two weeks after our walk, Henryk had to stop working at Hiram House. "My father needs me at the store," he explained. "I'll be writing receipts, not letters." Of course he had to help his family. But sometimes I imagined his voice in the Babel of scribing tables that winter.

*One windless Sunday* in early April, Yolanda agreed to take my place at Hiram House so Irena and I could go to Edgewater Park. "She does look pale," Roseanne observed as Irena pulled on her hat, gloves, and scarf. "But what can you talk about all day with her?"

"Lots of things, Poland and Naples and what she'll do when Casimir comes. I'm teaching her English."

"I see."

I kissed Mamma good-bye. She was sitting at the player piano, as she would be on our return.

The streetcar, the sights, and people out walking all delighted Irena, but she tired easily and leaned on my arm as we walked to the shore through a blaze of daffodils. Then we started our game. "You first," she said, "tell me about the sitting room in your villa." So I described again the light, the sea sounds, the oil paintings and marble busts, the glitter of crystal and silver. One day we'd take tea there, I promised. After

Casimir and Anna came and we all were rich, we'd go by steamship to Naples and even climb Vesuvius.

"Your turn," I said. We sat on a bench, where with halting English and little sketches in my notebook she told a folktale of an ancient dragon by the river. "It's a happy story," Irena insisted. "Not all dragons are bad." We debated this point in pictures and words, laughing until a coughing fit overtook her. People walking past frowned and hurried on, pulling their jackets close.

"I'll bring Casimir and Anna here to the park," Irena said, panting. He had finished his apprenticeship and bought a fine set of butcher knives for America. Once they came, Anna's secret recipe for sausage would make their fortune in Cleveland. "Everything will be good," she gasped. "We'll all dress up to see you graduate from high school."

That would be wonderful, I said, so wonderful. When we got home late in the afternoon, Irena said she'd rest a little before dinner. I watched her slowly mount the stairs, gripping the banister.

"She looks more flushed," Roseanne whispered. "And isn't she coughing more? Was there wind by the lake? Maybe you shouldn't have taken her." I swear I hadn't noticed the change. Irena was happy that day, freed from her prison of buttons. She'd said so over and over.

"You did well," Donato told me later. "If she was happy, that's the important thing. Don't mind Roseanne. Come, look what I just bought." He showed me traveling clothes he'd send to his wife and daughter in Italy. "They're coming soon. I'm such a lucky man." *No,* I thought, *his wife and daughter, they're the lucky ones.*

Irena and I never took another walk. Each day after school when I hurried upstairs to her room she seemed weaker. Her fevers grew more frequent. Sweat beaded across her forehead, and small efforts made her pant. "I'm sorry," said Roseanne, "but she'll have to eat alone. I can't let her infect the other boarders."

I got a visiting nurse to come. "It's pneumonia," she told me in the parlor. "Lucia, I won't lie to you. More than one in three die once the panting stage begins. Keep her warm. A pot of steaming water in her room might ease the breathing." Scarcely breathing myself, I confessed our walk. Was she sick because of me?

"No, of course not," the nurse said kindly. "Pneumonia comes creeping up. It's been with her for weeks, perhaps months. Give her rest and calm and we'll hope for the best."

"How can she have rest and be calm if she has to work and pay rent?" I demanded of Miss Miller. "It's impossible."

"Is it really? Can't *anybody* help your friend?"

Perhaps the situation wasn't hopeless, I realized while walking home. If one in three died, then two in three did not. Irena might still make *some* buttons, and the others might be negotiated. Iszak, one of our boarders, knew a little Russian and spoke to her dealer. He seemed truly sorry for her illness but had already done Irena the favor of buying her embroidered jacket at "an excellent price."

"She sold it?" I gasped. Anna's wedding present, her great pride? So often, after the night's last button, she'd unpack that jacket and run her fingers over its fine embroidery.

Iszak and the Russian conferred. "She has been behind in her quota for weeks," Iszak explained. "And there are other women who want this work."

"I see. Thank him please, Iszak. But tell him the buttons will be made."

For two weeks, Irena delivered her quota. On warm, moist days she could still rouse herself to work. I raced through homework to help her at night and made buttons on the weekends instead of scribing. Yolanda sometimes helped, eager to leave her crowded flat. Henryk brought over a pot of his mother's cabbage and chicken soup. "She says it's magic," he reported. "For sure it's very good." Irena thanked him gratefully.

"We all have to help her make buttons," I announced in the parlor while Irena lay coughing upstairs.

"And just why do we *all* have to help her?" Roseanne demanded.

"Because she has nobody else, because—"

"Because Lucia will keep asking until we agree," Donato finished.

"I'm not dipping all day and making buttons at night," Mamma said, "but I'll sing for you." In the end, even Iszak helped, and Roseanne let me pop corn for a treat.

"Thank you," Irena gasped when we met the week's quota. "When Casimir comes we—make you—Polish feast."

I felt her racing pulse. "Yes of course, but try to sleep now."

Donato stopped me in the hallway; on that kind and somber face I read his thoughts. "Lucia, you made a party out of nothing and we helped for a week, but you know this can't go on." Yes, I knew.

On a windy Monday morning she was so much worse that I stayed home from school, dosing her with warm tea and honey. A tree branch tapped against the window glass. "Death Angel knocking," she whispered. "Bury me in—dark blue dress." She pointed weakly at a drawer. "Tell Casimir I waited."

"Irena, don't talk that way."

Roseanne called me to the kitchen. "Lucia, I've done all I can for your friend, we all have. Now you know what you have to do." I knew.

When Mamma came home, we bundled Irena in blankets and took her to Saint Vincent Charity Hospital. Her voice was a terrible rasp. "Lucia, candle—in hand—light my way."

"Dear child," said the nurse, "Our Lord's holy light will lead you into glory when that time comes." As she dressed Irena in a linen gown and tucked her into bed, I saw how deftly she took the pulse and felt her brow while brushing back the damp hair. "I am Sister Margaret," she whispered. "You're warm and safe with us."

When I asked to stay the night, the sister refused. "You did quite right to bring her here, but now you must go home and rest to stay healthy yourself. You're still in school?" I nodded. "Good. Then come tomorrow afternoon. And God bless your care of the sick."

We took the last streetcar home. When Mamma had gone to bed, I rummaged in the kitchen for a thick candle and hid it in my pocket. Night passed slowly and the school hours crawled. "I said a rosary for her," Yolanda said at recess, "but only one because then my little brother hid the beads. You look terrible, Lucia. Your eyes are red, and rain makes your hair too curly. Pinch your cheeks at least, so you aren't so pale."

After school I ran to the hospital. Sister Margaret had me hang up my wet jacket, take off my soggy shoes, and drink a cup of hot tea. Irena had passed a difficult night and was struggling for breath by morning. "The priest gave her last rites and she has morphine for pain. It won't be long now, poor child. See her picking at the bedsheets?"

I sat by Irena's bed, lit the candle, and wrapped her damp fingers around it. When her hand jerked, I managed to blow out the candle just as it fell clattering to the floor. Rummaging under the bed to retrieve it, I was overwhelmed by the closeness of death. Sister Margaret found me sobbing.

She helped me to my chair. "There now, if she wants a candle, she'll have one, but let's not start fires. What's your name, child?"

"Lucia D'Angelo."

"Precisely, your friend's guardian angel. But, Lucia, if you are to be her angel, you must remember that the dying can still hear, almost to the end. Your tears will hold her back. The Call is coming very soon, and you must not keep her from Our Lord."

"Sister, I've never . . ."

"Never sat at a deathbed?" I shook my head. "Wait here." She hurried away and returned with a sturdy candlestick holder, relit the candle, and set it by the bed. "Our Lord will not suffer us to walk in darkness. He is even now preparing a place for Irena, beyond all trouble and pain. You can remember this for her sake?" I nodded. "Fix on the light, Lucia, and know that He is near."

*Breathe, breathe,* I heard Mamma's voice repeating. Somehow the hours passed. After work, Henryk came. Mamma came, Yolanda, Roseanne, and Donato. Irena died soon after the chapel bells tolled nine o'clock. Sister Margaret closed her eyes and let us kiss her. "But you all must leave now," she said firmly. "We need the bed for another patient. We'll wash her body and give her a good pine coffin. Our hospital priest says a funeral mass for the week's dead on Sunday afternoon and she'll be buried decently."

"With a headstone?" I asked.

"The field is consecrated, but it's a common grave."

"We can buy her a plot and a headstone," I began, but Mamma, Roseanne, and even Yolanda shook their heads.

"They're expensive, fifty dollars or more," Sister Margaret warned.

I swallowed. So there would be no headstone, no marker of Irena's life. "Sister, she asked to be buried in her blue dress. Can we do that, at least?"

"If you hurry. We have many bodies to wash. If you're not back in time, we'll have to put her in a linen shift." Donato ran with me to the streetcar, home and back to the hospital. By then the others had left. The sisters took Irena's dress but wouldn't let us see her.

"You're exhausted, poor girl," said Donato. "Let me take you to Lula's Tavern for a hot cider. It's nearby." At first I hesitated, never having been inside a tavern, but he and Paolo, Roseanne said, were two men one could trust in the world, so I let myself be taken to Lula's and settled in a corner booth of the smoky, wood-lined room.

I assumed that Donato would open his wallet and show me yet again the photographs of his wife and baby girl. Then I would tell him once more how beautiful they were and how happy I'd be to meet them. Instead he took my hand and said earnestly: "Lucia, she had a priest at the end and will have a funeral mass. She'll be buried in consecrated ground. If her brother comes, perhaps he can buy the headstone. Or later on, if you finish high school and get a good job, perhaps you could buy one yourself."

So much perhaps, so many ifs pressed on me. I slumped in the booth. "Donato, she had such a sad life in America. All the things we'd planned—"

A big-boned Negro woman of uncertain age eased her way to our table. "Looks like someone had herself a hard day."

"She did, Miss Lula. We just came from the hospital where Lucia's good friend died."

When Lula leaned down, her gas-lit face glowed like amber. "What took your friend away, child?"

"Pneumonia," I managed.

"Ah, just like my man Albert. Sweet Jesus rest his soul. It's a hard way to go, but they're both in a better place now." I nodded wearily. "You need something warm in you," Lula said, signaling to the waiter. "My melted beer cheese on toast won't fix your heart, but it's good for the rest of you." When Donato reached for his wallet, she shook her head. "On the house. If it was anybody else with such a pretty little girl, I would have thought, Uh-uh, trouble coming. But, Donato, you're different." She smiled and nudged him. "You got a nice young brother back home for Lucia here, or an old one for me?" Donato reddened but shook his head. She laughed. "Never mind, but you take this child back to her mamma soon, hear? We get a rough crowd with the shift change. Now, Lucia—"

"Yes, ma'am?"

"You call me Lula, like everybody does, and you stop and see me anytime you want in the daytime. I've been around Cleveland a long time. I know some things. And I like Italian girls. I knew one years ago. That Irma saw some trouble, like you're seeing now. But she's doing good these days in California." Lula touched a brooch with roses twined through a golden heart. "She sent me this when my Albert passed." A wave of new customers drew Lula away, but the melted cheese and warm cider were comforting.

We sent a telegram to Casimir at an address I found in Irena's room. Sunday was rainy and cool when Yolanda, Donato, and I went to the hospital chapel for Irena's funeral. Henryk's father needed him; Mamma and Roseanne were feeling poorly and hadn't come.

Ten pine coffins had been neatly stacked in the sanctuary with their names painted on the lids. Four were full size; six held children. Families of the dead clustered together as a sleepy priest gave the mass. Then he hurried away through a side door. A sexton loaded the coffins on a cart. The common grave site would be announced "in due time," he said, but we must leave now. The chapel was needed for a wedding.

"You did all you could," Yolanda reminded me as we walked home. "She died with friends. And you're not alone now; you have me. *We* don't have to draw pictures to understand each other." Of course a common language and memories of home were powerful bonds. Yet with pictures and buttons and stumbling English phrases, I'd given Irena secrets I'd never voiced in Italian. She knew my dreams for college and never laughed at them. When I spoke of Mamma's fits and temper, she held my hands and let me fret. I didn't know until that cold, wet walk home how much I owed and needed her. But Yolanda's anxious face was searching mine. "No," I agreed, "we don't need pictures for talking."

Of course I understood that Irena's room couldn't be left empty. Roseanne would store Irena's things for a while in case Casimir came, but the room must be cleaned and rented out again. "We'll take it," Mamma announced.

"It's fifty cents more a week," I protested. "We can stay where we are until we've paid back the countess."

"Come outside, Lucia. We'll talk about it." Walking up and down our street, we had a furious argument, our worst yet in America. "Listen to me," Mamma said loudly. "We deserve that room more than the countess deserves our fifty cents."

"We promised to pay her back. And that room was my friend's."

"Now it can be ours. Don't you care that after working all day to keep you in school, I have to sleep in a coffin?" Her voice rose. When neighbors came to their windows to watch us like a show, I gave up, exhausted and embarrassed by her fury.

After relating "our" decision, Mamma hugged and kissed me. "You'll see, Lucia. We'll be happy." That evening she scrubbed the front room until it reeked of borax, ammonia, and lemon oil. I still saw and felt Irena in the shadows, but Mamma was right: the old room *was* a coffin, and the bright morning light in the new one was a blessing. Donato dragged home a battered desk from his shop. I boxed up a cache of Irena's buttons, her rosary, Bible, and framed prints of Poland for Casimir and wrote to Countess Elisabetta, explaining that we would repay her but needed a little more time. She thanked us for our diligence and sent a spray of dried lavender to perfume our room.

"You see?" said Mamma. "That wasn't hard."

Casimir never answered our telegram. If he had made other plans, perhaps it was better that Irena never knew this. I went back to scribing and studied hard to make up for missed schoolwork. As we drew close to the end of the year, the school principal said I might skip a grade if I studied on my own that summer. Yes, I said, I'd gladly do that. If Mamma lost her job or quit, as she often threatened to do, if she was hurt or sick, I'd have to go to work. Skipping a grade would hurry my graduation.

"Why does a diploma matter so much?" Yolanda asked. "You don't need it for a job."

"For a good job I do. And I *want* to graduate." I wanted it for myself; it was the first prize I'd wanted so steadily. I wanted it for Irena's sake. I wanted to be able to care for Mamma if I had to work for both of us. And if I had a chance for college, I'd need a high school diploma.

"Well then," said Yolanda loyally, "I hope you get it."

*On a warm* July evening, Mamma was singing a silly popular song, "The Moon Has His Eyes on You." I'd translated the lyrics for her and any American would have imagined that she understood each word. I was curled on the divan with my battered dictionary and *A Tale of Two Cities*. A knock at the door brought Roseanne rushing, for new boarders often came at that hour from the last New York train. In fact, a weary young couple stood on the porch, a neat stack of luggage behind them.

"Yes, I have a room to rent," Roseanne said loudly before they could speak.

The man looked past her into the parlor. "Irena?"

My dictionary hit the floor with a thud. The piano slowed and stopped. Casimir was square-shouldered as Irena might have been before her accident, with the same blue eyes, thick blond hair, and open face. He carried a wooden box that surely held butcher knives.

"We need a translator," Roseanne said quietly. "Lucia, go get your friend Henryk." Then she explained to Casimir loudly in Italian that I would bring over a friend who spoke Polish. Meanwhile he and his wife should come in and make themselves comfortable in the parlor.

"Irena?" he repeated.

My shoes were too small, I remember. They pinched as I ran the few blocks to Henryk's flat. When I blurted my news, Henryk said something to his mother, who used the *"shiksa"* word again. His father spoke in a steely, low tone of command, more unnerving than any Neapolitan shouting. I heard "Polski" and "Irena" in Henryk's answers. Finally his mother and then father appeared to relent. Neither spoke to me.

"I'm sorry," Henryk said as we left his flat and hurried down the foggy street. "They just didn't like a girl calling on boys at night."

"They thought I was—"

"Yes, *that* sort. But I said you scribed with me, study hard, good girl, respect your mother, all those things. And they want to help other Poles, even Gentiles."

"Your mother sent over the soup," I remembered.

"Yes, her magic soup." He slowed his walk for me. "This brother must be exhausted, and now he'll find out his sister's dead."

"Roseanne's probably shouting at him in Italian."

"My mother does that too. I keep telling her that Americans aren't deaf. They just don't speak Yiddish."

By the time we reached the boardinghouse, Roseanne had brought Casimir and his wife wineglasses and little plates of *chiacchere*, the fried sugared strips that were her pride. They held these things on their knees, not eating or drinking as she rattled on about Cleveland.

Henryk bowed slightly to Anna and shook Casimir's hand before taking a chair in front of them. When it seemed their glasses and plates might slip to the floor, Roseanne quietly took them away. Henryk leaned forward, speaking softly, his eyes fixed on them, even when asking me for details of Irena's slender story. Their faces turned to wood; their hands sought each other. Finally Casimir spoke.

Henryk listened, nodded, and told us. "He never got your telegram. They must have already left for America. He'd like to see her grave." Silence filled the room like thick new snow.

"Tell them," I began. My voice cracked. Four blue eyes fixed on mine. "Tell them that Irena was given last rites and a funeral mass and buried in consecrated ground." Donato mouthed the word *dress* and I added as Henryk translated: "The sisters put her in a good blue dress she wanted for the end." Anna whispered to Casimir. Perhaps she knew the dress. "We're very sorry that we couldn't afford a headstone."

Another exchange and Henryk reported: "Casimir says he'll buy one as soon as he can. They brought some Polish earth." When we looked startled, Henryk explained: "Three handfuls, one for each of their graves." Nobody spoke.

I brought down Irena's box. Casimir opened it and touched the buttons avidly, as if they still held her heat. I told them the jacket she made for Anna had to be sold. "Describe it," said Roseanne, and I did: the deep red velvet, gold braid, and embroidered flowers. Anna smiled.

Then Casimir spoke at length and Henryk translated: "He wants us to know about Irena. She was always a happy child. She won footraces in their village. He made her a wooden doll and she dressed it." He and Casimir conferred. "She dressed it in a gown of feathers and bits of moss. He wanted to emigrate first, but Irena said he should finish his apprenticeship. She said she'd be lucky in America." Tears pooled in Casimir's eyes.

Anna spoke and Henryk translated: "She says he loved his sister very much." *How redundant words can be,* I thought, *how unnecessary.*

"Tell them I happen to have a room available," Roseanne said finally, "if they'd like to stay here where Irena lived." Henryk conveyed this, adding some words and then giving Casimir's answer.

"He thanks you all, especially Lucia, for your kindness to Irena, and the offer of a room. But I told him that in our building we're all Poles, Jews and Gentiles, and we have space. He said he'd rather stay with us until he finds a flat. He hopes you understand. When they're settled, they'll invite you to a *stypa*, a feast in Irena's honor. Now I'll take them home with me. The journey has been difficult and they're very tired."

"You can use my handcart," Roseanne offered. We helped load their bags and Irena's box and watched them move slowly down the street. In the fog their bodies merged. I was ashamed of my flash of envy: Casimir and Anna would live near Henryk. They'd see him every day, hear his laugh and see the particular way he knit his brow when working figures. He might tell them about the bread-wearing pigeon. *Stop this. Stop.*

"So many buttons Irena made," Mamma said softly. "For nothing."

"Henryk seems like a nice young man," Donato said, glancing at me.

"He's *Jewish*," Roseanne announced.

"Oh. Well then."

"He's just a friend," I added quickly.

*Casimir settled quickly* into Cleveland, working for his cousin, the Polish butcher on Forman Avenue. Anna made sausages and was soon producing great quantities for Polish customers, Lula's tavern, Roseanne, and other boardinghouse keepers. When Anna fell briefly sick, Lula sent over a special "reviving brew." Her customers wanted Anna's sausages, she said, and accepted no others.

After Casimir and Anna moved to a flat of their own, Henryk came to invite us to Irena's *stypa*. "They'll be months repaying the feast," he predicted, "but it's tradition. He owes her this honor."

"Wear something nice," Roseanne advised Mamma that evening. "You might snag a fella."

"I have work, I have Lucia. Not everybody needs a fella," Mamma snapped. In fact, her few evenings "walking out" with men who met her at church had ended badly. She came home early, said nothing, and the men never returned. She wore a work dress to the *stypa*.

Casimir's flat was packed with Polish families and customers for Anna's sausages. Lula came too. "That man loved his sister, but he's one good businessman," she noted. "All these folks will remember him." We'd surely remember the tables heaped with sausages, stuffed cabbage, potato pancakes, smoked and pickled fish. A picture of Irena, young, straight-shouldered, and beaming, hung on a wall. She might have just won a footrace and perhaps already begun dreaming of America.

Yolanda came with a tall young man whose sandy curls covered his head like lamb's wool. "This is Charlie Reilly," she said. "We met in a candy store three weeks ago."

"Yes, she's my little Italian sweet," said Charlie. His hand strayed to her waist as if he were constantly assuring himself of her presence. "And here I am at a Polish party. God bless America!" Yolanda had spoken mysteriously of a "fella," never mentioning that he was American.

When I asked if he was also Catholic, Yolanda looked at me sharply. "Not that I know of," Charlie said with a laugh. "Actually, my parents don't even like Catholics, but that's only because they don't know Yolanda. Look, little rolled-up pancakes."

"Blintzes," I corrected primly, but they didn't seem to hear me.

Charlie fed Yolanda a blintz. Her blissful smile, the soft curve of her body toward his, and the rich freedom of his laughter made a mesmerizing show. I watched them move along the tables, tasting every dish. Yolanda's face caught the light. In a plain shirtwaist dress transformed by lace, new buttons, and a subtle band of tucks, she seemed as elegant as any young woman on the stretch of Euclid Avenue that people called Millionaires Row.

"They look so happy," Roseanne observed. Yes, perhaps, but I couldn't help being rudely critical of this fella. What would Dr. Galuppi have thought of the slight scoop of Charlie's temples, the slope of his forehead? Could he be trusted? My teachers said phrenology was a bogus science, best forgotten in this century. I didn't care. A handsome young man was leaning close to Yolanda while I stood by with my landlady?

Across the room a slim, dark-haired girl with lavish curls stood with her back to me, talking to Henryk, his father, and Henryk's friend Abraham. Her rippling laughter skittered over the room. The men seemed bewitched. "Who's she?" I asked Roseanne.

"Some Jewish princess from Pittsburgh, just moved here. Look at your mother. Why is she facing the wall?"

I hurried over. "Mamma, what's wrong? Come, I'll get you something to eat."

"It's Polish food."

"Yes, everything's delicious. And there'll be singing later."

"In Polish."

"Yes, but you sing in English all the time. What's the difference?"

"It's so crowded with strangers."

"It's a wake for Irena, our friend. I'm glad so many people came. Look," I said, pointing. "Even the Russian is here, her button dealer." But Mamma was rigid and her eyes too wide. "Did someone say something to you? What's the matter?" For a frantic moment, I thought she'd conjured Toscanini.

"I want to go home." A film of sweat covered her face, and her breath came fast, like Irena's at the end.

"I'll tell Roseanne—"

"Take me *now*."

"Fine, Mamma, we'll go." Halfway down the narrow stairs, we heard the singing start, rich and rolling, buoyed by violins. She looked back as a hungry man strains toward a feast, even took a step up toward the flat again, but at a burst of laughter, her face clouded and she hurried me out of the building.

On the sidewalk, her breathing calmed, the seeming fever passed, and she spoke calmly of a new piano roll she wanted. "Mamma, shouldn't we see a nurse? You looked so sick."

"Because I wanted to leave," she said sharply. "Don't you ever want leave someplace?"

"I suppose, but—"

She began humming the tune we'd heard on the stairway. Mamma never explained the attack, why it came or how it passed, but that evening began a new time for us in Cleveland.

## Chapter 6

### FROZEN WAVES

*By the chill* autumn of 1906, Mamma was the fastest dipper at Stingler's, earning eleven dollars for a sixty-hour week without fines. However, possible fines were many: for being late or covering a friend's lateness, dropping or miscounting chocolates, making imperfect swirls, damaging equipment, slowing the line, talking excessively, singing inappropriate songs, or for the vaguely defined "insolence."

"Old Mr. Stingler's gone soft in the head as a caramel," Mamma said. He had started the company in his kitchen and designed every machine in the production line, but now between flashes of clarity, he wandered the factory, somberly studying the operations as if each was of the most astonishing interest. Sometimes he saw his dead wife sitting with the dippers. "Milly, you don't need to work," he'd say, tugging at a young girl's sleeve. "Come home. We have servants now and a big house on Euclid Avenue."

"Some girls would gladly be Milly," Mamma said, "if they could stomach Little Stingler, that nasty little cock who never dipped a chocolate in his life." In our parlor, she mimed him pacing the line, chest thrust forward, short, thin legs as stiff as rods, arms flapping as he urged the workers to be more industrious and attentive to their swirls. "Someday a cat will tear that cock to pieces," she took to muttering.

"The other girls might tear *her* to pieces first," Yolanda warned. "Little Stingler's always telling them to work as fast as Teresa D'Angelo. She needs to slow down." But as we dressed for bed in our chilly room, Mamma said she *couldn't* slow down. "If I do, my head fills up with bad thoughts about Little Stingler. Besides, if I'm learning a new song with a quick beat, I *have* to dip to that beat."

"Perhaps you could talk to the priest about your thoughts."

"They're *mine* and I'll think them."

"Be careful, Mamma." When did that tone of mine begin, that patter of advice, as if I were the mother and she the child? I didn't ask again. After all, that autumn began as an easy time. We chipped off bits of rent by doing chores for Roseanne; we were faster and more exacting than her cleaning girl. We had finally paid our debt to Countess Elisabetta. This meant nothing to Mamma, but it was a triumph for me. I stood straighter, wrote to the countess more often, and received longer letters back from her.

In October she trusted me with her great secret: lurking beneath Count Filippo's malarial fevers was syphilis. His rages had grown worse and more frequent with the pain of his great disease. His mind half gone, he gambled wildly, signing notes against the estate. The countess didn't know how many or to whom. "He spent the summer with us, which was a torment, as you know. At least he gambled less. Paolo turns away the 'gentlemen' who come like vultures to profit from his weakness. But tell me about school and all the wonderful things in America. I want to hear that you and Teresa are happy."

"He won't last long, she can hope," Mamma observed.

"What should I write about?"

"Anything except that bastard." I wrote about Cleveland, the parks and grand stores and the noisy immigrant quarters. I described Central High School. Students constantly left to find jobs in the factories, mills, and limestone quarries south of Cleveland. Little was done to keep them. Only eight in one hundred Americans had high school diplomas, our teacher told us. I was determined to be one of those eight.

Having skipped tenth grade, I was now in eleventh, gorging on speeches and poems to memorize, chapters to read, essays to write. When my first dictionary broke into pieces from constant use, I won another for reciting Mark Antony's speech to the Romans. I wrote to the countess about algebra's secret language of $x$'s and $y$'s. My geometry lessons made the city an intricate mosaic of shapes: arches of doorways, cones and pyramids of gaslights, cylinders of smokestacks, tangents and trapezoids of pathways and streets. In those days, I dreamed less of finding a fella than of holding a diploma in my hands.

"Don't waste your chances," Yolanda warned. "You need to get married in high school. Your friend Henryk's family wants a Jewish girl, so don't bother with him. Maybe Charlie knows somebody good for you. Should I ask?"

"Not yet. I don't have time anyway, with school and scribing and work in the boardinghouse." I saw Henryk often, for he too had skipped a grade, and we sometimes worked in the public library together. Sitting across from him at a long oak table, each in a pool of light, I tried to nail my eyes to books, away from the glossy falls of his black hair, wide mouth moving slightly as he read and long fingers scribbling. When we did our math together, droll little stick figures marched up and down his notebook pages. "They help me think," he said, but they couldn't help him think how to keep up these library hours when he had to work more afternoons with his father.

"Charlie wants me to graduate," Yolanda was saying, "but school is so boring. I want my own hat shop. Charlie says . . ." She talked constantly of him: where they'd gone, what he said, how he'd own a factory or limestone quarry one day and they'd have servants.

"Have you met his family yet?" I interrupted.

"No, but I will at Christmas."

"Why not now?"

"Because Protestants announce big things at Christmas. That's how they are. Lucia, you should be worrying about your mother, not about me. She keeps saying things about Little Stingler, crazy things she shouldn't say, even in Italian."

I fretted for days about how to ask Mamma about the "things," afraid she'd slip into another of the dark silences that often encased her. Finally one night I blurted my worry. She backed away from me and snapped: "The girls make up stories. Everyone's crazy with this cold. And your friend Yolanda is crazy with Charlie."

It's true that the cold pushed into every corner of our lives. The last winter had been mild, with barely more snow than we saw on Vesuvius. Now ice froths rimmed the lake; we stuffed paper in our shoes and wore coats in the house. I wrote to the countess that the Alps couldn't possibly be this cold. Even Miss Miller, born in Cleveland, remembered no winter so hard.

By December Lake Erie had frozen in ragged silver-gray waves as the wind drove icy chunks into hummocks. The sky shook down snow, paused for breath, and shook again. Frigid gusts raced down the streets, drilling through the boardinghouse walls, laughing at our coal stove. Every floor, table, door, book, and plate was cold. "Even the fire's cold," said Donato. Much as I missed Irena, I was grateful she was spared this suffering. Like a great plug pulled from a washtub, color drained from the city. Green was long gone, of course, and now constant frost dulled each surface to a dingy gray. New snow turned quickly black from coal and wood ash. Under a milky sky we scuttled to and fro, swathed in coats and mufflers. "How can we stand it?" I asked Miss Miller, wrapped in my coat for scribing.

"What can we do but stand it?"

Donato spent his evenings at Lula's, drawn by the comfort of her potbellied stove, many bodies, warm beer, and hot cider. When demand drove up the cost of coal, poor families huddled under blankets. Coroner's trucks passed each morning; black-garbed men plucked stiff bodies from the gutters outside taverns and hurried up apartment steps, returning with small bundles as mothers followed, weeping into their shawls.

In school we ran in place each hour to keep our feet from freezing. Rich women knit scratchy gray mufflers that signaled us as charity cases. "If they *really* wanted to help poor folks, they'd send around free coal," Roseanne muttered. Exactly as she had predicted, clothes froze on the lines outside as fast as we could hang them, creaking in the wind like metal sheets. How could it be that once on Christmas day in Naples, wearing only shawls over linen gowns, we sat on our flat rock without freezing, drinking wine and eating marzipan? Last summer we slept soaked in sweat. It seemed that heat had left the world forever.

Hard cold brought Mamma new troubles at Stingler's. First came the day she was late to work because a horse pulling a load of beer kegs slipped on ice and fell across the streetcar tracks, overturning his wagon. A keg split open, slicking the ice with beer. In the tumult of men slopping after rolling kegs and frantic, rearing horses, her streetcar couldn't pass. She ran to work but was late and fined a half day's pay. Still she had to dip all morning or lose her job completely.

"Promptness is paramount," Mamma mimicked that evening at dinner, thrusting out her chest and peering down her nose at us. "They say every cockroach is beautiful to its own mother. Ha! I bet even Milly hated Little Stingler."

"It's not fair they didn't pay and still made you work," I protested at dinner. Mamma flared at me. "*Fair!* You think that little bastard cares about *fair*? Of course I worked without pay. Don't you have to stay in school? Don't we have to pay our rent? Pass the potatoes!" In bed that night, she turned against the wall, her shoulders heaving, her muttering like distant, roiling water.

Guilt washed over me. She had raced down icy streets only to be fined. She sat for hours hunched over steaming vats. She had no Vesuvius for comfort, no warm bay for swimming, no fella or friends that I knew of, only an old player piano for pleasure. I had school, books, the company of friends, and my diploma dreams. How could I ease her life? Even if I went to work, I'd never make enough to support us. Girls were paid less than women, who earned less than men or even boys for the same work. As she drifted to sleep, I wrapped my arms around her against the piercing cold.

*Wrapping her.* Yes! I could buy her a warm coat like the ones in Higbee's window for seven dollars. Watching the first flakes of yet another snowfall, I pawed through schemes to earn seven dollars. Not scribing: that money went to Roseanne for the rising cost of coal. As the night sky gleamed with snow, it came to me that I could polish silver for pay.

Last week, I'd overheard Miss Miller complaining to a wealthy Hiram House patron that the family's silver was a disgrace; their butler was quite incompetent. Paolo had taken pains to train me for this task. I knew just how much fine English polishing cream to apply, how long to let it sit, and how to buff with soft cloths until my face pooled in every spoon. I could clean neglected silver, uncovering intricate designs in what had seemed merely gray knobs of tarnish.

The next day I drew Miss Miller aside to make my offer: I'd polish two cabinets of silver until they shone like moons for seven dollars, streetcar fare, and lunch on the two days I estimated this work would require.

"Three and a half dollars a day!" whistled Yolanda. "My father makes less than that. Does she feel sorry for you?"

"I don't care. I just want a coat."

The next Saturday I went to the Millers' back door and was bustled in by Agnes the cook, a sharp-angled woman whose odd accent, she explained proudly, came from Boston. She brought me to the butler's pantry, where a long table was heaped with platters, tureens, vases, pitchers, candlesticks, and silverware. Jars of English cream had been set out, neatly folded flannel cloths, and a plate with two thick slices of buttered bread. "No point working hungry," she said. "I'm in the kitchen if you need anything."

I set to polishing. With blessed warmth, a steady kitchen chatter of servants, and an abundant lunch of veal stew with cabbage, it was deep into the afternoon before I stopped to shake out the cramps of work. "You've been slaving like a Trojan, my girl," Agnes called from the kitchen. "Come get some hot cocoa and oatcakes."

She was an eager gossip and I was a fresh ear. "If Mr. Miller had known his daughter would come back all fired up to teach immigrants," Agnes began, "he'd never have sent her to Vassar College. But she'll marry soon and have a great house of her own. Richard Livingston's family made a fortune in limestone. He's sweet on her, and Miss Edith's a lovely girl. As you could be, Lucia, if you got yourself fixed up."

I thanked her, took another oatcake, and exclaimed over it to hide my astonishment. Miss Miller had told us often and earnestly that teaching immigrants was her life's calling. Now it seemed we were only a private charity before a splendid marriage, a harmless diversion, like tennis, golf, or watercolors.

The butcher's boy dragged in crates of meat, stamping his feet and sniffing cocoa in the warm kitchen air. "It's the blasted Arctic out there," he announced. "A dozen dead dogs and cats I saw today, frozen stiff as boards, a sight to sober up a tinker. Thank you, missus, very kind," he finished, as Agnes handed him a steaming mug. He gulped it and left, hunched into the cold.

Anxious now to finish work and be home, I was buffing the last platter as Miss Miller swept into the pantry. Her lush red velvet gown dipped low in front, pinched at the waist, and flounced behind. Her hair was a mass of ringlets and loops. "There you are, Lucia," she said in a high, breathy voice I'd never heard before. "Richard will be so cross that I'm late, but I just had to see those silver moons you told me about." Hanging lights did make moons on the platters, while vases, tureens, and pitchers reflected the gleaming red of her gown, black sheen of hair, and long loops of pearls against a creamy chest. At Hiram House, Miss Miller was always modestly, even severely dressed in high starched collars and dark woolen skirts. Was that penance for her other, gilded life?

"Mother will be delighted," she said, counting out my first day's pay and streetcar fare from a beaded purse. "Someone who served *a countess* is cleaning our silver. Be careful in the cold now, Lucia. Hurry home and we'll expect you in the morning." With instructions to Agnes for Sunday's tea in the conservatory, she was gone, trailing a heavy scent of roses. Her voice turned high and tinkling as she called out to Richard.

Out of the habit of constant work, my arms were stiff as stone as I put on my coat, gray muffler, and the woolen socks I used as mittens. In the long wait for a streetcar, cold winds flew down Euclid Avenue, drilling me like icy spikes. All the warmer inner seats were taken; I was pressed against ice-caked windows. Stamping my feet, clenching my fists inside the too-thin socks, I endured the ride, consoled by the weight of $3.50 in a cloth bag around my neck.

I reached the boardinghouse just before Mamma returned from her Saturday shift. Roseanne sat me by the kitchen stove. "Don't move until you thaw," she said, "and don't rub or your skin comes off. You'd think rich folks would send you back in one of their fancy automobiles. Ask if they will tomorrow." I didn't ask, and in Sunday's bustle of service for Miss Miller's tea, there was no break for cocoa and oatcakes. Still, in the frigid ride home, I had something better: the rest of my seven dollars.

Yolanda came with me to Higbee's so I wouldn't choose "something awful." She had been moody and anxious since Christmas. Charlie was still hovering, kind and attentive, still calling her his "dear Italian sweet," but, with various vague excuses, had never taken her home.

"Why can't I meet his parents? What's wrong with me?" she demanded as we went through the racks at Higbee's. When I suggested that Charlie's mother might prefer an American "sweet," Yolanda announced that she didn't want to talk about Charlie anymore. She pulled me toward a black coat with a short gray cape attached. "They call this a 'capelet,' new this season," she explained. "Very *dashing*, don't you think? That's what Americans say: *dashing*. But it's seven and a half dollars."

A clerk bore down on us. "Are you girls just looking or are you here to buy?"

I set my heavy purse of quarters on the counter with a thud. "To buy," I said, "here or in some other store."

"I was only asking, miss, since I heard you talking Eye-talian."

"I'll buy in American if you have that style in a *dashing* color."

He stepped back. "We do, yes, miss, over here." We chose burgundy with a deep blue capelet, not the winter's endless black and gray. With fifty cents more from my scribing, I paid and had him wrap my prize. It made a satisfyingly bulky bundle as Yolanda and I walked the long way home.

"Remember, don't talk about Charlie," she warned. But I saw how hungrily she stared at an American couple stepping out of a motorcar and an Italian couple laughing as they scrambled over ink-black humps of frozen slush.

"Thank you for helping with the coat," I said to distract her. "My mother will love it. She'll have the finest coat at Stingler's."

Yolanda's eyes swung back to mine. "She might need another job soon."

"What?" My stomach clenched.

"Stingler's could be making peanut clusters instead of chocolates and caramels. The swirls don't come right if the dipping room's too cold, and Little Stingler's too cheap to heat it. Anyway, peanut clusters cost less."

I hugged my bundle closer. "How do you know all this?"

We were crossing an icy patch. Yolanda walked cautiously as she spoke. "My friend Marta heard Little Stingler talking to the foreman about letting some of the dippers go. She could be wrong. Her English isn't good. But if she's right, your mother's in trouble. First: anybody can make peanut clusters. Second: he likes dippers with small children. Even better if they have small children and no husband. Those women have to work."

"So does Mamma."

Yolanda veered around a shoeshine boy. "So you really don't know?"

I grabbed her sleeve. "Know what?"

She dropped her voice, nearly hissing. "The other dippers make Little Stingler *want* to keep them. They do, let's say, private things for him. Your mother won't. He's kept her on so far just because she's so fast at dipping. But with clusters everything's different."

"Private things?" I repeated dully. "You mean the girls have to—" A heavy weight filled my stomach, as if I'd swallowed lead.

"Yes. They do different things, depending on what he can get. Of course, on Old Stingler's good days, Little Cock has to behave himself."

I stopped, nearly vomiting onto the black snow, sucking at the frigid air until I could walk again. I imagined Little Stingler lurking by the washroom, ordering girls to his office, keeping them late, making them come early, even pulling them from the dipping line as friends pretended not to see. I saw greedy hands pushed under skirts or resting paternally on shoulders and then slipping down. I saw red-faced girls returning to their posts, frantically smoothing skirts while others looked away, each one thinking: *Will it be me tomorrow?* I saw Mamma twisting free, dodging, snapping, snarling, making him turn to easier prey, but stirring up resentment at her "insolence." Perhaps each girl's shame reminded Mamma of what she'd endured on the seaweed. Meanwhile I'd curled around my books, suspecting nothing. Being so ignorant of Miss Miller's gilded life paled to nothing; I didn't know my own mother's life.

"Does Marta do those things?"

"She has to," Yolanda said quietly. "The family needs her pay. Charlie promised that I'll *never* work for Stingler's."

"I see." No wonder Mamma sang and talked to herself. No wonder she came home bad-tempered and exhausted. We'd reached Yolanda's flat.

"Maybe I shouldn't have told you. I talked about it with Charlie. We weren't sure."

"No, you did right. And don't worry. You'll meet Charlie's parents and they'll love you." We kissed at parting as we always did, but quickly, brushing icy cheeks before she flew upstairs to her crowded flat.

How could I study, waiting for Mamma's return? And what recompense was a wool coat with a silly capelet? Still, I laid out the coat on our bed and straightened our room until I heard her in the entryway speaking to Roseanne. When she came in, her face stiff and shoulders stooped, I pointed at the coat.

"For me?" She walked slowly to the bed and stroked the thick, soft wool. "You polished silver for this?" I nodded. "It's perfect, Lucia. Thank you. I never had anything so beautiful."

When she bit her lip, turning away, I couldn't hold on to my secret: "Yolanda told me what Little Stingler makes girls do."

She sat down, wrapping the burgundy sleeves around her waist. "Why talk about that bastard? It would just make me want to hurt him, like I hurt Count Filippo. Or worse, because he hurt so many girls. Then where would we go? But it doesn't matter now." She pushed the coat away. "He said he had to get rid of some girls and he was already paying me too much. Then today . . ."

"What about today?" I heard my own heart pounding.

She stood up so suddenly the bed thumped. "Nothing. I don't want to talk about it. I'm fired but at least I got paid for the week. Old Stingler made him do that much." Her eyes were wild and frightening. "I'll never make the same money anywhere else. My English isn't good like yours, and I can't trim pretty hats." She looked at the coat. "We'll sell it." She paced the room, walking into my desk so hard that my chair fell over.

"No. I'll leave school and work." Anything, anything to calm her.

She shook her head. "You have to finish and get that diploma." The dinner bell rang. We said nothing to the others, but afterward Mamma sent me upstairs while she spoke to Roseanne. I stared at my book until she returned and announced: "The kitchen girl was fired for stealing coffee. I'll clean here for two weeks. If you help on weekends, we can almost pay our room and board. Roseanne will forgive us the difference 'for Paolo's sake.'" Mamma smiled slightly. Then her face stiffened. "I'll look for work at the garment factories. Cold doesn't matter there."

"Mamma—"

"I need to walk."

"Let me come with you."

"No!" She yanked on the new coat and was gone. I sat with my book by the drafty window until past midnight, when I saw her coming home. That was the beginning of her night walks and my long vigils.

"So, I'm a servant again," she said in the morning, pulling her Naples work smock from our trunk, binding her hair tightly, and covering it with a scarf. I ached to see her do these things.

"When I finish high school," I promised in what became my steady litany, "I'll get a good job and you won't have to work. We'll have a piano—"

"The rugs need beating," she said. "At least here nobody touches me."

That afternoon I was late coming home after scribing for a new wave of immigrants. When I opened our front door, cleaning smells poured out: ammonia, linseed and lemon oil, borax and bleach. The parlor shone. The wooden banister gleamed like honey in sunshine. Even the brass coat hooks were polished. Roseanne showed me the dining room. The oak table was a sleek golden pond; windows sparkled. She ran her finger along the wainscoting and looked around in wonder, even dismay.

"What's wrong? Everything's clean. Isn't that what you wanted?" I demanded.

"She's so fast. It's not normal."

"She had to be fast at the villa. It was big and had to be clean all the time. Aren't you grateful? Look at this room. Look at the glass on this china cabinet, like you could reach in and touch the plates."

"That's true," Roseanne admitted, "but it's like she's angry at the floors, at the glass and furniture, as if she's possessed somehow. Was it like this in Naples?"

"There's nothing wrong with her," I said as crisply as I could. Wouldn't anyone enduring work and then the loss of work at Stingler's be angry? And wouldn't it be natural to hurl that anger against furniture and glass?

I tried talking to Mamma after dinner, but she merely snapped: "I'm tired of cleaning. I'm going out." When she finally came to bed, the bleach on her skin stung my eyes. On the third day she attacked the cellar, hauling out years of broken furniture, moldy books and clothing. I described to Yolanda this frenzy of work and refusal to talk about Stingler's.

"It's *not* normal," Yolanda agreed. "And she'll run out of things to clean."

The next week, we found relief. Mamma got work at Printz-Biederman, and Roseanne hired a somber Irish girl named Elsie with good references. Mamma would be making ten dollars a week. The bosses didn't ask for "favors"; all they wanted was finished coats and dresses. But she'd have to rent her sewing machine from the company and buy thread and needles. It would take years to own the machine. "It's harder work than dipping, for a dollar less," she said, walking wearily to the piano. I'd help, I promised. I'd start right away.

Agnes arranged weekend work for me at the Millers'. Dressed in a crisp black uniform, I became a waitress for parties, teas, and dinners. I had another job as well: when ladies gathered in the conservatory, they wanted tales of Countess Elisabetta, the count, and "all their noble friends." At first I resisted. My people weren't storybook figures. As much as I hated the count, his pains were real. But Mrs. Miller expected these tales and, Agnes hinted, might reward them with tips.

"Will those silly ladies ever meet the countess?" Roseanne demanded.

"No."

"Well then?"

I read my answer in her smile. Of course! Invent. On streetcar rides to work, I concocted tales of fabulous parties and midnight dances with moonlight frosting the bay, picnics on Vesuvius and balls at the palace of King Victor Emmanuel. Maestro Arturo Toscanini played piano for my countess; he adored her. I described precious gifts from an adoring count: cameos the size of my palm, ivory combs and coral vases, enormous bouquets of delicate porcelain flowers, marble busts of her as the Greek goddess Diana. The ladies were entranced. Before banquets I was to suggest points of "refined service" to the butler, which he attended politely when his mistress was nearby and then blithely ignored. For this I was paid well, fed, and given food left over from parties.

Between work, homework, and scribing, I had no time for dances at Hiram House. "I saw your fella Henryk dancing with Miriam, that pretty girl from Irena's *stypa*," Yolanda warned. "People say her family owes his a favor."

"He's not my fella," I said too loudly. "And the rest is just gossip."

"Of course. Anyway, I'm sure he missed you at the dance. Look what Charlie gave me," she said, showing off a slender ring she wore on a ribbon under her chemise. "We're engaged," she whispered. "It's a secret. But it's wonderful. We really have to find *you* a fella."

"I told you, I don't have time."

"You should *make* time," she said somberly. "It's important."

Henryk and I still saw each other at school. He was always kind, asked after my mother, and gave me news of Casimir and Anna before hurrying off. He was busy, of course. But he did have time for dances. In any case, he was just a friend, I steadily reminded myself, and I had no claim on his time. I asked Yolanda not to tell me any more about Henryk.

"I won't, Lucia, but *you* could go out sometime. Cleveland's a big city. People do have fun here."

She was right, I thought, and laughed at the coincidence when Donato came back that night from Lula's, beaming. "Look! I have four tickets to vaudeville at the Empire Theater. The show didn't sell out and the manager wants a full house. Maybe this will cheer up Teresa. You can bring your friend Yolanda." Donato blushed when I kissed him in thanks. Mamma was at the player piano, practicing the latest of her piano rolls, "Are You Coming Out Tonight, Mary Ann?" I waved the tickets in her face.

"We're going to the grand vaudeville, Mamma! Singing and dancing, popular songs, comedy acts, pieces of Shakespeare, opera." She snapped her head away, staring at the piano keys going up and down. I turned her face to mine. "I know what you're thinking, but Toscanini won't be there. It's just *pieces* of opera, entertainment like a circus but with more music. It's for families. Americans love it."

"Singers?" she asked finally. "Like Caruso?"

"Well, not Caruso, but others. You'll hear new songs. We'll have a good time."

"What can I wear?"

"Whatever you want. Put your new coat over any dress. You'll look beautiful."

I had no fine coat, but Roseanne helped me put my hair up and loaned me a velvet neckband. We teased Donato that we'd tell his wife he'd gone to the theater with *three* pretty girls. Only later did I find any meaning in Yolanda's distraction, the constant pressing of her hand to her belly. She said she was worried about Charlie. He'd left school for a job with the United Salt Company. Last week, two men had died at the loading docks, crushed under tons of salt. "He *has* to find safer work," she kept repeating.

Mamma barely spoke as we walked through the Empire's grand lobby and handed our tickets to a smartly dressed usher. We marveled at the plush seats, burnished brass, gilded festoons and cupids, sashes, loops of braided hangings, and organ rising by magic from a pit. "Imagine," she whispered, "singing in a place like this." I had never been in a grand theater but had read of them in books.

"You know, Shakespeare's Globe Theater was actually round and—"

"Be quiet, Lucia," Mamma said sharply. "It's starting," Juggler clowns emerged from the crimson curtain, tossing clubs and balls and silky flags. She glared at a noisy squad of young men arriving late. "Don't they want to see all the acts? Idiots."

She patiently endured a dramatic recitation beyond her limited English. Then came a storm of acts: ventriloquists, Blackstone the magician, acrobats, tragic scenes from Shakespeare, tap dancers with black-painted faces, and fast-talking comics who had the audience howling with laughter. Of course it was the singers who transfixed Mamma, first Nora Bayes and then the White Tscherkess Trio, a man and two women who with deft changes of costume and scenery created opera scenes as effortlessly as Blackstone pulled garlands of flowers from the air.

"Look at your mother," Yolanda whispered. "She's like one of those Egyptian things we read about, the finks."

"*Sphinx*," I corrected, but it was true that Mamma hadn't moved since the show began. At the intermission, she shook herself as if waking from sleep.

"Did you hear people cheering for Nora Bayes?" she demanded. "Let's come back next week when I get paid." Donato explained that Miss Bayes could be gone next week to another city. Mamma's eyes glittered. "Really? The singers travel?"

"They probably don't have families," I added quickly.

"They could," Yolanda said. "They might send money home. Imagine how much, with all these people buying tickets."

Mamma nodded thoughtfully. Her eyes glittered as they did at the flush of laudanum, wide and wet, cut loose from reason. I wished the vaudeville show were over and we were back in our room. It seemed as if a thick velvet curtain had slipped between us.

## Chapter 7

## NAPLES NIGHTINGALE

*A late snow* had fallen during the show, as if winter, having once nested in Cleveland, had no mind to leave. We walked home through a froth of slush. "Sara and little Clara will be here soon," Donato announced, explaining yet again how their life would be. After mass each Sunday they'd go to Lake View Park for Clara to play with American children. They'd see moving pictures at the nickelodeon and vaudeville at the Empire. My tales of villa life reeled out for Mrs. Miller's ladies were scarcely more distant from my own childhood than his happy plans, yet these were no fantasies: Donato already knew which streetcar lines went to the park and which playgrounds drew the most American children.

"Maybe Charlie's parents could come to a vaudeville show with us," Yolanda mused. "Even Protestants would like vaudeville, don't you think, Signora Teresa?"

Mamma barely looked up from her feet imprinting the slush, only asked again if we'd heard the applause for Nora Bayes and her harvest song. The next day she came home with a piano roll for "Shine On, Harvest Moon" and fed it into the player before taking off her coat. "Teach me the words," she demanded. I was often exasperated by my mother's blithe refusal to improve her halting English, yet she drank in English lyrics like water, perfectly pronouncing every word. "Silly song," she concluded after my translation. "And a sleepy tune. But you heard how people like it."

After dinner, she set herself to practicing while I studied mathematics. This semester we were learning to graph equations. "You *like* that work?" Yolanda often asked, astonished. I did. I found peace in letters and numbers. I buried myself in equations on days I saw Henryk with Miriam or heard her laughing and talking with girls who clustered around as if her beauty could be contagious. As Mamma sang "Shine on, shine on, harvest moon," I set myself a problem: If moonlight comes at angle $x$, traveling $y$ distance to earth, how far above us is the moon?

Three days after the vaudeville show, Mamma missed dinner. I fretted, then panicked and tried to persuade Donato to go out with me and look for her. "Look where?" he asked reasonably. "It's a big city. Maybe she's with a friend."

"She doesn't have friends."

"It's only eight o'clock. Show me some geometry." Reluctantly, I brought down my notebook, pencil, compass, and ruler. Distracted, constantly checking the parlor clock, I constructed right triangles as Donato feigned great interest in the Pythagorean theorem.

Mamma came home past nine, swept me upstairs, and pushed the warped door tightly closed behind us. "Lucia, listen. I could be the Singing Angel of Naples!"

"The what?"

"The Singing Angel of Naples, my new stage name," she explained as if to a simpleton: "Toscanini kept me out of opera, but I could do vaudeville. I sing as well as Nora Bayes, don't I?"

"Yes, of course, but vaudeville singers travel, remember?" Away from Cleveland. Away from me.

"Yes, all the time, just like Donato said. Who'd come if the acts were always the same? In a big city like this, they stay a week and in a small one a day or two."

"How do you know all this?"

"I went to the Empire and heard two men speaking Italian. So I—"

"You went to the Empire?"

"Yes, listen. One was Mario, the juggler clown in blue. Remember him?"

"No, but never mind. You met Mario."

"Yes, he's from Sorrento. I sang the harvest song for him on the street, and then we went to a tavern and he told me all about vaudeville."

"I see." If my mother had begun reciting Shakespeare or revealed a passionate interest in mathematics, I couldn't have been more astonished. When had she ever gone to taverns with strange men? "But, Mamma, I thought after the San Carlo and the guards—"

She waved this memory away like a bothersome fly. "That was *opera*. Vaudeville is different." I nodded, a little dazed.

With growing fervor she explained how smaller acts might be picked up or switched with other troupes in new cities. The first number was always a "dumb act" of jugglers or clowns as latecomers straggled in. Big names, who earned more, came after intermission. She explained the sequence of acts and how nothing in bad taste or risqué was permitted, so the clergymen in small towns wouldn't preach against vaudeville. In fact, clergy often got free tickets.

The ground rocked under my feet. Since we'd come to Cleveland, her life had spooled between work, home, church, Hiram House, Catalano's for Italian foods, and music stores with Italian clerks where she bought and traded piano rolls. Once again new truths about my mother dashed over me like a bone-freezing winter wave.

She sat on our bed, the luster fading from her face. "Lucia, the truth is, I *can't* work in factories anymore. It's too dangerous."

"Dangerous? You mean the machines?"

"No, my danger's here." She pointed to her head. "Even now, in this room with you, I'm still *there* at Printz-Biederman, passing sleeves left to right. I could die, still passing sleeves left to right. I sing and talk to myself to keep from melting into my machine. The other girls stitch, stitch, stitch. They never make mistakes. Sometimes I make mistakes on purpose just to prove I'm not one of them. Maybe I *am* a hysteric, like Dr. Galuppi said."

"Mamma, he was a—" What did Americans say? "A *quack*."

She shook her head. "The bad thoughts don't go away here, even at the lake. There's no Vesuvius. It's cold and the water's gray." Her eyes were very big. I moved closer and put my arm around her.

"Let me work more, Mamma, and you rest awhile. I can finish school later, when you feel better."

"No. The bad thoughts can't get out." She beat at her head. "They're like claws inside. You know what I mean?"

"No, Mamma."

"It's Little Stingler's fault." She held her hand in front of her face. "He's *here*, all the time, what he did, what I wanted to do to him."

I froze. "What did he do?"

She looked out the window at a maple tree just starting to haze with green. Her voice went flat. "On my last day, he said I had to get paid in his office. I was ready. I'm always ready. See?"

I gasped as she lifted her skirt. A slim-handled street fighter's knife was strapped to her calf. She put this on each morning and I never knew? When did she even buy it? The skirt dropped down. "He said I could still keep my job if I let him take me like a dog, from behind, against his desk. A dog because I was insolent, not 'appreciative' like the other girls. He takes *them* from the front."

"The bastard." I tried to picture him with Mamma, but all I saw was blackness.

Her voice went on, fierce and driving. "I pulled out my knife and showed where I'd cut if he touched me. I'd geld him. No more little stallion. He understood that much Italian."

"Mamma!"

She laughed. "The cock messed his trousers. Served him right. He said he'd have me locked up forever. The old man happened to come in just then. It was one of his good days. He made Little Stingler pay me and let me go." She grabbed my shoulders, shaking them until my head rattled. "Lucia, if the old man hadn't come, if his brain had been soft that day, I would have cut Little Stingler. You understand? My hands burned to do it. I could have gelded him and walked away. Then what? I'd be in jail or worse, an asylum with doctors like Galuppi. At Printz-Biederman, sometimes," she continued, as if noting that the parlor needed dusting, "it's all I can do not to tear my machine apart. The one I'm *renting*," she finished bitterly. "So I have to try for vaudeville. It's my only chance, Lucia. *Our* only chance."

Her rages had frightened me at the villa, but this placid calm was more terrifying. *Reason*, I thought frantically, *have her be reasonable*. "Remember Toscanini, Mamma? You tried to sing for him and we ended up in trouble. A vaudeville maestro might be rude like him. Then what would you do? You said yourself that if Old Stingler wasn't there—"

"Mario said nobody's rude at auditions. When the manager, Mr. B. F. Keith, is in town, you go onstage and show your act. If he says 'Next,' he doesn't want you. 'Have a seat' means he might want you.

He'll tell me to have a seat." Her eyes blazed with certainty, as if Mario had given her a magic spell for Mr. Keith.

"But you thought Toscanini would take you and he didn't."

"That was because I surprised him. And," she rushed on, "when I'm in vaudeville I'll send you money. You can finish school. You can buy all the books you want. Mario said the pay starts at thirty dollars a week *with* room and board. Thirty, Lucia!"

With thirty a small family could eat chicken on Sunday and buy coal all winter. The mother wouldn't need to work. They could have four rooms and the children could finish school. But we didn't need thirty dollars, I thought frantically. We needed the life we had right now, with her happy, just that one change. "But, Mamma, we'd be apart." Difficult, unstable, unreasonable, sometimes selfish, still she'd been my world. I'd never slept apart from her. If she left me so easily to sing for strangers, what was I worth? Who would truly care for me in Cleveland? I'd be one more immigrant girl, adrift like an abandoned boat.

"I'll see you when the show's in Cleveland, or you could take a train to Chicago when I'm there. I'll be happy. I won't have to go walking at night," she went on, as if spinning out one of her tales of poor fishermen transported to bejeweled mermaids' palaces. Just as Paolo had arranged our leaving Naples, a new life was being arranged around me. She took my hands. "Lucia, of course I'll miss you. I've never loved anybody but you. I have a bad temper. I don't say sweet things. But when I sing, it's for you. Can you understand this?" She stood up suddenly. "Anyway, I *have* to try vaudeville. Factory work makes me crazy. Do you want me to be a servant again?"

"No, Mamma, but—"

"You do your homework. I have to practice."

And then she was gone, back downstairs to the piano. A good daughter should be happy for her mother, I told myself. But would a good mother leave? Were her needs so much greater than mine? Had she kept me from the rich Roman lady only to leave me now? Still, in my waves of anxiety and fear came the utterly selfish thrill of youth: I could stop serving Mrs. Miller's lunches and buy a dress for dances. I could finish high school and even go to college. I could stay at the boarding-house, easily paying room and board. Mamma wouldn't be dead, only distant. She wouldn't have to work like a machine, paying rent on her own machine. She would be singing, her one true joy. How could I be-grudge her this?

But all these outcomes, good and bad, rested on the slightest chance that she'd be accepted in a vaudeville troupe and this would bring her peace. Rage had stalked her from Naples to Cleveland. Could she out-run it on the stage? Wasn't it more likely that Mr. B. F. Keith would say "Next," forcing her back to Printz-Biederman? With no escape, a new provocation might call out her knife. Disappointment could break her spirit. That evening I didn't work a single equation. I opened the door and lay on our bed as her gorgeous voice floated up from the parlor, the voice that had serenaded me all my life and now might leave for cities I didn't even know. I wished I was far away, not on this narrow bed, but on the warm waves of our other life when we swam in the moonlight. Would we ever have such peace again?

A week ago, I could have easily shared my fears with Yolanda, but she had quit school to work in a hat-trimming shop. It was Sunday af-ternoon before we could go walking together. First I had to hear about hat shapes and styles, ostrich, parrot, and partridge feathers, dried and silk flowers and the subtly distinctive traits of each. Yolanda even looked different now that she was working, more solid and matronly. She saw me studying her. "So you know. You can see it. Anyone can."

"See what?"

"That I'm pregnant."

It's true that this thought had flitted by, but I'd dismissed it. Yolanda belonged to *my* world, not the somber realm of mothers. I stumbled through the obvious questions. Yes, she was sure. Yes, Charlie knew. He had not denied her. "He wants to get married. He found a new job at the Bessemer Limestone Company in Youngstown. By the time the baby's born, he'll have the down payment for a company house. I'll live with his parents until then." Her voice dropped. "My mother says I've shamed our family." I found a bench, and she sat down heavily, pressed against the wrought iron.

"But you're going to be married. Isn't that enough for her?"

"No, because the child was conceived in sin." Yolanda's voice dropped, and she drew closer to me. "Everything's happening so fast, Lucia. I'm afraid."

"Did you want the baby?"

She wove her fingers into the metal slats of the bench, her head bent down so far I could barely see her face. I held her as she trembled. "It was just once that we were, you know, *together.* Charlie said he heard that nothing happens to the girl her first time. He was so sure, and I didn't know anything. Nobody ever told me how it is."

A storm of questions came to me. Where were they "together"? What did "it" feel like? Did "it" hurt? Did she lie naked with Charlie? Instead I asked: "When is the wedding?"

"Next week in City Hall. My parents won't come because he's Protestant. His parents are busy. And everyone but Charlie's angry that I'm pregnant. Angry at *me,* not him." She was weeping now, heaving like a child, wiping her face on her coat sleeve. "I can't stop crying at night."

I gave her my handkerchief. "I'll come to your wedding, and Mamma and Donato will too, I'm sure. *We're* not angry with you. Maybe Henryk will come. We'll make a little party." When the tears finally stopped, I walked her slowly home.

"Lucia, what did you want to talk about?" she asked at the door of her noisy flat.

"Nothing. It's not important."

In those days before her audition, Mamma wolfed dinner and nailed herself to the piano, practicing American popular tunes, arias, and Neapolitan songs. Then she slipped out for solitary walks around and around our block. "I have to be alone," she said. "It drives out bad thoughts." Everyone in our neighborhood knew her, I reminded myself, and she'd kept the street-wary habits from years in Naples. Still, I waited anxiously at the window.

When I passed his father's vegetable shop and found Henryk working by himself, I told him about my mother's audition and Yolanda's coming marriage at City Hall, saying nothing of the cause. I said she'd live with the Reillys after her wedding.

"Not at home?" Henryk asked quietly, arranging the frilly tops of carrot bunches.

"No, not at home."

He nodded, hearing what I hadn't said. "Well, they're getting married, which is the important thing. And they love each other. Anyone can see that. If I can get off work, I'll come. Miriam would too, but she's in Pittsburgh."

"I'm sorry." *Stay in Pittsburgh,* I thought peevishly as I hurried home. *Be beautiful in Pittsburgh.*

On Saturday afternoon, Donato, Henryk, Mamma, and I met Yolanda and Charlie at City Hall. They were the last in a line of couples being married that day. I'd dismissed Charlie as a selfish, handsome American who wouldn't present Yolanda to his parents, made her pregnant, and then had her live with them. But now I saw him solicitous and attentive. He brought her a fruit ice as we waited, found her a chair, and called his older sister's fine church wedding "a waste of time and trouble." Every extra dollar, he said, was better saved for a house of their own.

Yolanda held the fruit ice as it melted. "Your parents hate me."

"They don't know you, Yolanda. Once I'm gone, Ma will miss me, so she'll fuss over you, and once she changes, Dad will too."

"Are you sure?"

"Of course. And today they had to work." When his sister married last year, I whispered to Henryk, his parents closed their store. A judge galloped through their vows, declared Charlie and Yolanda man and wife, and reminded them to pay the clerk before leaving. We stood awkwardly in the hallway until Donato suggested we celebrate at Lula's.

"What's this, another funeral?" Lula asked as we settled in a corner booth.

"It's Yolanda's wedding day," I said. "Charlie's leaving for Youngstown tomorrow."

Lula's knowing eyes scanned Yolanda's belly and her nervous hands upon it. She studied the young husband. "So you have a job in Youngstown, Charlie?" He nodded. "And would you have married this pretty little girl if she *wasn't* in a family way?" No judge was ever so somber.

"I surely would, Miss Lula. I'd marry her and count myself the luckiest man in Cleveland." Yolanda reached for his hand and the stiffness in her body melted away.

Years after, Charlie and Yolanda would say their real wedding was in Lula's tavern. I didn't envy Yolanda's belly, but I wondered if I'd ever find the happiness that lit her face that evening or the bright expectation that wrapped my mother like a cape.

Laughing and telling jokes, sharing stories of our first days in Cleveland, we gorged on Anna's sausages, fresh bread, cheese, pickles, and warm beer. When Henryk politely asked Mamma about her audition, she hummed her songs. I'd never seen her so easy and relaxed in company.

In the next days, she practiced walking across the parlor, setting her feet, and refining her gestures. "Mario says Americans need to *watch* you sing. You have to act," she informed me. "Otherwise they get bored." I had thought she rehearsed me hard for the talent show, but she was relentless now, starting over for tiny mistakes I swore I couldn't see or hear.

"I *dream* those songs," Roseanne grumbled. Even Donato began slipping out to Lula's when Mamma headed to the piano after dinner. She cajoled Roseanne into letting her borrow a fine indigo dress with black trim and a frill of lace. Yolanda offered a hat she'd made splendid with partridge feathers.

On the great day, Mamma and I took a streetcar to the theater, but she wouldn't let me take her hand or speak. "Please, I have to concentrate." Fears spun in my head. If after so much work and rooted hopes, the maestro said "Next," what then? Would the knife come out?

At the Empire she gave her name to a clerk, who told us where to sit until "Ben" came for us. We watched a tubby man who called himself the Great Regurgitator. His act was to swallow gasoline, spit it out, and light the flames. Unfortunately, his shirt caught fire. He howled in pain until stagehands rushed out, rolled him in a canvas and hauled him away. "Next," shouted a man in shadows, "and he owes me for the canvas." Through all this Mamma sat motionless, mouthing words.

A girl my age presented four little dogs that leaped through hoops, jumped as high as her head after balls, and danced on their hind feet to the rhythm of her clapping hands until one brown terrier darted off after a mouse. "Have a seat," said the voice, "but get rid of the brown one."

A somber unicyclist waved flags as he rode in circles. "Next."

A magician brought out a table, stood behind it, and made flowers, scarves, and stuffed birds appear and disappear. Now accustomed to the dark, I made out a slim figure sitting by an unmoving, square-headed gentleman I took to be Mr. B. F. Keith. The slim one whispered constantly in his ear, perhaps the secret of each trick. "Next."

The Tumbling Turks, bare-chested acrobats in silky pantaloons, tossed one another through the air, springing from the stage as if it were India rubber and their bodies weightless. In their final stunt, a little boy came flipping from the wings and scrambled up a tower of men. "Take a seat." As the Turks hurried off, glistening with sweat, stagehands dried the stage with rags.

A dapper ventriloquist with his dummy dressed as a ragged newsboy traded jokes in breathless patter, so outrageous and unrelenting that even the square-headed man guffawed. "Take a seat," he said, "both of you." Mamma didn't laugh. Doubtless the English was too fast for her, but neither had she been listening. Her hand beat the air in time to music only she could hear. Two tap dancers performed with blurring speed, precise and elegant with top hats and canes.

"Next."

Now I was sinking in a pool of doubt. Did I want "Take a seat" because Mamma did, or because I was afraid of what she'd do after "Next"? Suppose she collapsed? Exploded? I'd watched her get dressed, but she might have somehow slipped a knife into her laced boot. Suppose she didn't attack but still seemed hysterical, "unstable"? Would Mr. Keith call for guards to take her away? Aside from these threats, did I want "Next" so she'd stay home with me or "Take a seat" so I could stay in school instead of working in a garment factory? I gripped the armrests so tightly that Mamma whispered, "Relax! It's not you that's performing."

I made myself watch the Whistler, a handsome young man with an astonishing repertoire, as if flocks of birds nested in his throat. He even mimed a comic debate, cleverly leaping back and forth between two stances until the whistles seemed like words. "Next." Why would these men want a foreigner who simply stood and sang? How could we have been so stupidly hopeful?

A dwarf appeared in the aisle, pointing a stubby finger at Mamma. She rose calmly and followed him. With every step her walk grew taller and more stately. She must have spoken to the piano man, for he announced, "Teresa D'Angelo, the Singing Angel of Naples," just as she glided onstage, set her feet, and began with "Sì, mi chiamano Mimì" from *La Bohème*.

How many times had I heard this aria? It was never so magnificent. Her voice effortlessly filled the theater, climbing and swooping, achingly sweet. Square-head never moved. Was he deaf? Stone-hearted? Then came "Maria Marì," poured out with such warmth that it seemed the Naples sun shone down on us. She had just finished a chorus when the voice called: "Give me 'The Star-Spangled Banner,' " and now the indigo gown was a motionless pillar.

The anthem wasn't in her piano rolls. She'd heard it once that I knew of, at a concert by the lake. The piano man slowly played the opening chords and then a long, looping introduction as the pain of held breath crushed my chest. My mother's shoulders dropped; her mouth opened. "Oh, say can you see," she began, and then, in perfect phase with the music: "da, da, da, da, da, da." After the first verse, she and the piano man closed like two breaths joined.

Square-head laughed. I closed my eyes against the surely coming "Next," picturing rage, screaming insults, or, worst of all, a grim and stolid silence, her last dream gone. She stood rigid as the men conferred in shadows.

Now the slim one spoke: "Miss D'Angelo, you've got fifteen minutes to learn our national anthem." The dwarf whisked Mamma away. I endured a minstrel duo, a soliloquy from *Hamlet,* and a portly juggler. Each received a "Next" before Mamma returned.

"Oh, say can you see," she began slowly, with grave deliberation. The piano man matched her tempo. She had reached the fourth line before "Have a seat. Please." Warm air filled my chest. *Have a seat. Please. Have a seat. Please.* My wet hands slipped from velvet armrests as the dwarf returned her. We sat together, attached, for the last auditions.

"You'll be called to the office for contracts. Wait where you are," the dwarf told those of us left sitting.

Mamma shook her head as I tried to speak. "I have to rest."

When the slim man came for her, I stood as well, announcing: "I'll translate."

"She doesn't speak English?"

"Not well enough to negotiate."

"*Negotiate?* My, my, a translator and *negotiator.* Well, come on."

"Teresa D'Angelo," intoned the square-faced, immaculately dressed gentleman who introduced himself as Mr. B. F. Keith. "The Singing Angel of Naples." He rolled out the words. "Don't like it."

"How 'bout Naples Nightingale?" the slim man suggested. "Like Jenny Lind, the Swedish Nightingale." Mamma shook her head. They ignored her. "Okay, Naples Nightingale it is. Who's this?" Mr. Keith pointed at me. "A sister?"

"Daughter," I said.

"Translator and *negotiator.*" Both men laughed. Mr. Keith leaned forward, delivering company rules to Mamma as I struggled to match Italian to his furious pace: Decency onstage always, in costume, gesture, and words in *any* language. Sick, well, or on women's days, one performed two, sometimes three shows a day. In certain cities, shows might be continuous. For *any* scandal, breach of local law or custom, public drunkenness, or any debts left unpaid when the show moved on, immediate release without pay. For pregnancy in or out of wedlock, release upon discovery without pay. For liaisons between performers detrimental to the peace of the troupe, release of both parties without pay. For insolence or insubordination to the manager or his agents, refusal to alter any act or costume upon request, immediate release without pay.

"And we'd be hiring *you*, Miss D'Angelo," Mr. Keith said firmly. "No translator, no negotiator. If you need more English, take lessons on your own time." Barely blinking, Mamma hadn't moved, seeming staked to the floor. "She understands, miss?"

"Yes, sir. Of course."

"Good. Let's see what she looks like. Turn around." My mother glared and stepped back. Mr. Keith bristled. "What does she take me for? I run vaudeville, not a burlesque. But men have to look at *something*." She turned, nearly spinning. "Good enough with some padding top and bottom. She understands twenty dollars a week? Room, board, costumes, two days off a month. Take it or leave it."

Mamma stiffened, clenching her fists. "Bastards," she whispered in Italian. "Mario said thirty. But I want this so much, Lucia. Should I take it?" My heart lurched for her.

"What did she say?" Mr. Keith demanded.

"She said I have to finish high school, sir. Right, Mamma?" She nodded slowly. "My father broke his neck falling from scaffolding in the Naples cathedral. Before he died, he told her to take me to America and have me finish school. So she needs enough for my keep at the boardinghouse, and books and clothes."

Mr. B. F. Keith glanced at the slim man. "Father's dying wish, was it? Cathedral painter? Well, I like women who think on their feet. 'Oh, say can you see, da, da, da, da, da, da.' Good try. Tell her she's welcome to B. F. Keith's vaudeville. Twenty-five at aforementioned conditions."

"Thirty-five," I said.

"Thirty the first month. If we like her, we'll raise it to forty."
Mamma nodded.

"She'll accept thirty, at aforementioned conditions."

"Good. Have Little Ben take you to the costume mistress. We leave town Monday morning early. Learn the anthem. We'll do a big number with flags and the Turks. That's all. And thank you for your service, *negotiator*." Laughter followed us to the door.

Little Ben was waiting outside. "You stay here," he told me. "Miss Emma don't like outsiders in the fitting room." For the next hour, I stood in the dark, narrow hallway as vaudeville people hurried back and forth. From inside the office, I heard the slim man say, "Thirty's a bargain for the Nightingale, Mr. Keith. The girl with the dogs cost us forty."

"I'll get my money's worth from both of them, but be careful, Jake. You might have trouble with that Nightingale. Something fishy in the eyes."

Jake gave Mamma fifteen dollars and she never went back to Printz-Biederman or even told them she was quitting. Instead she spent the next days in the parlor, learning new songs, practicing in front of the long mirror, going out only for costume fittings and walks. When I read a letter from Countess Elisabetta, she barely listened. "You paid her back. What does she want now?"

"It's a *letter,* Mamma. She's just being friendly."

"Well, she can be friendly with you. I have to practice."

Count Filippo couldn't last much longer, the countess wrote. He took morphine constantly for the pain. He'd ordered a coffin with an elaborate system of pulleys and bells to raise an alarm if he chanced to be buried alive, now his all-consuming fear. "Paolo and I" had discovered that the costly "Eastern powders" Dr. Galuppi peddled were merely clumps of dirt scooped from the villa's own garden. "Paolo and I" denounced him.

"Paolo and I," the phrase turned in my head, calling up sheaves of memories: Paolo's devoted attention to the countess; their long evenings in her sitting room "reviewing accounts," his effortless anticipation of her needs, her eyes falling gently on him. I remembered hearing her weep behind closed doors after one of the count's cruelties and Paolo's voice, low and soothing until the weeping ceased. Had they been lovers all these years?

"Of course," said my mother impatiently. "Were you blind?"

"*Everyone* knew about Paolo and the countess," Roseanne added. So this too I hadn't seen, as I hadn't seen Yolanda's condition or Charlie's kindness or my mother's knife. Countess Elisabetta's letter made me feel young and raw, unfledged in the world and soon to be alone. I followed Mamma like a puppy in the days before she left, but she barely seemed to notice me.

She packed and repacked her bag and picked at the American feast of roast chicken that Roseanne made on our last Saturday night, suddenly fretful and anxious: "I could forget the words. Maybe the audiences won't like me. They'll want an American." She worried that Toscanini might speak to Mr. B. F. Keith, that "bad thoughts" would trail her.

"You can come home if you aren't happy," I reminded her.

She told the wall: "If I'm not happy in vaudeville, there's nowhere else to go."

"You'll be happy, Mamma. You'll be a great success. Everyone will love you. Nothing bad will happen." *Nothing, nothing, nothing,* I repeated to myself.

On Sunday we bought food for a picnic at Catalano's and lugged our heavy basket to a pine grove along Lake Erie. The breeze was chill, but sunlight glittered on nearly blue water. We shared bread, prosciutto, cheese, and olives, and scooped artichoke hearts from marinade sharp with garlic. We drank red wine and ate *pastiera*, a rich and heavy ricotta pie that brought sweet memories of home. Then we stretched out on the mossy bank with a bag of candied almonds.

"Tell me about Palazzo Donn'Anna," I begged. It was one of my favorite stories. Our rock by the villa looked out on the old palazzo's ruins, whose macabre and tragic history gave me delicious shivers on the warmest summer nights. Fishermen avoided Palazzo Donn'Anna's mussel beds. "They do well to stay away," Mamma began as she always did. Long ago a princess of great wealth and insatiable sensual appetites had beautiful young fishermen lured to her palazzo at sunset. They must have thought themselves in an earthly paradise as servants bathed, perfumed, and dressed them, fed them the choicest sweets and wine, and took them to the royal bed for a night of unimaginable passion with the lusty princess, serenaded by unseen musicians. "At the first rays of dawn," Mamma always whispered, "servants roused the fisherman, still half drunk from his debauch, and brought him to the highest window." Closing my eyes now as I always did, I pictured the naked figure against a violet sky, a quick thrust from behind, and the wild howl as the not-bird falls, flailing, to jagged rocks below. The battered bodies were weighted in bags under the palace moorings, and their restless souls still haunt the ruined galleries where seabirds nest.

"Wasn't there *one* fisherman she let live?"

"No, not one."

"More," I begged. Mamma told a tale of a good fisherman who *did* marry a grateful mermaid and another of a hungry soldier who bought a fish with his last coin and found a precious ring inside that caused him both joy and pain. She sang me "Santa Lucia" and then, both weary, we slept a little under our shawls. When we woke, she said dreamily: "If I made seventy or eighty dollars a week, maybe a hundred, we could have our own house."

"Here in this grove."

"With a piano in a sunroom looking out on the water."

"Yolanda and Charlie and the baby could visit. We'd have a tide pool over there." I pointed to the rocky shore.

"Let's go back," she said suddenly. "It's getting cold." She tied a scarf around her neck to protect it from wind. "I'm leaving at dawn. You know how much I'll miss you, Lucia?"

"Yes, Mamma." *Tell me you love me. Tell me my life will be good here without you, that I'll find my way as you have now.*

"I *have* to do well in vaudeville."

"You will," I repeated. "Of course you will."

## Chapter 8

## AT THE HAYMARKET

*The troupe would* go east to Pittsburgh, then south and west through Ohio, Indiana, Illinois, and Michigan. I wouldn't see my mother until September, when she played in Chicago. Even Yolanda was drawing farther from my life. She worked at Mrs. Halle's millinery shop, where fine ladies came for hats or brought their own to be more elegantly trimmed with feathers, tiny stuffed birds, dried flowers, ribbons, and lace. She didn't mind the long hours, even as her belly grew. "I have a padded chair and a footstool; I can walk around the shop when my back hurts. She *smiles* and jokes with me. She doesn't stare like Charlie's parents do when I come in the door."

"It's quiet in their house at least," I said, remembering how eager she'd been to leave her parents' noisy flat.

"I'm not used to quiet. Charlie's father is nearly deaf, so he doesn't speak. His mother has nothing to say, so she doesn't talk. She just cleans. How much can you clean three little rooms? She sleeps with that dustcloth. I wish *she'd* go away to vaudeville."

I got penny postcards from my mother in childlike script, bits of messages that broke off when space ran out and rarely returned to explain: "Mario had a new act that . . . Jimmy the piano man is teaching me . . . I eat in restaurants but . . . I have a new stage hat but it's so heavy . . . People clap too much for the dummy and ugly little dogs . . . loved my 'Star Spangled' anthem . . . I get forty a week now but the fines . . ." She crossed out a note on winning at dice but sent the postcard anyway. "No Toscanini!" she declared from Detroit. Still, she seemed happy. I sent her letters through Mr. Keith's office, but if she received them she never said. She was becoming like the immigrants I scribed for, whose lives moved ever farther from their old country and families.

Yet into that space that divided us came new pleasures. On Sunday afternoons, while Yolanda wrote to Charlie, I roamed the city on street-cars, searched for treasures in used bookstores, or curled in the quiet parlor with my homework. Each time our teacher said "Next spring, when you graduate," bolts of pride and pleasure shot through me. I would be in the eight of one hundred with a high school diploma. When Miss Miller announced that a civic-minded benefactor was offering a prize of thirty dollars for the best essay on "Cleveland, a True American City," I wrote and rewrote my entry, fretting over every word, determined to win a diploma *and* the essay prize.

Free from my mother's complaints, I let books puddle on my bed. Papers carpeted the unwashed floor. "Teresa would scream if she saw this," Roseanne warned. I didn't care. All my life I'd scrubbed and dusted and put things away neatly. Disorder was a happy luxury that said: "This is Lucia's room."

Along with the penny postcards came money wired home and a note that said "Buy something pretty." I did: a softly tucked blouse and flounced burgundy skirt for a Saturday night dance at Hiram House. Roseanne arranged my hair in a pompadour bulked by a horsehair pad she called a "rat." All fashionable women used rats, she said. "Don't you know?" I didn't, having vaguely supposed that great wealth brought opulent masses of hair.

Embarrassed by her bulk, Yolanda wouldn't go to the dance, so I went alone, startled at my own reflection in dark shop windows, so elegant and American. Would the countess know me now? I didn't see Miriam with a chattering knot of girls by the door, tying and adjusting ribbons, carefully setting ringlets to frame their cheeks. She'd gone to Pittsburgh to tend a sick aunt, someone said. *Don't smile. She'll be back soon enough.* Henryk wasn't with the stand of boys across the room furtively watching us. Why should I care about this? He wasn't my fella. I didn't need a fella. I was too busy for fellas.

A put-together band of Italian, Irish, Polish, and Russian musicians played, grasping one another's tunes with uncanny speed. Casimir and Anna demonstrated an intricate polka that had been Irena's favorite, he said. "Here, Lucia, I'll show you the steps." He was a good teacher, patient and encouraging. In his sweat-soaked blond curls and wide smile as we spun around the room, my dear friend seemed alive again.

Donato's wife and daughter had finally come to America. He'd taken a furnished flat and was now proudly presenting his cheerful, exuberant wife, Sara. She was quickly learning our names, laughing heartily at jokes and sharing stories. "Cleveland is wonderful. Everyone's so kind," she exclaimed. In her bright presence, the tense, shabby city *did* seem charmed. Their daughter, Clara, slipped into a pack of children vigorously debating an elaborate game in a jumble of languages. "Look at her!" crowed Donato. "When I left Italy she couldn't speak at all."

In a ring around the dancers, knots of newcomers grouped themselves by country, talking, smoking, or playing cards. Some girls still wore their Old Country dress, but most were decked in American styles, with bright plaids and stripes. All were smiling now. When I scribed,

I often recorded bitter complaints to friends and cousins back home: "I give all my pay to Mamma, but she won't give me enough for nice clothes."

"You could ask your boss for a raise," I'd suggested to one girl. "You shouldn't be getting half a man's pay for the same work."

"I can't talk to him. I don't speak English."

"If you learned, you could get a better job," I persisted.

"I'm too tired for night classes. And after work there's laundry and cleaning and watching the little ones." Every family suffered long workdays: six, six and a half, or even seven days a week. Children rarely saw their fathers awake. They became strangers, awkward and stiff. Mothers locked small children at home, left babies in the care of five-year-olds, or even tied them to table legs. What else could they do? Garment workers often slumped wearily at my scribing table as if I were another sewing machine arm endlessly pricking cloth. They might not have my mother's plague of "bad thoughts," but work engulfed and dulled them. Only nights like this cracked the weary sameness of their days.

"Casimir says he taught you Irena's polka," announced a voice at my shoulder. I turned and saw Henryk.

"He's a good teacher." I stepped back, for the room was turning hot. A barbershop quartet sang "Sweet Adeline."

"Will you dance it with me?"

First I thought no and then, *Why not? It's a dance; that's why we're here.* "If the band plays another polka," I said. Away from his shop and our school, I felt stiff with him, my skirt too tight, my pompadour too heavy. What could we talk about? "Are you writing an essay for the Cleveland contest?" I asked.

"I would if I was going to college. I'll finish high school, but then I'll work with my father. You should go, though, for all of us."

"Roseanne says I'd be lonely; I'd be the only Italian girl."

"Maybe, but then you'd be the first and others would come after you."

"Then who'll make all the clothes and hats and chocolates?"

"Yes, Congress must consider the consequences of educating Italian girls. What *will* Americans wear?" The furrowed brow, thoughtful rubbing of his hands, and sly smile melted my reserve. We joined a circle dance that swept us apart. When the circle brought us back together again, he asked after Yolanda. I said she and I would be out walking on Sunday.

"You should go to Western Reserve campus and see if you feel at home."

"It's allowed?"

"Of course it's allowed." He was called away to greet an aunt but came back for the polka. Without a word we moved into Irena's steps, spinning, sliding, turning, my feet where they needed to be, the room a bright smear of color and sound. "Anyone would think," Henryk panted as the music ended and we pulled ourselves apart, "that you were a Polish girl." But I wasn't. Watching eyes raked over us. Donato was coming toward me.

"Hello, Henryk. May I borrow Lucia for a minute?" He drew me back to my people. "I was just telling Sara that we must invite you for dinner. Perhaps you can help with her English. You must be lonely with your mother so far away."

A group of young men closed around Henryk. I didn't see him for the rest of the evening.

*Yolanda wanted me* to come by the Reillys' flat early on Sunday morning; she wouldn't be going to mass. Children spilled down the steps of their apartment building. Bunches of boys shot marbles; girls played jacks on the landings. Small children raced up and down the halls. Voices poured through flimsy walls: laughing, talking, shouting. Furniture scraped over wooden floors as beds were shoved aside or dismantled for the day. Babies cried.

No sound at all came from the Reillys' flat. I knocked softly. Nothing. At last a neatly dressed woman with a face as still as clay opened the door. She studied me somberly, saying nothing. Yolanda stood behind her, ready with hat and gloves, strangely shrunken despite her bulging belly. She too said nothing.

"Good morning, Mrs. Reilly. I'm Lucia D'Angelo." When the woman didn't move, I added: "Yolanda's friend. We're going walking this morning."

Was she deaf as well? No, her head tilted slightly, considering me. "You speak pretty good English," she conceded, "for an Italian." I nodded, unsure how to answer this. A pale man at a spotless table watched us, immobile. Words dried in my throat.

Toneless as a sleepwalker, Yolanda announced: "We'll be leaving now, ma'am. You needn't wait lunch for me."

"You're not going to *mass*?"

"No, ma'am, not today." Yolanda eased her belly past the folds of her mother-in-law's dress. Infected by the Reillys' silence, we didn't speak all the way down the stairs and into the next block. Then, like a clogged pipe bursting open, Yolanda gushed out her troubles: "See how they hate me? If I sit in a chair, it's like I'm wearing it out. If the floors creak when I walk, she looks up. If the baby next door cries, she complains. What happens when a real baby's *inside* their flat? I don't think she'd talk to her husband even if he wasn't deaf. He just looks at me and grunts. What does *that* mean?"

"Yolanda, they're quiet people."

"No! They're people who hate Italians. And Catholics. The longest 'talk' we ever had was when they asked if I believe the Blessed Virgin Mary is greater than Our Lord. Does the priest *really* drink blood at

Holy Communion? Do I want the pope to rule America?" Her voice rose. "They think I made Charlie marry me. And he can't come on weekends like we planned. He works twelve-hour shifts every day so we can buy a house. If we all have to live with Charlie's parents . . . Lucia, I can't think about it."

"Do you want to go home?"

"Yes! I want the noise, the fights, the twins yelling, people *talking* to me, even if they're angry. But I can't even if they'd let me. My uncle just came over from Calabria. He's got my bed. And I shamed the family, remember?"

How to answer this avalanche of laments? "At least you like your work."

Yolanda blinked at the effort to recall that happy corner of her life. "Yes, *work* is wonderful. I made a hat with Brazilian blackbird feathers, and Mrs. Halle loved it so much she got more of those feathers for me. If I could, I'd be there now," she said fiercely. "When I go 'home,' the table's set for two. Then she *slowly* gets up, sets out another plate, and pulls out another chair as if she's surprised *again* that I'm living there." Yolanda stopped walking. Her voice rose. "No Italian would treat a guest that way. And the food! Everything's boiled to death: potatoes, cabbage, beans, stew meat, potatoes, cabbage, more beans. No salt, no garlic, no herbs. No wine ever. I asked if I could cook, and she said, 'Don't trouble yourself.' Is she afraid of eating something good?"

We were close to the Western Reserve campus now; fine stone buildings cut into the blue sky. American students hurried by. "I don't know what's wrong with the Reillys, Yolanda. Maybe they don't talk, so you don't talk, so they don't know you. If they did, they'd love you like Charlie does, like I do."

She hugged her belly. "I'm being punished because our baby was conceived in sin."

"So was I. So were lots of people. You're married now, that's what's important. Charlie loves you and you'll be together soon. When there's a beautiful little baby, you'll see, his parents will fall in love with both of you." Her path was so straight, I thought: make hats, mother her coming child, and tolerate these silent people until she could move away.

"I don't know where Charlie learned how to *talk*, let alone how to love somebody. What's *wrong* with them?" Yolanda's voice rose again and cracked. Passing students looked at us sharply, as if to say: "We speak English here and we speak *softly*."

"They're blond," Mamma had said, when long ago we passed the campus by mistake. Was I here again by mistake in this land of square-shouldered, light-haired people? My hair was heavy and dark, rolling with waves; my cheap wool dress hung stiffly; my boots slapped the brick pathways. Their clothes swished and their fine shoes tread softly. Yolanda's discomfort had weakened my resolve. "Let's go home," I said, taking her arm and turning her quickly around.

"I can't go back to the Reillys'," Yolanda declared. "I can't breathe there."

"Then come live with me."

"How? It's impossible."

"We'll find a way."

At the boardinghouse I convinced Roseanne to let Yolanda take Mamma's place in my room. Roseanne finally conceded, on the condition that Yolanda paid her share of room and board.

"But you'll have to let me keep the light on late to study," I warned my friend.

"You can read all night if you want. Just talk to me sometimes." We got her small bundle of clothes from the Reillys, who received without comment the news that she'd be leaving. "You see?" Yolanda demanded. "They're so strange. Suppose Charlie turns out like them?"

"He won't."

"I hope you're right." After dinner, Yolanda stretched out on my bed and watched me study, then closed her eyes and fell asleep. For the next months we lived companionably together as I finished eleventh grade, then scribed and worked for the Millers in the summertime when Mamma's money home wavered. By mid-July we had to wedge a cot into the room to leave my bed for Yolanda's bulging girth.

At last, in September, I could see Mamma. I left on a Friday, hurrying to the station before dawn to catch the first train for Chicago. The flat green miles sped away as I memorized sonnets for English class. "Any two you like, one from Shakespeare, one from Milton," our teacher had said. "Just learn them so they're yours and no one and nothing can take them away." I pored over the lines until we passed into the great stain of Chicago, cupping its lake. Then I closed my book and waited.

By good fortune Mamma saw me first on the platform. How could I have recognized the stately woman in a crimson walking suit bursting with lace at the bust; a wide-brimmed, black-plumed hat; kid gloves; and a massive pompadour? Men drew back as she came toward me, leaving an awed channel between us. "I know," she said after we'd kissed. "I look different. People are supposed to recognize me on the street and be excited. Are *you* excited?" she demanded of a gawking, red-faced young man. "Then come to the show tonight." She pulled two tickets from a velvet purse. "You can hear the Naples Nightingale." I was speechless. Was this my mother, hawking herself with such aplomb? And where were these hovering men for all the years when I saw that she was beautiful and all they saw was a house servant?

"They'd be panting after you too if you dressed like this," she said, sweeping me toward the great sunny mouth of the station. No, it wasn't just the lace and nipped waist. Her walk was different: straight shoulders, high hips, and a forward tilt of bulging bust. If she took off her gloves, would I recognize her hands at least, rough and red from years of bleach and soapy water?

"Look at this!" Mamma declared, drawing out a hatpin as long as my forearm. She waved the pin at one of the hovering men, who jumped back. "Who needs knives with a weapon like this? And look how strong it is." When she jabbed a wrought-iron girder, the hatpin barely bent. "Should have had one of these at Stingler's," she muttered. I gripped her arm as she shoved the long pin through her hat and hair. *Come back, Mamma. Stop being so different and strange.*

We went to the Hotel Burnham, an opulent palace for businessmen. "That one maybe owns slaughterhouses," Mamma said, pointing out a stocky gentleman in a top hat. "And those at the table could have railroads and banks and shipping companies. This is where I'd stay if my act came *after* the intermission. See? It's finer than the villa." She paraded me around the lobby, past the velvet-papered walls, carved ceilings, elevator cages in metal as delicate as lace, porters, busboys, waiters, and doormen in blazing white gloves gliding soundlessly over thick carpets. How many gloves would each man have, and what an army of laundresses must be working for them? "Enrico Caruso stayed here," she announced, "and Jenny Lind, the great Swedish Nightingale. Arturo Toscanini will sleep in the Burnham if he ever comes to Chicago." Her face darkened. "Maybe he'd tell Mr. Keith what I did."

I wished then and a thousand times after that Maestro Arturo Toscanini had never come to Naples. Years later a great doctor would insist that my mother's anxious fear of the maestro sprang from a deep hurt in her childhood, probably connected to her father. Perhaps so, but at that moment she seemed to be conjuring the maestro himself; his swooping black eyebrows were like the wings of a hawk seeking her out for destruction.

At least she was easily distracted. Passing the hotel's grand piano led her to speak of Jimmy the piano man, with whom she shared a language beyond words. Under his prodding, her voice was stronger now, her range, repertoire, and performances more assured. "Still, I'm always afraid onstage," she whispered. "Suppose the words don't come? Suppose the notes are flat, or people hiss or throw things? We have to go," she announced, peering at a lady's watch dangling from her belt. She never owned a watch before or cared much for time. So many small things declared: *Your mother has changed.* Was I changed too from living without her? She didn't say. Perhaps she hadn't noticed.

We hurried to the Haymarket Theater. "Look," said Mamma, pointing to the playbill with a gloved finger: "Teresa D'Angelo, The Naples Nightingale." Of course she'd be on the playbill, but to see her name in print, there on the street of a great city, nailed me speechless to the pavement until she pulled me away. "Come, I have to get dressed." We passed through the stage door. With every step she became even less Mamma and more an act in Mr. Keith's troupe, a tightly woven family that knew nothing of me. Strangers greeted her warmly, women in feathers, acrobats, a ventriloquist with his dummy, clowns, and a spindly memory master. Only Lydia, the girl with trained dogs, passed silently. "Those nasty dogs make more than I do," Mamma whispered. "Wait here. I always get dressed alone."

Alone? We had slept, dressed, and bathed together all my life. I knew every freckle on her back. I knew when her monthly flow began and ended and her six strands of gray hair. The dressing room door clicked closed. I pressed my back against the wall, away from a buffeting flow of performers. It was there that Mario found me, announcing himself with a funny rag-doll dance.

"Teresa has her ways," he said kindly. Yes, and every way was new to me. As I followed him through a maze of scaffolds, ropes, props, and players to my seat, he revealed that she spoke earnestly to herself in dialect before each show. She vomited after each performance, setting a bucket offstage for this purpose. In each new city she found her way to a nearby river, canal, or lake. "I followed her once," said Mario. "She stands there a long time, and if she thinks nobody's around, she sings."

"What does she sing?"

"Always the same: 'Santa Lucia.'" Joy shot through me. "She talks about you and how well you do in school."

"Really?" *Really?*

"Of course. But"—and now he lowered his voice—"she's playing cards too much with the acrobats. They cheat. Mr. Keith doesn't mind a friendly game, but if he catches you gambling, there's a fine. He says gamblers lose their edge onstage. I warned Teresa, and she said it's not my business. Perhaps she'll listen to you." I doubted that.

Mario pulled me into a niche between potted palms. "And here's an odd thing. Memnon the memory master always goes on before her. He says she showed him a picture from an Italian newspaper."

I sighed. "A handsome man with dark eyes and eyebrows like a hawk's wings?"

"That's what Memnon says. She always wants to know if this guy's in the audience. Memnon keeps telling her he doesn't do faces. He remembers cards, numbers, things like that. She got angry once and nearly wouldn't go on, screaming that he'd *have* to remember this face once he saw it. Mr. Keith fined her for 'backstage disruption.' So what's up? Did Hawkeye do her wrong?"

The jostling crowd had turned us face-to-face. Mario put his stubby hand on my arm. "I see. Long story, none of my business. Well, nobody gets into vaudeville without a long story. But, listen, Lucia"—he stepped closer and lowered his voice—"to *stay* in Mr. Keith's troupe, she can't let her story be a backstage disruption. She has to keep her grip. Well, enjoy the show. I have to put on my face." Mario slipped away. His own act came after the intermission, where Mamma longed to be.

Acts floated by. Lydia and her dogs, tap dancers, a hypnotist and a mime, acrobats and a tightrope walker, a joke-telling juggler and President Theodore Roosevelt impersonator whose story of big-game hunting laced with political jokes had the audience howling. Finally Memnon came on, flawlessly memorizing strings of numbers, dates, and random objects shouted out from the audience. Mamma would be next. "Breathe, Lucia," she would have said. A piano flourish and the master of ceremonies demanded applause for "the Naples Nightingale, direct from Europe." I clapped so loudly the woman next to me leaned over and asked: "Have you seen her before? Is she good?"

"Yes," I said. "She's wonderful."

A golden spotlight beamed down on Mamma, frosting the plume of her creamy, wide-brimmed hat. A violet gown draped in swirls to her feet with ruffles of lace at the breast and sleeves. Her hair was huge with swirls and loops. The hands in long, dawn-gray gloves lifted gracefully and pressed her heart in thanks for the applause. Men whistled, bringing scurrying ushers, for at Mr. Keith's vaudeville, audiences must be decorous. I drank in the glorious sight of her.

She settled her feet, a gesture so slight under the swirls of skirt that only a daughter would notice. When she opened her mouth, a huge voice flowed out: "Give My Regards to Broadway," a rousing song that many knew. How was that voice possible for any woman? It was so much richer and more soaring than I remembered or could have imagined. The heave of her breasts, lift of her hands, and sway of her body, how had I not seen this mastery in the boardinghouse? When she sang "Take Me Out to the Ball Game," the audience joined in, but her voice floated effortlessly over theirs. She sang "In the Shade of the Old Apple Tree" so earnestly that one would think we had apple trees around the villa. For "My Wild Irish Rose," she sounded pure Irish. Her last number was "America the Beautiful." She might barely know the meaning of these words, but one could swear she'd lay down her life for the country. A graceful curtsy rewarded the thumping applause. When had she learned to curtsy? I clapped until my palms stung. People would go home now, of course. What act could ever best hers?

No, they sat and cheered a fire-eater. At intermission people excitedly spoke of him, a young magician, and the Roosevelt jokes. "That Nightingale was pretty good," a woman said.

"Sure," her companion agreed, "but why Naples? She's got to be American."

Beaming like a fool, heart pounding, I made my way backstage after the show, worming past ushers and guards with "My mother is the Naples Nightingale."

"Don't keep saying you're my daughter," Mamma fretted as she washed out her sick bucket. "They'll think that I'm old."

"You were wonderful," I said over and over. The glaze of performance was fading, and she was becoming herself again. I could come in the dressing room now because "nothing bad" had happened in the act. So I sat on a wobbling stool and watched her remove hat, gloves, and a mass of rats, hairpieces, and hairpins. She applied a thick cream to her face paint, washed and wiped until her own olive skin appeared where American white had been. I helped her out of a boned, padded American Beauty corset and into another one less formidable, and then a dark green walking dress.

"You see?" she said earnestly. "I'm still your mother. Let's go eat."

Aside from Lula's, I'd never eaten in a restaurant before, never been waited on or had doors opened for me. Mamma seemed accustomed to all this, even impatient when the waiter was slow with our plates. She ordered my first sundae and watched me devour that fabulous concoction of airy whipped cream, dense chocolate syrup, and silky ice cream. "Do you want another tomorrow?" I did, yes, absolutely. "There's no gold on the streets in America," she noted, "but you can get ice cream sundaes."

It was late when we finished eating, and I was tired after the early rising for the train, the thrill of the show, and the opiate bliss of my sundae, but she led me between monstrous buildings at the heart of Chicago and then along Lake Michigan, where whitecaps frothed the dark waters. Finally as we circled back to a small hotel by the theater where the players lodged, I asked: "Mamma, are you happy in vaudeville?"

"Yes, mostly. Mr. Keith says we have to take care of each other like family because we're out on the road alone." In the gaslight, her eyes glittered. "But there's fighting all the time, Lucia. Who's higher on the playbill, whose act is longer? Who gets more applause? We're all paid differently. Why do those nasty, yappy dogs get more than I do? Why?"

"I don't know." She was silent until we reached our room.

"The magician says I should sing 'The Bee That Gets the Honey Doesn't Hang Around the Hive' because it suits my voice. But Memnon says no, it's a trick because the pastors will complain and then I'll get a red card from Mr. Keith. You see? Who can I trust? And Toscanini could be watching. He could shout something during my act."

We were in our nightgowns now. With her hair tied neatly back, she still looked young enough to truly be my sister. "Toscanini's in Italy," I said wearily. "Can't you forget about him?"

She sat down stiffly on the edge of our bed. "Any American opera house could bring him over."

*"But he's not here now!"* I said much too loudly. Her shoulders curled in, her head bowed down. Ashamed, I took her hands. "Mamma, I meant, don't worry about things that haven't happened. Isn't this better

than factory work? You eat in restaurants, sleep in hotels, and people clap for you."

"Yes," she said finally. "I'm not on my knees, scrubbing. And there's no count, no Galuppi. So yes, it's better." With that, weariness covered her like a blanket. She kissed me, stretched out in bed, and was asleep. Lying awake in my first hotel room, I wondered if some deep hurt had gouged away her capacity for joy, as a bad break in the leg leaves a constant limp. *Better*, I concluded sadly, would have to be good enough for her.

We slept late in the morning and went out for what Mamma called "brunch" and my second sundae. Hurrying back to the matinee, I asked the question I couldn't frame the night before: "Mamma, you wrote that you'd won money gambling."

"I never gamble," she said flatly.

I studied her face cut into the crisp blue sky, calmly absorbing admiring glances as we passed taverns and street corners. "You played cards for money, but that's *not* gambling?"

"No, because I'm not a gambler. Besides, we played Italian games, *scopa* and *briscola*, not poker. This is America, Lucia. Everybody plays for money. The dollars I sent you for new clothes came from *scopa*. Didn't you know?" How could I know? "I just have to make sure Mr. Keith doesn't find out."

"But he *could* find out, or someone could tell him."

"One of my enemies?"

"Just someone."

"Don't worry so much. Besides, don't you want a beautiful graduation dress?"

"A dress doesn't matter," I said hastily.

"*I'm* your mother," she said sharply. "I can decide what matters." We walked the next blocks in silence until we reached the theater. Then she stopped by the stage door and took my hands. "I'm sorry, Lucia, but listen. Suppose you come travel with me? I'll be calmer if you're here. Mario could get you work in the office. You could have sundaes every day."

Yes, to travel with the vaudeville would be exciting. I could eat in restaurants, sleep in hotels, and wear fine clothes. I could see America and not just the streets of Cleveland. Mamma might be calmer and perhaps she wouldn't gamble. But to give up graduation, to yank out a dream so deeply anchored? She studied my face. "Never mind," she said finally. "I have to get ready. Mario got you a seat in front so I'll see you when I'm on." She disappeared into a milling crowd of performers.

Mario found me outside my mother's dressing room. He was already in costume. "There's a telegram for you, Lucia," he said, holding up the frail yellow envelope. I stepped back. "It *could* be good news." But the little mouth inside his painted smile showed how unlikely this might be: everyone knew telegrams brought only bad news.

I read the few words: "Yolanda's labor started early. She's asking for you. Come home soon. Roseanne."

I knocked on my mother's door and explained why I had to leave. She frowned. "They can get a midwife. You're going tomorrow anyway. At least stay for the show."

"I'm sorry, Mamma. If I leave now, I can just make the next train. Yolanda needs me. She's alone."

"Fifteen minutes, Nightingale," somebody called. "Don't be late."

"When will I see you again?"

"Soon, very soon." We kissed. She stroked my hair, held me, and whispered, "Never mind about what I said. You wouldn't like this life." And she was gone, closing the door firmly behind her.

Mario assigned a lanky young stagehand named Harold to help me get my bags and catch the train to Cleveland. As we hurried off, Harold related how he'd run away from his father's dairy farm to join Mr. Keith's show in Cincinnati. "What I want from life," he announced, "is never to milk a cow again and never to shovel cow shit." I said I hoped to finish high school and then somehow go to college. As we waited by the tracks he cocked his head, observing me. "You're different from your ma. She's always jumpy, like somebody's after her. She does sing bully good, though. Anyway, here's your train. A-river-dare-chee, like you Eye-talians say." As I stepped on the train, he bolted away.

I worried about Mamma's "jumpiness" and fears as we barreled east through cornfields and small towns, first in sunshine and soon in a drizzling rain.

## Chapter 9

## YOLANDA

*I sent Charlie* a telegram and arrived soaking wet at the boardinghouse. Roseanne met me by the door. "We've been waiting and waiting for you. Hilda the midwife is on her way. Hang up your coat and go to your room. Hurry."

Yolanda lay heaving, clutching a crucifix. "Lucia," she gasped. "Nobody told me it hurt so much."

I mopped her brow. "When Hilda comes, if you want, we could take you to the hospital."

"Where Irena died?" she gasped. "No."

"Should I get your mother?"

"She's sick."

"Mrs. Reilly?"

Despite the pain, Yolanda managed a grimacing smile. "Noise? Blood? Mess? She'd hate it. Ohh, another one." Her wildly waving hand caught mine and crushed it as the next cramp came. The whites of her eyes blazed. "Stay with me, Lucia," she groaned.

"Of course, of course, I'm here. I won't leave."

"All I want is to hold my baby." Yolanda tore her hand from mine, arching her back, beating the mattress. I wanted a diploma. How different our dreams were.

"You'll have the babe in your arms soon enough, love," said a new voice, Hilda, the midwife. White hair framed gray eyes as calm as a foggy morning. So much changed with her coming. Yolanda's panting eased. She shifted her bulk, watching avidly as Hilda set out supplies on a starched linen cloth: herbs, oils, a neat stack of clean cloths, thin cord, needle and thread, pulling ropes, rubber bulb, stethoscope, listening tubes, scissors, and a basin. Her niece Claire sponged Yolanda's face and arms. In the coming hours, Hilda had only to hold out her hand for Claire to put in it the proper tool as if she were Hilda's own thoughts taking bodily shape.

Hilda passed her hands over and within Yolanda's body. "We'll be here awhile," she finally announced. "It's not time to worry yet, but the baby's in the wrong position. We need to have it head down."

"How can we do that?" I asked.

"You'll see." Humming softly, she oiled her hands and massaged Yolanda's belly, her humming easing in and out of speech. She asked a few questions, nodding at each answer. When Yolanda groaned, the humming deepened.

Exhausted by travel, the drumming rain outside, and the anxious strain of Chicago, I was kept awake all night by constant errands: to the kitchen, to another midwife for certain herbs and once for a medical book. When Claire asked for cushions and a blanket, I ran off eagerly, sure they would serve the baby. But they were for me to rest in the corner. Yolanda called for Charlie, moaned for him, swore she saw him, and cried that she'd die without seeing him.

The baby would not turn. Hilda and Claire considered and rejected bringing Yolanda to a hospital for a cesarean cut. Dangerous as a breech delivery could be, they feared the cutting more. "We just have to make it turn," Hilda repeated.

Yolanda was utterly spent. When I bent over the bed, her eyes seemed weighted, too weary to meet mine. Dawn brought no break in the rain. The road outside was a streaming swath of mud. The baby did not turn by ten in the morning, or by noon. Listening to Yolanda's belly, Hilda reached out a free hand. Claire produced a damp cloth that Hilda used to wipe her own face. "The heartbeat's down," Hilda whispered.

Yolanda hadn't spoken for an hour. "Trouble?" she whispered.

Claire turned away.

"You'll hold the baby, love," Hilda promised.

So it might not live. I might see the stillness of Irena's deathbed, the last heave and stop of the chest. With the pale excuse of bringing more hot tea, I fled to the kitchen, trying to think of nothing at all. Then under the pounding rain I heard a furious knocking. "See who it is," Roseanne called, "but don't let anybody wet my floor."

"Coming!" I shouted. When I opened the door and a staggering, dripping man pushed past me into the hall, my screams brought Roseanne with a fire poker raised.

"Yolanda!" gasped the man. Roseanne set down the poker as Charlie pulled off his dripping cap and bent over, panting. "Didn't get— another telegram. Afraid—trouble. Boss gave twenty-four hours' leave. How is she?"

"She's fine, fine," I said too earnestly. "The labor is just slow." I peeled off his coat and made him sit to catch his breath.

"Got a ride with a coal truck—streetcars flooded. Ran forever." He looked down at his shoes, leaking muddy water.

"Just a minute," Roseanne said, returning with slippers left by a former tenant.

"I'll take you," I began, but he was already bolting upstairs. I ran after him and was there when he opened the door.

Yolanda's face blazed like a moon suddenly blown free of clouds. "Charlie! Charlie! Charlie! You're here!" He lunged toward the bed and buried his face in the crook of her arm.

"So here's the father. Maybe the babe will turn for him," Hilda said.

Charlie lifted his head. "Turn? What's wrong?" He listened carefully to the risks of breech birth, never ceasing to stroke Yolanda's brow as Hilda related their options. How had I so misjudged him? "Let me stay" was all he asked.

"Will you faint at blood?"

"No, ma'am."

"Will you leave if I tell you, no questions, just leave?"

"Yes, ma'am."

"Lucia, bring a chair." My chair, she meant. I was to leave and wait in the parlor with Roseanne. Claire came down soon after to say the baby had turned.

"How?" we both asked.

"Charlie told it to. Sometimes that happens." Then: "Soon, very soon." Yolanda's screams were louder now, but without the desperate terror of the night.

A half hour passed before a sudden roaring howl shot me to my feet. Roseanne followed, and like sneaking children we slipped upstairs and stood outside my door.

"Good, good, we're coming," Hilda was saying. "Another push, love, and we're there. Push! Yes! *Yes!*" And now a hush.

We stood shoulder to shoulder, and Roseanne's hand gripped mine as we heard that raucous cry like no other, that imperious "I am!" beyond the magic of any vaudeville show.

Charlie: "Yolanda! Look!"

"Yes, love," said Hilda, "a perfect baby girl." Then loudly: "Come on, you two. We know you're there." We slipped into the crowded room. Hilda and Claire were washing the baby. Charlie had collapsed across Yolanda's chest, shoulders shaking. We glimpsed a tiny red face as the bundle was passed to her parents. "We'll leave them alone now," said Hilda, herding us into the hall. "It's their time."

Downstairs in the parlor, Roseanne brought out her best crystal and we toasted the little one's health. "There's no work like mine," said Hilda. "It's the best in the world." The oiled table reflected our weary, happy faces. Upstairs, Charlie and Yolanda were beginning their new life. When would mine begin?

An hour later the rains ceased so suddenly that the last day and night might have been a dream except for the baby upstairs. Sunshine blazed, and the earth began sucking in the waters she had lately refused. A young boy running by shouted: "Streetcars are moving again!"

Upstairs Yolanda slept quietly with little Maria Margaret, named for her grandmothers. Charlie paid Hilda. In two days, Roseanne would arrange for a cab to take Yolanda and her daughter to the Reillys' flat. The birth had been exciting, but her boarders didn't feature living with a baby. Meanwhile I'd sleep in the parlor.

Charlie had me come with him to see his parents before he left for Youngstown. He seemed taller since going away, and older. "I got a promotion at Bessemer Limestone. I'll be a loading foreman. The last one didn't lock a pulley and was crushed to death. There's a little company house. We'll need a boarder at first, but if Yolanda earns enough with her hats, we'll be fine."

"But isn't the work dangerous?"

"That's why it pays well. The last man was careless. I won't be. I have a family now. And if I get to be a boss, it won't be dangerous at all." He had a dazzling smile and buoyant certainty. I knew why Yolanda loved him, but how did that sunny soul come of age in his parents' grim flat?

We reached the Reillys' block and began threading through children sprinkled on the wet sidewalk. They greeted Charlie, hung on him and begged for pennies. When he'd amiably shaken himself free, I stopped him on the landing. "You know that Yolanda was miserable here. She thought your parents hated her."

"They didn't. They're quiet, I know, but it's just their way."

He was about to mount the stairs, but I held his sleeve and persisted: "*Why* is it their way?"

He looked out at the noisy street. "Four children died, two after my sister and then two after me. The last had a fever that my father caught, and he lost most of his hearing. Then my mother stopped talking. All she did was clean. When Yolanda complained about how noisy and crowded and dirty her flat was, it almost made me jealous."

"So you kept putting off bringing her home? You thought she wouldn't love you if she met your parents?" He nodded sheepishly. "And you never told her what you just told me?"

He had the grace to blush. "I didn't know how. Then I was working so hard and I couldn't write all that in a letter. But everything will be different now in our own house. Will she forgive me?"

"If you talk to her. If you don't keep secrets."

He shook his head in wonder. "I have a *family*. Can you believe it?"

Charlie knocked loudly. Mrs. Reilly opened the door, saying, "You're here," as if he'd ducked out for bread. He rested a hand on her shoulder, a barely grazing touch, shook hands gravely with his father, sat down, and began slowly, loudly explaining the difficult labor, his race to Cleveland, and then the birth and naming of their baby girl. The father closed his eyes. Mrs. Reilly rose, went to the second room, and returned with a dusty bottle of sherry perhaps left over from Charlie's birth. We drank without toasts or clinking, our eyes fixed on the scrubbed oak table. Count Filippo would have pounded that table, shouting: "Celebrate, you fools! You'll be dead soon enough!" For once I would have agreed with him.

Mrs. Reilly turned, the first she'd acknowledged my presence. "You saw Maria Margaret?" Only in "Margaret" did her voice rise slightly to the palest hint of wonder.

"Yes, ma'am. If you'd like to visit, I'm sure Yolanda would be happy." Or rather, Yolanda's joy was so great that not even Mrs. Reilly could distress her. A nod, then silence swallowed us again. Any comment seemed pointless or overdrawn. We had been sitting for twenty-one minutes by the kitchen clock. Occasionally, Mrs. Reilly asked about Charlie's work. He answered and we all fell silent again. I touched my empty glass, then jerked my hand back lest they think I wanted more sherry.

Finally: "Yolanda will stay here before she moves to Youngstown?"

"Yes, Mother, she'd like to come in a couple days, when she's strong enough."

Was this truly a smile, an upward lift in the lips? "We'll be glad to see them."

At Charlie's urging I spoke very loudly of Maria Margaret's beauty. Mr. Reilly's blank face made me wonder if he recalled a baby's general appearance. When Charlie rose, saying he'd have to leave for Youngstown now, his mother fetched a neat brown package. "It's our family's christening gown, for Maria Margaret." A stranger might have missed the tiny tremor and misting of her eyes.

On the stairway to the street, Charlie took my arms and shook them. "Did you see how happy they were? How proud? The christening gown, it's all we have from Ireland. Everything will be different when Yolanda comes back, she'll see." Church bells tolled in the gathering dusk. "I have to go, the boss is waiting. Kiss my wife and daughter for me, we'll be together soon!" Charlie cried, darting away. Looking up at the lighted window, I saw two figures, each raising a hand. I raised mine back at them.

Two days later, while I was at school, Roseanne helped Yolanda take the baby to the Reillys' flat. Roseanne reported that a dresser drawer had been emptied and lined with cloth. A basket of snowy diapers sat in the corner of the room and next to it a knit afghan.

Six weeks later a telegram came from Charlie: he had furnished the little house and was ready to receive his family. I would see Yolanda and the baby off at the Cleveland station.

The Reillys brought them, hovering over Maria Margaret. In the crisp morning each building and tree seemed cut from the blazing blue sky. Yolanda was incandescent with happiness. She would at last have a home of her own, a fella, a baby, and a job that she loved. "Miss Halle will send me everything I need and sell the hats for me. I'll work while the little one sleeps."

When the train came, both Reillys kissed Maria Margaret, shook Yolanda's free hand, and stood with me, almost waving as the train pulled away. Then we looked at one another, awkward without the baby's presence. Were they reluctant to return to that silent flat in a buzzing hive of families? For the first time, I pitied them.

"Will you come to my graduation in spring?" I asked suddenly.

"We've been invited to Lucia's graduation," Mrs. Reilly shouted to her husband. "Yes, we'll come." As if exhausted by this flurry of emotion, they solemnly shook my hand and left the station without touching or speaking.

And then I was alone. In the roar and rattle of the station, I felt like the smallest gear in the great machine of Cleveland. But if I *was* a gear, I had a task, even if no one cared for it but me: to graduate from high school. That afternoon, I cleaned my room, washed the sheets, and straightened my piles of books. Late nights followed to fill the emptiness of Yolanda gone to the cocoon of her little house. I studied, scribed, and finished my essay on the "true American city," explaining how Cleveland's factories clothed America, built her automobiles, forged her steel, and cut limestone for monuments to her greatness.

## Chapter 10

## UNACCEPTABLE GESTURES

*During the next* months, the money my mother sent home began varying wildly and without explanation. An extra twenty dollars might appear, or only half her usual funds. I swerved between guilt for dependence on her pay and grating irritation. I was working too, and wasn't it our plan that I'd finish high school and get a job that might one day support her? Her penny postcards grew fewer, harder to read and understand. If people asked after her at church, there was little to report. "She's having a wonderful time," I always said. "Everyone loves the Naples Nightingale."

Certainly she wouldn't come to my graduation. The troupe had begun a long loop across the Dakotas, through the western states, and perhaps back to Chicago, where I could see her again. A note from Bismarck said, "Cowboys cheat." At cards, I assumed, for she sent half the usual funds that week. I missed her. I was angry with her, worried for her, and tired of so much worrying. When Roseanne pressed me for room and board, I bundled up the piano rolls and sold them all. I worked more and more often at the Millers' house.

A note from Mario warned that Mamma had been fined for coming onstage late and complaining loudly about cowboys in the audience. "They buy tickets like everybody else, and tickets pay our salaries," he wrote. "Please remind your mother of this." As if she were my child, as if she'd listen to me.

I walked to Lake Erie, gray under a chill, dull lid of sky. Pebbles trapped in dried algae fringed the shore. When I tried to console myself by reciting Leopardi, the lines wouldn't come. How was that possible when once they were nailed in my head? Had my English sonnets chased them out? I'd brought pen and paper, but trying to relay Mario's message to Mamma, I was overwhelmed by the hopelessness of finding words that would somehow work a change in Bismarck.

I decided to go back to the boardinghouse, fish out my volume of Leopardi, and read until every trouble of these last months was washed away. I did read Italian that night, but not Leopardi. A letter had come from Countess Elisabetta. "Count Filippo died in his sleep. May the Lord rest his troubled soul," she began. His last days were marked with breathless "little deaths" in which he seemed to cross into another land and then return and reach for one of his Capri women.

After the funeral, she and Paolo spent a week by Lake Como. I imagined them traveling north by train, she in first class and he in second until they'd passed north of Rome and were sure they'd meet nobody who knew them. Then Paolo might have donned his gentleman's attire and they could sit together, her purse in his pocket, fine manners masking his common birth. I pictured them in the mountain mornings, watching mist rise off the lake. Surely she deserved such pleasure after so many years of subterfuge and pain.

But the pleasure was brief. Returning to Naples, they found the count's death had triggered a new flood of debt notices. Some claims were false, merely vultures' forays, but now their days were consumed by meetings with lawyers, creditors, and bankers. As they feared, the villa was heavily mortgaged. In dark hours, the countess wrote, she remembered how I'd repaid her when it would have been so easy to escape this burden. "I will follow my Lucia's example. The debts *will* be paid, and interest on the debts. Somehow we'll keep my family's villa."

They could sell the house in Capri, I reasoned, the count's erotic statues that so repulsed her, and the land she'd managed to buy on the hills over Naples. Would that be enough?

"Why is it your problem?" Roseanne demanded. "They'll sell what they can and live more simply. They don't have to eat on silver. *You* just keep up with your room and board." Yet the count's debts *were* my problem for a reason I couldn't share: my plan of asking the countess to help me pay for college. Now even raising the question seemed unkind. How could I add to her burden?

I could hardly bear to hold the three tinted photographs that came with the letter. The first was captioned "To remember your distant friend." Fresh and glowing, the countess sat in a ruffled gown of apricot and cream, framed by the great parlor window with the blue of the bay behind her. "All of us" showed the countess, Paolo, Nannina, Alma the laundress, Luigi the gardener, and two new servants in front of the villa, flanked by potted geraniums. "Your Vesuvius" she'd written on the last image, taken from our flat rock.

My hand shook at the smell of sea and lemons this photograph recalled, the sound of lapping waves and distant cries of fishermen. If I could show them to Mamma, would they bring her joy or pain? I truly didn't know. She was so distant and mysterious now.

I bought frames at a secondhand shop and hung these pictures of the Old Country in my room as Irena had done, as immigrants did all over the city. Yet even with pictures, it was so hard to picture myself in Naples. Where was the Lucia who once lived there? The villa itself was becoming a place of fables, like the Palazzo Donn'Anna, grist for stories served up at Mrs. Miller's afternoon teas, no more real than a mermaid's romance.

My true home was Cleveland now, and not just to anchor my mother in her wandering. Somewhere in this city of brick and steel, monstrous wealth, and blocks on blocks of scrabbling poor, there must be a place that needed me. Not in a factory, although that might come. Not at Hiram House with those like Miss Miller who labored charitably, if briefly, for the poor. Somewhere else, a distant image wrapped in fog.

"For now, only study," said Father Stephen when I brought my anxious questions to his confession booth. "Finish high school. Then we'll see." It was true. I was so close. That spring I was called to serve at a round of garden parties, teas, and banquets for Miss Miller's coming marriage to Mr. Livingston. I visited Yolanda, Charlie, and little Maria Margaret in Youngstown. They were kind and fussed over me, but their world was limestone and hats and the tiny girl's varied triumphs. Better to study, to wrap myself in books and papers.

My graduation date had nearly arrived. Maria Margaret was sick with whooping cough, so Yolanda couldn't attend, but Roseanne would come, the Reillys, Henryk's family and Miriam, Casimir and Anna, Donato and his family. When I invited Lula, she patted my face. "Thank you, sugar, but why would I go someplace I'm not welcome?"

"All the graduates have tickets. I'll give you one."

She roared with laughter and pressed me into the white apron stretched across her chest. "Everybody, here's the most ignorant child ever to leave high school," she called out to the early drinkers. "Look at this," she said, putting her dark arm against my light one. "Understand?

That's why I can't come. But never you mind. You bring your friends here afterward and we'll have a little party. I'm proud of you, just like I'm sure your mamma is." In truth, Mamma's only comment was the word *Brava* marooned on the face of a Denver postcard that perhaps referred to my graduation.

The countess sent me as a graduation gift the cameo I had loved most in her collection: a perfect head of the goddess Diana set in a filmy veil. My hand shook when I held it. She had sold so many jewels, paintings, and silver pieces, yet saved this one for me. "We're so proud of you," she wrote. "Wear it to remember us."

"You've studied hard," Roseanne observed. "You deserve it. And who else would have repaid a countess? Not Teresa. And not me," she added emphatically. "Put it on and look in the mirror." I hardly saw myself behind the cameo, as if the swirling veil eclipsed my face. I set the lacquered box on my dresser and opened it at night, when the pale face glowed by streetlight and I could imagine my distant friend saying, "Come to the sitting room, Lucia, and let's read from Leopardi."

In truth I rarely read from Leopardi now. "*English literature,*" our teacher insisted, "is the crown of European culture. We must honor our Anglo-Saxon heritage and remember that we are heirs to Shakespeare, Milton, Keats, Browning, and Wordsworth." I studied hard. In the last months of school, my grades edged over Henryk's. I would be the valedictorian, our teacher announced.

Mr. Steinblatt, the principal, wasn't pleased. "Boys make better valedictory speeches," he grumbled.

"He's a fool," Henryk said. "*You* won the Cleveland essay prize." I had indeed, but that prize money was sucked away so quickly in the weeks when no money came from Mamma that I hardly felt the triumph of winning. I was determined to savor my valediction.

I wrote out a graduation speech and went early one Saturday morning to Lula's, seeking Mr. Hardwig, a rheumy-eyed regular who'd once taught rhetoric in Boston. Fortunately, I caught him sober. He had me read each sentence aloud, tapping his finger at ungainly constructions until my changes satisfied him. Then I practiced in front of our parlor mirror and in the kitchen for Roseanne.

"It sounds good, but don't you want to say something else?" she asked.

No, I wanted *this* speech. Remembering Mamma's lessons, I even marked where I must breathe. On graduation night, I put on a new dress that Roseanne had helped me buy with a sudden spurt of money from my mother, dark violet with soft pleats down the front. My cameo shone at the collar like the moon on a clear night.

At last my time came. I began the valedictory by listing all those in my first American class who were not with us onstage: Yolanda, Carmen, Ciro, Herman, Benjamin, Antonio, Joseph, Gabriella, Patrick, Bronya, Anna, Salvatore, Mary, Maria, Sarah, Johan, Domenico, Angela, Jakub, Robert, and Roberto. "*Why* are they not here?" Everyone knew. Most were working. Many of the girls had families. Domenico and Joseph had died in the quarries, Patrick and Jakub in the mills, Maria in one of the workplace fires. "Was *this* the golden future for which their parents came to America? If they had stayed in school, they could have one day helped to educate their own children." Young faces turned to mine. Power surged from my feet. *Here's the joy my mother finds in singing,* I thought, *the stunning power of one's own voice.*

I took a breath where I'd marked my page and went on: "From educated citizens could come inventors and scientists to design machines for relieving the tedium of work, artists, writers, scientists, and gifted craftsmen. What is needed for these benefits? Only that parents earn enough to keep their children in school and not have to thrust them into the working world too soon. Can our rich country not give her young people two simple gifts: the pleasures of a childhood without labor and the solemn discipline of education? Yes, we on this stage are proud indeed to be the eight in a hundred with diplomas in our hands. We will treasure this evening forever. Yet, how proud, how great our land would be if we were eighty, ninety, *a hundred in a hundred,* crowding this stage, bathed in the light of learning!"

My speech was brief. Not brief enough, said Mr. Steinblatt's scowl. The polite applause was brief as well, but I was flushed with pleasure to have done the whole only glancing at my notes. I had remembered to breathe and passed my eyes over every quarter of the audience just as Mamma did in Chicago. I had made myself smile at parents who stared back not understanding English. I had looked to the front row of wealthy patrons who paid my working schoolmates so little, whose wives knit children scarves in winter but hired their parents for pennies an hour. They looked at one another, whispering, their gloved hands tightly folded.

Only Mr. Richard Livingston, Miss Miller's fiancé, sought me out after the ceremony. "Well done, Lucia. America needs more clever men to invent new machines. Just be careful not to veer."

"Veer, sir?"

"Into socialism."

"Oh, Lucia's no socialist," said Miss Miller with a tinkling laugh. "She only meant that young people should stay in school. Isn't that right, Lucia?"

"Yes, Miss Miller. They should be *able* to stay in school."

"What would you like to do now, Lucia?" Mr. Steinblatt inquired stiffly. "Teach young immigrants at Hiram House?"

"No, sir. I'd like to go to college." There, I'd spoken my dream to a stranger.

He frowned. "That would be difficult, don't you think? Do you have funds?"

"No, sir. I'd need a scholarship."

"Certainly. Well, congratulations on finishing high school. That in itself is an achievement." For an immigrant girl, he surely meant, for the "daughter of a showgirl," I heard him say to a patron.

Clutching my diploma so hard that the paper creased, I joined a milling cluster of new graduates and their family and friends, their voices loud and strident in the rich June air. The Reillys shook my hand, gave me the present of a steel-tipped fountain pen, and walked slowly home, wrapped in quietude.

"Let's go to Lula's!" someone said, and we moved in a jubilant crowd, *graduates,* we who had endured. On that balmy night we believed our teacher's promise: "Now you can do *anything!*"

"There must be scholarships you can get," said Henryk as we crowded around a table.

"Couldn't Miss Miller help?" Miriam asked, her creamy white hand resting on Henryk's forearm. "You did shine her silverware."

Henryk slipped his arm free to pass around a plate of toasted cheese and pickles. "Miss Miller may not have her own money," he said. "And she has a fancy wedding to think about."

"A lot of parties means a lot of vegetables," said Miriam thoughtfully, taking a pickle. "Will your father be getting some of that business?"

"I doubt it. That's a big contract and we're a small shop."

"It never hurts to ask, does it?" she said sweetly and I wondered, not for the first time, how he could love her. Yet he seemed happy.

While the others drank ginger beer and talked eagerly about a country weekend organized for us by Hiram House, I cobbled together a plan. I wouldn't go to the country if Henryk and Miriam were going;

I'd visit my mother in Chicago before the troupe swerved west. I'd get a job in a shop, for my English was good enough now. Then I'd wait until after the wedding, when Miss Miller would have forgotten my speech, and ask her for a scholarship. Annoyed as I was with Miriam's constant little lessons, she was right in this: it never hurts to ask. If Miss Miller couldn't help me, she might know someone who could.

Mario had written that it would be "useful" if I visited Mamma soon. He hadn't said why. So I was anxious all the way to Chicago. When she didn't meet me at Union Station, I made my way to the Haymarket Theater and then backstage through a gauntlet of eyes and murmurs: "There's the Nightingale's daughter." Yolanda had given me a fine straw hat with silk flowers, the rim skillfully shaped for my face. With a trim striped shirtwaist bought for the trip, I could hold up my head against any voices.

I looked for Harold, who'd taken me to the station on my last visit, and found him in a warren of ropes, set pieces, and performers in costume. He was dressed in a white shirt with a crisp celluloid collar, carrying a notebook, a pen tucked behind his ear. "I'm the backstage manager," he announced proudly, "coming up in the world."

"That's wonderful, Harold. I'd like to see my mother."

His face clouded. "She's locked herself in her dressing room since last night. Claimed some Eye-talian gent was bothering her. But it wasn't no gent, just an old drunk at the stage door. Your ma was going on about his eyebrows." Blood pounded in my head as I watched Harold force her lock with a skeleton key and usher me in. "Good luck," he whispered.

The dressing room was meticulously ordered, I saw with relief. At least this much was unchanged. "Lucia, you're here," my mother said wearily. "I'm so glad. Nobody talks to me now." *Because you locked them out.* "I couldn't meet you at the station. The maestro's waiting outside the theater."

"Mamma!"

Her arms wove like vines around me. "I'm so thirsty," she said in a tiny voice. "*So* thirsty and cold."

"Wait here." I darted out to ask Harold for some hot tea.

"She's mostly drinking wine these days."

"Tea, if you would, please."

"She's on in an hour. She knows that?"

"I'm sure she does. She'll be ready." When I returned, Mamma was listlessly putting on her costume. "Can you sing? Are you well enough?"

"Of course," she said sharply. "I'm just tired of people asking how I am. Tired of being whispered about and worrying about *him*. Why can't he stay at the opera houses? This is vaudeville. He should leave me alone." She tugged at the corset straps. "And my act is *still* before inter-mission. Fasten my dress behind. I don't want to ask the girls." My fingers struggled with the tiny buttons. Her once-glorious emerald dress showed constant wear: small rips in the seams, a ruffle unstitched, a dirty hem, and several buttons replaced with pins.

"Let me fix the ruffle at least, Mamma."

"No, it doesn't matter. The audience is far away, and all they want is a show. They don't care about us. They're so stupid they think the clowns are really smiling. They look at acrobats jumping and spinning like tops and think it's easy. Backstage, the young ones cry. There's some *on crutches* between shows." Her voice turned shrill. "Crutches and canes. The dancers' feet are always bleeding. Vaudeville's a sad world, Lucia. That's why performers are so mean. When *he* comes backstage looking for me, of course they're scared."

I made her sit down. "Mamma, it was just a drunk. Maybe it looked like Toscanini, but it wasn't." Harold came with tea, and I watched gratefully as she arranged and padded her hair with practiced hands, painted her face, and adjusted the heavy plumed hat. Perhaps she was only agitated about my coming or in a woman's time of the month. But I feared worse. Nannina's word, *unstable*, rolled inside my head. The darting eyes, loosened fingers, the shrill edge to her voice made me feel unstable myself, perched on a rock in a rising sea.

When a ruffle of applause had her cock her head and stand up, I pounced on this good sign: she still knew the pace of the show by heart. Harold rapped on her door and called "Five minutes." She smoothed her gown and squared her shoulders. "Tap dancers, then me. Lydia and her ugly dogs come *after* the intermission." She hurried away.

Nobody led me to a seat this time, so I found a spot to watch her from the wings. My fingers sought the folds of my skirt, squeezing tightly. Would her voice crack? Would her old fear come true and the words run away? Would the audience laugh? *Blessed Mary, Mother of God, be with her now.* The curtain rose. From my nook I saw the fray of her gown. Yet the marvelous familiar voice was the same, rich and rising, warm and strong as ever, the high notes held to impossible length. The glorious Naples Nightingale. I sank gratefully onto a coil of rope.

Then I panicked. The hands were going wrong. The left one, which first had been rising and falling with practiced grace for "Sì, mi chiamano Mimì," now lay flat on her chest and then—*No, Mamma, no!*—cupped her breast, rubbing. The audience hooted. When her right hand copied its mate, men whistled and stamped. In the front row, a dark-suited man lifted a red card, and the piano man jumped his tempo.

With the slightest flinch, Mamma righted herself. Both hands floated modestly down, then gracefully lifted, airy with longing. Cheers, calls, and whistles filled the hall. Sweat ran under my cotton dress, which now seemed made of heavy wool. *Mamma, how could you?*

A boy ran across the stage with an enormous American flag. A change in the sequence, obviously. Red and blue lights flashed. Drums beat backstage. Catching time with the music, my mother began "The

Star-Spangled Banner," knees lifting slightly in a march, arms stiffly swinging. My heart ached for her frozen face and toy soldier act. What did she care about the rocket's red glare, the dawn's early light?

Behind me acrobats were assembling, recalled by Harold and grumbling at the forced reprise. So she'd have just two songs? How many had she sung before? Frantic, I tried to remember. Four? Five?

She took her bow with hoots from the cheaper seats. Elegantly dressed women in the first rows did not clap. The acrobat master barked "Alley-oop" and clapped his hands. The troupe smiled in unison like a single string pulled tight across their faces as they flipped themselves onstage.

Mario was waiting in Mamma's dressing room. When he held up a red card, her face paled to white. "It's your second warning, Teresa," he said severely. "Mr. Keith could turn you out today for unacceptable gestures. You know this. You signed the contract. Vaudeville is a *family* entertainment. Teresa, what were you thinking?"

I moved to her side. "She was singing from opera, Mario. She was taken by emotion. It was a dramatic gesture. Please, give her another chance. Where can you find a voice like hers? And the national anthem, have you ever heard it sung so beautifully? Mamma, you won't do that again, right? Right? You won't make unacceptable gestures?" She nodded so stiffly that it seemed her neck might creak.

Mario sighed. "Teresa, next time I'll have to telegraph Mr. Keith. If there's one more incident, *one* gesture, *one* late entry, *one* more angry word with Lydia about her dogs, *one* more scene about that maestro—"

"Toscanini," Mamma muttered.

Mario ignored this. "*One* more problem and you'll be traded to the Loew circuit as a warm-up act to one-reelers. Five shows a day. You'll share the bill with *movies*. Do you understand?"

"She understands," I said.

"I'm speaking to Teresa. Do *you* understand, Teresa?"

She nodded. Mario went over some bits of business: new lyrics, changes in staging, a shuffling of songs. When he left, we slumped in chairs, more spent than we ever were after a summer day of cleaning.

"*Do* you understand, Mamma?"

"Yes, yes, of course. Stop talking about it. Let's go out."

We walked along Lake Michigan. Against that mass of water she seemed frail and uncertain, tentative in her step. "Vaudeville isn't what I thought, Lucia. All these rules. Always watching for *him*. And nobody's kind to me anymore, not even Mario."

"Mamma, the problem is the way you touched yourself. You know they don't like it."

"Americans!" she exploded. "They hate their bodies. They hate women. The churchmen see filth everywhere. Whatever I did, it just happened. It's not my fault." Useless to remind her that she practiced every gesture, every crook of the finger and bend of the wrist. Nothing in her performances "just happened."

"Mamma, I'm worried. Why don't you come home and rest? I can get a good job. I can't go to college without a scholarship anyway."

"No, I'll stay here. I feel better now. Look." She pointed to a boulder by the shore. "We'll sit over there." In the hour we had before the next show, I told her about Yolanda's baby, the cameo, and my graduation speech. She held my hand, barely listening. When I had no more news to share, she announced: "Maybe it *was* just a drunk backstage. I'll keep singing, Lucia. It's the best thing for me. After all, I *am* the Naples Nightingale."

"Of course you are. And you're wonderful." She sighed as we leaned together. In the next day and a half, there were no incidents, unacceptable gestures, or talk of Toscanini. Mamma didn't gamble, which annoyed the acrobats who won from her regularly. "You see?" she said.

"I'm fine. If they would just treat me well, everything could be easy. Or if you came with me," she said wistfully.

Mario said there was no possibility of my traveling with the troupe, none. Mr. Keith would not tolerate an unwieldy crowd of spouses, children, lovers, and "others." He did promise to work harder at enforcing Mr. Keith's rules against backstage gambling. That in itself might help, for losing made my mother anxious and angry. Perhaps the gestures were only a passing error, an operatic excess. Lying awake in our hotel room, I could think of no better work for her than singing and no better world than vaudeville. If only she could stay.

"I'm fine," Mamma insisted at the station as I left. "You worry too much, Lucia." I went back to Cleveland, hovering between hope and helpless worry.

"You did your best," said Roseanne. "You can't be her mother forever. The best thing for both of you is work." Perhaps she was right.

*My diploma earned* me a trial post as junior clerk for $11.50 a week at Mr. Kinney's Dry Goods. I didn't mention my hope for college, and of course Mr. Kinney had no suspicions. In a stroke, every lesson in geometry, grammar, history, rhetoric, civics, and geography was replaced by principles of shopkeeping, constant reminders and instructions. I must be attentive, he warned, for respectable-seeming customers might slip unpaid-for items into commodious purses. The most trusted employee might take merchandise, sell it at lower rates to friends, or simply give it away for favors. *Loyal employees,* Mr. Kinney reminded us, could expect due recompense. Others would be fired immediately.

"You'll work hard," other clerks warned, "but he does appreciate diligence." I tried to make myself useful. Sales to Italian customers increased. I grasped the knack of running a sharpened pencil down a list of prices and summing them in my head. I had no talent for artful arrangement of merchandise but could bargain hard with wholesalers. When a dealer from Boston agreed to my price for strong cotton thread and fine steel needles if I bought two cases, I pressed the point on Mr. Kinney. "You'll see, sir, Italians will appreciate quality."

"And if not, you'll buy the overstock yourself, Miss D'Angelo?"

"Yes, sir, of course."

I began quietly speaking to friends and sisters of friends and those who came for scribing, showing the strength of the thread, the smooth finish and keen point of the Boston needles. "Why buy from your bosses at twice the price and half the quality?" Factory girls hesitated, afraid of fines for dealing outside the company store. "I need my job," said Yolanda's cousin Giovanna, who sewed for Printz-Biederman. "*My* mother isn't a vaudeville star."

"I work too," I reminded her. "And I can help you, if you want."

Giovanna's shoulders sagged. "I'm sorry, Lucia. We just have to be careful." With some trouble, I had Roseanne, Donato's wife, and two of her friends buy needles and thread and sell them at cost to the factory girls.

"Strange," Mr. Kinney mused. "Italians buy my needles and thread, but no yard goods. Why is that, Miss D'Angelo?"

"You know how they are, sir. Yard goods cost more, so they deal in Italian stores, where they can bargain."

He was pleased, though, for the shipment sold quickly. He began asking my advice on other goods and pricing and soon raised my salary to twelve dollars a week. With the few dollars I still got from Mamma and scribing money, I could even save a little. I felt useful and clever, helping my friends and furthering my own ends.

Then Giovanna was fined for using outside materials. Someone had seen needles in her purse. When she protested that Printz-Biederman was profiting from workers, she was fined for speaking socialism. Coming in late one morning after nursing her mother's raging fever all night, she was fined again.

"It's not your fault, Lucia," Roseanne insisted. But the first two fines *were* my fault: my thread, my words, my clumsy maneuvering without considering what consequences others would shoulder. In that summer and fall of 1908, I brooded on my mother's brittle moods that I couldn't ease and workplace injustices I couldn't heal. I longed to go to college and learn to be of greater good—or at least less harm.

I went to see Miss Miller, now Mrs. Richard Livingston. Married and settled in her husband's grand home, she might have money of her own, or at least some claim on his. She met me in the marble entryway. In a pearl-gray morning dress, tightly pleated and overworked with embroidery, she took little bird steps, anxiously looking around. Where was the assured, driving presence that staged a lively talent show at Hiram House?

"This house is a present from my father-in-law. Limestone money," she announced, indicating the marble, gilt, brocade, carved woods, and crystal, all even finer than her family's magnificent furnishings. "*Everything* comes from him," she whispered, "and I am to be grateful. He lives with us. He watches us. He was never like this before, Richard says, never. Now he's convinced he'll die in the poorhouse, that I'll ruin him with ten-cent tips to the butcher boy or a birthday present to the scullery maid. Look around, Lucia. Is that possible?"

"No, I don't think so, Mrs. Livingston," I said obediently, already fearing my mission was hopeless.

"Let's talk in the sitting room. *His* servants are cleaning upstairs."

We sat on a delicate French divan. "It never hurts to ask," Miriam had said. I had come to ask. I had to ask. I poured out my longing for college and joy in reading, the pleasures of school and skipping grades, my first sight of an American college. "I know not many Italian girls go, but I *could* do it, Mrs. Livingston. I'm sure I could."

She sighed. "I'd love to help, Lucia. You were made for college. But *he*"—she jerked her head toward the grand stairway with such force that the puffed pompadour shook—"put us on a 'charity budget.' We gave to the new park in Shaker Heights. I'm afraid to ask him for another cause." She leaned toward me. "Richard won't have his own money until the old man dies. I'm so sorry." She did seem sorrowful, deflated as a child. When she offered streetcar fare from a tiny dangling purse, I refused. "I'll tell Richard you stopped by. He heard you're working for Mr. Kinney. It's a fine post for you. Congratulations. I'll be sure to tell Agnes." She leaned forward. "At least the old man let me bring her with me." There was little more to say. I thanked her and left. Walking between rows of mansions set in velvet lawns, my shoes beat out "No college. No college. No college." Father Stephen was right. All I could do now was to make the best of my work.

At least that fall was splendid, with bright blazes of leaves and balmy days deep into October. I pried my face into smiles when customers said how fortunate we were with the weather. "Yes, we certainly are, ma'am."

Not everyone was fortunate that season. Giovanna was fired from Printz-Biederman. Now the best she could find was a place in a dusty, wood-framed workshop behind Kinney's where Mr. Lentz contracted with wholesalers for piecework: cutting patterns, sewing bodice fronts and backs, and making sleeves. Giovanna earned less for this rough work and had to lease her machine from Mr. Lentz. Her mother was bedridden now; her ten-year-old brother got five dollars a week as a messenger boy. I offered to make up her difference in salary.

"That's charity, Lucia. I can't take it." Only Yolanda could help, for she was family; she sent a dollar a week. I was ashamed for my part in her troubles and seethed with anger at Printz-Biederman's rules and greedy fines.

*Just after New* Year's in 1909, Mario wrote: "I'm sorry, Lucia. We may be a family, but we can't be nursemaids. Your mother needed more attention than we could give. Mr. Keith had to let her go." I never knew why. Months later, a passing statement, "They didn't like my hands," made me think she had repeated the "unacceptable gestures."

There had been some kindness, I'm sure arranged by Mario. She might have been turned out on the street in a small midwestern town. Instead, she was kept on until St. Louis and traded to Mr. Marcus Loew's People's Vaudeville Company in return for a juggler. Exactly as Mario had warned, Mamma's beautiful voice would introduce one-reel motion pictures of chase scenes, cowboys and Indians, and newsreels of Chinese mandarins, Indian rajas on decorated elephants, and the pomp of Russian czars. To lure vaudeville lovers, Mr. Loew provided a few singers and comics, perhaps a mimic for his shows, easy acts to pack and move.

If she got good reports from Loew's, Mario wrote, Mr. Keith *might* take my mother back. But with new acts auditioning in each city, why reclaim a problem? Questions flew at me. How would she fare with the castoffs of vaudeville houses? How long would Mr. Loew even keep live acts? Moving pictures didn't need to be housed, dressed, and fed. They didn't jockey for better billings or higher wages. If she failed with Loew's, what then? Mamma hadn't confessed her situation, so how could I comfort her? I didn't even know where she was. Frantic letters to Mr. Loew went unanswered. A theater manager in Cleveland said "New York" arranged performers' itineraries; he had no idea how to find the

Naples Nightingale. All I could do was wait for her next postcard. "Bad things come in threes," Roseanne was fond of saying, as when three boarders in sequence stole from her and slipped away at night.

In Mr. Lentz's shop, where Giovanna worked, girls sat surrounded by stacks of unfinished garment pieces. The air was thick with snips and fluff of thread and fabric. Even foremen couldn't smoke; the risk was too great. There were so many fires and causes for fires in those days: a hobnail shoe striking an iron plate, a cracked electrical wire, or wadded oily rag set in a sunny window.

In a March mid-afternoon as I was finishing an inventory, someone screamed into the store: "Fire in Lentz's, right behind you!"

I raced toward the workshop, shouting at the girls who got out first. "Giovanna Fidelli, have you seen her?" Dazed, they shook their heads. Perhaps they couldn't hear me amid shrieks and sirens, fire bells and shouts of policemen pouring into the alley, pressing back the gathering crowd. Smoke billowed from the doors and windows as dark shapes of girls appeared, staggering, some trailing streams of flames.

"There's another!" People shouted and pointed. Firemen turned their hoses on the blazing dresses.

"Blankets!" someone cried. Mr. Kinney was already coming, his arms full of blankets and heavy coats. Firemen snatched them to wrap the burning girls.

A girl I knew from scribing raced by. "Adele, where's Giovanna?"

"Machine," she gasped before a policeman pulled her away.

Of course, the sewing machines. Everyone knew what happened after garment shop fires: girls who survived lost all they'd invested and had to begin again. A dark shape appeared against the tumbling smoke: a girl hugging her machine. Two firemen doused her with water. A third pulled the machine from her arms. But the girl wasn't Giovanna.

Starting toward the building, I was yanked back. "You can't help," someone shouted. I barely recognized Giovanna when she finally came reeling out, her sooty face darker than Lula's. The steel in her arms would be blazing hot. I saw the seared, scorched skin, smelled the stink of flesh. When someone brought a soggy coat, she howled as it touched her. Two men carried her to Kinney's back lot, where the wounded lay on blankets. Other blankets covered the dead. Three more girls were found charred inside the building, cradling their machines.

The fire chief ordered his men back just before a surge of flame brought down the roof and the four walls fell in like a collapsing house of cards. Now the crowd ringed a new spectacle: a black-suited, dazed man, Mr. Lentz.

"My daughter died for your damn machine!" a mother screamed. Boys spit on his suit. The first girl who had escaped, her dress merely singed and arms blistered, moved through the parting crowd toward Mr. Lentz. She opened her mouth. Nothing. When someone brought her a cup of water, she drained it. "I paid seven dollars into my machine," she croaked in an old man's voice, horrible to hear. "Tell me." She gestured for another cup and drained it. "Tell me I'll get that back."

Filled with all I had seen—the blackened girls, the dead beneath blankets, and Giovanna's scorched arms—I pushed to the front of the crowd. "Tell her!" I shouted, startled by the force of my own voice. "Tell her!"

Voices behind me repeated: "Tell her! Tell her! Tell her!" When Mr. Lentz tried to back away, boys blocked his path. A smoke-darkened fireman silently joined the ring.

We were sweating freely now with the crackling, hissing fire behind us. Mr. Lentz wiped his face with a white handkerchief and faced the girl. "Rachel, you and the others will have full credit for what you have paid into the machines when I rebuild my shop. I'll have to trust your word on how much you've paid. My account books are in there." He pointed to the ruin. "But you'll have jobs when I rebuild."

"Give your hand on it, sir," I said, and he did. Someone passed around a Panama hat for funeral expenses. When it came to Mr. Lentz, silence fell over the crowd. He took out his wallet, hesitated, and put it in. The hat sagged. Fifty dollars, I heard later. A murmur of content swept around the circle as I pushed my way toward Giovanna.

If Mr. Lentz had rebuilt his shop, he might have kept his promise. But he didn't rebuild. Two weeks after the fire, declaring bankruptcy, he joined the wholesale firm of Joseph & Feiss. He did write letters of recommendation for the survivors and paid them two, three, or four weeks' wages, depending on the severity of their injuries. Giovanna received four weeks'.

Chapter 11

## Paradise Lost

*Finally Mamma wrote* again, not penny postcards but notes on the backs of used tickets from the People's Vaudeville Company, mailed in Memphis. She never explained her change of company, only commenting that she would be "south," safe from "him."

Where could I find a lever long enough to pry Arturo Toscanini from her head? Her imagined enemies grew on every side. A ticket from Little Rock spoke of Lydia and her dogs. "They follow me too." She stayed in the theater between performances to watch the moving pictures. "Safer than the street." She didn't play cards. "Everyone cheats." I'd waited so long to hear from her. Now this little stack of tickets made me sick with dread. Far away, was her mind unraveling?

"Lucia," Father Stephen said severely. "She is using His gift, her marvelous voice, to earn her bread. She renounced the vice of gambling. You must trust His protecting hand." He seemed so sure.

Walking home from church, I counted Mamma's other "protectors": the comfort of song, a smaller company, and moving pictures to safely entertain her. Mr. Loew's audiences were surely less exacting, his rules less austere. Her "unacceptable gestures" might be acceptable, even welcome in his theaters. Without a schedule of her tour, I couldn't arrange a visit, but she sent a few dollars home every week. That constancy was reassuring: she wasn't fired at least. Yet when nobody wrote to warn me or complain of her behavior, I shared a new worry with Roseanne: perhaps she had no friends to fret over her. Had she even given Mr. Loew my address?

"Stop it!" Roseanne snapped. "You're making yourself sick. Teresa's working and sending money. And look at you with a high school diploma and a fine job in a downtown shop. What could be better?"

College would be better, but perhaps Roseanne was right: work in the shop brought some quiet satisfaction and paid my room and board. Mr. Kinney had begun teaching me the rudiments of double entry bookkeeping, "invented by your Italian ancestors five hundred years ago." The craft demanded perfect concentration, he warned, for a single transposed or misplaced number could bring havoc. He began cautiously entrusting me with more complex tasks. In quiet hours bent over the broad pages of ledgers, I didn't fret about Mamma, absorbed by the clatter of adding machine keys, the handle's ratchet, and that first giddy moment when the day's transactions fell neatly into balance. "To the penny, Miss D'Angelo, to the penny!" Mr. Kinney crowed. Delighted, he gave me the pick of a new shipment of ruffled blouses. "If my Olivia and I had a son," he said wistfully, "I couldn't have asked for a better hand on my books."

Yet despite Mr. Kinney's praise, bookkeeping wasn't enough. I yearned for college as much as Yolanda ever yearned for a fella and release from her family's flat. I devised a plan, ironed my best shirtwaist, and puffed my hair in a pompadour.

Mr. George Bellamy, the director of Hiram House, was known to have wealthy friends. He dined with Rockefellers, bankers, and mill owners. He knew me and knew my work as a scribe. Perhaps he could help. I went to his office and found him seated behind a gleaming walnut desk. Gold studs glittered in his cuffs. The lapels of a finely tailored jacket were cut in the season's fashion, and his shirt was of English weave, stiff-collared and perfectly starched. Surely friends of such a man could provide a scholarship. I scarcely cared to which college; they all blended together. A young girl dreaming of marrying a prince would be happy with any prince.

He listened, folded his hands, and fixed me with an avuncular gaze. "You graduated from high school, Lucia. Most immigrant girls do not. Your parents surely sacrificed for your education."

Was he taunting me? He must know that Mamma had no husband. "My father was killed in Naples, sir. He was a cathedral painter who fell from a scaffold and died."

"Ah, I'm sorry to hear that."

"He wanted me to be educated. It was his last wish. And for this I'm applying to you." I stood very still, hoping he wouldn't notice the flush of heat from passing on my mother's lies again.

Mr. Bellamy turned a heavy ring. "Don't you want to get married, Lucia? If you go to college, your chances will diminish." Because most Italian boys don't go to college, he must have meant, and American men wouldn't consider me.

"I hope to marry someday, sir, but I want to go to college *now*. If someone provides the means, I'll make my patron proud." Mr. Bellamy drummed his blotter. I remembered to breathe.

He sighed. "I will try, young lady. I make no promises, but I will inquire."

I thanked him and left quickly. Once clear of the Hiram House grounds, I raced to the boardinghouse and threw myself into the arms of an astonished Roseanne. "There now," she said, patting my back. "Here's our Lucia again."

Restlessly waiting for Mr. Bellamy's response, I persuaded Giovanna to visit Yolanda with me that Sunday. Her singed hair had been cut short and her throat was still raw from smoke, but her spirits lifted on the short train ride south. Joy filled Yolanda's tiny house and flavored the amiable disorder of baby Maria Margaret's toys and clothes mixed with piles of feathers and flowers, entire stuffed tiny birds, hat forms and lace. Finished hats perched rakishly on chairs. "Isn't she clever?" Charlie demanded. "She sells to all the owners' wives."

"Look at her!" demanded Yolanda as she lifted up the gurgling baby. "She's so adorable!" Charlie had designed a new pulley system and was bound for greatness, Yolanda insisted. I had stumbled into a storybook.

Charlie's friend Frank came for dinner, a slender, cheerful man, clearly brought to court Giovanna. He leaned close to catch her whispered story. Her dark eyes glittered; curly cropped hair framed the perfect oval of her face. "No woman who doesn't want to should have to work outside the home," Frank announced. She beamed.

"We could have invited someone for you," Yolanda whispered when Frank and Giovanna had gone out walking. "But—"

"I don't want to be married yet, and you didn't have space for another chair."

Yolanda laughed. Nothing troubled or offended her now. I was happy to see her happiness, to play with the cheerful baby and admire the new hats, but I felt out of place in the little house and eager to go back to my life.

A month after I'd visited Mr. Bellamy an envelope arrived from his office. "Open it," said Roseanne, but I took it to my room instead and held it, turned it over and over, warmed it, finally opened it and drew out a single monogrammed sheet. An anonymous donor had offered funds to send a "worthy young woman" to college and I had been selected for this honor. Mr. Bellamy recommended his alma mater, Hiram College, just south of Cleveland, for which Hiram House was named and where I might receive an excellent education in the wholesome country air. President Bates had arranged my lodging beginning in midsummer so that I might have private readings before the next semester. My patron was most anxious that I do well but did not wish to be identified.

Happiness whirled inside me like a great wind. I was certain that Mrs. Livingston was my patron despite her father-in-law. Perhaps she had argued for Hiram House to be added to their "charity budget," having made private arrangements with Mr. Bellamy that I receive these funds. How could I thank her without betraying the elaborate subterfuge? Not in writing, for the old man might intercept my letter. If I went calling, one of his servants could reveal me. Finally I determined a means: I put on my drabbest dress and battered straw hat, approached the grand house through a back alley, and knocked at the kitchen door, asking Agnes for scullery work.

She peered closely at my face and then said gruffly, "Sorry, girl, we're not hiring." Leaning forward, she whispered: "I'll tell the missus you came." Agnes pointed to a reddened finger where a ring might be and made a sign for money. "Sold?" I mouthed, and Agnes nodded. Then aloud: "The Winstons next door might need a maid. Wait, here's a fresh oatcake. Good luck to you, girl." It was warm and sweet under the rough grain, the taste of hope and secret kindness.

When my time for college finally came, I wrote to Mr. Loew, imploring him to forward a letter to Teresa D'Angelo with my new address. Then I took a difficult leave of Mr. Kinney, who doubted finding a better clerk, "even among Americans." Finally I visited those who had filled my years in America: the Reillys, Casimir and Anna, Donato, and then Yolanda's and Giovanna's families. I went to Hiram House, to church for Father Stephen's blessing, and then early to Lula's before her first customers stumbled in from the night shift.

She was scrubbing the front steps, for she took particular pride in a gleaming limestone entry. "Girl," she said, setting down her brush, "I've been hearing about your good-byes. You're going thirty miles away, not to Timbuktu."

"I won't be back until Christmas, and you're the only people—"

"The only people you know in America?" she said, patting my cheek. "Well that's true. And your mamma's not here. You're a good girl, Lucia. We'll have a grand graduation party someday." She went back to scrubbing, working at a stain. "Now in all these good-byes, did you happen to give one to Henryk?"

"He's busy," I told the limestone step. He *was* busy in the shop. I'd also heard that he was often out walking with Miriam. I had stopped going to Hiram House dances, not wanting to see them there.

"Well, I'm busy too, Miss Lucia. I'm not sitting around eating chocolates, but I've got time for a friendly good-bye. How would Henryk feel if you blew out of town like a bad breeze?" I mentioned Miriam. "So what? He's still your friend."

Henryk was stacking apples in a neat pyramid when I told him of my scholarship. Apparently he already knew. "You've worked so hard for this, Lucia. You deserve it. I'll miss you though." He looked up from his apples. "You *could* write me a letter, since you don't need a scribe." His wide smile and warm, dark eyes melted away my stiffness, as they always did.

"You mean, you want to know what books I've read? Would that be interesting?"

"Well, sure. And I'll tell you the fruits and vegetables I've sold. Everybody wants to know things like that." He slipped an apple to a hungry-eyed street boy who darted off, chomping.

"And what fruit you gave away."

"Right, I'm a famous philanthropist, like Andrew Carnegie, but don't tell my father." A customer came in for onions. As furtively as he'd fed the street boy, he reached out quickly and squeezed my hand. "Congratulations, Lucia. Do us proud." Then to the impatient woman: "Yes, Mrs. Rothbard, sweet new onions right over here."

I crossed the street to put automobiles, pushcarts, and wagons between us, my hand clenched to hold in the heat of his touch. It was good that I was going away, better that than seeing him out walking with Miriam.

I left the next day with a rudely hasty thanks to Roseanne. She laughed. "I felt the same when I was leaving for America. All I wanted was to go." On the crowded local train I stared out the window, so immobile that when I stood up to leave the woman beside me commented, "Miss, you looked frozen."

"I'm going to college."

"Really now? Well good for you."

I should get off at Garrettsville, President Bates himself had written; his wife shopped that day and could bring me to college. She was waiting at the platform, a gracious, motherly woman who bundled me into a carriage. "Mr. Bates *does* have an automobile," she assured me, "but with these muddy roads, a horse is more reliable." Summer rains had washed the land until it shimmered. I saw green in crossing Pennsylvania, but not these soft hills of velvet grass, startling against fields gold with grain, mounds of maple and oak trees and lush hedges. Black-eyed Susans and orange daylilies grew wild along the roadsides. "This is God's country," Mrs. Bates observed. "In the spring, with the flowers, it's like Mr. Wordsworth's poem. Do you know it, dear?"

"Yes, ma'am." I recited: " 'And then my heart with pleasure fills, and dances with the daffodils.' " She smiled, gazing across the fields.

Describe a dream too closely and it scatters like milkweed. Here is what I remember from my too-brief time at college. I was given a small room whose window opened so near to a giant maple tree that I might have been lodged in its limbs. Two afternoons each week I was to work in the library. Walking through those hushed canyons of books was a pleasure as great as any sunset on the bay. "Joy delights in joy," said Shakespeare in one of my sonnets, and my joy circled upward in those weeks. Busy with reading and work, I wrote no letters, despite my promises, so no record remains, as if my college time was indeed a dream.

I came on a Saturday. On Monday I met my three professors: Dr. Sutton for English, Dr. Peckham for classics, and Dr. Bancroft for mathematics. They were grave, courteous, bearded men with faded frock coats; Mr. Kinney would not have been unimpressed by the cut and quality of their waistcoats and collars. But I loved how carefully they opened each text and showed where my reading began. Dr. Sutton announced: "We will commence, Miss D'Angelo, with a review of Milton's sublime *Paradise Lost*, with which you are doubtless familiar." I was overcome by embarrassment, first that I had read only fragments of this work, and second that I was presenting myself with a false, invented name. The alias had never once troubled me before, but in this book-lined office I felt like a fraud.

"I'm really Lucia Esposito, sir." Dr. Sutton sat back, hands woven together, smiling slightly, awaiting an explanation. "I changed my name in Pennsylvania, near the Susquehanna River."

"And what exactly caused this change near the Susquehanna River?" Words tumbled out. I explained how my great-grandfather Domenico was given away in a churchyard, my mother's shame over this story, and how, having learned how easily names could be altered in America, we had shredded our old documents and thrown them out the window.

Dr. Sutton tapped his fingertips together. "So you made yourselves angels?"

"Yes, sir, for—protection in America."

"I see. Very original. Now to return to the matter at hand, since Milton's *Paradise Lost* concerns the nature of angels, perhaps your chosen appellation fits our purpose. You will read the first fifty pages for our next meeting, paying close attention to rhetoric. You are familiar with standard rhetorical terms?" I nodded. "Excellent." He dictated a formidable list of poetry and plays which I would read in the coming years. We would meet the next Monday. "I am certain you'll be well prepared. When the semester begins, I would suggest joining the Alethean, our women's literary society." He smiled. Unsure of the appropriate response, I smiled back and, when he said nothing further, excused myself.

Dr. Bancroft was next. "We will review your algebra and pass through trigonometry into calculus and higher realms of geometry. You are prepared for this journey, Miss D'Angelo?"

"Yes, sir."

On a small chalkboard he set me a problem in algebra. Once again the play of numbers was a balm, fading other matters into shadows. "Unconventional," Dr. Bancroft observed of my method, "but effective. I suggest you prepare the first two chapters and as much of the third as you're able."

With Dr. Peckham I'd read the classics, including selections of Ovid, Horace, Cicero, and Virgil. "As you know, Miss D'Angelo, Virgil was buried in Naples. You have seen his grave?" I hadn't. "A pity. In any case, we begin with the Greeks."

In our next encounters I was thrilled, horrified, and entranced by *Oedipus Rex*. Even now I remember Dr. Peckham's slight lift of the eyebrow, urging me on to more precise and defensible analyses: "Understanding emerges from the *text*, Miss D'Angelo, not from personal speculations on the text. Now, at what point precisely does Oedipus begin doubting his identity?"

Yet much as he revered the ancients, Dr. Peckham brought a lively, affectionate interest to each of our encounters and seemed in no hurry to shoo me away. After our discussions of *Oedipus*, readings from *Ovid* and *Herodotus*, and the first chapter of the *Iliad*, he leaned back in a creaking oak chair, lit his pipe, and asked about my life. No one ever listened with such attention, bemused at times, and without judgment.

I told him about our work for the countess and first encounter with Maestro Toscanini, the rock where Mamma sang to Vesuvius, Count Filippo's sickness, Dr. Galuppi's horrific "cures," and the calamitous circumstances of our leaving Naples. I described Irena's death and my scribing, my mother's marvelous voice, her troubles with Mr. Keith's vaudeville, my longing to finish high school, and the Lentz factory fire, when garment workers died for their machines.

"Considering such a history, Miss D'Angelo," he said, brushing tobacco flecks from his trousers, "what is your purpose now?"

"Sir?"

"There is a purpose for our life's journey. Is that not why we're here?" He waved toward the tall window looking out on lawns and blue sky puffed with clouds. "It is a question which bears contemplation whilst continuing the *Iliad* for next Monday."

We would never finish the *Iliad*. The next day, before I had begun my assignment or considered his question, I was summoned from the library to Dr. Peckham's office. "This telegram just came, Miss D'Angelo, and, thinking it might be urgent, I sent for you." He handed me the envelope and then tactfully busied himself at a table heaped with manuscripts. I opened the envelope: *Dear Lucia. Teresa home, nervous collapse. Won't speak. Dangerous condition. Can't stay alone. Needs you. Roseanne.*

Mute with shock, I showed my professor the telegram. He left immediately, telling me to await his return. Alone, I bent into the anchoring weight of the great oak desk and cried. The demons that chased my mother from Naples had caught her at last. Who could repair the shards of a broken mind? The magnificent voice hadn't saved her. *Needs you.* I would surely have to leave this kindly paradise of books and scholars. Where would *my* dreams go? Would Mamma's demons find me too? *Can't stay alone.* Could she even stay at the boardinghouse? And if not, where would we go? Who, in a great city consumed with its industry, would shelter a lunatic and her daughter?

Dr. Peckham returned with a train schedule and a document from President Bates granting me an emergency withdrawal until "personal conditions permit." Dr. Peckham himself would take me to the station in the president's carriage. I packed my few clothes and left within the hour. That leaving was like the wrenching away of skin, far harder than leaving Naples, for I was young then and on a grand adventure.

I said nothing on the road to Garrettsville. "Farewell, happy fields," Milton's fallen angels cried and I cried too, turned away from my teacher, who gave me a silent space for grief. At the station, he helped me from the carriage. "Miss D'Angelo, we shall expect a letter from you with news, good or bad, of your situation in Cleveland." I nodded. "Listen to me, my dear. From the classics we know that families great and small have known the fragility of the human mind. There is no shame in this, any more than in sickness of the body. Those who say or think otherwise are mistaken. You must only find a way to care for your mother or have her cared for. I am confident that you will. And you will find us awaiting your return."

I had never wanted a father so much as I did then. And what could I do but extend my hand? He gripped it in both of his. "Miss D'Angelo, I'm sorry that life has found you out so quickly." He took an envelope from his pocket. "Here is forty dollars. It is a gift." When I protested, he shook his head. "I was helped when I was your age and I trust you will help another young person in your time." The Cleveland train clattered in. I ran to get it. Through the dusty window I waved at my slender, bearded friend until the station vanished behind me.

*"She's in your* old room. It happened to be empty," said Roseanne when I came home. The stairway rose like the Himalayas before me. She rested her hand on my shoulder. "Would you like to rest before you see her?"

I shook my head. "How did she get here?"

"A man brought her from Georgia in handcuffs." I leaned against the stairwell. "He had orders not to remove them until she was out of his care. He wanted five dollars."

"I'll pay you back. When she came, how was she?"

"She didn't know me. I sent for Donato and we managed to get her up to the room."

"She was violent?"

"At first, yes. Stomping, throwing things, pounding walls. Then nothing for hours. She hasn't eaten. We put a lock on the door from the outside."

"Like a prison?"

"Lucia, she was wild! Screaming. Anybody else would have—"

"I know." Anybody else would have called the police and had such a lunatic taken away. I had walked out of my old world and into a new one in which my mother was caged like an animal. The ground rocked beneath me. "Give me the key, please."

To mount the looming stairs, I summoned the acrobats' command:

"Alley-oop." It beat in my head: *Alley-oop. Alley-oop. Alley-oop.* But acrobats know where to put their feet, where to bend, and where to find a hand to steady them. I knew nothing about lunacy. Whatever I expected when I unlocked the door, it wasn't this: someone once my mother sitting in the burgundy coat buttoned high despite the late-summer heat. The once-glorious hair hung tangled along her ashen face. All the bedclothes, every object that belonged on shelves, walls, in the closet or drawers lay crumpled and stomped on the floor. She didn't lift her eyes or in any way note that I had entered.

Here was the Naples Nightingale, stripped of feathers, an angel fallen and crushed. No, she wasn't here. *Here* was a shell of the slender beauty who'd floated with me on warm waves in moonlight. The wild disorder surrounding her inhuman stillness churned up nausea so intense that I turned, ran, and retched into the toilet.

I couldn't go back to my room; that was impossible.

No, think of the warriors of Troy, the heroes and great lovers. Of what possible use was my college reading if not to shore up the courage to join the battle that called me? I made myself return, close the door, and lay a cautious hand on her shoulder. "Mamma, it's Lucia, your daughter. Let me bring you something to eat." No response. I touched her horribly tangled hair. "Or brush—"

Her balled fist, whipping full and hard into my stomach, slammed me into the wall. When I struggled to my feet she was a statue again, as if I'd conjured the blow. Panting, I realized my folly. I needed a doctor, a guide and interpreter of the mind's underworld, the inferno my mother had entered. I left the room, locking the door behind me. Now I was her jailer. No, no, I was only protecting her until the storm passed away. It must pass away. How could she stay like this, like a lunatic, a madwoman? I went out to look for help.

A nurse at Hiram House promised to send Dr. Ricci, a noted neurologist who could speak to my mother in Italian. She took my hand. "I'm so sorry, Lucia."

I thanked her and hurried home to wait in the parlor for Dr. Ricci. Roseanne brought a glass of brandy. "It will calm you," she promised. What could calm me when so much had changed so suddenly? Or *had* the change been sudden? Perhaps this state was merely the logical end of her rages, obsession with Toscanini, manic cleaning, and night walks, the "gestures" and odd behaviors that had disgraced her in two troupes. The strangeness of her cards and letters had been a clear enough sign, if I'd chosen to read it. Just as Irena's coughing, which I'd taken as chronic but innocent, steadily slipped into pneumonia, my mother's strangeness had transformed her into an ashen statue with a flying fist. *She hit me.* No, she must have meant to do something else. Or did she "mean" nothing at all? Was she even capable of "meaning" now? Once she'd said her love for me was like Vesuvius, always there, even if hidden behind fog. *Vesuvius, Vesuvius, Vesuvius,* I repeated until the word only timed my breathing. No sound came from my mother's room.

Roseanne appeared at the parlor door. "You do understand, Lucia, that if Teresa frightens the boarders, she can't stay." Yes, I said, miserably, I understood.

Dr. Ricci came in the early evening, apologetic for his delay. He was a small, dapper man, who spoke a precise and cultured Italian. Yes, Roseanne could take his hat and coat. Yes, he would care for tea. His fee was three dollars for a house call. From the elegance of his dress, I assumed that he charged wealthy patients more. Graciously, firmly, he had Roseanne leave us, closed the parlor doors himself, and began "taking the history": Mamma's grandfather, the sordid tale of my conception, our time in Naples, why we left, her work in America and a detailed account of her strange behaviors.

He wrote without comment until I burst out, half rising from my chair: "Dr. Ricci, what's *wrong* with her?" She was the first, the central person in my life, and, like Oedipus, I didn't know my mother at all.

Dr. Ricci smiled gently. "Miss D'Angelo, if we can be strangers to ourselves, how much more can we be strangers to each other, to our own parents and children? But first we complete the history. Then I speak with the patient."

"She doesn't speak! She screams and punches, throws things on the floor. She came home in handcuffs!"

"She will speak to me," Dr. Ricci said with such calm assurance that I sat down, tamed by the force of his certainty. "Now, Miss D'Angelo, shall we return to the last time you saw your mother? It was"—he glanced at his notebook—"in Chicago, at the Haymarket Theater." After more questions and a careful study of Mamma's "letters" home, he announced that he would visit her.

Incredulous, I watched Dr. Ricci mount the stairs, unlock the door, knock politely, and enter as calmly as one might enter a bakery. He got her to speak: a steady murmur of two voices filtered through the door. Hers rose and fell; his never changed. No crashes or thumps, no bodies thrown against walls. Had the danger passed, like a wild drunkard grown sober? An hour later, Dr. Ricci came downstairs and again closed us into the parlor. From his grave face and gentle manner I knew the danger had *not* passed or perhaps even truly begun.

"Lucia, is there no one else in your family I can speak with? An older relative?"

"I'm her only family, here or anywhere. Tell me, please, sir. What happened to her?"

Dr. Ricci helped me sit and then sat himself, thoughtfully smoothing his jacket as I gripped the chair arms. "Your mother is exhibiting multiple symptoms: paranoia, hallucinations, nervous prostration, neurasthenia, hysteria, aggression, sexual anxiety, and catatonia, the rigidity you noted on first entering her room."

"Catatonia," I repeated dully, dazed by the chain of terms, each like a surgeon's knife laying bare the deformity and disorder of my mother's mind, making her an *esposito*. Whether I understood each one hardly mattered.

"More precisely, transient catatonia, since she attacked you."

"Not really attacked—"

He opened his notebook and read: " 'She hit me in the stomach with her fist.' Those were your words, Lucia? You were thrown across the room?"

"Yes," I whispered.

"Then we are speaking of an attack. Your mother is seriously ill."

"Dr. Ricci, why did this happen?"

His grandeur diminished. He lifted empty hands. "We are profoundly ignorant of the workings of the human mind, both its glories and its troubles, the injuries it suffers. Dr. Freud and his colleagues would look for explanations in your mother's childhood and," he said delicately, "the circumstances of your conception. Yet others with a similar past might show different symptoms, or none at all." He tapped his brow. "*Here* is the unknown land, the Dark Continent, the mystery to plumb in this new century."

"And my mother, sir?"

"Yes, of course, the practicalities. How is she to be cared for in the next months?"

"She won't improve? Perhaps after a rest—"

Dr. Ricci leaned forward. "Mental illnesses, and we may call your mother's case an illness, build gradually for years, as you yourself have indicated." He indicated his notebook. "We cannot expect a rapid cure, *if* cure is even possible. Still, we can't be hopeless. Patients have recovered from cases worse than this. However, at present, she must be kept from harming herself or others. A private sanitarium would provide perfect rest in peaceful, comfortable surroundings. However, such establishments are costly, hundreds of dollars a month." I crumpled in my chair. "Precisely. They cater to the wealthy and are not universally efficacious. Often they are family expedients, places to house the infirm or inconvenient. There is the Cleveland State Hospital, which is free"—he coughed slightly—"for those in need."

"No, not there! Never!" Yolanda's aunt had worked in that place briefly and told us what she saw: rats, chains, straitjackets, filth and feces, food slopped in trenchers, cages where men and women howled day and night, women abused by keepers hired from jails or pulled from the wards themselves. The aunt took lower pay in a factory to escape that "human zoo." Whatever else I wanted for my life would now come after keeping Mamma out of Cleveland State Hospital.

"Could she"—my mouth struggled to frame the words—"get worse?" Lines from Milton loomed: "And in the lowest deep a lower deep."

"She *could* worsen," Dr. Ricci agreed. "And that would raise new conditions, of course, but for now, there may be a place for her, a third option."

A crack of light. "Where?"

"Here, if you are willing and your landlady agrees. With daily doses of laudanum she could be kept quiet and might sleep a good deal. She fears 'the outside,' which is fortunate, for all that is 'outside' will agitate her, possibly creating violent reactions. She must not leave this house alone. She must have quiet and calm in familiar surroundings, with no obligations. We are speaking of a grave charge, Lucia."

"I can keep her. For how long, do you think?"

In the lift of his hands and shoulders, I saw my hope of college gone, my portal to a different life closed and shuttered. "Let us not speculate now. Rest *has* cured some difficult cases. She needs bland, wholesome food. Sweet and spicy tastes inflame the passions. Dr. Kellogg of Michigan gives his patients toasted cornflakes of his own devising. You may find this helpful." He wrote out a prescription for laudanum and his own address for emergencies. He did not say what I knew: if our plan proved insufficient, Cleveland State Hospital would be my only option.

And so began my life as a caretaker. I wrote to my professors, who sent lists of books I might read. When could I do this? My life was whittled down, spare and tight. I read a little poetry or sonnet before sleep, other chapters of the *Iliad,* and sometimes solved a problem in geometry, nothing more.

Mamma slept in the daytime while I worked; at night she paced the room, watching me sleep or try to sleep. Mr. Kinney hired me back, generously paying thirteen dollars for a fifty-four-hour week since I had attended college, however briefly. I bought grains and cornflakes, brown bread and beans, which my mother ate in our room, chewing loosely and dropping food. I cleaned her afterward and took her plate away before she threw it. *Don't think about this. Don't remember how she thrilled hundreds from the stage with the warmth of her voice and the lift of her hand.* Now she was stiff and silent as a wooden doll when I washed her. Exhausted, ashamed, afraid, I saw nobody. "She's much better," I told Father Stephen. He nodded gravely, and I felt like those who dictated fanciful news at my scribing table: "Everything is wonderful in America. I have a good job. We live in a beautiful house. The streets are paved in gold."

October brought a strange relief. I awoke with a start past midnight, horrified to find myself alone, and raced downstairs. Had she run away? Where would I find her in the dark? But she was on the kitchen floor, scrubbing. "What are you doing, Mamma? It's not your job. Come to bed."

"I'm not finished." She had spoken a whole sentence! I backed into the cabinets, stunned. No clean floor had ever brought such joy. I watched her work until, convinced that she was calmly cleaning, I retreated to our room. Before dawn she came upstairs, undressed, and fell into peaceful sleep beside me. She did the same the next night and the next.

After a week, Roseanne accepted my proposal. She would put out supplies, and Mamma would do whatever cleaning she chose at night, or none at all. Money proportional to her work would be deducted from our board. This was far from vaudeville's glory, but there was no shame, for nobody would see her on her knees. She took no orders and faced no expectations. Tired after hours of furious cleaning, she slept easily and I could sleep myself without her restless, looming presence. Mamma didn't speak again for weeks, but we had found a peaceful order that could last, I thought miserably, for years to come.

If rest had cured difficult cases, then I must simply wait. I wrote to my professors of the hope that my mother could someday return to vaudeville and I to college. Then I would find happiness. "We wish the same for you," Dr. Sutton wrote back, adding a gentle admonition drawn from Milton whose sense evaded me then: "The mind is its own place and in itself, can make a Heaven of Hell, a Hell of Heaven." What could be heavenly in Cleveland? Was he speaking of my mother or of me?

## Chapter 12

### USEFUL WORK

*By the end* of a cold, bright January 1910, Mamma had been home more than five months. In that time she had not gone out the front door and only occasionally ventured into the tiny backyard to hang our clothes. Her skin had paled to paper whiteness, and her gaze was vague. She spoke rarely, and her phrases were as disjointed as her letters: "Which is why," she might begin, and then lapse into silence. "Before the dogs." Or: "The third time." I couldn't prompt a finished sentence. Her thoughts surfaced as dolphins leap from the sea, and descend where we cannot follow. *She's getting better,* I kept telling myself, despite all proof. *She must be.*

Anxious fear folded back on me: all I knew of my father was that he brutally raped a serving girl. Would a sane man do this? If sickness infected me on both sides, what could my future be? Could my own mind crack? *Don't think of this, don't, don't. Think only of her.*

Cleaning was good for Mamma, said Dr. Ricci. "Wholesome, useful work in familiar surroundings brings self-respect." This was true enough, but the work gave me new tasks. Mamma disliked certain of Roseanne's pictures and hid them or turned them to the wall. She put chairs, china figures, or books in strange formations. When she came to bed before dawn, I slipped downstairs to reset the rooms.

Still, those months held a small, unexpected pleasure: Mamma began cooking. I never knew she had watched Nannina so closely. After the first minestrone appeared from beans and vegetables in the pantry, Roseanne began casually leaving ingredients on the kitchen table. In the morning we might discover a warm frittata, spicy ragù, baked pasta, lentil soup, vegetables roasted with Anna's sausages, or stuffed manicotti. The boarders were delighted. Yet sometimes ingredients would be ignored or hidden. I found pasta thrown against a window, tomato sauce splashed across the floor, or forks jabbed in the purple flesh of eggplants. I studied her footsteps coming upstairs before dawn like wives straining to hear in their husbands' tread if they were returning happy or drunk, injured or laid off from work.

Those who knew of Mamma's collapse pressed me curiously for details. How much, exactly, of her reason was lost? Could I relate odd things she said or did? Some wanted to see her, as if she were a circus sideshow. Others backed away as if I bore sickness on my breath like smallpox. "I appreciate your concern. She's resting from overwork," I always replied. Some ceased asking, but when I slipped into Sunday mass late or left early, they watched me, perhaps wondering: Is Lucia turning strange as well?

I couldn't bear to face Mrs. Livingston and say she'd sold her ring and risked the old man's anger for nothing. Even to knock on the kitchen door, whisper to Agnes that my mother was ill, and then have Agnes ask what kind of "ill"—I couldn't bear that either.

"Your patrons will be disappointed," Mr. Bellamy intoned after extending his deepest sympathy. Leaning back, he explained how hard it often was to help immigrants, how hopeful he had been of my success before this unfortunate problem. *Doesn't he know how neatly great wealth can ease away problems?* If we were rich, Mamma could be kept in a beautiful sanitarium until I finished college. By his avid concern for my mother's health, I knew he'd heard the gossip and wanted more.

"She was overworked," I said stiffly.

"Have you considered the Cleveland State Hospital?"

"No, sir." And more boldly: "You've heard about that place. Would you put *your* mother there, sir? In any case there's no reason to confine her. She's recovering at home."

"Surely those horror tales are exaggerated. Besides, the infirm must be restrained and isolated for their own good and society's. Remember, Lucia, the deficient aren't like us. Most likely they aren't even aware of their predicament."

I gripped my chair. By good chance, a messenger boy appeared. "I see that you're busy, sir. I'll leave you."

At Lula's, I spun out my rage. "Now, now," she said. "He built Hiram House and keeps it going. He *does* a lot of good. Just don't mind what he *says*. Keep telling yourself your mamma could get better."

I was doing that, conjuring scenes of miraculous recovery or at least a steady softening of her symptoms. Meanwhile, I struggled to understand how this disaster had happened, and where my own guilt lay in not averting it. In that tangle, I lied to the countess. She had described her trip to Rome with Paolo, how they'd wandered through the Forum and the Vatican and watched a moonrise over the Colosseum. In turn I related all I'd read and learned in college. I said that I'd left because Mamma was "sick." Why not tell the whole truth? The countess would not have scorned us and might not even be surprised. There would be no blame or coy reminders of past misdeeds.

No, my lies were born of pure superstition. In Naples, Mamma had

been "difficult," often bad-tempered, "unstable," but not *mad*, not catatonic, paranoid, or any of the other terrible words that defined her condition now. If that image changed in Naples because of what I wrote, I
was darkly convinced that somehow her fate as a hopeless lunatic would
be sealed. "Words create our world, Miss D'Angelo," Dr. Sutton had
intoned. I knew I distorted his meaning when I considered my own condition and Mamma's, but since the why of her collapse and the how of
her healing were unknowable, I clung to magic.

I called up images of my old life as if they could somehow protect me
from the new one. These images were perfect as painted postcards: the
magenta blaze of bougainvillea and soft hills beyond the city, marble
fountains, children playing on jetties by the sea, daily miracles of sunset
over water and the floating green island of Capri. Yet even more than I
missed all the beauty of Naples, I longed to be a child there again with
many duties but no responsibilities, no deep dreams, and nothing that
I'd wanted so deeply and then lost.

Fixed as she was on her boardinghouse economies, even Roseanne
saw my isolation and offered a small release: "There's a Valentine's Day
party at Hiram House. I heard they're teaching American dances. Why
don't you go? I'll watch your mother." Dr. Ricci agreed that I could try
an evening event.

I protested, they both insisted, and in the end I went. A cheerful American couple demonstrated the turkey trot, a sliding ragtime
step with scissor kicks that left us convulsed with laughter when too-
exuberant dancers scissored themselves off their feet. In a break between dances, Henryk's mother and aunt pulled me aside to ask about
Mamma. I said she was getting better, even starting to cook. They hovered between curiosity and fear, plying me with questions yet keeping
their distance. "Probably a *dybbuk* got her," the aunt announced. The
conversation swerved into Yiddish.

Henryk spoke to them sharply and drew me away. "They shouldn't talk to you like that."

"What's a *dybbuk*?"

"Just a silly superstition from the Old Country. A spirit with unfinished business takes possession of people and makes them mad. It's nonsense. My aunt's sister in New York went hysterical last year and drowned herself in the Hudson River. My aunt thinks a *dybbuk* must have gotten her because she'd always been so docile."

"Mamma *could* have a *dybbuk*," I said as we watched couples line up for a cakewalk. "According to Dr. Ricci, nobody knows why madness comes or how it can be healed."

"Whatever happened, I'm sorry it's happening to you," Henryk whispered. I looked away and asked about Miriam.

"She's in Pittsburgh again to take care of her aunt. Maybe this aunt has a *dybbuk*. Miriam is the only one who can stand her."

"Everybody loves Miriam," I said, staring out at the turkey trot.

"They do. My mother says we're perfect together." *Breathe*, I told myself, *just breathe*. "Our families were close back home, and we helped them emigrate."

"I see."

"I'm the only son, you know."

"I'm the only daughter," I blurted. This talking was too hard. "Should we try the dance?"

"Yes."

We were awkward and out of step at first. In the second round we improved. *Fix on the dance, only the dance*. Scissor-kicking past the frowning aunt and mother, I heard that foreign word again. "What's a *shiksa*?"

"It's a Gentile woman."

"That's bad?"

"Well, it's like: you have your best apples set out and a stranger steals one." His smile spun past me. "Italians are the worst. They look like us, so a boy could be fooled."

"If he didn't know."

"Exactly."

"Change partners!" the caller shouted. The rest of the evening was a swirl of faces: Italians, Czechs, Germans, Poles, and a shy Bohemian. I didn't dance with Henryk again.

I came home late, and Roseanne met me at the door, distraught. Mamma had hidden in an unheated alcove off the kitchen and nearly froze. "I thought she was upstairs. When I found her and tried to bring her inside, she hit me with a broom handle. What could I do? I left her there. I thought you'd be home sooner."

With difficulty, I got Mamma into the kitchen, sat her by the stove wrapped in blankets, and put her hands and feet in warm water as once had been done to me. She was stiff as wood. Her eyes were dark marbles. Had anger or spite kept her in the cold? Did this mean I could never go out to dances? A cage was closing around me.

Help came unexpectedly. When Giovanna's mother died, her father left the younger children with relatives and drifted out of town. Giovanna found work with Mrs. Halle. She had no particular artistry, but could precisely copy any design and had a pleasing way with customers. Frank was her fella now; she meant to stay in Cleveland until he was promoted, move to Youngstown, marry him, and help make hats. Meanwhile, she would board with us and graciously offered to watch Mamma some evenings while she made hats for extra pay.

When I introduced Giovanna, my mother had no response. But I noticed that she ate when Giovanna urged her, seemed to listen when she spoke, and could sit for hours watching her work. I fought a niggling jealousy. Wasn't it good that Mamma at least responded to someone, even if that someone wasn't me? Of course it was.

What could I do in my free evenings? Miriam had returned, so I stopped going to dances. Looking around for other diversions, I was intrigued by notices tacked on walls and posts: TWELVE REASONS WHY WOMEN SHOULD VOTE, said one. SISTERS UNITE! said another. WOMEN'S SUFFRAGE IS GOD'S WILL AND NATURE'S TRUTH. A rally had been announced for a warm spring evening.

"Go if you want," Giovanna said. "Even if it's a little silly, all that shouting and carrying on. Frank said that when we're married we can talk over who he'll vote for, so it's almost as if I'm voting myself. Besides, I didn't finish school, so what do I know about politics?" Frank hadn't finished either, I might have mentioned, but I only thanked her for taking my place. When I left, Mamma was sitting rigidly, watching Giovanna sort feathers.

In Public Square, women in elegant dresses and hats waved signs for suffrage. How beautiful America would be if women could vote, one speaker said. "*Our* true American votes could cancel out those of the lower class of men." A speaker for the Women's Christian Temperance Union promised a pure and sober world if women voted. More speeches followed, despite heckling from clots of drunk or idle men. Drums beat; we carried banners and chanted as we marched to City Hall. I was thrilled with the power and rightness of our cause: why *shouldn't* women vote? Yet where were the workingwomen, the thousands on thousands in Cleveland who bore the weight of laws favoring factory bosses and owners?

"You mean factory girls? They're always welcome to come," said a woman marching beside me. "But I think immigrants don't care about suffrage. Or they don't understand what it means."

I wasn't exactly their image of a typical immigrant, I gathered from talks with suffragettes. I had finished high school and spoke good English now. Soon I could even be a citizen. But still I wasn't like these ladies; I could be useful for their marches but not precisely welcomed in their parlors.

"I *do* want a vote," I told Mamma that night as she faced the wall. "It's wrong that we can't. But women's suffrage seems so far away. There needs to be change *now* to make life better at Stingler's or Printz-Biederman. Making new laws takes years and years. There's a meeting of garment workers at the union hall. I think I'll go." Of course she didn't answer.

"Keep talking," Dr. Ricci said, "even if she's silent, she's listening." So I chattered on, feeling foolish, as if speaking to a doll. There was a second, less worthy reason for my rambling: to show that *I* was the always-present daughter, not Giovanna.

"I heard a speaker at the union hall," I reported the next week. "It was Mother Jones, the great organizer, talking about mill children. She brought up a little worker, just eight years old. Mamma, her face was already old. Machines mash their fingers and tear off limbs. Four- and five-year-old children work from dawn to dark. They fall asleep on the floor and get kicked awake. Boys work in the mines pulling carts. Can you imagine?"

"*You* worked. What's the difference?"

"It's different because housework isn't dangerous—" I stopped. She'd listened and asked a question! "Mamma!" But she'd already turned away, smoothing the sheets. *Keep talking.* I described how in 1903 scores of children walked from Pennsylvania to Long Island to see President Theodore Roosevelt, show him their bodies, and have him feel the shame of a country that used its little ones so cruelly. When I said the president refused to see them, Mamma pushed a pillow to the floor. Was she outraged by Roosevelt or only angry at my talking? Annoyed by the pillow? Discouraged, I fell silent. Mamma wrapped herself in a sheet and slept.

I started going regularly to meetings of the International Ladies' Garment Workers' Union. Standing in the back, I studied workers' faces. Many were my own age but already looked aged and drawn, their young shoulders curved. Several had lost fingers; many had chronic coughs from the lint-filled air. I saw workers scarred by fires. Everywhere I felt the bitterness and confusion of those who wanted a better life in America.

"You're *right* to want more," cried Miss Josephine Casey, who had come from New York to help us. We were all to call her Josephine because we were brothers and sisters through the union. My sister? She was elegantly tall, or seemed so, with a fine black dress and wide hat trimmed in velvet. Her voice was astonishing: softly rounded and stretched like taffy candy. It seemed to speak inside my head. People said she came from a wealthy family in the South, where people talked like that. She'd gone to college. Yet she chose a life with us. Josephine could silence hecklers with a glance and pull from a babble of voices a neat assemblage of all that we meant to say.

"I hear what you want," she told a rumbling crowd. "You want a fifty-hour week. You want time with your families. You want no more than two hours overtime on weekdays and higher pay for those hours. You want repose on legal holidays and equal pay for equal work."

"The machines!" a woman yelled from the back.

"And you refuse to pay your bosses for sewing machines, needles, and thread. Why should they take back the little they give you? You deserve fifty hours and a decent wage!"

"Fifty" flew through the great hall like a flock of wild birds. "Fifty, fifty, fifty!" we repeated until it seemed almost within our reach.

Mr. Isadore Freith, our local union president, spoke. "Cleveland workers must claim their rights. George Washington, Simón Bolívar,

St. Joan of Arc, Abraham Lincoln, Giuseppe Garibaldi, all the great liberators would join our struggle." Songs and chants began. In Chicago I had thrilled when a great crowd sang with Mamma. This was even more glorious. Simple tunes with strident beats bore the longing, rage, and bonded hopes of those whose bodies ached from making clothes they'd never wear. A buttonhole maker taught us a song by Mr. Joe Hill:

> You will eat, bye and bye,
> In that glorious land above the sky;
> Work and pray, live on hay,
> You'll get pie in the sky when you die

I sang too, despite the crow voice that so embarrassed Mamma. I felt light and thin-sided as a rubber balloon, no longer Lucia the clerk or Lucia, my mother's keeper, but a voice among many. We were Joshua's warriors, whose cries tore down the walls of Jericho. I told Josephine that, yes, of course I'd put up signs at Hiram House for the next union meeting. If children could walk from Philadelphia to Long Island, surely I could hang signs.

"Come to the meetings," I urged Elena, who lived on our street and did piecework at home.

"Lucia, I have three little ones. If my contractor finds out I go to meetings, he'll give my work to the Bohemians. Anyway, it's their fault my wages are low."

"Bohemian bosses tell their workers it's Italians who keep their wages down."

"What? That's crazy."

"Exactly. Workers have to stick together."

Elena's face cleared, then darkened. "But we *aren't* together. You have a steady desk job, and my sister lost her contract to a Bohemian. How do you know what it's like for us? I'm sorry, I have to feed my babies." Her hand on the door told me I must leave.

Bohemians had just starting coming from the western fringe of Poland. They lived in tight clusters, and the women did contract work. When fires ripped through their quarters that spring, the Cleveland *Plain Dealer* reported many home workshops ruined. "Did you hear?" Jewish and Italian women whispered in the markets and union hall. "How horrible." Yet the news brought a guilty shiver of relief. Now more jobs might come back to the factories.

"If the pieceworkers and factory workers got together, they'd *all* earn more," Mr. Kinney observed. He had taken to stopping in my upstairs office, at first to check my sums, but often to smoke his pipe, drink tea, and gaze through a balcony window down at the shop floor. He left more and more tasks to his assistant, Mr. Wells: installing displays, choosing merchandise, greeting customers, and overseeing an army of clerks. "He's hungry for work. Like I was once," Mr. Kinney said. "But we were speaking of the Bohemians. Now if wholesale prices on our dresses were to go up, what then, Miss D'Angelo?"

"Our prices would have to go up as well."

"Naturally. *But* if working girls had more to spend, we wouldn't do so badly, would we? Now Mr. Wells wouldn't agree, but if you're old like me or young like you, you can see some sense in raising wages." He tapped out his pipe. "What was the balance yesterday, Miss D'Angelo? And the plaid shirtwaists, how are they selling?"

Another day, reading in the *Plain Dealer* of union demands for a fifty-hour week, he mused: "I worked seventy hours a week when I was young. But it was *my* store and the time never bothered me. Now Olivia wants some of that time. Born as mewling babes, all we have in this world is time, Miss D'Angelo."

"Sir?" But he had closed his eyes and leaned his head against the back of the chair. I had meant to ask why he hadn't ordered more dress stock in the last weeks but instead returned to my pile of sales slips, handling them carefully so the rustling paper wouldn't wake him.

Some minutes later, he opened his eyes, stood, and straightened his collar. "I think I'll go home to Olivia," he announced. "Do you think she'll be pleased to see me in the middle of the day, Miss D'Angelo?" I nodded, perplexed by the sudden bustle. "If you have questions, Mr. Wells is quite capable. You know the poem by Robert Burns: 'My Luve's like a red, red rose, that's newly sprung in June'?"

"Yes, sir, we learned it in school." Years ago, it seemed, my work was books and poems. Now it was ledgers and numbers and worry for the workers whose children would never go to school.

"A lovely poem. I believe I'll bring my Olivia a red rose. Good day to you, Miss D'Angelo." I could barely fix on my work then, thinking of Olivia, who had been loved so well and for so long.

A week later, as we were closing, Mr. Kinney called the staff together. The store was ending, he said simply, as if announcing a new line of shirtwaists. The inventory would be sold to Higbee's, which had also bought the building. We stared at him, stiff as statues. What about us?

Mr. Kinney smiled, even rubbed his hands. "I've arranged posts in other establishments for every one of you, similar to those you now hold so capably. When Mr. Wells hands out your pay envelopes, you'll find two weeks' salary in lieu of notice as well as your new position, should you choose to accept it. Mrs. Kinney and I will be moving to our lake house in Ashtabula, where we'll be happy to receive you as visitors. Now I must go home. Good evening. I thank you all for your faithful service and wish you well." And then he was gone, never looking back. Even Mr. Wells was stunned as he handed out our envelopes.

"I didn't know anything," he answered each query. "The old man never said a word. But look in your envelopes. I'm sure he told us the truth."

"Miss D'Angelo," said a note in Mr. Kinney's elegant hand, "Your position is in the accounts department of Printz-Biederman. In light of your high school diploma and other estimable qualities, Mr. Printz has agreed to pay a dollar above your present salary. Please give my best regards to your mother. Yours respectfully, Herman Kinney."

We lingered in the stockroom, comparing notes in our envelopes until four gentlemen from Higbee's came to take inventory with a small army of clerks and hurried us out of the building. The door was locked behind us.

*In the days* before my new job began, I decided to spend a Sunday by Lake Erie and managed to persuade Mamma to come with me. She leaned against a tree, wrapped in the burgundy coat. Her face mirrored the water's heavy calm. "Are you tired?" I asked. She shook her head, never turning her gaze from the lake. At least she nearly smiled as I set out our lunch from Catalano's: provolone and salami, crusty bread, paper cones of fava beans, and the salty black olives she loved. When an afternoon chill skimmed over the water and I was packing our basket to leave, my mother walked along to the water's edge, trailing a murmured wisp of "Let Me Call You Sweetheart."

I stopped, so happy to hear her voice again, but when I turned, she fell silent. Still, she *had* been singing.

I visited Dr. Ricci, who agreed that her willingness to go to the lake, the almost-smile, and the bit of song were positive signs, but not, alas, indicative of significant healing. Another matter troubled him. "Lucia, there is much bitter talk now in newspapers and Congress and even great universities of 'deficients' arriving from Southern Europe."

"Deficients, sir?"

"Immigrants such as ourselves." Dr. Ricci adjusted the drape of his fine wool trousers across his knee. "Apparently we bear 'germ plasma' which might infect pure American stock. 'Scientific study' shows us disposed to insanity. Many insist the condition is hereditary, even if there is little evidence for this claim. There is talk that this germ plasma must be removed from the healthy population."

His words rang in my head like a leaden gong. "Removed—"

"We must do what is necessary to keep your mother at home."

Fear churned through me. "How? What else can I do?"

"Talk to her as you have been, even if she makes no response. Treat her as one who *could* be healed. Encourage useful work." Feeble counters to the threats around us.

Dr. Ricci asked about her color and appetite, hygiene, the few words she said, what she cooked, and how she behaved around Giovanna. "Her condition has not worsened," he concluded. "We should be grateful for this. More I can't say."

Discouraged and anxious, I made my way home. Mamma was staring out the window. In a pale rose shawl, she seemed to fade into the wallpaper. "Mamma, can we talk?" I pleaded, but she pushed me away like a bothersome cat. "You *must* get better, Mamma. I can't afford a sanitarium." No response. I recited a happy sonnet, "Shall I compare thee to a summer's day?" Nothing. I talked about the union: "You remember how factory work made you feel like a machine? How bad the pay was?" Nothing. I mentioned the "services" Mr. Stingler demanded. She glared and then looked away. Finally: "I want to help the workers. And I want to go to college when you're better. I want you to sing again, Mamma, and smile and hold me."

She didn't move, and I couldn't be still, head-clogged with all that I wanted. That evening, when the frantic cleaning began, Giovanna said she'd be up late making hats and could watch Mamma. So I became the nightwalker, trying to beat out dark fears with the tread of my shoes. I passed families sitting outside in the spring air and boys playing marbles by streetlight. What did they know of germ plasma or deficients? I came home near midnight and sat on our front steps as a half-moon rose and the last streetcars rattled off. A couple passed, laughing, turned a corner, and disappeared. In that warm spring night with maple leaves unfurled against a violet sky, blood pounded in my head and I vowed to make my place in America, even while I kept my mother safe.

*Chapter 13*

## "WHAT'S WRONG WITH ME?"

*Yolanda arranged for* her second child to be baptized in May, just after Giovanna and Frank's wedding, so guests from Cleveland could attend both ceremonies. If we wanted to come early, Yolanda's letter said, she'd find a friend to host us. "It would be like a vacation."

*Vacanza.* I stared at Yolanda's rolling script. "We can't even go for the ceremonies," I told Roseanne. "It's impossible. Yolanda and Giovanna will understand."

Roseanne shook her head. "No they won't. They're your friends. You can't give them up just because your mother's sick." *Just because!* Did Roseanne live in this house and not know how much I was already giving up?

Still, I asked Dr. Ricci for his advice. "It is a risk," he agreed. "However, these would be pleasant occasions with no demands on her." In the end, he said I should try. We would go and return on Sunday; Mamma should take a stronger dose of laudanum, and I'd have the name of a Youngstown doctor in case of "disturbance." I must choose front seats on the train and aisle seats in church so she didn't feel surrounded by strangers. "You both deserve a happy day," he said earnestly. Yes, I determined. I would somehow *make* us a happy day.

The morning started badly. I had chosen a plaid shirtwaist from Kinney's and had laid out for my mother a navy blue walking suit she wore in Chicago. Instead, she rummaged through her trunk for a flounced crimson gown from the stage, gaudy and low-cut, ripped in the back, with a rim of grime at the hem.

"You can't wear this; it's dirty and not right for a wedding," I protested.

"Nobody sees!"

"It's a *church*, Mamma, not a show! People will talk."

She stomped on the floor until Roseanne came.

"Lucia, let her wear what she wants. If people don't know she's not right, they will soon enough." Roseanne and I sewed up the rips and arranged a shawl to cover the gown's worst indiscretions.

At least our train was nearly empty. In the foggy cool of the Youngstown station, Mamma seemed calm enough. She carried our presents: a linen tablecloth for Giovanna's new home, a stuffed Teddy Roosevelt bear for little Charlie, and *The Tale of Peter Rabbit* for Maria Margaret, so she wouldn't feel neglected in the celebrations.

At the baptism, guests studiously ignored Mamma's gown. Even Mrs. Reilly said politely: "Good day to you, Mrs. D'Angelo," gathering from Mamma's clenched fists that she would shake no hands. The kindly circumspection brought me to tears.

"I know just how you feel, dear," Frank's mother whispered. "I always cry at baptisms and even more at weddings. See?" She opened her purse, filled with snowy handkerchiefs.

The priest made much of the confluence of sacraments, the purpose of holy matrimony being the creation of Catholic children to be raised in the loving cradle of sanctified union. Little Charlie squalled. When ripples of laughter passed through our crowd, Mamma gripped my arm. Was she overcome with emotion like Frank's mother, grieving that a sanctified union was so far from her life, or simply afraid of the crowd? "Don't worry," I whispered. "I'm right here."

Frank and Charlie had arranged for lunch in a dining hall overlooking the Mahoning River, strangely colored from the mills and stinking slightly, but moving water at least. I settled my mother in a chair by the window, where she sat immobile for so long that when she finally stood up, Frank's little niece shrieked.

Someone calmed the child, and I brought Mamma to the table, talking softly in a way that sometimes calmed her. "Let's eat," I urged. "See? It's an Italian-American feast." The pairings were Yolanda's gift to Charlie's parents: pasta, chipped beef, eggplant Parmesan, and boiled potatoes. Giovanna was beautiful that day, beaming with happiness.

"Are you next to marry, Lucia? Do you have a fella?" many women asked, although some, watching Mamma rearrange her food in angry jerks, put on sympathetic smiles and swerved the talk to Yolanda's good fortune in having two healthy children, one of them a boy. Yes, I agreed, she was indeed fortunate. When jealousy washed over me, I reminded myself of even worse cases that Dr. Ricci described: the violent, cruel, or depraved afflicted. This wasn't a Greek tragedy, I reminded myself, only a common case of insanity.

"Oh dear," someone said. I spun my head toward Mamma. The waiter was collecting plates. She had jerked hers from his hand, scattering food on the tablecloth. When he edged away, she folded her arms in apparent triumph. There were small children who behaved better, I thought grimly as I gathered scraps while she stared out the window.

Before the wedding cake, talk turned to work: the long factory hours and how fines and rising costs of thread and renting their machines ate away at women's salaries. There was whispered mention of "services" bosses demanded of pretty girls.

"My wife will *never* work for strangers," announced Frank, draping his arm around Giovanna. Her face lit with relief. After the Lentz fire, the heaped bodies and burned flesh, why would she want to work?

"Strikes only bring strikebreakers, and then the workers always lose," Frank's brother announced.

"That's not true!" I said loudly. "After the International Ladies' Garment Workers' Union struck last year, the workers have a shorter week, more pay, *and* better conditions." Charlie repeated this loudly to his father, who swiveled his heavy head toward me and seemed to smile.

"*I* heard," Yolanda interrupted, "that Little Stingler's marrying into the Union Salt Company. Her daddy's men mine salt, and he grinds it into gold. She and Little Stingler can eat chocolates while they're counting money." Everyone laughed. Mamma scowled and stamped her feet. I glanced a warning at Yolanda, who deftly brought the conversation to the kindness of Mrs. Halle and the funny hats that little Maria Margaret made from scraps around the house.

All talk of strikes and bosses ceased when the cake arrived. Now came toasts, cheers, and songs in Irish, Italian, and American. "You could sing, Mamma," I whispered. Wasn't it still possible that *somewhere*, perhaps in this dining hall by the Mahoning, was a bridge back to her other life? Wine must have gone to my head, for I kept pressing, even using her gown as a prop: "See, Mamma, you're dressed for the stage. Sing whatever you want, English or Italian. People will love it." She looked at me as if I'd unaccountably spoken a foreign tongue. And I had: the language of those who believe in magical cures.

Mamma didn't sing. She did eat the cake. Hunched over, she crammed it into her mouth as if to punish me. Icing smeared her face and fell into the folds of her shawl. "Mamma! Stop it!" I whispered. When I tried to ease the plate away, she snatched it back.

"Mine!" she snarled. By now the room was watching us.

"Look how that lady eats!" Frank's niece demanded shrilly. "Like a monkey in the zoo."

"Hush," her mother hissed. "She's sick." In the silence someone started "By the Light of the Silvery Moon," and at last the many eyes swung away from us.

Mamma stopped eating and began winding a napkin between her fingers, making intricate loops. "You could have her knit," said Yolanda behind me. "She might enjoy it." Mamma "enjoying" something seemed far-fetched. "Try," she persisted. "Yarn doesn't cost much."

Frank stood up. "For my beautiful new wife," he announced. The swinging melody of "Let Me Call You Sweetheart," Giovanna's blushing pleasure, and the smiles around the table could have made a nickelodeon show: "The Wedding Dinner." But I wasn't an actor in that show.

Suddenly Mamma scraped back her chair and stood facing Frank, who affably ceded the floor. "Ladies and gentlemen, I bow to the Naples Nightingale." The room fell silent as Mamma's shoulders drooped and her arms unbent. The modest black shawl slithered to the floor, revealing her gaudy dress. Rips and stains I hadn't seen in the morning dimness of my room were now in glaring evidence. She didn't sing "Harvest Moon" or any Italian song or tune from her vaudeville repertoire. Horrified, I recognized "The Bee That Gets the Honey Doesn't Hang Around the Hive." Parents moved uncomfortably, trying to distract their children as she pointed in apparent warning to Yolanda and Giovanna. Then her arms bent, and the fingers, spread wide, cupped her breasts.

"*Basta*, Mamma!" Murmurs grew around us. I stood up, moving toward her. Still today, I don't know my intentions. To block her from view, hug her, or lead her away? None of this was needed, for she sank into a crimson puddle, rocking, her hands slapped over her face.

"Mamma!"

"What's wrong with me?" she sobbed. "Why am I like this?"

I put my arms around her. "The doctor says it's a sickness in the brain."

"Why? *Why?*"

"I don't know, Mamma. Nobody knows."

"Help me!"

"I'm trying, Mamma. Dr. Ricci's trying." I realized later a sad irony: in this exchange we came closer to "conversation" than in all the months since her collapse, even if the only answer I could offer was ignorance. "The mind is its own place," Milton had said. That "place" had consumed my mother. She tore at her hair and gown, sobbing full-throated, not to be hushed. Behind us children whimpered at the strangeness of an adult so reduced.

I tried to lift her and couldn't. Then Yolanda and Charlie, each taking an arm, helped me half lift, half drag her to a chair by the window. A waiter brought water. I held the glass so she could drink. Slowly, the sobs faded to babble and then silence.

"I'm so sorry," I said over and over to Yolanda. "We ruined your dinner."

"No, no. Everyone knows she's not well, and nobody blames either of you."

This kindness in a sea of troubles brought me close to tears. I leaned on my friend's shoulder. "It's so hard, Yolanda, and she's not getting better. If I can't keep her, she'll have to go to—"

"The state hospital. I know. It's horrible. And if she stays with you—"

"It's like this, or worse."

"We're so sorry, Lucia."

"I have to get her home."

Mrs. Reilly watched their children as Charlie and Yolanda helped me wrap a shawl around my mother and pin up the worst of the rips in her dress. Limp as a doll, she offered no resistance as we maneuvered her to the train station. In Cleveland I hired a taxi, saving us from streetcar stares. I leaned against the taxi window. We were so far, so very, very far from that last warm night at the villa, when we floated in our linen shifts, so happy in the moonlight.

Roseanne saw us come in, saw Mamma's vacant eyes, torn dress, my own exhaustion, and never asked what happened at the wedding. She helped me bring my mother upstairs, where we undressed her and put her to bed.

Terrified that we had begun a new, worse phase of illness, I sat for a long time watching her sleep. *Do something,* I told myself. Moving slowly, I folded the ruined dress and was about to lay it in the vaudeville trunk that had sat for months untouched in a corner, heaped with books. What else was inside?

I began a silent exploration. Here was the lace-trimmed walking dress I'd seen on my first trip to Chicago, then magnificent hats, gloves and hatpins, corsets and hair rats for performance. I pulled out plumes and fans, gorgeous memories of her triumph. Then at the bottom I found the catalog of her collapse: a thick roll of playbills from every city where she'd performed, so meticulously ordered by date that I could follow a zigzag line through Ohio and the Midwest, north to the Dakotas, south and east again. At first "Teresa D'Angelo, the Naples Nightingale" was inching up the playbill. Then the name began steadily creeping down, always in smaller print. The night of "unacceptable gestures" in Chicago was reflected in the next city's listing: "The Swiss Yodeler *and* the Naples Nightingale." She'd lost her own line. In Springfield, Missouri, her name appeared in a stream of "other acts." Loew's notices said only "Live dancers! Singers! Clowns!" In each venue, she must have hastened to find her listing; each would bring new dismay.

Yet in that downward odyssey she had the methodical will to acquire each clean, unfolded playbill and carefully preserve it. Perhaps Mario or Harold helped. While sending shreds of "letters" home, still she kept evidence that strangers cheered and clapped for her, even if less wildly every time. Her last "performance," at Giovanna's wedding, would have no playbill. I folded the dresses and carefully set the hats so no plume or flower would be crushed, rolled up the playbills in their sequence, and closed the trunk. "Why? *Why?*" she had cried in Youngstown. And now I cried myself. "Why? *Why?*" Why had the nightingale fallen so far? Why was her wondrous voice held captive by a broken mind? The boardinghouse was very quiet. I made my way to the parlor and sat alone for a long time. No answers came, only the grim fear that this solitude could be the shape of the rest of my life.

*In the days* after Youngstown, Mamma was pitifully silent and subdued. Desperate, I followed Yolanda's advice and bought her yarn and knitting needles at the May Company: bright blues, greens, yellows, and reds. Knowing better than to *ask* her to knit, I simply set these things in our room. Three days later she began balling the yarn. "Remember those scratchy gray scarves church ladies made for us that cold winter, all of them the same?" I asked casually. "Wouldn't it be nice if the children had prettier ones?"

Mamma said nothing. I tried, as Dr. Ricci constantly suggested, not to let her silence wound me: "When a consumptive coughs, it's no attack on the loved one, merely the disease expressing itself. Her silence *is* the disease. Keep talking to her."

Two days later a scarf appeared. She worked quickly, yet was as severe with herself in knitting as she once was with singing, fiercely examining her work, unraveling rows on rows for a single dropped stitch. Hiram House desperately needed warm clothes for immigrants unprepared for Cleveland winters. "Children won't notice little problems. Or you could work more slowly," I suggested. Or else, I finally chided myself, she could work as she pleased. Remaking scarves kept her calmly occupied and saved money on yarn. In fact, each was more accomplished than the last, beautifully designed, marvelously soft and warm. These "Teresa scarves" would come to be passed from child to child in families, carefully washed after each season and packed away in mothballs.

On those summer evenings I studied in my room as Mamma knit. When Mr. Sutherland at Printz-Biederman suggested that "increased utility" could bring higher pay, I enrolled in a correspondence course on the elements of bookkeeping. "Like before," Mamma muttered one night, pointing with a knitting needle to my books and then quickly bending over her work again. But we weren't quite like before, when I was in school. "Before," I had my college dreams. "Before," her mind wasn't sick.

Dr. Ricci had found a small consolation in the Youngstown collapse: "She is aware of her own condition. That is a hopeful sign."

"But eating like that, touching herself, that song—"

"Inappropriate, yes, of course. Not normal. Yet you brought her home and no physical harm was done. Lucia, you must remember that every day you care for her is a day saved from this inferno." He showed me a photograph of a woman confined to an asylum by a husband who'd found her inconvenient. She looked hardly human: shriveled to bones, skin crusted with scabs, hair chopped off, bruised where she'd been tied for days and burned by electrical shocks. Perhaps she was beautiful once. Now she'd likely die of syphilis contracted from her keepers if other ailments or sheer misery didn't take her first. At night images of her scabs, burns, bruises, and those wild and haunted eyes come at me like cards dealt by a manic player.

"You are doing well," Dr. Ricci insisted.

"But *will* she get better?"

"I'm sorry, Lucia. I don't know. Try to find a way to live with her in this state and include her in your life." I must make a heaven of hell, Milton would say.

How? I had thought we'd be safe in Youngstown among people she knew. Clearly now I couldn't take her among strangers. Mrs. Kinney had invited us to their summer home in Ashtabula on Lake Erie. I longed to go, having seen pictures of American country homes with deep lawns and mounded shade trees, arbors thick with roses and children running by with hoops. I imagined Mamma well and healed, magically returned to "before": we drink iced tea on a porch looking out at the blue lake. Knitting quietly, Mamma sings "Let Me Call You Sweetheart." Mr. Kinney explains a puzzle of double entry bookkeeping. The dream reels on. We eat roast beef on fine plates in the dining room and an American dessert, perhaps lemon meringue pie. Talk flows pleasantly around the table. Mamma sings an aria after dinner. The Kinneys are charmed. We spend the night in a canopied bed with crisp sheets, and windows open on a sweetly flowering locust tree.

But the dream ends badly and always in a new way: the Kinneys may have a little dog that resembles Lydia's in the vaudeville troupe. Mamma attacks this dog. She makes "unacceptable gestures." She walks into the lake, bound for Vesuvius, and must be rescued. She hurls insults at the Kinneys. She stabs them with knitting needles. In the end I sent Mrs. Kinney my regrets: "My mother is ill and can't travel."

At least I was absorbed by work at Printz-Biederman, constantly given new tasks in the elaborate puzzle of entering, verifying, and balancing accounts for a business of nearly a thousand people, one of the largest garment makers outside New York City. "A great company is built on accounting. We are the foundation, the steady core of this establishment," declared Mr. Sutherland. Sometimes I barely raised my head from the books for hours, hearing only my adding machine's ratchet, whirl, and ding.

When I was sent to other offices with account statements, I passed through the factory and saw garment workers doing hand tailoring on lines of straight-backed chairs, women in dark skirts and white shirts, faces alike in solemn attention, bent over their work. Sometimes the finished piece went to the next woman, sometimes into great baskets collected by young boys. The tedium, close space, stuffy heat, and constant harangues to work more quickly, more neatly, to appreciate their stake in the good name of Printz-Biederman, how did they endure these days? When bosses ordered long lines of stitching torn out, what pain this must cost those who had bought thread from the same bosses.

I counted the quirks of fortune that separated me from this line of labor: Mamma had taken easily to chocolate dipping; I could add to her pay by scribing at Hiram House and serving at the Millers'; her voice had brought dollars to buoy me to graduation; I worked easily with numbers and had been well trained by Mr. Kinney. Lacking any of these chances, I'd be bent over a shirtwaist now, tearing out thread.

My department loaned me to payroll one week when a clerk was sick. Now I truly saw the heavy toll of fines these workers bore, sometimes taking home nearly nothing. "They'll learn," the head payroll clerk said crisply. But how could they live in the week of such learning?

"Why are these five sleeve setters paid five different rates?" I asked.

"That's what they took when we hired them." Filling out pay envelopes, I pictured the scene of each woman's hiring. Perhaps one spoke more English and thus was bolder. Another might have been more desperate for work, perhaps with a sick child at home. One who earned a dollar more may have offered some "service" for her job. I knew workers never compared their pay. When I scribed, they leaned over my table to whisper a number. "We aren't supposed to tell the others what we earn. They'd be jealous." But how could *each one's* pay be higher than the others'? Ignorance kept them pliable.

"Look at this," I said. A pattern cutter was fined for bloodstained cloth when the mechanical blade cut her flesh instead. "It's not her fault the machines are old."

"Miss D'Angelo," the head clerk snapped, "since we have nine hundred pay envelopes to prepare, perhaps we needn't comment on each one."

"No, sir." But I *did* comment, over and over in my head as I worked.

## Chapter 14

## Reading the Names

*In the weeks* after our problems in Youngstown, I spooled between home and work, terrified that Mamma's sickness might worsen, deepen, or take some new and terrible shape and I must be there to help or shield, divert or, if nothing else, be present for a new decline. But we seemed to have reached an endless plateau. By day she knit, slept, and stared out the window. At night she cleaned, sometimes cooked, or paced barefoot through the kitchen, dining room, parlor, and hall. "She's not much trouble, really," Roseanne said. So for now we could stay at the boardinghouse. By midsummer I began slowly expanding my circuit, going to church, attending some union meetings, and scribing again at Hiram House.

"See?" said Lula. "You can breathe a little." Autumn was early and glorious that year. When the maple trees blazed red and yellow, I stopped by Henryk's store for apples. Or rather that was my excuse: I'd told Roseanne that Mamma might make a tart if we left some apples in the kitchen.

"Is Henryk your fella?" Roseanne had asked. No, no, I'd protested, just a school friend and bound to another woman besides. Still, I couldn't deny even to myself that I'd missed his easy presence, patient way of listening, and gift for bringing pleasure to the simple act of buying fruit.

Colors mounded everywhere in the shop: squash and pumpkins, beans of many kinds, strings of peppers, golden braids of onion, heaps of bright red cabbage, and everywhere bushels of apples. The shop was nearly empty, just Henryk and a young helper. "Lucia, I haven't seen you in weeks," said Henryk, setting down his clipboard.

"No. I've been busy."

"Yes, of course." If he'd heard of Mamma's scene in Youngstown, he gave no sign. He said some words in Polish to the boy and ushered me into a tiny office, meticulously organized and astonishingly clean. "My little kingdom," he explained. "No onion peels or old cabbage leaves. Let's see how Samuel does by himself. He just arrived last week from Poland."

"He's a relative?"

"Sort of a cousin, very clever. He's already learned some English. He's taking lessons at Hiram House."

"That's good."

"He wants to be a doctor."

"Wonderful." How long would we talk about Samuel? I stepped back in the cramped space. Where else to look but at the wide dark eyes? I smoothed a pleat in my skirt and studied an ink spot.

Henryk rolled a pen between his palms, put it down, and picked it up again. "How's your mother?"

"Fine. She's knitting scarves."

"It's good that she's busy."

I agreed. Then, as if a gate had been cracked open, we talked a little more easily. I told him about my work and correspondence course. The shop was expanding, he said. Casimir and Anna were having a baby. Neighbors on both sides had just come from Bohemia. We agreed that many, quite a lot of Bohemians were coming to Cleveland. Then we both fell silent, absorbed by the swept floor.

Henryk looked up. "I'll be marrying Miriam next year. The dowry's set. I wanted to tell you before you heard it somewhere else. If you hadn't come by, I would have stopped by your house."

The words were gongs: *Marrying. Miriam.* What did I expect? I was a Gentile, a Catholic, Italian, with a mother known to be insane. Miriam was a rabbi's beautiful niece; her father had property. A "splendid catch," as Americans said. Henryk and I were friends. Wasn't that enough for me?

"Congratulations." Other kind and customary responses tangled in my head but I couldn't say them.

Henryk rolled the pen in his hands. I watched sunlight flick off the steel nib. "I'm the only son, like I told you," he was saying. "I need to, you know, continue the line. And she's a good girl. Very capable. My father says she's the perfect wife for me."

"I'm sure you'll be happy." Americans constantly shook hands. Should I do this now? I held out mine, stiff as a marionette.

Henryk did the same, forgetting his pen, and the steel nib nicked my palm. At the tiny stab, I jerked my hand back, and we watched a rivulet of blood snake across the skin. "It's nothing," I stammered.

"No, look, you're bleeding." He pulled a white handkerchief from his pocket and pressed it to my palm. "Oh, Lucia, I'm so sorry." The office was shrinking, the air dense with our breath.

"I have to go. Roseanne's watching Mamma."

"But your hand—"

"It's nothing." The handkerchief fluttered down. He didn't pick it up. I turned to go.

"Wait, your apples." He hurried away and returned with my basket heaped with apples and a pineapple besides. "It's from Hawaii, very sweet." Holding the heavy basket between us, our hands touched. His was warm, despite the cool of the day. I feel that warmth now and smell the pineapple's heady sweetness and the lighter spice of apples. We might have stood forever, studying my basket, if a clatter of pumpkins that Samuel stacked too high hadn't startled us back to life. I darted from the office, forgetting to pay.

I ran all the way to Lula's despite the heavy basket. Panting, I gasped out the news. "Well," she said finally. "You knew it was coming, didn't you? Her family has money and you're no rabbi's niece."

"No."

"And if those things weren't true, would you even want to get married right now?"

"What?"

"You heard me, girl. Would you?" She went back to polishing. I stared at my apples. It was true that being with him could sometimes make my whole chest ache. But even if Mamma could be miraculously cured today, would I truly want to live Yolanda's life in Cleveland, circling around a man's coming and going?

"I guess you don't have a mother telling you things, so I will. You know that some women just got to have a fella or they're miserable?"

Like Yolanda. "Yes."

"Well, there's others that don't ever want a man. And then others have times when what they need is to be alone. Maybe this is your alone time."

"But I love him, and he's marrying Miriam." *Yes, there, I'd finally said it out loud.*

"So you love him and you can't have him. You want your mamma to be well so you can go live your life, but you can't have that either." Her dark face was frank and full of kindness. She patted my cheek. "Honey, you've got an old soul and you got to be alone with it awhile."

"But . . ."

"Yes?"

A wall of buts rose up around me: *but* I wanted college now; I wanted Henryk *but* his family surely didn't want me; I wanted the comfort of unity and love, an old man bringing me a rose, leaving work to be with me. *But* did I want all the tasks of domesticity that had been mine since I could first carry a dustcloth? Did I want my world so shrunken?

The tavern seemed silent despite the crowd behind me. I ran my wounded hand over the dry pricks of pineapple. "I better go home."

"I guess you better. Here. I can't help your heart, but it's sure good for the rest of you." She slipped me one of her rounds of dark bread with beer cheese. I was about to go when she reached for my arm and gently pulled me close, whispering: "I know it's hard, honey. Sometimes it seems like just about everybody else has got somebody." I nodded. "But like I said, maybe it's just not your time for loving. Maybe it's some other time for you."

I nodded, hoisted the heavy basket, and made my way home.

All I could do was work, it seemed. Learn bookkeeping, do my job, and care for Mamma. Scribe. Write to the countess and my professors and read from the list they gave me.

When I finished the course in November, Mr. Sutherland raised my salary to sixteen dollars a week, only six dollars less than the male clerks earned. Living carefully, I could save a little money. "When your mother has recovered her health," Dr. Peckham wrote, "we look forward to your return." Tuition, room and board would cost two hundred dollars a year, but I could work for board with a family in town. Or my secret patron might help me again.

*Look forward to your return.* I looked forward constantly, picturing my mother healed and myself free. There were good days and bad days. On good days we walked around the block, although sometimes she'd insist that Maestro Toscanini was lurking behind a tree. "Look, he's coming!" she'd bark, pointing wildly. I'd smile and hurry her on. Mothers pulled their children close.

Of course they were afraid. Everything strange frightened parents then, for diphtheria was stalking the immigrant quarters. A child who was simply feverish in the morning would be gasping for breath by nightfall. When a gray membrane coated the throat, death was near and inevitable. A ghastly blue cast crept over little bodies. Necks swelled horribly, hot to the touch, boiling with poisons. A young couple lost all three of their children in a weekend and collapsed at the triple funeral, senseless with grief.

The health department blamed invisible germs and toxins, against which cleanliness was the best defense. "Against the invisible?" many shot back. Children were dying, clean and dirty children in equal numbers. One Sunday after mass, Gloria, a slender girl from Calabria who had left school early to marry, turned on me. "You don't know what it's like to lose a child, Lucia. You have no idea." Her voice rose. *"No idea! Your life is so easy."*

"Our little boy just died," her husband apologized. "He seemed better, and then in an hour he was gone."

"Gloria, I'm so sorry," I began, but she spun away from me.

"Give me back my Robertino!" she shrieked, pounding the statue of

Our Lady. Father Stephen came flying down the steps, his black robe like great wings as he and her husband closed around her.

Everyone had theories about the disease: Bohemians brought it on boats. No, the crowded flats of Jews or Italians bred the germs. No, scoffed others: it came from the city's bad water. The food was infected. Frigid winds from Canada weakened children and so they fell to the scourge. A new "antitoxin" would cure diphtheria, doctors promised, but false or diluted mixtures were peddled everywhere. When even the purest preparations sometimes failed, many lost faith. Some feared an American plot to kill all immigrant children. Didn't they call us "germ plasma"?

Because I seemed immune, I helped translate for one of the American nurses on her Sunday rounds. "You must act at the first signs of infection: sore throat, coughing, or fever," we told Rita, who had just come from Sicily.

"But *all* children cough in winter," she protested. "Do they all have diphtheria? Will all of them die?"

"What does the antitoxin cost?" the father asked anxiously.

Doses were free to the poor, the nurse explained. "Lucia, make them understand. They *must* get the antitoxin. If a child is badly stricken, there's nothing we can do. Nothing."

"God sent the strangling angel; He's cursing us for leaving Sicily," Rita cried, clutching her tightly swaddled infant.

"No, Father Stephen says—"

"Father Stephen is Irish! What does he know about Our Lord? And the wind will kill my baby if I take her outside." When I said we'd bring her a dose, she hugged me, sobbing, "I'm so afraid of this cold. There was nothing like it back home."

"Lucia," Nurse Lynch warned. "I can't bring everyone the antitoxin. They *have* to come to Hiram House."

"But Rita talks to other Sicilians. If we help her child, she may convince them for us."

"Perhaps." So we went on, cajoling, urging, sometimes bribing parents with bread given by wealthy donors.

"Look at you," Roseanne marveled as I came home from my rounds. "The whole city's coughing and you're healthy as a horse." I swerved between gratitude and guilt. Gratitude for my health, since who would care for Mamma and help Nurse Lynch if I sickened? Guilt that I had so neatly escaped the plague.

In church Father Stephen organized a collection for the stricken families. I got beer cheese from Lula and pounds of Anna's sausage to distribute. I couldn't bring myself to ask for Henryk's help, to enter that tiny office again, but I didn't have to. Mr. Bellamy found crates of potatoes, onions, cabbages, and beets on the steps of Hiram House.

Hollow-eyed mothers received the vegetables silently, too spent for civility. Sometimes we knew by the wailing behind doors that we'd come too late and could only note the address and flat number for health department men who gathered the dead.

After weeks of this work, I was worn out by death and sickness. Early on a cool, damp Sunday morning, I roused my mother for a walk to the port, where we could watch the familiar bustle of ships and fishing boats. But death was there too: a barge had just come from Canada loaded with little pine coffins. Even the gulls fell silent, and a line of burly longshoremen crossed themselves. Mamma watched curiously, as if she'd never seen this gesture before. She looked at me leaning against a wooden pillar and tugged at my arm to keep walking.

I wanted to shake her. "Those are *children's coffins*, Mamma. Don't you see how many there are? That many children are dying!" Once again I described my home visits with nurses and the terrible scenes I'd witnessed in this epidemic, the torrent of loss. But she seemed unable to grasp pain outside her own, as one might watch ants scrambling in the dust and feel no connection with their troubles. She pointed to a fisherman unloading his catch. With a sigh I turned away from the coffin barge.

"Is this part of her sickness?" I asked Dr. Ricci.

"Lucia, didn't you say she had very little empathy for the countess, even knowing the count's abuse?"

Yes, those were my words. "But when she sang, people *cried*. She must have—"

"Watched people. Observed other singers," Dr. Ricci supplied. "I believe that she loves you, Lucia. But parts of her heart are blocked; it's a symptom of her sickness. Those scarves she knits, does she make them *for* the children?" No, I admitted grudgingly. She knit to knit. If everything she ever knit ended up in Lake Erie, she wouldn't be distressed. He took my hand. "As for the coffins, Lucia, you are doing all you can for this city. We must endure the waiting."

So we waited. The coroner's wagons rolled by all through January. By February, the number of new cases began falling. We went days without seeing a wagon. One by one, children came outside, blinking against the sunlight. Schools slowly refilled, and street markets bustled again.

When new orders dropped slightly at Printz-Biederman, workers who had taken days off to care for their children were fired. Mr. Sutherland had me hand out final pay envelopes. "If we couldn't count on you in January, you're the first to go in February," he told them. Speechless, I followed him to our office, not responding to his usual banter on the weather, President Taft's latest blunders, or the week's tally of shirtwaists.

Eventually he noticed my silence. "I was only relaying Mr. Printz's orders, Miss D'Angelo."

"I assumed that, sir. But they were good workers."

"Then they'll find other posts."

Most became contract workers, making collars or cuffs at home, setting sleeves or constructing the tedious tight pleats so fashionable that year. Their miserable pay drove down factory salaries and pitted workers against each other.

"Why do they do that? They *all* have landlords and grocer bills," I lamented to Lula. "Why don't they fight the bosses instead?"

Lula was mixing biscuits. "You figure it out, child, and poor black folks and poor white folks will get together against rich folks." Her wooden paddle slapped the side of her bowl. "Long, long time from now," she added grimly.

That evening I screwed up my courage for a great risk. I brought Mamma to the union hall and set her in a corner far back from the crowd where she could knit undisturbed. I managed to stay for an hour before she grew agitated, rattling her needles and rocking rhythmically in the chair. It was a rainy night, and we took a streetcar home. She sat quietly at least, staring at the floor. A man in front of me read the *Plain Dealer*. A headline caught my eye: Arturo Toscanini was conducting in New York City. Suppose he took his company on tour? My mind raced. So often oblivious to English speech, Mamma would surely seize on the word *Toscanini* in any conversation. Suppose he came to Cleveland and by a terrible string of coincidences she saw him? Suppose she pounced on him with no countess to save her and nowhere to flee?

I must have leaned too close. The newspaper snapped closed. "Why don't you buy your own," the man said sharply, "instead of reading over people's shoulders?"

Mamma's head jerked up, attentive to any insult. I hurried us off the streetcar, bought a paper from a newsboy, and read the article as Mamma clattered in the kitchen. The maestro wouldn't be touring, I learned with relief. But now at night his hawk eyes softened to Henryk's, and both men watched me as I tossed in bed. *Go away, you two, let me work at least.*

*With the passing* of the epidemic, rage seethed in the union hall. My professors might have argued with fine logic that diphtheria did not *cause* this rage but only preceded it. Still, I noted that those who had lost children were inflamed more quickly against the owners. A litany of complaints filled the hall: poor lighting, cold and drafty workrooms in winter, heat and stench in summer, inadequate lavatories, the rising cost of needles, thread, and sewing machine rent, random fines, and wildly unequal pay for the same work.

Luisa, who worked in a small company making men's shirts, complained of forced overtime. Of three children, only her youngest was left alive. "When can I see my Salvatore?" she demanded. The nursery at Hiram House teemed with babies and tiny children watched for hours by a few harried attendants.

Young boys roamed the streets causing mischief. When I caught two overturning our ash can, Roseanne and I hauled them into our kitchen and extracted their names: Enrico and Pepe. They didn't go to school because it was boring. They turned over ash cans because they had nothing better to do.

"You could join a boys' club at Hiram House," I suggested.

"That's for greenhorns."

"If public school is boring," Roseanne said, "what about reform school?" They looked at each other in alarm and fell silent.

"Meet me at the union hall tomorrow night," I announced.

"Why should we?"

"Two reasons. First, if you don't, I'll tell your mothers what you did." They swallowed hard. "And second, because there *is* something better to do."

"What?"

"You'll find out."

They came to the meeting. I had sent a message to Josephine, who first terrified them with the fate of two boys she knew well who went from overturning ash cans to worse crimes, broke their mothers' hearts, and ended their miserable days in prison. She leaned down so far that her black hat shaded them. The soft, driving voice popped out beads of sweat across their brows. When she stood up suddenly, their mouths dropped open. "However, I *could* use two boys to paste up meeting notices and hand out leaflets at the factories. They'd have to be brave, smart, quick boys who aren't scared of bosses. Are *you* those boys?" They were, so excited they didn't ask for pay.

Josephine straightened her hat. "You see, Lucia, everyone wants to help if you just find the right job."

The boys' mothers thanked me heartily for "saving" their children. Workers' troubles were less easily solved. Forced overtime brought weariness and accidents. Supervisors found errors and laid fines. "We're *tired,*" women protested. "Hire more help if you need more dresses." With a fifty-hour workweek, many sighed, life would be so good. When I walked through the factory floor, breathing in the weight of hours, weary eyes followed me and whispered words scraped my back: "Office work."

Strikes in Chicago had won standard wages at some factories. That meant, Josephine explained, that desperate women couldn't be frightened into taking lower pay. "Maybe in Chicago," someone called out. "Cleveland's different." We heard that suffragettes in New York City had supported strikers, marching with them, sometimes paying their bail. Rich women made a "Mink Brigade" and fed the strikers. Would rich Cleveland women do the same? Or would they side with husbands who owned the factories and mills?

Talk spun through the union halls, debates raging until midnight. Even Josephine's rousing speeches couldn't lift the dreary certainty that bad as conditions were, change was impossible here. I began finding excuses to miss meetings, stay home, read or work out equations in algebra. At least I could solve *these* problems. What was my place in the vast machine of contractors, factories, the splintering of immigrant groups, cotton prices and garment markets? Equity, justice, even solidarity seemed as impossible as healing my mother's broken mind.

*Everything changed in* late March. I had risked taking Mamma to Youngstown for the day. The air was sharp with foundry smoke and the dust of limestone quarries, but in Charlie and Yolanda's messy little house we played music on Charlie's new Victrola. After dinner, Mamma watched our card game. Pleased by this sign of sociability, I casually dealt her in. She played a little, then slammed down her cards and hid, claiming that Toscanini watched us through the window. I had to take her home. But she *had* played two hands of gin rummy.

That trip was on March 25, 1911. On the twenty-sixth, I saw no newspapers and noted only a strange hush among the clerks. I gave it no meaning and worked more quickly without the normal clatter of voices. When Enrico brought news of an emergency union meeting the next day, I nearly didn't go. But passing through the factory, I overheard whispering: "girls . . . fire . . . jumping." Mamma was in bed sick with a headache. Roseanne said she'd watch her, so I went to the hall alone.

"Lucia, can you help us onstage?" Josephine asked. She didn't wait for my response but sat me with Isadore Freith, Father Stephen, and Rabbi Rosen before a large, murmuring crowd.

"What happened?" I asked the rabbi. He shook his head and pointed to Josephine.

"Yesterday afternoon," she began, "one hundred forty-six workers, mostly young women, died when fire broke out on the eighth floor of the Triangle Shirtwaist Factory in New York City. Stairways were locked. To escape the inferno, girls jumped from eighth-, ninth-, and tenth-floor windows to the sidewalks below. Why were they locked in? Because no law compels owners to provide fire exits. Because workers' lives are cheap." Eyes closed, I saw girls like human torches, pausing briefly in the window before that desperate leap. I heard thuds on pavement and saw the crushed and burned and mangled bodies, heads turned wrong, limbs splayed out.

"Now we will honor the dead," Josephine announced. "Lucia D'Angelo will read the names and ages of those who have been identified. Think of the fallen, their families, and those who loved them. Think of their tireless work for the Triangle Shirtwaist Company and think of their reward."

I was handed a list and walked to the podium. "Weren't you nervous?" Roseanne asked later. No, I was only astonished by my own calm and the ranks of upturned faces watching me, quiet and expectant, even small children in their parents' arms. I settled my feet as Mamma did onstage, took a breath, and began.

"Julia Aberstein, thirty; Lizzie Adler, twenty-four; Anna Altman, sixteen; Anna Ardito, twenty-five." After each name and age, Father Stephen rang a bell. Ignazia Bellotta's father identified his daughter by the heel of her shoe. Two Brodsky sisters, sixteen and twenty-one. Dosie Fitze, twenty-four, survived the jump for a day and then died. Pausing for bells, I caught movements in the crowd: signs of the cross; flutters of handkerchiefs; children hushed; adults nudging boys to pull off their caps; bearded Jewish men folding their arms and rocking. "Mary Goldstein, eleven." Children's heads jerked up. A woman gasped. So many names were familiar: Sara, Vincenza, Rose, Jennie, Abraham, Ida, Jacob, Max. We could have been the ones falling in flames.

Catherine Maltese died with her daughters, Lucia and Rosalie. Bettina Miale, eighteen, and Israel Rosen, seventeen, identified by their rings; Sophie Salemi, twenty-four, by a darn in her stocking. Someone brought me water. "Should I finish?" Isadore asked. I shook my head.

Candles were handed out and flames passed from person to person. Damp eyes glittered. The lights of the union hall dimmed as I finished the list: Joseph Wilson, twenty-one, found by his fiancée. Tessie Wisner, twenty-seven. Sonia Wisotsky, seventeen. Zeltner, no first name, thirty, died of injuries in St. Vincent's Hospital. After the final name, Father Stephen and Rabbi Rosen offered prayers for the dead.

"We will have time in the coming days to determine our course in Cleveland," Josephine said. "Tonight we must go quietly home, remembering those who have fallen, praying for strength that from their deaths will come justice for all workers." I was given a candle and followed the others to the street, a river of light in the chilly darkness.

## Chapter 15

## WE ARE THOUSANDS

*In the months* after the disaster, stories streamed west. Witnesses on the street had thought owners of the Triangle Shirtwaist Company were throwing bolts of burning fabric out the window until they realized in horror that the "bolts" were jumping girls. Nineteen bodies were found melted against a locked door. All the victims had been working overtime; their miserable wages could not support decent life in New York City. Brave men made a bridge of their bodies from an eighth-floor window to another in the next building. A few girls safely crossed before the "bridge" broke and all fell to their deaths. There was one unlocked door at the west end of the factory, but it opened inward and a crush of desperate girls forced it closed. The owners had never installed a sprinkler.

"Because they weren't forced to," Isadore and Josephine tirelessly reminded us, adding that strikes and walkouts in other companies had won higher wages, safer factories, and the right to arbitrate grievances. *Those* workers didn't have to rent sewing machines or buy costly thread from owners. They enjoyed Saturday afternoons with their families.

Workers who did the same job got the same pay. Fines were listed, not imposed at will.

"We could have all this, Mamma," I related one hot April night after a meeting. She didn't look up from the dance of her knitting needles. "Remember the fines you paid at Stingler's?" She jerked her head away. Dr. Ricci had warned me to avoid distressing subjects and follow her lead. But she gave so little lead. On many days, she barely spoke. Yet sometimes she stroked me as one might stroke a pet, small comfort to light the years of caretaking that rolled out before me.

Much of that spring she spent in our darkened room, plagued by headaches with no one to sing them away. Chamomile tea didn't help. Even the tread of stocking feet pained her. I confess to using her troubles for my purposes. I ran home after work, ate quickly, helped her to the bathroom, sponged her with rosemary water, and then hurried to a union meeting.

There were many meetings, for the plan was to call a general strike in early June. Success would require meticulous organization. "If we build the will to strike," said Josephine, "we must prepare the means to win." The strike might last eight weeks. We hoped for five thousand strikers. Few would have savings. Even now, on nights before paydays, many ate only beans and bread, especially those still paying off doctor bills and funeral costs from the epidemic.

"How will we eat when we strike?" many asked anxiously.

Supporters in Cleveland—wealthy women, suffragettes, enlightened industrialists, philanthropists, the Women's Christian Temperance Union, and Jewish charity groups—would all help, Josephine replied. With this support and union dues from other cities, we could give out strike pay: four dollars per week for single workers; six for those with small families; eight for large families. With exceeding care and union soup kitchens, nobody would starve.

Josephine asked me to keep the ledger books for strike pay. They must be meticulous. Hungry, tired, and frustrated, some might try to collect twice. Then others would have nothing. All the ledgers I ever kept for Kinney's and Printz-Biederman, the streams of money I tracked, even my studies in college seemed so insignificant now. *This* work could help families hold on for justice. "Yes," I told Josephine, "I'll do it."

"Good, or *brava,* as you say." Her accent stretched the word, eating the *v,* kneading the *a*'s into soft and windy *ahs,* little chills in the stuffy room. She needed a translator to help recruit Italian workers. When had I been included in great plans? In Naples, aside from reading to distract my mistress from her headaches, I was needed only to clean. As Mr. Sutherland often told me, bookkeepers could be easily replaced. The fact that Josephine needed *me,* Lucia, was thrilling. For the first time I was swept into a cause larger than my own troubles. Perhaps my strength would grow to meet this challenge.

Yes," I told Josephine, "I'll translate too."

There were so many tasks: finding a printer for signs, leaflets, and bulletins to report the strike's progress; collecting water barrels, cups, and wooden stakes for picket signs. We'd need bandages, iodine, smelling salts, splints, stretchers, and crutches. We must enlist messenger boys and translators in other languages, observers and photographers to record disturbances, sympathetic lawyers, doctors, and nurses, reporters who might support the strike, rabbis and priests to lead prayers and speak well of us to their congregations.

"You're writing this down, Lucia?" Isadore asked. My fingers had cramped around the pen. I shook out my hand and kept writing. When he and Josephine stopped to debate a point, I read over the list. Splints, stretchers, and crutches? Outside, the streets seemed peaceful enough. Women passed in feathered hats, men in homburg hats and straw boaters. Two boys raced by with their hoops, dodging an ice wagon. We'd soon be at war, needing bandages? Here in Cleveland?

"Don't worry, Lucia," said Josephine as we hurried to a shop on Woodland Avenue to meet ten dressmakers from Calabria. "That's why we're planning, so we can build a great swell of support, a tide to carry us to victory. Because we *are* right. We *will* win." That May was buoyant with promise. I was lifted up by speeches and songs, even by the tedium of pay lists I prepared in our parlor after work.

Late at night, when cool breezes finally curled into our room, Mamma and I took turns brushing out each other's hair. It was a good sign that she would do this, Dr. Ricci said. I recounted the speeches and how an Irish piano player had made up funny strike lyrics for "Frankie and Johnny" and "By the Light of the Silvery Moon."

"Before Mr. Keith," Mamma muttered at breakfast. The boarders stared, for she rarely spoke in public. When I asked what she meant, she pushed a spoon around her oatmeal, saying nothing.

Roseanne drew me aside. "I think she meant that you're like she was before she joined vaudeville. Happy and excited."

I was. May's unseasonable heat didn't bother me. Neither did Roseanne's constant accounting of the cost of every foodstuff, as if we ate boiled pennies. Even stopping at Henryk's shop was possible if the purpose was to enlist assurance of good prices on vegetables for our soup kitchen. I smiled at Miriam standing by the beets, ignoring her icy stare. I even felt sorry for her, for anyone not busy organizing.

"Will Bohemians join the strike?" Henryk asked.

"They said they would. They didn't know how much less they were making than factory workers. They didn't realize that contractors pay each of them differently and pit them against each other. They're angry now."

Miriam had moved to a pool of light where her glorious black hair glistened. "I wouldn't trust Bohemians. They don't mix with anybody. They don't want to be American and they can't keep their word."

"Not all of them," Henryk said quietly.

I managed to smile, thank Miriam for her concern, wish them both a good day, and leave, feeling triumphantly above petty issues of the heart. The Bohemians *would* strike, I reminded myself. More than promised, they *understood* that even if they lived apart and worked for contractors, only unity could save them from misery.

We would begin the strike on June 6, 1911. A letter of demands was sent to the owners and ignored. "Of course," said Josephine, "if they answer it, that means they think we're worth answering." We would be absolutely peaceful and orderly, trusting in the virtue, modesty, and logic of our cause. New York owners had agreed to these demands. Why shouldn't owners in Cleveland? I was sent home early the night before. I'd done enough, Josephine said, and needed rest.

I didn't rest. I watched gaslight from the street throw shadows on our wall, imagining problems that might unfurl in the morning. Workers would not come to their posts as we'd instructed, or would not leave in a mass at ten o'clock, taking their tools. There would be heckling or fights with those who refused to strike. The factory doors would be locked so we couldn't walk out. Yiddish workers had raised their hands and vowed: "If I turn traitor to the cause I now pledge, may this hand wither from the arm I now raise." Suppose they foreswore? Suppose only a pathetic scattering of us rattled in the union hall, looking foolish?

Nothing I'd seen in America, not the first snow or any blaze of autumn, was as beautiful as that day. A crisp breeze had scuttled across the lake that morning, pushing heat and clouds away, scrubbing the air. Workers found the promised red cards calling for a general strike and calmly left their stations at the stroke of ten. I stood in a balcony over the factory floor to watch that thrilling sight: rows upon rows of women and girls pushing back chairs; dropping scissors, needles, thimbles, and thread in their waist bags; and walking calmly out of Printz-Biederman, their faces alight with purpose. Have you ever wanted arms enough to gather in hundreds of fearless women, a massive chest to hold your swelling pride? The entire fleet of ancient Greece sailing out to vanquish Troy could not have been more glorious.

We were six thousand Italians, Poles, Jews, and Germans, a thousand more than we had fondly hoped for. The Bohemians came together, a glorious show in blazing white, puffed-sleeved blouses, embroidered crimson vests, and blue skirts. "New Americans wearing the flag," I heard a striker say approvingly. Women brought babies in beribboned carriages. Lines of finishers, shirtmakers, dressmakers, and tailors swelled our stream. We were a "joyful parade," the *Plain Dealer* reported, and indeed we were. Enrico carried the union flag, head high, sunlight frosting his dark curls.

"He's so proud," his mother told me. "And I'm so proud of him. I just hope we can go back to work soon. The strike pay isn't much."

"I know."

"Still," she said loudly in English toward a hovering reporter, "I'd rather starve fast than starve slow at Printz-Biederman."

"It has been an orderly strike," the *Cleveland Press* acknowledged in an editorial read aloud at the union hall, "and orderly strikes, when waged in a just cause, are almost certain to end in a victory for the wage earner." We cheered and sang. On my way home, I stopped at an Italian bakery for little almond cakes to celebrate with Mamma that night. The baker wished us well and slipped an extra cake in the neat package.

The Cloak Manufacturers' Association's statement came three days later in the *Plain Dealer*. "I could have written it myself," Josephine huffed. The full page announced that our strike was useless, even foolish.

We enjoyed "optimal" conditions and pay. We were dupes of the East, stirred up by outsiders and radicals to price Cleveland cloak makers and dressmakers out of business and thus enrich New York manufacturers. Thinking only of our welfare, the association urged us to return to work and in that way avoid reprisals for our ill-considered actions.

We marched again. This time hecklers stood in clumps. "Socialists! Go home if you don't like American work!" they shouted. Alda, a clerk whose desk was near mine, called from the sidewalk: "My little boy's sick, Lucia. How do I pay the doctor if we can't work? How?" Men and women whose faces I knew from church or scribing watched grimly. How could they not see the rightness of this strike? Yet I had no answer for Alda. How had everything that seemed so clear yesterday now become so murky?

As we turned from a shaded street to a blast of sun, my head swirled. In that instant, a bull-shouldered vagrant named Roy who was often thrown out of Lula's charged our line, flailing like a drunkard seeking a target. Over and over Isadore had warned: "There must be no violence. Whatever the provocation, *do not fight back.*" Newspapers, suffragettes, churches, and city leaders who might support our cause would turn away if we behaved like ruffians.

"Lucia, do you know him?" Josephine whispered. I nodded. The gesture must have caught his eye, for he lunged at me. A heavy hand pawed my shirtwaist. "Ex-cuse *me!*" he muttered. When I stepped aside, he followed. From the sidewalk, people watched as if we were a vaudeville show.

Steeling myself to Isadore's orders, I stood like a post until Roy's heavy hands gripped my head as Dr. Galuppi once did, fingers driving through my hair. A voice thick with beer whispered: "Eye-talian girl, go home to your crazy mamma." *Basta!* I wrenched myself free from his grasp. How could I know that he would stagger, trip, and fall, cutting his head on a curb?

Police had been watching. Stepping over Roy, they seized me and Josephine. "Both of you, under arrest for assault."

"We have been exercising our right of peaceful assembly," Josephine announced, "with permission to march signed by your chief. This young lady was avoiding a ruffian who touched her indecently. He tripped, that's all. How is that assault?"

"Under arrest," the police repeated. This was worse, far worse than being taken from the San Carlo in a carriage. This was handcuffs. We were pushed into an airless Black Maria; the door locked behind us as if we were criminals. Nobody listened to my protests. Nobody cared. Josephine's beautiful hat slipped off, and we couldn't retrieve it.

In the stifling darkness I cried in anger and shame. "When he touched me like that, when he talked about my mother, I had to get away."

"Of course you did," said Josephine's calm and steady voice, "and if they want arrests, they get arrests. Roy was paid. I just didn't think they'd bring in strikebreakers so soon. But don't worry. Isadore will bail us out soon."

"*Soon*? If I'm not home for dinner, my mother will worry. She'll go looking for me." I panicked. Would *she* be arrested? I pounded the walls, screaming, "Let me out! I didn't do anything wrong."

"Stop that. It doesn't help. Someone will go to your house and explain what happened. Lucia, we never claimed a strike would be easy, only that we'll win in the end. Now sit back and try to relax. Here's what I do. I imagine I'm a smooth stone in a riverbed. Cool, clear water runs over me." I peered at her face in the gloom. Cool, clear water? This was a nightmare.

We were hauled from the Black Maria, pushed into the station, and fingerprinted. *Cool, clear water,* I repeated to myself. But this water roiled; it was dark and bad-smelling. I was in prison, a criminal. The countess,

Mrs. Livingston, my professors, and Henryk, what would they think of me now?

"Put 'em in cell three," a clerk grunted. Two burly officers hauled us along, a hand on each of our arms. Nothing in my life could have prepared me for that sound: an iron gate creaking open and locking behind us with an echoing thud.

The constant bustle at least distracted me as our cell filled up with strikers crowding onto narrow benches against the wall. "So, what's our first song?" Josephine demanded. How could she be so cheerful? We were in jail! Two women offered a pretty tune in Yiddish. Others sang "Casey Jones," their voices echoing off brick walls. Police wandered by to hear "America the Beautiful," "Battle Hymn of the Republic," and "By the Light of the Silvery Moon." Swept up in the noise and fellowship, I slipped my voice into the bouncing flow. "Do 'Alexander's Ragtime Band'!" a policeman called out. We shouted back:

Come on and hear, come on and hear,
Alexander's Ragtime Band.
Come on and hear, come on and hear,
It's the best band in the land!

In pauses between songs, we told stories. I shared the tale of the fishermen killed by the lascivious princess of Palazzo Donn'Anna, expecting gasps of horror. Instead, a woman in the corner shared a lewd joke on the length of a fisherman's "hook." Talk spun into other tales of lusty excess. Translations flew across the room, followed quickly by guffaws. I remembered bits of such talk between Nannina and her friends before they shooed me away. I'd never been welcome in a circle of such freely talking women.

"Look at Lucia," a voice called out. "She's red as a berry."

"The poor child hasn't had a proper liberal education," lamented Josephine in a tone so prim and somber that everyone laughed. Thus began another round of jokes on schools and "proper education." As we howled after a wild story of a priest in the Irish countryside, a Polish woman suggested we get ourselves jailed all together again.

"No lack of opportunity," Josephine commented, and we talked in easy good humor about tactics for the strike, allies we might tap, and slogans for our marches.

Near dusk, Isadore bailed us out as if the process were as perfunctory as buying onions. An assault charge hadn't been recorded. "It was all for intimidation," he said. "Were you intimidated, Lucia?"

"At first, yes."

"Of course. So was I, the first time."

"How often have you been jailed?"

"Can't remember. Let's say often," he answered lightly. "It comes with the job."

At the boardinghouse, in the markets, and around the neighborhood, everyone knew where I'd been, as if a sign around my neck read: "Arrested. Been in jail." Friends fluttered with questions: "What was it like? Did they beat you?" Enrico and Pepe hovered around me, demanding: "Did you break out? Did you see real criminals? Did you have bread and water? Could you scratch through the wall with spoons?" Basking in unaccustomed glory, I didn't mention the songs and jokes I'd blush to repeat.

"Never mind criminals, we need rich women," Josephine said briskly. We would speak to them with two workers: Amelia, a young Italian mother with a cherubic baby, and Hannah, a Jewish woman whose arm had been scorched by the Lentz fire. I would translate for Amelia. Hannah spoke English well, and her dramatic tale of the fire, many said, could make a polar bear sweat.

I expected audiences like my mother's in vaudeville, thrilled and expectant, listening avidly. Ladies of the Cuyahoga County Women's Suffrage Association were polite, even distressed to hear Amelia's stories of a worker's life and to see Hannah's arm. "However," said their leader, "we come together for women's suffrage. To win this fight requires focus, as does yours." Individuals might sign a statement of personal support, but the association could not publicly endorse our strike. The ladies passed a pretty basket for donations. I saw many of them later in that long summer bandaging strikers, cheering, handing out sandwiches, or giving lemonade to weary children. But none wrote letters to the *Plain Dealer* or marched with us.

"Rich bitches," Hannah muttered as we left the meeting. I explained our failure to Amelia as she soothed her hot and fretful baby.

"Well yes, but they did contribute," I pointed out. On a secluded bench I counted our take: $547.50. If the suffragettes were so generous, how could they not see that the rightness of our cause was as clear as water, as indisputable as gravity?

"We'll keep asking," Josephine announced. "We'll go back each month for more." *Each month?* Hannah glanced at me. "Next, we ask the WCTU."

We went to the Women's Christian Temperance Union, arguing that strikebreakers were being issued alcohol and the workers' misery led many to drink. Again, some gave money or promised letters to the manufacturers' association, but the group itself could not publicly support the strike. In the gathering heat, our dresses clung to sweaty skin and the weight of each no dragged at our feet. This must be a singer's nightmare: a perfect performance that nobody cheers.

In all we gathered $970.56 that day for our soup kitchens. Hannah said she'd visit her father's cousin who owned a fine haberdashery near Public Square.

"Ask for two hundred," said Josephine. Hannah gulped. "And, Lucia, the Livingstons live off their limestone quarries. It's nothing to them if garment workers get more. They can easily give five hundred." The number bloomed before me, almost the cost of a Model T Ford. "You can do it. If you don't ask, you'll never get. But go tomorrow."

I'd have to take Mamma with me to the Livingstons', Roseanne said. She had been restless all day, looking for me, and might slip out the door to find me. "Besides, she makes me nervous wandering around the halls, looking in all the rooms." How could I protest after all of Roseanne's favors for us?

We went in the morning, when Mrs. Livingston might be reliably at home. I had persuaded Mamma to wear a somber dress and bring her knitting, even if was hard to imagine needing a woolen scarf on such a warm, sticky day. We went to the back door, where I implored Agnes to keep Mamma while I talked to her mistress about the strike. Mamma's eyes darted around the fine kitchen. She tugged hard at my hand, straining to leave.

"No, no," I said quickly in Italian. "Not to work here, just to wait. Remember what I told you? I have to speak with Mrs. Livingston. We'll find you a quiet place to knit."

"Your ma's touched?" Agnes asked warily.

"No, no, she's just nervous in new places," I said, briefly explaining her condition. With difficulty we settled Mamma in the cool of the stone-lined pantry with a glass of iced lemonade.

"You left college to take care of your ma and now you're helping with the strike? You've grown, my girl. Don't you worry, I'll watch her." Agnes leaned closer. "You'll find the missus in a better mood. The old man died last month. We all thought he'd be tormenting us forever and making the missus miserable. Then bam! Having breakfast in bed he was and the maid goes in to collect his tray. There he is, facedown in oatmeal, stone dead. Scared her silly. I was afraid they'd think I poisoned him. In fact, I'd wanted to often enough, but no, just a heart attack, the doctor says. You go around to the front door now, love, since you're seeing the missus."

I passed through a shaded rose garden to the front door. Even Betsy the housekeeper seemed more cheerful. Massive bouquets filled the house; carpets had been replaced and the grand staircase freshly waxed. Mrs. Livingston came floating into the morning room with the smile of her Hiram House days. Masses of curls framed her lovely face, balanced by swoops of pearls against a lacy morning dress. She directed me to a bright brocade divan.

"Oh, Lucia, it's been like a honeymoon," she gushed as if we were the dearest friends. "Richard never complained, but his father rode him like a horse, begrudging every penny."

Betsy brought iced tea and little cakes. In the flurry of setting out dishes and glasses, she whispered that all was quiet in the kitchen. Mrs. Livingston listened sympathetically to my tale of leaving college to care for Mamma, never mentioning the ring she'd sold to send me. It was delightful to talk in that lovely room, to pretend I was a leisured lady with nothing to do all day but receive calls and plan for the evening's entertainment.

*The money, ask for the money,* I heard Josephine whisper. How much money was here in furnishings and art, in Mrs. Livingston's dress, jeweled watch, lace and pearls, and translucent porcelain plates for the little cakes? How many thousands? But to ask again for help, why had I told Josephine I could do this?

I asked instead if she'd heard of the Shirtwaist Factory fire. "Yes, it was terrible, ghastly. Those poor, poor girls. We gave fifty dollars to a fund for their families." My mind raced: was this good that she was sympathetic or bad that she had already given to the fund, and so why support another labor cause? I took a breath and spoke about the Cleveland conditions, the long hours, fines, rented machines, illicit services demanded of young girls, and how factory workers were pitted against the even-worse-paid contractors. She listened avidly and asked careful questions. Was she moved by the tale or only being kind to a former student, perhaps proud of my English vocabulary?

I plunged on, explaining the benefits of strikes in other cities, the aid given by the suffragettes, WCTU, and Mink Brigades in New York, educated and far-thinking women who saw in strikers both sisters and the builders of a great nation of work. I cited Mr. Kinney's argument: workers paid decently could buy more, uplifting every store and business. I explained how workers suffered even in a short strike. I told her the dilemma of those like Alda with sick children and how much depended on the support of the wise, compassionate, privileged citizens of Cleveland.

Mrs. Livingston put down her iced tea, seeming much younger, like a hurt and disappointed little girl. "You came here again for *money*, Lucia? That's all you want from me, first for college and now this?" She had thought I dared come on a social visit? Words rattled in my throat. Sweat trickled between my breasts despite the cool of the morning room.

"The workers are suffering, Mrs. Livingston, and I—"

She sighed and held up a hand to stop me. "I'm sorry, but since Richard's father died, do you realize how many people come or write or stop us at church wanting money for good causes? We gave to the diphtheria fund because the need seemed so desperate."

"I know. These are difficult times."

"Now the union wants money."

"It does. If the workers can't hold on long enough to convince the owners, then all their suffering will be for nothing."

She sighed. "How much, Lucia?"

*Say the words. Think about Alda.* "We need five hundred dollars, Mrs. Livingston. We've raised some, but it's not enough. There are six thousand strikers and their families to feed." I was holding my glass too tightly and set it on the marble table. "I sing to the eyes," Mamma had said on my first trip to Chicago, when her star was rising. I made myself look in Mrs. Livingston's eyes, reposing my face, smiling slightly. She relaxed a little, becoming almost the Miss Miller of Hiram House again.

"I'll have to speak with Richard. I don't know how much we can give, but it will be something. And I'll talk to friends who might be sympathetic, those whose husbands aren't in the garment business."

"Thank you so much, Mrs. Livingston." I let my breath out slowly so she wouldn't notice I'd been holding it.

"Now," she said briskly, pouring more tea from a crystal pitcher tinkling with ice, "tell me about yourself. You *are* keeping up with your studies?" She explained why I must read the novels of Mrs. Edith Wharton. I told her I certainly would. Then she glanced at a dainty watch.

"Thank you so much for your time and generosity, Mrs. Livingston. I'll be going now."

She rang a bell, conveyed her best wishes for my mother's recovery, and had Betsy thread me back to the kitchen.

Agnes was waiting. "So, she'll ask the master for money, will she?"

"How do you know?"

"Now don't look so surprised. When you were in service, didn't you listen at doors?" I nodded sheepishly. "So Betsy happened to be dusting nearby and happened to hear you talk. The missus asks him *everything.* 'This sauce or that one, darling? Which necklace tonight?' But he's a good man. And for sure your strikers need help. I'll be sending over some of my oatcakes tomorrow for the children. And this"—she held up a little bag—"is from all of us here in service. Eight dollars. Payday's tomorrow, so that's all we could raise right now. But everything helps, no?"

The weight of it lifted my heart. "Thank you, Agnes. Thank everyone for me. It's a week's strike pay for a large family."

The scullery maid looked up, startled. Agnes gasped. "Well, may the Lord hold you all in the palm of His hand."

When we went to get my mother from the pantry's cool, she almost smiled and even asked if I'd spoken to the countess. "She's no countess, Mamma, but I think she'll help us."

A week later, Josephine told me that four hundred dollars had come from Richard Livingston's account. "Just four? I wanted five," I said, deflated.

"I never thought they'd give five, but if I'd told you three, they'd never have given four. So you did well, Lucia." She left me to ponder my first lesson in organizing.

*At our next* march, on blazing July 4, four Bohemian women were arrested for "promoting anarchy." One was pregnant. After she shoved aside a strikebreaker who charged at her belly, she was jailed in a different precinct, and had started bleeding by the time Josephine found her and paid the bail. She lost her baby that night. A few days later, workers loyal to Printz-Biederman broke windows in striking Bohemians' flats.

"It's terrible. They're new in Cleveland and mostly poor," Henryk said. I had stopped to order vegetables for the soup kitchen. We talked as he sorted potatoes in the slight cool of his shop. Miriam was in Pittsburgh again, visiting her aunt. "There aren't enough rich Bohemians to help the others. Some of the Jewish strikers are getting aid through a fund at the synagogue. Wealthy families in other businesses have been very generous."

"Bohemians have the union," I said stoutly.

"Yes, but who's in the union? Jews and Italians, some Poles. The Bohemians feel alone."

"Yes, maybe so." The announcement of his engagement, difficult as it was, had one small advantage for me: with impossible hopes gone, only friendship was left. Perhaps that was enough. When I spoke of my mother's good and bad days, Henryk listened with none of the pity or random advice that so many showered on me in those days. The constant coil of worry in my chest began to loosen.

"On bad days the *dybbuk* has her?" he asked lightly.

"Yes, the terrible *dybbuk*." We spoke of the strike: I told him about my morning with Mrs. Livingston, how the old man had died in an oatmeal bowl, how difficult it was to ask for money, and yet I'd raised $408 between wealthy masters and poor servants. I described how the confident Miss Miller now deferred to her husband even in matters of sauces.

"I have an aunt like that," said Henryk. "She left her brains at the altar when she married."

"Why didn't someone remind her?"

"Good idea. We should have said, 'Excuse us, Aunt Gertrude, are you forgetting something?'" We laughed until a string of customers arrived, and then I slipped away.

*Henryk was right* about the Bohemians. Their union ties were unraveling. Arrests, the loss of the baby, and broken windows frightened them. Their contractors, often deeply in debt to factory owners, pressed and threatened the women relentlessly. A week after the broken windows, Isadore announced what we all feared: Bohemian workers had voted to return to work at the same miserable rate.

Josephine's voice rose over the waves of angry, fearful talk. "Defectors *do* return when a union seems about to win. We must hope for this."

"So *we* do all the starving," someone shouted, "and they sponge off our rewards?" Songs and speeches, impassioned arguments on the strength of union, and prayers of compassion for the Bohemians slowly eased the angry talk. Still, walking home on that hot, muggy night, I couldn't clear away the fear that we traveled over shifting sand.

Congregations could be swayed against the strike by a single priest who counseled reconciliation. Our numbers were chipped away as workers went to contractors or simply left for other cities. Newspapers breathlessly recounted reprisals against Bohemians, painting us as rowdies, anarchists, socialists, thugs, and bullies, immigrants with nothing better to do than chant and make trouble. If supporters believed this talk and turned from us, how could we keep on striking?

As I walked down Woodland Avenue, now as familiar to me as Via Roma, Cleveland felt fearsome, fraught with risks and dangers. I had grown, as Agnes said, but so had my troubles. From this distance, Count Filippo seemed almost benign. I saw now why so many immigrants longed for home, even with its poverty. But how could this Lucia go back? I couldn't fit in my old life or ever be only a servant again.

"What's wrong?" Roseanne demanded when I got home. "You saw a ghost?"

"No, just problems at the union hall."

"Is the strike ending soon? You're behind in rent, you know."

"I'll pay on Friday," I told her. But how? I'd already used all my college savings. As I helped my mother with her bath, the only solution that came to me was to sell my cameo, the one beautiful thing that I owned. That night when I opened its velvet box by our window, moonlight frosted Diana's creamy face. Mamma looked over my shoulder. She must have had a very good day.

"Keeping for your daughter?" she asked, almost smiling.

"Yes, Mamma, for her." I closed the little box. "Let's go to bed."

*Chapter 16*  ♔

## RAIN ON THE LAKE

*The next morning,* I went to a jewelry store on Bond Street. When the owner poked at my cameo with his pudgy fingers, Diana's delicate face and swirling veil were suddenly so familiar and dear to me that I took her back, stammering that I'd changed my mind. "Miss," he called out when I'd reached the door. "Happens all the time. Let me know if you change it back again." I walked around the block to gather strength.

Heat swirled around me like Diana's veil. My mind swirled as well with anger at the factory owners who'd pushed us to this strike, and at Josephine and Isadore, that they hadn't magically won it for us. Anger at Roseanne that she dared charge so much for room and board, and anger at my poverty. Mrs. Livingston could have a tray of cameos if she chose. Why couldn't I keep my one treasure? When I'd nearly circled the block, the anger turned to shame: What of mothers with hungry children and nothing to pawn? On a side street off Public Square, I saw a sign for Cramer's Jewelry.

Countess Elisabetta had taught me to recognize poor cameos. Cramer's was full of them: cheap carved silhouettes glued to dyed shell or coral bases, priced by size alone. Mine would get little here. I walked on to Mr. H. W. Beattie's store on Euclid Avenue. Velvet-lined trays cradled exquisitely crafted gems. His cameos were of fine sardonyx stone like mine. I took a breath, squared my shoulders, and went in. Mr. Beattie carefully studied the deep carving and many layers of my Diana, the perfect beauty of her face, veil, and tempest of curls, and the fine bezel mounting. His pupils bloomed. He noted the plainness of my dress and asked gently if the cameo were a gift. "Yes, from—a friend."

"Made in Torre del Greco, outside Naples, before 1850. I know this artisan's work. I call him Carlo because there's always a curl of hair in the shape of a C. Look closely; here's the C." His forefinger hovered over the curl. Mr. Beattie looked at my face as carefully as he'd studied Diana's. "I've seen you before, miss. On the picket line, was it, with Miss Casey?" When I nodded, he dropped his voice. "A just cause. I wish you well. Let's say forty dollars. I know a collector who appreciates fine work."

A month's reprieve. "Thank you, sir," I stammered. "Thank you very much." He let me hold the cameo one last time before gently setting it in his case and counting out my dollars. The thrill of my sale lasted barely a block. Walking home, I pictured my dingy bedroom's worn wooden floors, cracked walls, and curtains grayed by coal dust. But yesterday it held my cameo, like a perfect diamond set in tin. *Don't think of this.*

I fixed on the villa instead, so intently that when I got home, paid Roseanne, and saw a letter for me from Naples, I was half convinced I'd conjured it. I fingered the creamy parchment, tracing the watermark with the Monforte family crest. While I sweltered here in Cleveland, golden plums were ripening in the villa orchard. Nannina would be picking tomatoes, eggplants, and sweet peppers, and canning her winter sauces. As I imagined the great window looking out to sea, a curl of cool slid through our open kitchen door. "Ah, a lake breeze," Roseanne said. If I'd told her no, no, my letter had brought it from the Bay of Naples, she would have thought me mad as Mamma. I closed myself in the dining room to read.

It was a long letter. The countess was making steady progress in paying off the count's debts. She had sold land on the Vomero hill over Naples for a good price, traded two unprofitable farms for a larger one with water rights, and given one creditor an ancient marble bust. This hadn't pained her: "Who needs a Caesar staring at you?" Paolo repaired a small guesthouse which was now rented to an English couple. Nannina had married Luigi the gardener and was selling her marmalade, a tiny business, but it turned a steady profit.

"We live simply," the countess wrote. "I don't have a box at the opera or go to balls anymore, so I don't have to buy new gowns. It's a great savings." Early that morning "Paolo and I" had taken a rowboat along the rocky coast west of the city. "Lucia, you're floating *inside* Roman ruins. Sunlight sparkles on the walls like a jewel box." After the count's cruelty and many offenses, how could she not deserve these pleasures on a glassy sea? "Paolo and I . . . Paolo and I." Peppered through her pages, those words brought an ache of loneliness. Where was *my* Paolo?

"Please tell me all your news," she wrote. "Your last letter was too short. How is Teresa? Is she feeling better? Has she gone back to vaudeville? Tell me about your day."

I wrote to her about the strike, but not my time in jail. At each new sentence, I thought: *now, now, tell her about Mamma.* But my pen wouldn't shape these words, neither Dr. Ricci's medical terms nor the common ones: that she was crazy, out of her head, not herself, or, in that strange American phrase, "gone screwy," as if her head were a small machine rattling itself apart. I recounted the pressing heat and how Bohemians had left the strike. I did not say I'd sold her cameo. By the fourth sheet, all that I hadn't said weighed on me like bricks. I wrote that a young man I cared for was engaged to another. Yet even without her, he'd never be my "fella." His family would refuse and he couldn't oppose them. "But there are many fine men in America, and when I'm ready, I'll find one, as you have found Paolo." I promised Nannina and Luigi a wedding gift from America when the strike ended, which would surely be soon with victory for the workers. When the letter was finished, I slumped in my chair, exhausted by the effort of so many lies and so much good cheer.

Roseanne eyed me acutely. "You didn't tell her the truth about your mother, did you?"

"No."

"Because you think she'll get better?"

Perhaps. Even Josephine knew only that Mamma was "not well" and for that reason I sometimes could not attend meetings, marches, or pickets. She didn't know why I cringed when we passed Cleveland State Hospital on our way to visit possible donors. Howls and curses poured from the asylum's barred windows. Inside the iron fence, wild-haired men and women in shapeless gowns drifted across the yard, sometimes walking into trees or stopping, immobile as trees themselves, until gruff attendants set them moving with a push. The patients' ages were vague. Rich and poor looked the same, as if madness washed away every sign of former rank.

Once I saw a pretty young woman staring through the gate. She seemed to be summoning me, but drawing closer, I heard only "Pigeons going away, pigeons, pigeons." An attendant shooed the others inside like chickens and then came back for her. His wide hand on her back moved as if soaped, down to her waist, between her legs, up her side, across her breasts. She never flinched, but the voice rose steadily as he drew her on, a steady cry of "Pigeons going away, pigeons, pigeons," until the door slammed shut behind them.

"Poor thing," Josephine had commented.

"Yes, poor thing."

Pneumonia had never destroyed what was Irena in my friend. Sick or well, she was one of us. Mamma's case was different. Friends from school and church ceased using her name or even saying "your mother." They asked how "she" was feeling, if "she" was any better. Did only Roseanne, Donato, and I remember the Teresa who once spoke and sang and worked as other women worked? I sometimes doubted my own memory.

At least the union hall and picket lines brought the comfort of company and a common vision. We buoyed one another with a constant flow of stories: outrages at work, other strikes, and peaceful victories. These stories reminded us that we weren't alone. We were part of a vast tapestry of American workers in cities, mines, mills, factories, foundries, and quarries, woven together in righteous cause.

On a July day too hot for pickets, Josephine went to meet a group of rabbis, hoping they would persuade wealthy Jews to support a kosher soup kitchen. "It was easier in New York," she grumbled. In Cleveland, too many wealthy families were linked by business, family, friendship, or marriage to the garment industry. As the strike ground on, their giving faltered. "Still," she said, "you have to ask. Nothing comes from not asking."

I'd never realized how tightly woven a city could be. Lula had to let her kitchen girl go because the tavern had fewer customers now. Shoeshine boys complained that office clerks and supervisors in the garment trades no longer used their services. Landlords, grocers, pharmacists, barbers, and peddlers all cursed the owners, the workers, or both for the lengthening strike.

Meanwhile the constant, astonishing heat touched every moment of our lives and every conversation. Yes, a hard winter's cold did the same, but who could imagine cold now? Scuffles came easily when hot bodies pressed too close in streetcars and shops, stairways or crowded flats. A splash of shade on a baking sidewalk became contested territory. Women waiting in lines for ice squabbled irritably. Garbage rotted in the street, and horse droppings seethed with flies. Through open windows one constantly heard parents shouting at children or each other. Clerks snapped at messenger boys. On front steps and porches, men and women sat in a dull torpor.

It seemed that only Pepe and Enrico were active, darting through the city, carrying messages between the organizers and pasting up notices of marches, pickets, and the owners' injustices. As quickly as they were torn down, the boys put up new ones. Josephine managed to pay them a few dollars a week, and they swelled with pride. They lifted our spirits, telling jokes as we marched, showing off handstands, and fashioning noisemakers out of scraps of wood and metal.

Moving constantly, the boys saw everything. They knew when wives of strikebreakers were cursed and mocked by strikers and their families. When the newspaper reported that a strikebreaker's window on Woodland was pelted with eggs, the boys knew otherwise. "Eggs?" cried Enrico. "It was rocks. And company thugs did it to make us look bad. *If* we had eggs, we sure wouldn't waste them on windows."

"I'd rather have potatoes," his mother said. "They fill the belly more."

The *Plain Dealer* made much of the egg-throwing report and a strikebreaker's wife who said, "I've got hungry babies at home. My man's working to feed them. What's the harm in that?"

"The *harm* is Printz-Biederman working people to death and stealing back their miserable pay in fines and fees. The *harm* is sixty-hour work-weeks, secret contracts, threats, and layoffs," Isadore said when he read the article aloud at a meeting.

"We need more money. You can't keep a strike going without it," Josephine added, regular as a clock. "We *all* have to think of who we know with money. Think and ask. I can't do everything."

The countess had sent fifty dollars by wire to help the strike. She would have sent more, she wrote, but new debts kept surfacing. Suffragettes were helping, but not enough to meet our "special needs": sick babies and children, wives whose husbands spent their strike pay in bars, and evicted families camped in parks or neighbors' flats. Strikebreakers drew idle young men into scuffles, battering faces with brass knuckles the owners provided. Josephine gripped the "special needs" cards, as if drawing strength from them. "A strike always looks worst before the end. We just have to hold on a little longer."

I decided to go to Ashtabula and appeal to Mr. Kinney. I'd leave on Saturday morning and be back by afternoon. When I explained this plan to Roseanne, Mamma gripped my wrist, her voice taut with panic: "Don't leave me."

"It's just for a few hours, and you don't like strangers."

"Take me!" Useless to explain that her presence would be distracting, that I was afraid of what she might do. "Take me! Take me!"

"You can't leave her with me like this," Roseanne warned.

So I gave Mamma laudanum and prayed for a good day. The morning started well. We walked quietly from the Ashtabula train station through streets lined with trees holding dense clouds of fluttering leaves. The nearness of water and the flash of bright birds on fresh-cut velvet lawns enchanted us both. A young boy on a bicycle pointed to an elaborate confection of turrets and porches surrounded by rose arbors and blooming blue hydrangeas. "That's their house yonder. Missus Kinney is in, she just paid me for trimming the hedges."

"And Mr. Kinney?"

The boy shrugged. "He's *always* in unless he's out walking with her, and she's *in*, like I said."

The Kinneys saw us coming and met us on the porch. "Who is it?" Mr. Kinney said, beaming and pumping first my hand and then Mamma's. He studied me with friendly curiosity.

"It's Lucia D'Angelo, dear," said Mrs. Kinney quickly. "She worked at your store. And here's her mother, Mrs. D'Angelo. I told you they'd be coming. Lucia sent a note, remember?"

"Of course, of course. Lucy, come sit on the porch swing with me. And your friend can take the rocking chair. Would you like some lemonade, my dears?" The right side of his face dragged a little. He held his right arm stiffly, and his speech was slightly slowed. A cast dulled his eyes, like those of pleasant drunks at Lula's. I watched with astonishment as Mamma, who always shied from strangers, sat readily in the rocking chair as if she'd just come home. I was the stranger now.

"Lucia, let's fetch the lemonade," said a gentle voice. I followed Mrs. Kinney through the cool, dark elegance of her parlor, where potted ferns and palms sprang from every corner and a cut-glass chandelier threw splatters of light across a flowered rug and polished upright piano. I wanted to curl into the divan, nesting in this room far from Cleveland's troubles. "You have a lovely home, Mrs. Kinney."

"We built it as our refuge, a place to come back to after the travels we'd planned. We had such plans." Her voice trailed off. "Well, the kitchen's this way. The maid's busy upstairs, we'll get the refreshments ourselves." But we didn't move, both of us caught by the scene outside: Mr. Kinney talking to Mamma, her face turned peaceably toward his. "Five minutes later, he'll tell her the same thing," Mrs. Kinney said.

"What happened, ma'am?"

"He had a stroke last spring. The doctor said we're lucky he's not paralyzed or lame. But he forgets everything. As soon as we go somewhere, he wants to come home. I think he knows he's not himself. He'll only walk with me early or late, when there's nobody around." Mr. Kinney was still talking; Mamma was still listening. "Does your mother speak English?"

"Not well."

"But they understand each other, I think."

"Yes, they seem to."

Mrs. Kinney rested her hand lightly on my arm. "Excuse me, Lucia, but did she have a stroke as well?"

"No, it was a—a nervous collapse."

"Sit down with me, dear, and tell me about it. He's already forgotten the lemonade." Nobody in Cleveland had asked for Mamma's story with such compassion. It loosened my tongue. I told how we had to come to America, Mamma's singing, her first triumphs and swift unraveling in vaudeville, how her troubles had wrenched me from college and back to work, my struggle to keep her from an asylum and daily fears of failing.

Mrs. Kinney was silent. Then she brushed a strand of hair from my face and pressed my hand between hers. Just that, but it seemed a crushing weight had lifted. "He'll be getting anxious now," she said finally. We brought lemonade and sugar cookies to the porch, where a warm breeze blew rose scents over us.

"I was telling your friend about my store," said Mr. Kinney. "I'll be going in tomorrow or the next day. We have some lovely shirtwaists, don't we, Olivia?"

"Yes, dear. Here's your lemonade."

"Rain's coming. Look there," said Mr. Kinney, signaling with his glass. Indeed, dark clouds had rolled across the lake. Birds called urgently. Butterflies and bees sucked at banks of flowers; branches bowed as if welcoming a great guest. "We love rain on the lake in Ashtabula," Mr. Kinney announced. "Don't we, Olivia?"

"Yes, dear, but we must go inside before our guests catch a chill."

*When the rain comes,* I told myself, *I'll talk about the strike and ask for money.* Until then, we sat in comfortable silence, Mamma and Mr. Kinney rocking, Mrs. Kinney and I on the creaking swing. The rain did come, first gently and then blowing harder. Heavy heads of hydrangea swayed; petals flew off rosebushes. Mrs. Kinney urged us inside, walking behind her husband, reminding him to step up from the porch. "I know that, Olivia," he complained amiably, although he kicked the door riser several times before stepping up. "We're going to travel," he announced. "When I close the store, I'm taking Olivia to Italy."

Mamma edged past him to the piano, her eyes flashing in the dim light. I darted to her side, whispering, "Mamma, come sit down with me." She stroked the keys. "It's not a player piano like Roseanne's. See, there's no rolls? You can't—"

"Would you like to play, Mrs. D'Angelo?" asked a gentle voice behind us.

"Thank you, Mrs. Kinney, but I don't think—" Mamma pushed me aside. "I told you," I hissed in Italian, "it's a *real* piano." She sat down hard on the bench, held her fingers over the keys, and froze. I froze as well. Would she cry now? Beat the keys? Walk out into the rain or start the steady rocking she did when most distressed? I couldn't ask for money then, perhaps couldn't even get her back on a train. Would someone set the police on a rocking, lunatic foreigner?

"I will sing 'Shine On, Harvest Moon,'" Mamma announced, in her nearly perfect stage English.

"Wonderful," cried Mr. Kinney gleefully. "My favorite."

"What a treat," his wife added. "Vaudeville in our own parlor. Come sit by me, Lucia." I took myself to the flowered divan, stiff as wood, consumed by fear. At home Mamma kept such distance from Roseanne's piano that she hadn't even noticed I'd sold her song rolls.

Her hands stretched over the keys, stopped, and shook. Was she just now realizing there was no button to start the music? "Shine on— shine—on," began Mr. Kinney, his voice deep and achingly slow, as if calling words back from a great distance. Pale fingers lowered to the keys, pressed one, the next, the next until a tune came halting out. I was stunned. Had the piano man taught her to play, or had she watched the player keys go up and down until the patterns pressed into her mind? She'd never told me. And of course I'd never asked.

"Harvest—moon—up—in—the—sky." Mamma joined him, her still-rich voice carving words from air. She or Mr. Kinney might repeat a word as the other one pushed on. Together they managed: "I—ain't— had—no—lovin'—since—April—January, June, or July."

A warm hand closed over mine. Tears glistened in Mrs. Kinney's eyes. She leaned close and whispered: "We were going to be in Venice on a full moon. Herman wanted to sing this to me on the Grand Canal."

*Have music bring Mamma back.* Could she feel once more the heavy drape of her vaudeville gowns, the weight of the puffed pompadour and hat, the thrilled breath of her crowds? *Just one step, just a little step back to me.*

The two voices, high and low, gathered their forces and finished together: "For me and my gal." Drumming rain filled the silence as we waited, breathless, for the next verse or song. Neither came. Mamma slumped, her hands sliding off the keys as if they'd been greased. Mr.

Kinney simply stopped, his mouth hanging open. We clapped. Mrs. Kinney caressed her husband, but he didn't move again, staring fixedly at his knees.

I ran to hug my mother. "*Brava,* Mamma, *brava*! Can you sing another? You haven't done 'Santa Lucia' in so long. I'm sure Mrs. Kinney—"

The piano bench scraped back, and Mamma pushed past me to a stiff little chair facing the rain. "So, the concert's over," said Mrs. Kinney.

"Yes." We sat in the dim room, drained by the upswell of hope and its sudden collapse. When Mrs. Kinney asked her husband and Mamma if they'd like some luncheon, he didn't answer, already deep in sleep, and Mamma shook her head.

Mrs. Kinney sighed. "We'll eat here then. I often do." She had the maid bring us cold chicken sandwiches, chilled broth, and cucumber salad. Alice set these things on little tables by our chairs. How many times had I brought lunch for ladies? I mouthed to Alice that she'd forgotten soup spoons and diverted Mrs. Kinney from her broth until the errant spoons appeared.

All through lunch our eyes strayed constantly, hers to Mr. Kinney and mine to Mamma. "Tell me about the strike, Lucia," she asked finally. "Are you involved?"

"Yes, I am." Carefully naming Mr. Kinney as a fair and generous boss, I outlined our grievances with the others. I tried to be calm, to stress how often and earnestly the workers had presented their complaints. I explained fines and fees, the long hours and dangers of work. She knew about the Lentz fire but not the Triangle disaster. I told her how suffragettes gave private gifts but refused public support, the strikebreakers and the fights they started, my own time in jail, the heat that eroded patience, and families without savings, hungry and soon to be homeless.

"So you're wanting a donation, Lucia? Is that why you came?" she asked gently, without Mrs. Livingston's bitterness or hurt.

"Yes, ma'am. The workers are desperate. Anything you can give will help."

She looked at her husband, his mouth slowly opening and closing, chewing air. A foam of spittle glistened on his lower lip. It seemed so long ago that he watched as I kept his books, attentive, even playful. Once he reeled off twelve random prices for my adding machine. Before I could pull the heavy lever, he announced the sum: $187.63. "You see, Miss D'Angelo," he said, tapping his head, "it never leaves you, never, never."

Mrs. Kinney wiped away the spittle with a lacy handkerchief. "He'd be distressed to wake up soiled. You know what a gentleman he always—" She turned away.

"Yes, ma'am. He was a true gentleman." Her shoulders dropped, and regret surged through me. Why had I said "was"? How much pain pressed into that little word? "I'm so sorry, Mrs. Kinney."

"Oh, Lucia. I fought it at first, but yes, he *was* a gentleman." She straightened her back. "And he was very fond of you and would have wanted to help. Just a minute." She left me with Mr. Kinney nodding and Mamma a glaring statue. I listened to the slackening rain and first birds chirping. So often in the next weeks I recalled that lovely room filled with loss and quiet sympathy.

In the streetcar back to Cleveland, I unfolded the bank draft Mrs. Kinney had given me. Three hundred and fifty dollars. "Look," I whispered to Mamma. "See how much? Josephine will be pleased."

I think she smiled, but I wonder now how many smiles and comprehending looks I'd simply imagined. "Home?" she asked.

"Yes, we're going home now."

Josephine received the money gratefully, but it melted like ice on summer sidewalks, gone for soup kitchens, bandages, to pay fines for "disturbing the peace" and reward the few policemen who favored our cause.

Two German mechanics who had boarded with Roseanne left for better jobs in Chicago. She had us pay more each week until she filled the empty rooms. "What can I do, Lucia?" she demanded. "There's no work in town, and other landlords are throwing people out on the street. How long will you keep striking?"

"Until we get justice," I said, as we'd been drilled to say. I took a dime to Henryk for a watermelon to mollify Roseanne. He gave me a cup of ice as well.

"Try this," he said, running a cube against the back of his neck. I did the same and felt the cool, delicious trickle down my back. When our eyes met, I took my melon and hurried home. Sweat burned away the trickle but not the image that filled my mind that night: ice cubes melting on our hot and eager skin.

When the strike crawled on, I slipped two of Mamma's best vaudeville hats from her trunk and sold them. Walking at night, searching for cool pockets in the city, I heard from every window the whine of fretful, hungry children. People slept on roofs, porches, and patches of parched grass. Picketers fainted in the heat. A portly man who used to jeer at us didn't come one day. He'd collapsed on the stairs of his boardinghouse, Enrico announced importantly. "He cracked his head and died. People say he was nice enough before the strike. His wife is lame and he's out of work."

Josephine used the story at a night meeting. "He should have joined us. We would have cared for his wife. Brothers and sisters, you'll tell your children stories of the Cleveland Garment Workers' Strike of 1911. They'll wish they were here with us, with the six thousand."

"We aren't six thousand no more," cried a voice.

"We will be, when the owners start to crack. A little longer, brothers and sisters. Let's sing." We sang "Hard Times Come Again No More" and a rollicking ballad of Casey Jones, "The Eight-Hour Day" and "Tramp, Tramp, Tramp, the Boys Are Marching." We sang loudly, clapping and tramping until we were roused again to solidarity and hope. Men and women, Jews, Poles, Italians, Czechs, Russians, and Serbs linked arms for "The Battle Hymn of the Republic." Pride in all the good our country could hold and our place in America eased our aching feet. We could march tirelessly and no trouble seemed a sacrifice.

But after the meeting, as I swept the union hall, I saw Josephine and Isadore speaking together. The curve of their bodies filled me with dread.

## Chapter 17

## Germ Plasma

*August was my* bitter month in a smear of heat. I'd forgotten the feel of clothes that didn't stick like skin to my body. Coal dust, street dust, and the grime of factory smoke mixed with sweat. I couldn't keep clean. Ice prices rose steadily. There was no relief.

Even the peace of Ashtabula turned sour, for in the days after our return Mamma was consumed by a grim frenzy, terrible to watch and live with. She scrubbed the front steps as sweat streamed from her face. She tirelessly opened and closed windows, doors, and curtains as if seeking magic combinations to pull in breezes. She polished the player piano until Roseanne pulled her away, saying, "*Basta*, you're wearing it out."

I asked Dr. Ricci if our trip had caused this change. He passed a snowy handkerchief across his brow. "I'm sorry, Lucia. Sometimes we're like poor billiard players who can't predict where a ball will go. Singing to the Kinneys was a great step forward, but perhaps it brought back a difficult memory. Or the change might have come in any case."

"What should we do?"

"I can't prescribe more laudanum. You might tire her with walking. Try to be patient. This manic phase had a beginning and it will surely have an end."

"And the next phase?"

He sighed. "We don't know."

I repeated the line from Milton: "The mind is its own place."

"Yes, Lucia, it surely is."

At night, when the heat dulled a little, Mamma and I walked along Lake Erie. A hazy moon swam in charcoal water. Languid waves heaved against the pebbled shore. She'd kick one small stone and then frantically search for it to kick again. By turns, I'd help, feeling foolish, or try to stop her: "Mamma, please. Pick another. They're all the same." Or I'd simply watch her rummage, grateful nobody saw us. When I'd had enough, I hurried her home.

"What's the rush, girls? Where's the fire?" men called out from tavern doorsteps, but nobody troubled us. Perhaps they had no energy. Dripping with sweat, we hung our clothes to air, washed our faces and arms in rosemary water, and went to bed still damp, hoping for slips of cooling breeze. Mamma slept in ragged patches, rising early to cook with a great rattling of pans, opening and closing doors, knocking furniture around. Dark circles bloomed around my eyes from constant worry and wakefulness.

"She's bothering the boarders," Roseanne complained fretfully. "You have to make her stop or else put her someplace while she's like this."

"You mean the state hospital? You know what happens there, Roseanne."

"Well, there's a reason for these places if people can't be kept at home. Maybe your rich friends in Ashtabula can keep her for a while."

"No, they can't. I'll find a way."

"Do it quickly. Two men with good city jobs came by yesterday, and she spooked them. I can't afford this."

Donato's wife was working. I telephoned Charlie and Frank in Youngstown. Both were kind but couldn't help. Yolanda met customers at home for her hat business. "If they're uncomfortable, they won't come. I'm sorry, Lucia," Charlie said. Frank and Giovanna had a boarder, a new baby coming, and no space for Mamma. I went to see Enrico's mother, Angela, thinking to hire her help, but in the tiny, stifling flat, a cot in the kitchen held her oldest son, paralyzed from a fall in the limestone quarries. Her husband couldn't rouse himself for the picket lines but sat hunched on a chair, rocking on the warped wooden floor and lamenting the family's lost land in Calabria.

"If I had money, I'd give it to him for drink," Angela said. "At least get him out of the house. Now what did you want, Lucia?"

How could I add to her troubles? "Nothing. I just came to say what a blessing Enrico is, what a clever boy. When school starts in September, he must go. I'll help him with his homework once we win the strike."

"*When the strike's over,*" she corrected me, "when there's work again." The invalid groaned, and Angela hurried to his side.

"He needs changing," she said over her shoulder, "and he's ashamed with a stranger here. Excuse us please, Lucia."

I let myself out. *Think, think, who else could help?* Not the Reillys. Even if they'd softened after the birth of Maria Margaret, the silence of that flat would terrify Mamma. Father Stephen offered sympathy and prayers, but the church was a place of worship, not a sanitarium. She couldn't stay at Hiram House, Mr. Bellamy said firmly. Consider the donors who funded the nursery school and children's clubs. "What would come next, Miss D'Angelo? First lunatics wandering in the halls, then drunkards and the demented? Should we expose our innocents to the depraved and syphilitic?"

"No, sir, of course not," I muttered. When he asked why I couldn't care for my own mother at home, I reminded him of my work with the union and how the union helped parents give their children a better life.

"But your method is misguided. This strike *must* end. The violence is unacceptable. Businesses suffer. The city suffers. For their own good, the workers must return. You've read the *Plain Dealer*?"

Yes, I said wearily, I'd read the latest diatribe condemning scuffles, fights, and general disorder, never mentioning ruffians paid by the bosses to batter us with insults, pick fights, and overturn water barrels so picketers regularly fainted from thirst.

"Bring your mother to the marches," Josephine suggested. "Remember: long picket lines make short strikes." How could I risk this? If Mamma had attacked Dr. Galuppi and threatened to castrate Little Stingler, why wouldn't she return the first insult, hurled rock or bottle?

Roseanne gave me half a day to "make other arrangements." Heat evaporated all thought. Who could help me?

Dripping with sweat, I reached Henryk's shop. He gave me a glass of cool water from an earthenware jug. I drank gratefully. Perched on a stool, Miriam watched as wind from an electric fan ruffled her silky waves of hair. I listened dully as she explained how a motor drove the whirling blades. She used the fan in her bedroom at night and brought it to Henryk each morning. "You should get an electric fan, Lucia. After the strike ends, of course." For so long I'd been intimidated by her family, beauty, charm, and promised future with Henryk. Now all this hardly mattered. I thanked her for the suggestion and relayed my problem, the fruitless avenues I'd followed and now my desperation. Out of the fan's breezy path, Henryk stacked crates of beans.

"Roseanne's right. Your mother does have to be put someplace," Miriam interrupted. "You know how Americans are, Lucia," she reminded me in her sweet schoolteacher voice.

Frustration made me bold. "I know how *people* are. They think mental illness is shameful. They don't realize that anyone can get sick in *any* organ, even the head."

Miriam looked away.

"What about Lula?" Henryk suggested quietly. "She has a storeroom behind the tavern for deliveries. It's cool and clean. There's even a bed she uses sometimes."

*Of course, Lula!* I hurried over, spilling out my plea as she washed a rack of glasses. "I run a tavern, honey. Not a sanitarium. There's a difference, even if sometimes I'm not so sure."

"Just for a few days," I pleaded, "until this phase has passed. You don't have to do anything. She'd just stay here during the marches. The tavern's full of men, so she wouldn't leave the storeroom. She could knit."

"Knit? In this crazy heat?"

"Or clean." Now Lula seemed interested. "You'll be amazed. The copper, the brass, the windows; once she starts, your kitchen will shine. Or she'll sleep. Even if she opens and closes doors, there's already noise in the tavern."

"That's for sure. Could be she's no worse than my regulars. Well, just a few days, mind you." I tried to hug Lula. "None of that. It's too hot." She put her hands on my shoulders. "You want so much, Lucia. I don't mean you're greedy. It's just—you want so much."

"What do you mean?"

"Dunno, I'm just sure of it. Wanting ain't a bad thing, but some folks have a lot of it. You better run along. Roseanne's waiting, right?"

Early the next morning, I brought Mamma to Lula's with her

knitting. The tavern was full of "very bad men," I had stressed, and she must stay in the storeroom or kitchen. The clean, closed spaces seemed to comfort her.

"Teresa did just fine," Lula said after the first day. "She knitted some and cleaned my stove better than new. I don't even want to use it now. Then she slept, I guess. I didn't hear a thing." I took her to Lula's for the rest of the week.

Those were hard days on the picket line. "Europe scum, go back home," street boys chanted. The few suffragettes who sometimes cheered us ceased coming. "Our fight is for women's votes," they reminded Josephine. "We must conserve our energy." This was a blow. Well dressed and well connected, they had quelled the worst language and attacks with the mere fact of their presence. Now we walked a gauntlet of insults, hurled pebbles, and sometimes garbage.

"Don't stop, don't answer, don't look at them. Think of victory," Josephine and Isadore said. We dodged when we could. When we couldn't we showed our stained clothing, scrapes, and bruises to reporters standing in the shade and drinking beer provided by the manufacturers' association.

Pepe and Enrico marched in front, heads high, beating drums they'd fashioned from cans. The lilt of their step gave us heart. They wiggled into taverns with strikebreakers to bring back news we used to reroute our marches. Nobody begrudged them full votes in union business. Once, when Enrico came panting up with a message, his eyes glittering in triumph that he'd outrun "six big thugs," I hugged him. "Hey, what's that for?" he demanded. "It's just a message."

"If I ever have a boy, Enrico, I'd want one just like you."

He grinned indulgently. "Well sure, Lucia. Maybe after the strike, you'll get a nice Italian fella. Oh, I have to tell Isadore something." He was off again. I smoothed my skirt, turning away from two garment workers standing nearby.

"Hard times," one of them commented. "But we're all marching for 'after the strike,' aren't we? Take a break, Lucia. There's a respectable tavern around the corner. Come have a beer with us." I went. We shared stories from the picket line and passed an easy summer hour, the kind I'd thought had gone away.

*The next day* a lid of white clouds closed over the city. The air was a tepid sponge, thick and hard to walk through. We were marching in Public Square, having pleaded with those who'd left the union to come back for one more push. Loyal priests and rabbis helped: "Our Lord is a lord of justice and will help the righteous," they told the faithful. Strikers came in droves, despite heat and hunger.

Our spirits rose. We made a sport of dodging clods of horse manure thrown into the line until the ruffians ceased their game. Someone began old "Peg and Awl," a cobbler's lament for changing times. Our voices drowned the litany of insults: we were traitors, socialists, lazy, dirty parasites, Europe's trash. Looking straight ahead to avoid the red-faced hecklers, I never saw trouble coming until Josephine tried to jerk me clear of a man charging head down like a bull at a matador. I wasn't fast enough. He hit me full in the stomach. Doubled over, gasping, I heard Josephine call for witnesses.

In the chaos, I didn't see Mamma. Then I heard her roar, the power of her voice quelling all the others: "Get your filthy hands off my daughter. I'll kill you!" That morning I'd pinned her hair into a pompadour. Now it hung wild around her shoulders. Lula was pounding down the sidewalk after her. But Mamma ignored us both, leaping at the thug, tearing his shirt, grabbing his arm, biting. I saw blood. I heard Josephine calling for strikers to curtain off the melee. She and Lula closed their arms around me as police pushed through the line and seized Mamma.

"No!" I shouted. "She doesn't know what she's saying! She's my mother, she's not well, let her go!"

But Mamma was a tempest of hair and teeth, her voice billowing over the crowd: "Bastard cops, *bastards*. Castrate them all!" Now the police had words of their own: *hellcat, bitch, crazy wop*. The Black Maria came, bells and sirens tearing the air.

"Be quiet!" Josephine shouted in my ear. "If you get arrested too, who'll help her?"

Enrico stared. "Is *that* your mother, Lucia? Is she crazy?"

"She's—"

Mamma was howling: "Lucia, help me!" as the police handcuffed and shoved her into the Black Maria. Josephine pulled me back. Confusion roared all around: hecklers, union songs from farther up the picket line, and Josephine still shouting that I must keep calm, keep calm.

"That crazy bitch bit me," the strikebreaker cried, showing his bloody arm. Then one sound pierced every other: the iron door thudding closed, trapping my mother in the stifling chamber that had so terrified me. I fainted into hot darkness.

When I opened my eyes, Lula's face hovered over mine. Josephine was there and Enrico behind her. A sticky wetness covered my face. "It's beer," said Lula. "I asked for water and your little friend here"—she indicated Enrico—"went to one of those no-goods standing around, snatched his mug, and doused you. You're back, that's the important thing."

"And not arrested," Josephine added. Her voice came from far away.

"Where is she?"

"At the station by now; we'll go bail her out. But first you'd better change into something that doesn't smell like beer or they'll arrest you too."

The case might be tricky, Josephine explained as she and Lula walked me home. "She *did* draw blood. And everybody heard what she said. But we have witnesses that she was protecting you. Don't worry, Lucia."

"There was a crowd at the tavern, and she must have slipped out," Lula explained, breathing hard. "Folks were talking about the picket route, so she knew where to find you. I'm so sorry, Lucia. She'd been quiet for days and never set foot inside the tavern. I didn't expect her to bolt."

"Nobody knows what to expect," I said miserably. "It's not your fault." No, it was mine. I'd left her for what I'd held to be the greater cause, my union "brothers and sisters." What was she feeling now, trapped in a jail cell, abandoned by her daughter? What had the police said or done to her? How far was she spiraling down?

At the station with Josephine, I waited in agony as a clerk slowly searched his ledger for a Teresa D'Angelo. "Nobody by that name," he announced finally. "But we got an Italian female, age about thirty-five, medium height, dark green dress, gave her name as Teresa Esposito. Deranged and incoherent. Bit two officers here. Is that who you want?" I nodded. "Hey, Mac, where'd we send that crazy Eye-talian lady?" he called out.

"To the crazy house," someone answered. "Captain said no mad dogs at the station."

In the rolling peals of laughter, I nearly fainted again. Josephine rapped the counter sharply. "When you're quite finished with your jokes, exactly where can we find Teresa D'Angelo or Teresa Esposito?"

"Cleveland State Hospital," the clerk said after a last guffaw. When his eyes settled on my face, the smile quickly faded. "She's a relative, miss?"

"My mother."

"Well, that's where you'll find her. You want some water? You look a little pale. Never mind the boys. Long, hot day, you know."

"We'll be going," Josephine said crisply. "Thank you so much for your help."

*As we hurried* to Cleveland State, my mind swirled with sickening memories of Dr. Galuppi's experiments and the horrible photographs that Dr. Ricci had shown me. In a gray-green receiving room the pale clerk informed us that an Italian female, self-identified as Esposito, Teresa, would be under observation for a week on charges of criminal insanity. Visitors prohibited. Muffled howls wormed through the walls. When the clerk took up his pen again, discounting us, my fury rose like lava in Vesuvius.

"This is my *mother*, sir. She was defending me from attack, as any mother would. She is being treated by Dr. Ricci. She's not a deficient. She's not germ plasma. She was a star in Mr. B. F. Keith's Vaudeville Company. There's no need to keep her here. I can take care of her perfectly well."

"But you didn't 'take care of her perfectly well,' did you now, miss?" the clerk asked archly. "She bit a citizen and two peace officers. She's a danger to herself and the general public. Therefore she must be observed. Then, *if* she can be released, we'll determine if you are competent to keep her. You are employed?"

I was about to explain the strike when Josephine interceded: "She is a bookkeeper."

"You have a responsible male here in Cleveland? Husband, father, brother, someone?"

Outrage surged through me. Was I nobody without a man behind me? Josephine's foot pressed mine and I nodded.

"Good. Come back next week with a responsible male and you can discuss the matter with our doctor. We'll need a declaration that she'll be adequately confined at home, not roaming the streets, biting people."

"She is not a dog, sir! She wasn't—" Josephine pressed again and I was silent.

The clerk closed his ledger with a thud. "There's nothing more to discuss. Bring this receipt." I was given a slip of paper. Mamma was No. 4389F, received August 16, 1911. Like a dry goods shipment.

I endured the next week in an agony of waiting and fear. For distraction, I walked the picket lines, going by habit, for loyalty, and to pass the time. But I couldn't eat; food was sawdust in my mouth. Between marches and meetings, I circled the hospital, trying to pluck out my mother's voice from screams and howls cascading down from the barred windows. Was she being beaten or shackled? Was she being used like the "poor thing," pawed by an attendant? Were they spinning her? Was she locked day and night in a Taming Box?

I called guards to the gate, asking for news. They didn't know or wouldn't tell me about Teresa Esposito. When Enrico brought me ice in a paper cup on the picket line, the pleasure of it made me gag. Even in the wildly improbable case that she was being exquisitely treated, respected, and spoken to in her own language, Mamma knew where she was. How could this not worsen her condition? Each day brought an agony of imagination and helpless guilt.

Dr. Ricci was in New York meeting great doctors, his housekeeper said. But even if he were here, he couldn't swear that Mamma posed no danger to others or that he was making progress in curing her. I thanked the housekeeper and left.

Who would be my "responsible male"? Donato had taken his family to the country. Casimir apologized but couldn't leave his shop and perhaps feared too close association with a madwoman. Charlie and Frank couldn't leave their jobs, or wouldn't. A union brother would gladly help, Josephine said, but I couldn't bear to expose Mamma's story to one more stranger. Anguish tore away my reserve. I walked past Henryk's shop three times before I found him alone.

He considered the issue as calmly as if I'd asked which potatoes were best for boiling. "I can't be your father, obviously. Since we don't look alike, I can't be your brother. So I'll be your husband. Samuel can run the shop while I'm gone."

"What will you tell your father?"

"That I've gone out to the country for apples. It's getting harder and harder to find good ones. Don't worry, Lucia. Just think about your mother."

"And Miriam, what will she say?"

"She's in Pittsburgh again with her aunt." He put a strange inflection on *aunt,* but in my distraction I assumed he was only distressed that she was so often away. I left without thanking him. Shouts from the street reminded me of inmates' howls, and I wanted to be back in my own room, where Mamma's presence still lingered.

"You have to look important when you go," Roseanne declared, and loaned me a deep purple shirtwaist, severe and respectable, and even her own wedding ring. Yolanda had given me a lovely plumed hat. The night before, Lula brought over a fresh peach pie because, she said, "A girl can face anything better with my peach pie inside her."

Henryk came to the boardinghouse in a dark suit, his thick hair combed neatly back. "What a fine-looking couple," said Roseanne, but on the streetcar to the state hospital anyone would have thought we were headed to a funeral.

We got a shimmer of respect in the reception office. A gangly clerk took my receipt and had a silent inmate bring two chairs. He ran a long finger down a column in his ledger and tapped an entry: "Esposito, Teresa, No. 4389F. Recovering from surgery."

*Surgery!* I hadn't guessed this, not in all my grim imagining. "She was healthy when she came. What did you do to her?" I demanded.

The clerk looked startled, excused himself, and after a lengthy wait was replaced by a tall, broad-shouldered woman with a forward-jutting jaw who introduced herself as Nurse James. She snapped the ledger closed and turned on us. Were *we* the inmates now? I folded my gloved hands and leaned forward. Her eyes flicked away, then back.

"Mister and Missus—".

"Weiss," Henryk supplied. "Where is my mother-in-law?"

"Mr. and Mrs. Weiss," Nurse James began evenly, "the woman identified as Teresa Esposito has been surgically sterilized and is, as I said, recovering—"

I bolted to my feet. "Sterilized!"

"You'll sit, please, Mrs. Weiss. There is no cause for alarm," she continued with patronizing detachment. I have never hated a voice so much. "Sterilization is widely prescribed for the protection of society and the patients themselves, male and female. Normally, of course, we obtain the family's consent, but unfortunately there was some confusion. Two women of the same name, Teresa Esposito, are inmates in this institution. Your mother, case number 4389F, was given the surgery in place of"—she flipped open the ledger—"number 4289, who had been scheduled for the procedure."

"You butchered my mother *by mistake?*" The shrill knife edge of my voice cut the air. Henryk gripped my hand in warning.

"Mrs. Weiss," said Nurse James archly, "we 'butcher' nobody. This is a standard procedure, done under hospital conditions by an experienced surgeon. While in this instance, it may have been technically premature, it would have been advised in anticipation of any extended stay by a woman of fertile age. You can appreciate the practical benefits. Mental deficients are often promiscuous, breeding more of their kind."

"My mother was *not* promiscuous. In twenty years she has not had a single—"

"Then, you see, Mrs. Weiss, there is nothing lost if she cannot breed."

"We are not speaking of animals, Nurse James," Henryk said sharply. "Human beings do not 'breed.' "

"We are speaking of a deranged woman who bit a peaceful citizen."

"Peaceful? He was a hired goon attacking her daughter!"

"A citizen, Mr. Weiss," the nurse repeated, "and two officers." She leaned back. "As you know, there is rising concern regarding germ plasma entering this country from Europe and weakening good American stock."

"*Germ plasma?*" Henryk demanded. "That's what you call immigrants? Germ plasma? When did *your* people come here?"

"A rising number of recent immigrants become public charges, and many, as I say, actively breed more of their kind. Sterilization is advocated by some of our finest minds: captains of industry like Mr. Henry Ford and Mr. Rockefeller, senators, doctors, and scholars at Harvard and other great universities."

Fury lifted me off the chair again. "I don't care about great universities. You butchered my mother! You know nothing about her, nothing! Not even her name." Nurse James stood as well now. I followed her large eyes to a buzzer prominent on her desk. Doubtless it would call a guard. Could I end in shackles myself? I sat down. Was this how Mamma's fits possessed her, the churning frenzy to silence a smug, cool voice, to make a jutting jaw tremble? In a whisper so low I felt it through my skin, Henryk warned: "Lucia, remember why we're here."

I gripped my chair and lowered my voice. "Nurse James, you have my mother. May I see her now? I've come with my husband, who will sign the necessary papers."

"That is impossible. She's recovering."

"She can recover at home."

"There are charges against her. She needs to be evaluated."

"I should give you more time and risk another butchery, *by mistake?*"

Henryk sat forward, his voice low and hard. "There may be charges against this institution and against yourself, Nurse James, if it is widely known that records are so poorly kept that women are butchered at random; if the newspapers, for example, investigate this case, or if certain officials were informed."

"She was not *butchered,* sir." But the nurse's voice had weakened.

Henryk pressed on: "Very well, she was *mutilated* against her will, against her family's will. Do your patrons know this? Would they like to know this? And doesn't your director constantly seek public funds, warning that the wards are dangerously overcrowded? We'll take this patient off your hands. You should be grateful."

"She needs medical care."

"Of course, after her shameful treatment in this institution. Nurse James, release her *now.*"

The woman opened and closed her mouth, took in Henryk's good suit and neatly brushed hair, my dress, hat, and gloves. She made a show of examining her ledger and finally said, "Wait here."

We waited an hour in that airless gray office. "Try to sit down, Lucia," Henryk said. "Tell me about Naples." He kept me talking until the nurse returned, pushing a woman in a rattling wheelchair. We gasped aloud.

My mother's face was bruised, her hair shorn. She was dressed in a shapeless gray gown, bent over, arms wrapped around her belly.

I knelt by the chair. "Oh, Mamma."

"Bastard—wore a mask," she said in a terrible voice, low and toneless.

Glancing at Nurse James, Henryk touched my mother's shoulder and began, "Mamma Teresa—"

She jerked away, growling: "He cut me."

"Yes, Mamma. We're so sorry." I turned to Nurse James. "We'll be going now."

Henryk took the handles of the wheelchair. "We'll need this to get her home. Obviously she can't walk. I'll return it later."

Nurse James opened her mouth to protest, closed it, then blurted: "There are papers to sign, sir. You'll have to assume responsibility for the inmate's care."

"Where are they?" he said sharply. "Bring them to me."

Henryk quickly signed pages of tight script, arranged for a taxicab, and helped me get my mother home and into bed. How could I begin to thank him? "Henryk, I don't—"

He took my hand. "Lucia, it's nothing. Anyone else would have done the same for you."

"But *anyone* didn't, only you."

He shrugged. "Then they're fools. I have to get some apples now. I'll come back later."

I got Hilda the midwife to examine Mamma, for I wanted only women near her. The cut was clean, at least, and not infected. They had "only" severed the Fallopian tubes and not performed a hysterectomy. Still, she'd be bedridden for days as the incision healed. Hilda looked sadly into Mamma's beaten face. "The other healing will take longer."

I combed the remains of her beautiful hair and fed her broth that

Roseanne brought upstairs. After she'd turned from me to face the wall and shuddered into fitful sleep, I stood at our window, breathing the thick night air. How long could I keep our secret from my oldest friend? This silence had to end.

I got a glass of water from the kitchen, took out an ink bottle and sheets of onionskin paper, filled my pen, and moved the chair to catch a thread of breeze. Then I undressed to a cotton chemise, straightened my desk, and when I could think up no more excuses, began: "Dear Contessa Elisabetta." I stopped. *Tell her. Write it down.* "My mother is very sick. You remember what we called her 'fits.' They became worse in the last years. Now she is afflicted by—" The pen froze. I made myself write: "hysteria and paranoia. The doctor fears she may not recover. It's true that she was happy at first in vaudeville, but nearly a year ago she had a nervous collapse and was sent home in handcuffs. It is for this reason that I left college. She believes that Maestro Arturo Toscanini follows her everywhere. She barely speaks and cannot control her behavior."

I walked around the room, stood at the window, and finally sat again. I described my struggle to keep Mamma safe and how I had failed at this task. "They took her to a hospital, a horrible place such as Dr. Galuppi would relish. There she was sterilized. If you saw your Teresa now, you would not know her. Pray for us. These are difficult times in America."

After these few pages my fingers cramped around the pen; my arm throbbed, and the paper was damp with sweat. Weeks might pass before an answer, but writing the countess had been like the slow release of a volcano, letting pent-up lava run harmlessly down the sides.

I slept more easily that night and stayed home for the rest of the week. Mamma stared at the ceiling and walls. Her eyes skittered across my face. When she spoke, it was a toneless drone against "the bastards," as if memories of all those who had hurt her were spreading like a stain, absorbing the man who had pushed her into the seaweed, Toscanini, Little Stingler, the surgeon who cut her, and now random men she spied from our window.

I ceased trying to reason with her and cared only for the wounded body. The red gash across her belly was pointing us both to a new land.

## Chapter 18

## DUSK BY ERIE

*September dulled the* press of heat, but still ice prices rose in the parched city. Underground storehouses in Michigan and New York were exhausted by the summer's heat, and, after the long trek from Canada, blocks arrived half melted. "It's not our fault! Ice costs, straw costs, barges cost, and we're not running a charity," icemen insisted when customers cursed them. Stones were hurled at wagons. Looking for culprits, icemen saw only grim-faced children or women standing by the road, empty-handed.

Like widening circles from pebbles thrown in water, troubles spread across the immigrant quarters. Nursing mothers exhausted by heat and hunger lost their milk. "What do I give my baby now?" they demanded at union meetings.

I appealed to Mr. Bellamy. "For this cause," he vowed, "I'll move heaven and earth." He did, wheedling funds from patrons to buy dairy milk and enough of the costly ice to keep it fresh.

"Look at that," said Josephine. "You have power."

"Not really, if I can't help my own mother."

When Dr. Ricci finally returned from New York and received my message, he hurried to the boardinghouse, but Mamma wouldn't turn from the wall or speak.

In the parlor, with the door closed, I described her treatment to the doctor. His kind face darkened. "There is no excuse, none!" he said fiercely. "Even if she were promiscuous, even then, to have robbed her of the chance for motherhood without consent or knowledge, *by mistake*, because one Italian woman is the same as the next to them, it's beastly. But these places *are* beastly. The filth and crowding and hellish noise, the mass of insane, demented, aged, and imbeciles, drunks and criminals crowded together strips the best doctor of his humanity. He forgets his calling. Feeling that he's among beasts, he becomes a beast himself. A beast with a scalpel. And your mother was subject to this."

I sighed. "What can be done?"

"For other men and women, we can try to stop this curse of sterilization. I'll write the director and the governor and protest her treatment. For Teresa, I'll go to the police, describe her, and give them my card. If she's arrested again, we'll be warned. Send for me when she's willing to talk. For now all we can do is let time bring its healing."

Everyone was sorry. Roseanne berated herself for having forced me to find day lodging. "But since now she's . . ."

"Catatonic."

"Yes, that, I can watch her, poor creature, when you're on your strike."

*My* strike? I seemed to watch the world through glass. Even union songs and chants couldn't lift my heart now when my mother's very presence seemed insubstantial, as if she might at any minute cease to be or melt away. I made her eat, bathed her, put yarn and needles in her hands, closed mine around hers, and had her "knit," cursing my clumsiness, for she was visibly pained when we dropped a stitch. At night she pointed wildly at the bedroom window. What did she see: Maestro Toscanini, the doctor who cut her, or only the beckoning darkness?

With whom could I speak in those days? Not Henryk in my dismal state, grateful as I was for his help in rescuing her. Not Yolanda or Giovanna. Nestled in their domesticity, how could they understand us? Josephine and Isadore were consumed by "the final push." Lula was racked by guilt that she had let my mother escape. How could I increase her pain? I'd expected an answer from Countess Elisabetta by now, but nothing came from Naples. Perhaps she was traveling. Or perhaps, like so many Americans, she feared the contagion of madness, even by post and across the ocean.

I was becoming as reclusive as Mamma when Roseanne ordered me downstairs to speak with a visitor in the parlor. It was Enrico. Strike rations had thinned his body and sharpened the lines of his face, but I couldn't help smiling at the soldier stiffness of his shoulders and his air of solemn importance.

"The first message," he announced, "is that Josephine says you *must* come back to the pickets. The path is not easy, but together we *will* win. The cause of the ILGWU is greater than any of us, and to be a part of this greatness makes us strong." He let out a long breath after his feat of memory.

"Thank you, Enrico. You know, if you can learn all that, you can easily learn your times tables at school."

"Maybe." He relaxed a little. "I might go back after the strike. Here's the second message. It's from Lula: you need to get your skinny self down to the tavern 'cause she's got some news." He grinned. "So now me and Pepe are going fishing at the lake."

"You mean 'Pepe and I.'"

"Yeah, us two." But he didn't go right then. The smooth brow furrowed and he stepped closer. "Lucia, you really don't look so good. Maybe you *should* come to the union hall like Josephine says. To get your mind off—" He glanced at the stairs.

"Other things?" I prompted.

"Right, other things. Well, Pepe's waiting." And he was gone in a whirl of churning legs.

So I went to the tavern with a bucket from Roseanne to fill with beer. Lula drew me aside. "Listen. You know how your friend Henryk's Miriam is always going to Pittsburgh to see her aunt?"

"Yes. The aunt is sick and Miriam's the only one she wants around her."

"Hum. I don't know about 'sick.' What I *do* know is this aunt has a young cousin, a bachelor, and this young bachelor cousin owns a bank." Lula folded her arms. "Did you hear me, girl?"

"Yes," I said dully, "the aunt's cousin owns a bank."

"Well, don't you think Miriam wants a bank? One of my regulars says *he's* the reason she goes to Pittsburgh. He gave her a diamond as big as your eye. And whatever her family owes Henryk's family for whatever they did in the Old Country, this banker can pay off easy. My regular says Henryk's father's so angry, it's like the girl was cheating on *him*."

Another time, this news would have mattered. Lula sighed. "I know, you can't forgive me for what happened at that place."

"It's not that." No, I couldn't be angry with Lula. Soon or later, my mother might have found her way to a madhouse, as surely as water is drawn to whirlpools. "I just can't think about fellas now. Like you said, maybe this isn't my time."

"I know, honey. Fact is, I just wanted to see your pretty face and get you out of that house."

"Thank you, Lula. And I am getting out. I'm going to the union hall tonight." I filled the bucket, brought it home, and made myself go to the hall. Still, I avoided Henryk's shop. Angry as his father was with Miriam, wouldn't he be more enraged by a girl who entangled his son with a lunatic?

A restive speaker at the union hall claimed to be a member, although I'd never seen him on the picket lines. He called himself Mel and accused the union sisters of acting too ladylike. "It's like you're wearing fancy dresses instead of making them. If you want victory, you gotta fight for it. Fight back! Fight back! Fight back!" Soon the hall was shouting too: "Fight back! Fight back! Fight back!"

Isadore began rousing union songs that finally overwhelmed the pounding chant. "We *will* fight, brothers and sisters," he promised, "for justice, not for anarchy. We are workers, not rabble."

But Mel's chant had charged the room. People were tired, hot, and hungry, weary of waiting for victory. I knew he was wrong, that fighting would only win us jail cells, yet it was something to do, some shift in our apparent stalemate. "Where'd he come from?" Josephine demanded as we gathered in a smaller group after the meeting. When Enrico offered to follow Mel, I quickly said I'd go along.

"Good idea," said Josephine. "Don't let him see you, but if he does, just say you're taking your little brother home."

We trailed Mel to an office building where the Cleveland Manufacturers' Association met. Hidden in a shaded doorway, we watched him speak to a man in a homburg hat, take an envelope that he slipped into his pocket, and then hurry away.

A small, warm hand slipped into mine. "Lucia, sometimes I'm scared."

"Me too, Enrico."

"What if the strike doesn't work?"

"We can't think that way," I whispered back. "Come on, it's late and your mother will be worried."

Like sparks on dry leaves, fights were breaking out everywhere that week: in taverns and soup kitchen lines, on stairways of apartment buildings where some supported the strike and others did not. When I saw Mrs. Reilly on the street, she first shared the latest adorable saying of little Maria Margaret before lowering her voice in warning: "Lucia, everyone says the strike isn't working. People just *have* to go back to work."

In the end, it was ice that changed so much, or rather a lack of ice. Icemen went on strike, infuriating Josephine and Isadore, who feared the city would turn against all workers now. In fact, newspapers throbbed with warnings of general strikes, anarchy, and Cleveland held hostage to socialist demands.

I was working at the union hall when Pepe came pounding in. "Mob at the icehouse. Enrico's there," he gasped.

Josephine ran with me. The icehouse wasn't far, but my chest burned as we drew nearer. A boiling crowd spread out from the warehouse steps, swearing there was ice inside not being released. "You're holding it to push up the price," a woman shouted.

"That's not true," the guard was saying. "I don't have *any*, but there's five tons coming tomorrow."

"What'll it cost then?"

Josephine stopped, took a breath, and shouted: "Brothers and sisters, let's talk to the bosses, not the workers!" The magic of her voice could calm any crowd, I told myself. People would listen. They'd calm down and go away. But afterward, few remembered that she was even there.

"We want ice *now*!" a man shouted.

I heard Enrico's high, clear voice: "He *said* they'll have a shipment tomorrow." Was he alone inside an angry mob? I pressed my way into a hot thicket of bodies.

"Look out!" someone said. Talk stopped as a brick sailed overhead, flying as if winged, smashing a high window to leave a black hole, a gaping O. Cheers exploded. Did they think cool air would pour out, chilling the city? Rhythmic clapping joined a menacing chant: "We want ice! Ice now! Ice now! Ice now!" I thought I saw Mel; certainly I heard his driving voice: "Ice now! Ice now! Ice now!"

Josephine cried: "Come back, Lucia. Pepe's getting the police." But the station was blocks away. Could they come in time? Wearied by endless calls to settle fights, would they even try? Burrowing frantically through the crowd, I finally glimpsed Enrico's rough curls. He was standing on the icehouse steps. For an instant, pride lifted me over fear. "The man said we'd have ice tomorrow," he was calmly reminding the women in front of the crowd. "Let's go home. The guard can't help. We'll talk to the bosses tomorrow." A woman in a red shawl stopped chanting and looked at him, considering. He could do it! A child could truly calm this crowd!

He saw me and smiled. I'll remember forever those bright eyes and that hand raised in greeting. He pointed to the woman who was saying to her friend: "He's right, Sarah. It's not the guard's fault. Let's go."

"Come with us, Enrico," I said. "Josephine needs you." I saw his worn shoe lift, about to step down, then pause and move backward, up a step. Now he was at eye level with the adults.

His voice rose. "Listen, everybody, let's just—"

A man cried out: "Get outta there, kid!"

"Enrico, come down," I hissed. "It's dangerous."

Behind me, a chant was swelling: "Ice now. Ice now. Ice now." Mel! Where was he? Turning to look, I saw the brick instead. How could I see it so clearly, turning so slowly?

"Enrico!" And then louder, shrieking, tearing my throat: *"Get down!"* But his eye must have been caught by the woman's red shawl disappearing into the crowd.

The brick met his bright, upturned face. A horrible jerk back of the neck like a breaking doll. The slender body spun down, headfirst on stone steps, bouncing. Racing forward, I caught the last jerked flail as Enrico tumbled limp into my arms, one side of his face a bloody mass. The other side was perfect, the eye glazed, slightly astonished. I reached for his hand. Perhaps it closed around mine. Perhaps I only imagined this from gripping his so tightly.

"She can still hear," Sister Margaret had said when Irena was passing. "Enrico," I whispered in his perfect ear, "don't worry, we'll save you. You'll go fishing with Pepe. You'll go to school." In the midst of horror so great, what's left to trust but miracles?

The crowd was deadly calm around us. A man pulled off his shirt and wadded it under the bleeding head. "Get a doctor!" I shouted. "Go!"

"Sure, a doctor's coming, or a nurse," the man said slowly, as one might speak to a child or crazy person. He removed his cap. He was a big man with an Irish voice that rolled over me: "The Lord is my shepherd, I shall not want. He maketh me to lie down in green pastures. He leadeth me beside the still waters." *Why is he doing this?* But I recited the psalm with him, slipping into Italian. Some joined us in English, others in their languages. Dark blood flowed over my hands; the glazed eye rolled back. "Surely goodness and mercy shall follow me all the days of my life."

Now a woman was kneeling beside me. "I'm a nurse," she whispered. Clean hands moved over Enrico's slender body, touching his chest and neck, closing the eye.

The man reached out long arms. "I'll take him home."

The woman with the red shawl wrapped Enrico. "So the mother won't see his face right off." She helped me stand. Now we were all moving, a slow river flowing toward Enrico's house. The woman's voice never stopped, gentle and insistent, leading me on: "You're Lucia, aren't you? I saw you at the union meetings. Step down here. *Brava.* This way, we're turning. Shall we rest a minute?"

"Take the shawl away. He can't breathe."

"Later, dear. We'll do it later."

Someone must have run ahead. Angela and her husband met us in the street. Neighbors had cleared the kitchen table to lay out the little body. A priest was called. A woman brought Pepe and then led him away, holding him tightly against her side. The thin shoulders heaved. People moved silently, as if in a picture show. Sitting in a corner of the crowded kitchen, I watched them come shuffling forward to gently touch Enrico and say a word to his family. So many knew him. He had brought them messages; they'd sent him on errands and watched him put up union signs and beat his drum at marches.

"For ice, can you imagine? He died for ice," I heard over and over.

Then Isadore and Josephine were beside me, one at each arm. "Lucia, we're taking you home."

"No."

"Yes. It's time."

At the boardinghouse they maneuvered me to the parlor, where I folded like paper into the divan. The news must have flown through the air like bricks. Roseanne brought a wet cloth for my head. When Isadore and Josephine left, images of the child came at me like cards: Enrico flushed with pleasure when he outran "six thugs," the guilty face when I first caught him turning over ash cans. Enrico in our kitchen when I persuaded him to help the strike. Persuaded? Hadn't I threatened him?

Enrico drumming, marching, skittering along picket lines with messages, pasting signs on walls, handing out notices, standing tall in our parlor to give his last message. His warm hand in mine as we followed Mel. Enrico at the icehouse, smiling at me. The brick. Enrico falling, bloody. A red shawl over the astonished young face.

Then I was crying. The sound brought Mamma downstairs, running her hands along the walls as she eased into the parlor, touching me curiously, as if recalling what tears might mean. "With a brick," I sobbed. "That beautiful, beautiful child. Why couldn't I leave him turning over ash cans?"

Roseanne held me. "Lucia, control yourself. You didn't throw the brick. You didn't hurt him. It's not your fault. You don't want to be—" She glanced at Mamma. *Like her,* she meant, *crazy.*

*I lost myself* in busyness, for when I stopped, the bloody face loomed before me. I translated for Josephine and Italian icemen. I went with her to the ice dealers, who finally agreed to a small reduction in price. Because Enrico's family had no funds for a coffin and headstone, I wrote an appeal. Casimir and Anna gave generously, remembering Irena's common grave. None of this brought comfort or relief.

Enrico's funeral brought the shamed city together, filling the sanctuary with strikers and non-strikers, Lula and many of her regulars, Henryk and his family, and the boys' club that I'd cajoled Enrico and Pepe into joining. I thought I saw Mel in a corner scanning the crowd, but when I looked again, he was gone. Had I conjured him? Was he my imagined Toscanini?

"Lucia," said Roseanne severely when I said I might have seen Mel, "you promised to control yourself." There was no control. The peace of Enrico's funeral passed quickly and the city itself swirled into madness. A strikebreaker was found stabbed. Sidewalks shimmered with broken glass. Perhaps *I* was part of the seep of germ plasma. Hadn't I pushed Enrico into the union, stored my mother in a tavern, setting her on a path to the asylum and from there to the cutting room?

"Stop!" Father Stephen ordered when I confessed my sins. "Think of the good you've done. Think of Pepe going to school in Enrico's place. Think of the funeral, so many lives touched by one child. Perhaps you have been called to this work, more than to a life of study."

"The work of killing children, Father?"

"Lucia! You must seek peace within yourself, the peace that passes understanding."

I tried.

"Teresa is healed enough to walk," said Hilda. "And it would do her good. Take her to Lake Erie. She can if you walk slowly and rest when she tires. You both need some air."

Late in the afternoon we made our way to the lake and walked east along the shore to a log pile near the water, where we sat. An abandoned warehouse fronted the lake, every window gone. "Look, it's like Palazzo Donn'Anna in Naples," I said dreamily. Mamma shrugged, as if she didn't remember the palazzo whose tale she'd told a hundred times. Had all the old stories had been cut away from her too? She looked around anxiously.

"Toscanini's not here," I said. "We're alone." She closed her eyes, shutting herself away. I was alone too, imagining fishermen at the palazzo. Did they know why servants roused them from that silky bed? Might they have heard the whispered stories, and did they perhaps walk almost willingly to the window in the early light? Were they pushed, or did they jump into the sea and rocks below? Why not? What end could a poor fisherman expect but water? What other pleasures in his miserable life could equal those he'd known that night? Why struggle on?

But the fishermen made their choices long ago. What of *us,* the germ plasma? All that Mamma and I had attempted in America had failed: college, vaudeville, and perhaps the strike as well. I hadn't saved Irena. What had my care of Mamma brought but a gash across her belly? Enrico had been happy enough before I set out to reform him. The thread I'd supplied to Giovanna had cost her job at Printz-Biederman and sent her into a terrible fire.

Father Stephen's consolations sank below dark waters as years of loneliness rolled before me. Lula was wrong; this was no "time" of being alone. This was my gateway to a life of endless solitude. The easy coupling that Yolanda and Giovanna enjoyed was impossible for me, shackled to a hopeless lunatic. Henryk had played my husband out of kindness, but he was right: any decent man can be kind for an afternoon. And what of Mamma? Dr. Ricci hadn't promised a cure even before her last assault. If a young fisherman felt doomed to draw up empty nets forever, why *not* walk to a tall window, mount the ledge, and leap, joining the mermaids forever?

Months of troubled sleep had dulled my mind, swirled my thoughts, and shaken my faith. Over the dark western rim of the lake, purple rimmed a towering cloud. I watched its summit slowly build to a cone. Was Vesuvius calling us home? Perhaps this was *our* high window, *our* leap to the end of despair, like burning girls at the Triangle factory. It would be so easy. Just walk to Vesuvius. Why not?

The strike would succeed or fail without me. Nothing could touch Enrico now. Henryk would find himself a faithful Jewish girl. Giovanna was settled and healing. Dr. Ricci would write an outraged report linking the doctors' careless arrogance to Mamma's death. Some might recall her vaudeville life or my little time in college. One woman would weep for us in Ashtabula, two in Youngstown, another in Naples, and my friends in Cleveland, but Roseanne would clean our room and rent it out again.

Three men had climbed onto an abandoned pier, sharing a bottle. Even if they noticed two figures walking resolutely into the lake, what could they do, so far away? The soft rim of Vesuvius blazed. It would fade soon and we must hurry.

I shook my mother's shoulder. "It's time to go." I believe she understood me. Why else would she have sat up? I took off my shoes and stockings and then hers. The habits of poverty are so strong: protect your shoes, they cost so much. We stood, and she took my hand like a trusting child. For an instant that trust made me falter. By what right did I make this choice for her? Yet what truly lay ahead for us besides more mistakes and failures? "It's better this way, isn't it, Mamma?" She turned to me. Golden light across her face made her beautiful again. She seemed to nod. I told myself that she nodded.

In water to our knees, I pointed to the cloud. "See, Mamma, it's Vesuvius. We're going there. Nobody will cut you again. Just a little more and we're home." Walking carefully through sucking mud, we were thigh-deep when a distant freighter sent chill waves splashing at our waists.

Holy Mary, Mother of God, thank you for that chill. Mamma's arms wrapped around her wounded belly, a simple act that shook my resolve. She still had enough aliveness to seek warmth. If we went farther and the heedless water stung her scar, what then? I slipped in mud. My feet found solid ground to hold us both, and we stood there a long time. Was I waiting for our bodies to absorb the chill, for my resolve to strengthen or for it to fall away? All I remember is an empty space of waiting.

As waves gently lapped us, a song floated over the water. From where? Oh, yes, those men on the pier, waving their bottle and rocking side to side, singing "Take Me Out to the Ball Game." That silly song. What difference did it or any song make now? And why, of all the possible tunes, should this one be our last? But Mamma turned her head to the music, solemn and attentive as a bird, pulsing with the clocklike beat. "Take me out to the ball game. Take me out with the crowd," she whispered, the words coming slowly, yet each a little louder.

I sang softly with her: "Buy me some pea-nuts and Crac-ker Jack." Our arms wrapped around each other in the rocking waves. "I don't care if I ne-ver get back." In the deepening dusk, a stray beam lit her eyes, tiny brimming lakes. She grimaced, and I nearly laughed, knowing what pained her: my terrible voice. Still I went on singing, and she too: "Let me root, root, root for the home team. If they don't win it's a shame."

The Vesuvius cone was flattening, its purple rim fading to charcoal. My resolve was fading. "Are you cold, Mamma? Shall we go home?" She nodded. We turned around and carefully picked our way to shore. An evening breeze was coming, and a second freighter sent new waves against us. We hurried, skimming over mud. On land again, we found our shoes and stockings, put them on, and walked quickly home, wet skirts slapping against our thighs.

"What happened to you?" Roseanne demanded at the door.

"Nothing. We went wading in Lake Erie."

"Wading in your clothes? Wet and walking in the wind! You're crazy! You want to get pneumonia and die?" I hugged her, and she stepped back, stunned. "Are you drunk, Lucia D'Angelo?"

"No. I just love when you talk about wind. Never mind, we're going to take our baths now. I know it's not our day." She stared after us, shaking her head.

I brought Mamma upstairs and drew her hot water. Exactly as before, she took my ministrations silently, neither helping nor protesting. That night in bed, she turned as always to the fading wallpaper. Yet she was *here*, and I beside her. I whispered thanks into the blessed night for the waves, the freighter, and the drunkards' song.

We woke to astonishing chill. Walking to the union hall, I passed men, women, and children in the street smiling and greeting neighbors. "It's cool!" they said in wonder. "And look at the sky!" It was clear blue, fresh against leaves shaken clean of the summer's dust. That afternoon, blankets fluttered on clotheslines, shedding the camphor of summer storage.

*Chapter 19*

## CORSETS IN KALAMAZOO

*When two people* from the same Old Country village meet by chance in America, a special bond unites them, close as no other. In the days after I led Mamma into Lake Erie and back, she often turned on me a piercing, knowing glance. We had been to a dark and secret place together where most had never gone. She grew less skittish around me. I was more patient with her—and more watchful of myself.

"You must be stronger, Lucia," Dr. Ricci warned. He was right. Often now, I imagined sinking through dark waters as floating leaves blocked the sky. I sometimes heard beguiling whispers: *You could try again, you know. The water's always there.* Sometimes by evening I barely remembered how I'd spent my day.

I often awoke, sweating, with Enrico's bloody face floating over mine. I learned to slip outside until the chill darkness brought back his other, eager, happy faces. Or I'd go to the dining room and work problems in mathematics until I'd worked myself back to peace. I had convinced Pepe to go back to school and reminded him of the many professions in Cleveland in which immigrant children had prospered. "You want too much for me," he grumbled, but promised to work hard and do his friend Enrico proud.

I bought good yarn and cajoled Mamma into knitting a shawl for Roseanne. She settled herself at our window overlooking a tapestry of leaves slowly turning red, orange, and amber. She'd never had the leisure to truly enjoy this American marvel, I realized with a guilty jolt. In other autumns she'd worked through the daylight hours or shuttled between stage, dressing room, and hotel. When could she watch trees?

She no longer cooked, for a morbid fear of knives had joined her other neuroses, but the dusting and polishing were even more relentlessly thorough. "Look!" Roseanne commanded prospective tenants. "You can't find a speck of dust in my house, not a speck."

With Mamma knitting and cleaning, I went back to the union meetings. The first night I watched children playing at the edge of the great hall, imagining Enrico with them, organizing a game. Who was the lunatic now? No, no, this was merely grief. Didn't people often glimpse the dear departed in familiar places? *Listen to speeches. Don't watch children.*

Isadore was reporting that garment makers had taken out loans to cover their losses and pay the strikebreakers. "You see? They're in trouble."

"So are we," returned voices from the floor. "We're four months without salaries, Isadore. We're hungry and winter's coming" Still, a slim majority voted to keep striking. After long debate, we determined a new tactic: wearing white and marching silently. Why bother shouting our demands? They were certainly known by now. Who could object to a peaceful witness for justice? In fact, when a man with his cap pulled low lunged at a line of women, bystanders yanked him back, chiding: "Give 'em a break, buster. They ain't bothering you."

Even the hecklers drifted away. Were they weary of their game or no longer bribed to keep up a gauntlet of abuse? Perhaps we'd shamed them. An anonymous donor, I assumed the Livingstons, gave a hundred dollars for striking families. The money passed quickly through our soup kitchen. "It's only beans and a little bread," the cooks complained. But at least we had food for another week.

I'd finished my cameo money, and Roseanne again recited her many favors. A few days after newspapers praised our white marches, Mrs. Kinney sent me thirty dollars. "I know these are difficult times," she wrote. "We're so sorry about the boy at the icehouse." When I showed the letter to Pepe, he whistled. "People knew Enrico all the way in Ashtabula!"

The silent pickets soothed me. Here was comfort and company. Linking arms with others who had their own sorrows, I found my mind straying less often to dark places. I slept better at night and woke stronger in the morning. "Suppose we'd started the white marches earlier?" I asked Josephine.

"Hmm." She scribbled this thought in her brown notebook. Lately she had been having me write letters to thank supporters or seek more funds. "I'm sure it's fine," she'd say, signing her name before reading. She watched me figure strike pay, order supplies for the soup kitchen, and encourage weary strikers. "You'd really go back to bookkeeping?" she asked one evening.

"What else can I do?"

"You could help organize a strike in Michigan."

A thrill rose and fell in me. "You know I can't leave Mamma."

"That's a pity."

October 14, Josephine and I were arrested for obstructing a public sidewalk. Even the policeman handcuffing us acknowledged the "obstruction" was trivial: I was steadying Josephine as she bent to tie her shoelaces. "Captain's rules, not mine, ladies."

"Since when is tying your shoes a crime?" Josephine demanded.

"Obstruction is obstruction, ma'am." The officer had us step aside as he whistled for a Black Maria.

Pepe ran up, tugging my skirt and whispering: "I'll tell Roseanne so your mamma doesn't worry. I'll tell Isadore too."

"Thank you, Pepe. But you better go now. Don't obstruct the sidewalk."

As he was darting off, the officer caught his shoulder. "Hey kid, weren't you pals with that boy at the icehouse?"

Pepe twisted to glance at Josephine, who nodded. "Yes, sir. Enrico was my best friend."

"And you are?"

"Pepe, sir."

"Well, Pepe, I'm real sorry about what happened. Heat makes folks act crazy sometimes." He fished two quarters from his pocket. "Here's one for your ma and one for you."

"Thanks a lot, Copper. Can I go now?"

Looking into bright, round eyes, the officer added another quarter and gave Pepe a gentle push. "Okay, scram before the captain sees you."

The Black Maria came. My second journey in that dark, airless box was less fearful. I knew to sit quietly. What else could one do? As before, we were measured at the station, photographed, solemnly informed of our crime, and told we'd have dinner soon. "How lovely," said Josephine. "Could that be beans and bread? Such an improvement over the union hall, right, Lucia?"

"Yes, so much better than bread and beans."

"Very funny, you two," said the officer. "Here's your cell. You can

sing, tell jokes, whatever you want. You've got it almost to yourselves."
Two disheveled women were curled together in a corner like puppies,
lightly snoring. Soon after, a guard brought us dinner on tin plates and
another two for "the sleeping beauties."

"Isadore will bail us out after the meeting," said Josephine when the
guard left us. "He's calling for a vote tonight. I'd like to be there, but
it doesn't matter. We're going to lose the vote. The strike will be over
tomorrow."

I stared. "How do you know? We had a majority a few days ago."

"We *barely* had one and it's gone now. We can't keep asking people to
sacrifice. Tonight they'll vote not to. I'm sure of it."

I'd never seen her like this, so calm, as if we were speaking of another
city's troubles. The strike had been my world since early June. Could it
be over so suddenly, like a summer storm?

"But the white marches were working. Didn't you say so yourself?"

"They *were* good, and we'll use them next time, maybe earlier. But
*this* strike is over. The owners promised to hire everyone back at the
same wages and terms. No reprisals at least." She leaned against the
brick wall, spent.

"The owners promised? You *talked* to them?"

"We've been negotiating. I'm sorry, Lucia. We had to do it secretly."

I put down the plate. My eyes burned. So much hunger, so many
sacrifices. Constantly telling ourselves we could win, urging women to
march one more time, one more time. I saw Enrico's bright face, then his
bloodied face, and finally the rigid little body before his casket closed.
The tears came now, sheets of them falling silently. Josephine gave me a
handkerchief and wrapped her arm around my shoulder.

"I know what you're thinking," she said finally, "that because we're
going back, we lost everything." I nodded. "But it's not like that. We
aren't stopping. In another city, in the next strike or the next one we'll

win. Workers will get a fifty-, even a forty-five-hour week. We'll keep going forward, for Enrico, for everyone who marched and all who couldn't. The owners suffered too: remember the loans they took out? They never expected us to last this long. Next time, they know we'll do better."

"Why will we do better?"

"Because of all the groups that *didn't* help us. If just one of those had been with us, we might have won. If the Cuyahoga County Women's Suffrage Association or the Women's Christian Temperance Union, the YMCA or the Federation for Jewish Charities had supported us, the others might have too. Imagine if they marched with banners or took out a notice in the *Plain Dealer*. Suppose we'd had a mink brigade of rich women like in New York? The owners would have noticed. If we'd had the newspaper editors on our side, if churches and synagogues had spoken more openly or the summer was cooler or the Bohemians had been here longer and felt more American, we might have won. Perhaps we moved too quickly after the Triangle Shirtwaist fire. We should have planned better to be sure of our allies."

"If we'd tried the white marches earlier," I said, joining the swell of possibilities.

She smiled. "You see? And even if the strike is over, we didn't completely lose. *You* changed, Lucia. Others changed. Don't you feel it?" She picked up her plate again.

Yes, I had changed. While Josephine ate, I thought back to that first glorious day when we left our posts in unison, to the marches, the songs and jokes my first time in jail. I had asked Mrs. Livingston and Mrs. Kinney for money and spoken boldly to Father Stephen, to pastors, rabbis, and ladies' groups. I'd managed strike pay for hundreds of families. Others had changed too. Young women whose lives had been ruled by bosses, fathers, and husbands, had convinced neighbors and friends to join the strike. They had marched for hours in public, chanting despite heat and hunger. Even Enrico's too-brief tenure in the great enterprise took on stately meaning. A street boy had been known as far as Ashtabula. His funeral filled a church. My appeal raised funds for a dignified casket and headstone. Pride in these things swept over my past pleasures of books and school. Perhaps Father Stephen was right: my calling was here.

Josephine set down her plate. "Lucia, I'm going to Michigan soon. The Kalamazoo Corset Company sells one and a half million corsets a year, but they won't heat the factory decently in winter." She opened her notebook and showed me a list. "These are girls who died of pneumonia." As her finger traced the line of names, I saw Irena's pale face in candlelight. "And here are those bitten by rats." She traced a longer list and closed the book. "The girls have to buy their own thread unless they make 'other arrangements' with the bosses."

"Like at Stingler's?"

"Yes, exactly. While the company sponsors silly songs about American Beauty corsets, workers get fondled in front of their mothers. They're fired if they speak out or won't 'cooperate,' and there's no other work in town. Some girls take poison to end their shame. Others smother the babes born in shame. Some jump off bridges. Three couldn't pay for a decent abortion and bled to death."

I thought of the girls at Stingler's, of Giovanna and Mamma. What right had any boss to treat his workers like whores?

"Some girls will testify," Josephine went on. "We can convince others. The clergy will march; they know how bosses use factory girls. This time the suffragettes will come with signs and the WCTU as well. Rich women are different in Michigan, everybody says. If we organize well, the strike will be short and we'll win. You'll see, Lucia. I want you to feel that joy."

"How will I feel it?"

"By coming to Kalamazoo with me."

"I told you I can't leave—"

"Bring her. We'll find lodging for both of you. Stay a couple months and then come back to Cleveland, if there's somebody waiting here for you," she finished slyly. "Once the strike is started, the union can run it themselves."

"Mamma's used to the boardinghouse. In a strange place she'd get worse."

"Is it really because of her that you won't go?" she asked mildly. "Are you afraid of something else?"

"Like what?"

"A bigger job than bookkeeping, a bigger voice." The women in the corner untangled themselves and sat up. Josephine brought over their plates, keeping her back to me.

*Was* I afraid? Going to Hiram had been easy. Because I was younger then, or because nobody depended on me? Confused in a new place, Mamma might wander and perhaps end in an asylum where the rest of her mind would fail. Yet if I stayed in Cleveland, how could my life be more than bookkeeping and caretaking? Even if I somehow went to college, would that solitary pleasure satisfy me, having once helped build a march of six thousand? If I went to Kalamazoo and we lost, how could I bear the weight of another failure? Was that a reason not to try? Another question loomed: was it better to never see Henryk again or to see and not have him? My chest tightened. I was trapped in a cell within a cell, a prison of questions.

Josephine came back to our bench. "You're thinking about your fella, that you'd miss him in Michigan?"

"There's no fella," I said too sharply. "Henryk is—" Josephine raised an eyebrow. Caught, I slumped against the wall. "Anyway, he's Jewish."

"That's what Pepe said, but he thinks a lot of this young man who's not your fella."

"Well, Henryk's family doesn't think a lot of a girl who's not Jewish, with no money and no father and a crazy mother. *They'd* like me to go to Michigan and never come back."

"Lucia," Josephine said casually, "it's a new century. Not everyone needs a family. And marriage isn't the only path. Men and women come together for pleasure and then go their separate ways. It's called 'free love.' "

I stared. Was that how she lived in the private life of which she never spoke? Of course I'd heard talk of free love all summer as union brothers and sisters coupled and uncoupled, as unfettered as Count Filippo in Capri. "But isn't that—"

"A sin?" Josephine finished, smiling. She opened her book and pointed to the names of girls dead or rat-bitten. "*Here* is sin. Being forced into 'services.' Working in firetraps. Sixty- and seventy-hour weeks. Free love is men and women living their lives as they choose, caring for each other. Think about it."

Just then a tubby officer rapped at the bars of our cell and said a friend had posted bail. "Isadore came early," Josephine said, brushing her dress. "Well, let's go."

The officer shook his head. "Not Isadore, some American: Harry White." Perplexed, we followed him to where Henryk was waiting in a striped suit and Panama hat.

"Ah, Mr. Harry White," said Josephine, "so good to see you."

Henryk grinned as we stepped into the street. "How's my American look?"

"Very convincing," said Josephine.

"Pepe said you were arrested," Henryk told us. "The strike's over. Two thirds voted to end it. Isadore read a statement from Printz-Biederman promising to rehire the strikers. They'll put up a list of fines so foremen won't invent new ones, and they'll supply the needles and thread."

"Pepe told you all this?" I asked.

"Yes, I pay for his news with apples."

"Henryk, shall we stop the little secrets?" Josephine interrupted. I looked between them. "Lucia, remember the last donation, the one you thought came from the Livingstons? It actually came from a grocer."

I turned to Henryk, who shrugged and smiled. "It was important to you, so I helped," he said.

"But you're saving for a new shop. And then you paid our bail."

"I'll earn it back. People always need vegetables. They'll buy more now that the strike's over."

Near Public Square, Josephine stepped aside. "I have to talk with Isadore. Henryk, will you walk her home?" He nodded. "And, Lucia, think about Kalamazoo." Then she was gone, dodging a truck unloading bundles of newspapers.

Left alone with Henryk, I felt the air between us thicken. Perhaps he felt it too. A newsboy ran by. "It must be a *Plain Dealer* extra on the strike," I said.

"Do you want a copy?"

I nodded, thinking that we could read as we walked. That would be easier than talking. My head spun with the end of the strike, the question of Michigan, and the strange, dizzying notion of free love. Henryk caught up with the boy and paid him. But he didn't unfold the paper. "I guess you heard about Miriam," he said instead.

"Yes, I'm sorry. Lula told me." Without discussion, we had taken the long way home, kicking through a crunchy blanket of leaves.

"Everyone said we were perfect for each other. She didn't think so, obviously. She thought she'd be better off with a banker than a grocer, especially if the banker loves her."

"And the grocer?"

"The grocer thought he did. But mostly he was a big fool. Is that what Lula says?"

"She didn't say."

"But she probably thinks so, and it's true."

"I see." We walked a block in silence. I didn't want to talk about Miriam.

"What's happening in Kalamazoo?" he asked suddenly.

I explained the corset makers' strike and that Josephine wanted my help in organizing a strike. I listed the grievances and how the workers could win. *Yes, just talk about Kalamazoo. It's easier.*

"What about your mother?"

"Josephine says to bring her, but I don't think I can. It's a problem."

"Michigan's far away. And cold."

"That's true." Far away, but wouldn't it be easier to have just one task: to win a strike for corset makers. Our feet sounded a beat on the slate sidewalk like the blacksmith poem from long ago: ta-*dum*, ta-*dum*, ta-*dum*.

Closer to the boardinghouse, Henryk took my arm. "Lucia, I'll miss you if you go."

Another time, his words and the warmth of his hand would have thrilled me, but I'd lost patience for half measures. Perhaps the walk to Vesuvius had done this, or the ending of the strike. "Henryk, we've been friends since we first played Simon Says."

"Yes—friends." He stumbled on the word like a greenhorn.

"Perhaps it was more," I said.

"It was."

"Is that why your father found Miriam for you? Because we're too different to be more than friends?" Henryk flinched. "We *are* different. And I won't convert, and I'd never ask you to be Catholic."

"The problem is my family. My father."

I pulled a dry leaf from a tree. "What do *you* want, Henryk?"

"I want to go walking with you and dance with you without a dozen people telling me the next day: 'She's not one of us.' I want a life with you, I want to marry you, but I need my father to stop—"

I crushed the leaf. "Then tell him! Tell them!" I was weary, shaken by the end of the strike and flushed with Josephine's truth: so much had changed. *I* had changed. "Henryk, we marched all summer. We went hungry and were beaten because we wanted a better life. We went to jail. Can't you tell your father who you want to marry?"

His face went pale under the streetlight. The newspaper crinkled. "I'm the only son, the only child. I'm everything to my parents. I know that's hard to understand because you don't have a father—" I stopped walking and spun to face him. He covered his eyes; the extra fell with a slap to the ground. "I'm so sorry, Lucia, I didn't mean—"

"To remind me that I'm illegitimate? You can do a good deed and pretend you're my husband to get my crazy mother out of the crazy house, but really I'm just a *shiksa*, and worse because I'm poor. Is *that* what you meant?" I had never spoken thus to anyone, never, never. The words tore my throat, but I was more than Lucia now. I was all the women born poor, born with no fathers, born germ plasma, born wanting too much. "Maybe you should get your father to find you a better Miriam. Then everybody would be happy." My words stopped. Tears were coming. I turned away.

A breeze blew his Panama hat off. He let it go. "You're right," he said quietly. "Enrico was just a child, but he fought for what he believed in."

I kicked at the dry leaves around us. I'd had so little of family in my life. How could I disparage his and the solid ground it gave him? Yet what pain, what aching loss to cast away those wide, kind eyes and lean face, the welcoming way of listening and easy jokes, his goodness and the comfort of his presence.

"Lucia, you want—"

"Too much, I know." We were walking again, dragging our feet as if we'd suddenly grown old. "Josephine says it's a new century and we don't need families. Love can be free, men and women coming together and leaving each other when they choose. But I need a place I can count on forever, where I can be *me* as I am, not me different. And you need your family. Why should you give that up? I wish I had one myself. So yes, I want too much."

Henryk stopped me, touching my shoulders as lightly as wind. Pain washed over his face. "I'm sorry, Lucia. I need time to think."

"There isn't much time." I grasped the lapels of his American jacket, then released them as if the cloth were burning. Night air filled me, blowing us apart, and suddenly I was running, my feet on the sidewalk drumming ta-*dum*, ta-*dum*, ta-*dum*, up the boardinghouse stairs and into our bedroom, where Mamma was already asleep.

*Don't think about Henryk. Stop thinking of him.* I paced the room, never lifting my eyes from the floor or looking out the window, afraid he might still be there on the sidewalk. *Look at your mother instead,* I thought frantically. *Think about her. Think about work, only work.* I'd need a job to pay the next weeks' room and board. Where could I find one? Not at Printz-Biederman, the memories were too painful. I paced the room until I was exhausted enough for sleep, still thinking of him.

*In the following* days I obtained a letter of recommendation signed by Mr. Kinney but surely written by his wife. With it I was hired in the accounts department of Taylor's department store for seventeen dollars a week. From Monday to Friday, bookkeepers worked nine-hour days: on Saturday afternoons we were free to "enjoy the pleasures of family life."

"Imagine, Mamma," I said, "we could go to the country or see a concert."

She shook her head violently. Of course, Toscanini.

I sighed. "That's true, *he* might be conducting." I'd ceased arguing with her. As Dr. Ricci said, she lived beyond logic and I must meet her in that land. We went to Garfield Park, far from Lake Erie or any concert hall. She wanted more yarn. I bought it, and she began making a shawl for "the dark lady."

"Lula?"

"The dark lady."

"Well, I'm sure Lula will love it."

The countess finally wrote that she and Paolo had just returned from Rome, where an aged aunt had died. They were sorry to hear of Mamma's "condition." She prayed for us both, held us close to her heart, and would write again soon. The single page was a thin blanket for a cold night, yet the simple words reminded me yet again of how far I was from my friend. Yolanda and Giovanna had written lately with veiled references to the asylum and for the first time did not invite us to Youngstown.

"You can bring her over here," Lula said. "It's not Youngstown, but it's someplace." I did sometimes bring her on quiet nights. I never loved my mother more than in that time when we learned to be alone together.

Chapter 20

## IN THE PARLOR

*The city surged* into lively action after the summer's languor. Josephine
went to New York for ILGWU meetings. She'd pass through Cleveland
again on her way to Michigan, hoping to take me with her. Isadore con-
fided that Josephine had a "friend" in New York, although each had
other "friends." So this was free love: freedom from this tearing, constant heart pain. *Don't think about Henryk. Don't.*

At Printz-Biederman and even in the smaller factories, salaries were
creeping up with rising demand for dresses, coats, and men's suits.
Workers began simply refusing forced overtime and banding together
to buy sewing machines at wholesale prices. Bosses complained and
threatened but in the end did nothing, knowing that a skilled seam-
stress could easily find work in other cities. As Josephine said, we were
changing and the bosses were changing with us.

I had successfully avoided seeing Henryk until a rainy November
day when Roseanne needed potatoes for dinner and brushed away my

excuses. "I am *not* letting my boarders go hungry just because Lucia and her fella had a fight."

"He's *not* my fella."

"Wonderful. Then go now, please. I have to start the stew."

"Couldn't—"

"Lucia, I need those potatoes!"

So I went to the store. Henryk and I were elaborately cordial, discussing the rain and Pepe's progress in school while his father noisily stacked cabbage crates, muttering in Yiddish. Henryk answered back sharply. Lamplight brushed his shoulders as he filled my basket. The light, his hands, the workings of his arms all were more than I could bear. I looked away. "What about Kalamazoo?" he asked softly.

"I still don't know how to bring my mother."

"I talked to Isadore about the factory. Those poor girls."

*Don't be good. Don't make me care for you.* When a cluster of women crowded into the store, I slipped away. Next time, Roseanne would have to do her own shopping. Or I'd pay a neighbor boy. I began scribing again and keeping ledgers for the union. The work was tedious but it filled my time.

The next Friday evening, I was hurrying home for dinner with a pack of receipts from Isadore. Boys selling late apples had tossed bruised fruit in the gutters. The air was bright with apple tang. I ran up the boardinghouse stairs, pulled off my coat, and was about to go check on Mamma. The parlor doors were closed, which was odd. Roseanne met me, hands on her widening hips. "You're late! And you have visitors in the parlor."

Police? A complaint about Mamma? Fear shot through me. "What happened?"

"Find out." Roseanne opened the doors and pushed me in so briskly that I stumbled over the rag rug, noticing nobody at first, but caught by familiar smells: lavender and English soap. I stepped back in terror, fearing that my mind had truly gone. Mamma saw Toscanini everywhere. I'd seen Enrico in the union hall. Now here were two visions from my past.

Behind me, Roseanne was laughing. "Lucia, have you forgotten my cousin Paolo? He hasn't forgotten you."

So they *were* real, Paolo and the countess in our parlor. He came forward and kissed me on both cheeks. The black hair was tipped with gray, but he was Paolo still, the steady ground of my life in Naples. "Elisabetta," he said, "just look at our Lucia, such a splendid young lady, all grown up!"

"Come here, my dear," said the kind, clear voice. Here was the countess in soft blue wool and lace, stretching out her arms to me. I looked between them, dazed.

"Elisabetta wanted to surprise you," Paolo explained. "Perhaps the surprise was too much?"

"My aunt in Rome left me enough money to pay for a trip to America," the countess explained. "We'd planned a spring visit, but after your letter, we knew we had to come now. That's why my letter was so short. We left that day."

I cried and laughed and couldn't speak. Roseanne brought a glass of water. Paolo handed me a spotless linen handkerchief scented with his soap. So it was real; they were here with me, and this was joy, pure joy, like a warm summer night on the bay. When the countess closed her white hands over mine, I saw a gold band on her finger, the mate of Paolo's.

"Yes, we're married," she said simply. "But in truth, we've been pledged since you were a baby."

Paolo sat beside us. "We're having our honeymoon in Cleveland."

Roseanne brought wine and her best glasses, announcing that my mother was asleep after a restless afternoon. In his silky way of smoothing out all trouble, Paolo proposed that we three visit until Teresa awoke. Then we could all go out to an American restaurant.

"You've grown, Lucia, even more than I imagined," said the countess. "You've done so much and learned so much. We've been proud to read your letters."

"You look well, Countess." I couldn't cease smiling to see them, the places of my life joined like broken china miraculously repaired. She did look well, the furrows of her brow smoothed, a ready smile, and no dark circles beneath her eyes.

"Call me Elisabetta. We're friends, are we not?"

"Yes—Elisabetta. How are Nannina and Luigi?"

"Very well. They're expecting a child and send their love." Elisabetta took my hand, excited as a child herself. "I can't wait to see Cleveland with you. And Teresa of course, if she'd like."

*If she'd like.* The simple words rolled in my mind. Who could know what Mamma truly "liked"? I asked instead if they wanted to eat at an Italian restaurant.

Elisabetta glanced at Paolo, who took a small leather notebook from his pocket. "Elisabetta and I have been reading about American foods we'd like to try. Shall I read you our list?"

I was young again, enthralled by his solemn grace. "Please."

"Some I will translate. For others I'll attempt the English." He cleared his throat. "Succotash, puffed rice cereal, and quiet little dogs—"

"Hush puppies," I corrected, trying not to stare at Elisabetta's face watching his, as if this were Leopardi himself, reciting for her.

"Thank you. Hush puppies, buttered toast with hash, biscuits, maple syrup and pancakes, peanut butter, frizzled beef, sliced ham, smoked bacon, fried clams, clam chowder, oyster stew." He looked up: "Shad?"

"A kind of fish."

"Ah. Shad. Campbell's soup; angel's cake and devil's cake; ginger-bread; strawberry shortcake; rhubarb, pumpkin, and blueberry pie; sweet potatoes; baked beans; corned beef; creamed corn; whipped potatoes; and roasted turkey, stuffed. That is all, Elisabetta?" She nodded happily. The familiar parlor was so charged with their presence that I felt like an intruder. "So," Paolo asked, "where can we find good American food?"

"The Forest City Hotel is very fine," Roseanne called from the hallway.

"Perfect," they said together.

"I'll see if Mamma's awake." When I stood, Paolo rose as he would for any lady. In that instant, the sheath of "servant girl" I'd worn for years fell away. I straightened my shoulders. A gentleman had stood for me.

Perhaps Mamma saw something new in my walk. She sat up and allowed the sheet she had wrapped around herself to be pulled away. "Mamma, Countess Elisabetta and Paolo are here! They're married and came to visit us." She said nothing as I brushed her dull hair and helped her put on a handsome woolen suit from her vaudeville days. It hung on her now. When had she grown so thin? "Isn't it wonderful to see the countess again?" I persisted. No answer. Perhaps she didn't believe me. Or perhaps she had truly forgotten our old life. "Let's go to the parlor," I said finally. She shuffled close behind me down the stairs.

Elisabetta and Paolo were standing, smiling. When I stepped aside and they saw her, color dropped from Elisabetta's cheeks. Paolo's hand braced her back. I realized then that I'd ceased noticing Mamma's flat-footed walk and wooden face or that her hair looked fresh-shorn because she'd taken to snipping off small bits when she was alone. Now I saw her as they did: a figure you'd avoid on any street. Could they even recognize in the gray face and vacant eyes the wild-spirited, lovely woman who left Naples six years ago? Could they believe she'd been a skilled chocolate dipper, much less a vaudeville singer? Was I insane to imagine taking her to Michigan?

Mamma's eyes slowly grazed the floor until they bumped into Elisabetta's shoes and then climbed upward. When they reached the pale face, she howled, a terrible, trapped animal sound. "Uhhhhhhh, the count!" She would have fled the room if I hadn't shut the parlor door.

"The count is dead, Mamma!" I said loudly, gripping her arms as she struggled. "We're going to a restaurant."

Paolo drew Elisabetta to a chair. "It's a pleasure to see you, Teresa," he said in the soothing voice that could turn black to white. "We've been visiting with Lucia. Doesn't she look well?" Mamma twisted around, her back to our guests, shoulders heaving.

"It's only Paolo and the countess, Mamma. You're perfectly safe."

"We don't have to go to a restaurant," Elisabetta murmured. "We could stay—"

"A restaurant!" Mamma said loudly to the wall.

"Well—" I began.

"Restaurant!" Mamma repeated.

"You have taxicabs?" Paolo asked smoothly. Yes, I stammered, we could find one nearby. "So we'll go out, if that's what Teresa wants."

"Certainly," Elisabetta managed.

The enterprise seemed bound for disaster. In an elegant restaurant, wouldn't people stare and whisper? Wouldn't we be made to leave? But Paolo's calm eased us all. I got Mamma's burgundy coat from the closet and hid her ragged hair beneath a broad-brimmed hat. Elisabetta composed herself, fixing a smile that never flagged all evening.

At the restaurant Paolo found an Italian waiter, whispered a few words, and deftly transferred a generous tip. The waiter gave us a corner table, obsequiously welcoming Countess Monforte and her party. Throughout dinner, he was unfailingly gracious, no matter what Mamma spilled or how often she stood, moved her chair, scraping it across the floor, and sat down hard again. Mortified, I barely ate, but Paolo and Elisabetta courteously ignored her, exclaiming over every dish. They included Mamma in conversations even when she merely stared at her plate or busied herself hiding knives beneath the tablecloth.

"My favorite," said Elisabetta as we walked home to digest our feast, "was the ice cream sundae you had me try." Under gaslight, I saw Mamma almost smile. We stopped at the hotel where Paolo and Elisabetta had taken a room.

"Thank you for a lovely evening," Paolo said. Mamma pulled away as Paolo, Elisabetta, and I kissed a good night. When a doorman ushered them into the lobby, Elisabetta buried her face in Paolo's jacket, seeming more exhausted by our evening than by their long trek west. Mamma watched curiously through the glass doors.

"They're staying here," I explained. "We'll pick them up in the morning."

"Why?"

"Because they want to see Cleveland with us."

"Why?"

I sighed. "Let's go home, Mamma. You must be tired."

The next day Paolo had the hotel arrange a touring car and driver. We glided past Public Square, "Lucia's union hall," Garfield Park, fine houses on Euclid Avenue, and the zoological park. Mamma was skittish, her eyes darting everywhere, watchful for "him," but quiet at least. In the afternoon, we brought her home to rest. "And now," Elisabetta announced, "we'd like to visit your friend Lula's tavern."

"It's just a place where people go to drink," I warned. "It's nothing elegant."

"We'd like to meet Lula. You've written so much about her."

So we went. Lula had somehow heard they'd come to town and pushed through knots of customers to reach "Lucia's countess and her friend." She made a group of regulars surrender a table and called for beer and sausage, beer cheese, smoked and pickled oysters. Then she sat herself down between Paolo and Elisabetta and I watched in astonishment as they conversed, she in English and they in Italian.

"Yes, yes, of course," Elisabetta would say over my translations. "We understood." They whispered and laughed together. When Lula was called to the bar, they looked at me, smiling.

"So," said Paolo, "Miriam left Henryk for a young man with more money."

"How do you know?"

"Lula just told us."

"Don't embarrass her," said Elisabetta. "I'm sure we'll find out more in good time."

"What else do you know?"

Elisabetta patted my hand. "Just that she's fond of you. And she's a very wise woman."

Paolo took out his notebook. "We'd like to see the eerie lake tomorrow."

On Sunday, a winter chill settled into Cleveland. Leafless trees spiked the white sky. I was glad for these changes, hoping that nothing would remind my mother of our terrible last visit to Lake Erie. Careful as I was to choose a vista point far from where we'd walked into the water, she hugged her waist and stayed far back from shore. Our guests tactfully made no comparisons with their own blue bay, exclaiming instead over the expanse of the lake, many times larger than any in Italy, and the scurrying traffic of barges and freighters. When I pointed out the distant abandoned warehouse that reminded me of the Palazzo

Donn'Anna, they nodded politely, for in fact, there was no resemblance at all.

Elisabetta had been watching Mamma all morning, perhaps searching for signs of the old Teresa. I'd done the same since her collapse, heartened by every trivial normality, pained at each new oddity. As we walked along the shore speaking of Naples, I hoped the talk would vault my mother back to what now seemed the golden days when she was a servant, but at least herself. We spoke of Nannina's sweet babas with rum, the season's first fava beans, brimming bowls of shellfish, the clatter of carts, fishermen's cries, church bells and glorious fireworks for our Feast of the Assumption. Sometimes a smile crossed Mamma's wooden face. Other times she turned away.

We found a lakeside café and drank freshly pressed apple cider: "As fine as any wine," said Elisabetta. She and Paolo and I were devouring warm doughnuts, comparing ocean crossings, when a waiter tapped my shoulder. "I'm sorry, miss, but that lady's scaring the customers." Mamma was splayed against a wide window, arms outstretched. Nobody ever called us sisters now, I realized with a start; she had so aged and changed that we scarcely seemed related. I hurried over and peeled her from the glass.

"So cold," she protested. "I need sun." I wrapped my coat around her.

"Elisabetta's tired, perhaps we should go back," Paolo announced. "I'll get a taxicab." When it came, Mamma peered through the window and jerked back, pulling me with her.

"You want my cab or not, gents?" the driver demanded. He had a thin, elegant build, a neatly trimmed mustache, and a gray homburg hat.

I sighed. "She thinks he's Toscanini."

"Tell her it's just a *taxicab* driver," Elisabetta whispered.

"She'll say he's in disguise to spy on her."

"Then I'll get another taxicab," Paolo said.

"For you and Elisabetta, if you like, but she'll be too anxious now. We'll have to walk."

So Paolo tipped the driver and we all walked home, stopping for roasted chestnuts from a vendor born in Naples within sight of our villa. But the long trip was difficult, requiring constant crossing of streets and detours when Mamma panicked at men in homburg hats or mustached men or certain alleys where, she whispered, "the maestro likes to hide." At the boardinghouse, after giving her a dose of laudanum and putting her to bed, I joined our guests in the parlor. They were perched on the divan, shaken.

"She wasn't like this yesterday," Elisabetta began.

"I know. She has good days and bad days. This wasn't a good day." I recited Dr. Ricci's diagnosis: paranoia, hallucinations, nervous prostration, hysteria, sexual anxiety, catatonia. The strange words pooled around us.

"She'll recover?"

"Dr. Ricci can't say. Being arrested, the asylum, and then the operation made her worse." I didn't speak of our own walking into the lake. That secret was best unshared, the doctor had said, locked in my heart forever.

"Would a sanitarium help?" Paolo asked.

"The good ones are very expensive, and the cure isn't certain. The sick are treated kindly, but even if I could afford that care, she'd feel abandoned to strangers. How could I do that?"

"So you'll care for her?"

"Yes, somehow."

Elisabetta took my hand. "Were we wrong to come, Lucia?"

"No, she's glad to see you both. Or, I think she is." I slumped in the divan. Was Mamma ever "glad" now? Could she still feel joy? "*I'm* very glad you came."

"Oh, Lucia, we miss you every day. With all that happened, are you happy here in America? Do you want to stay? You *could* both come back to Naples with us now that the count is gone."

The last six years flew across my mind: school and scribing, my happy time in college, vaudeville and Mamma's collapse, the terrible cold and heat, the failure of our strike, Cleveland's acrid air, the steady strain of needing money, the lack of my blue bay. Yet I had grown and graduated. I was Lucia D'Angelo here, not a servant girl or *bastardina*. I'd helped six thousand march for justice, and even if our strike had failed, some gains were made and more would come. "Yes, I want to stay."

Paolo and Elisabetta glanced at each other. She took my hand. "Well then, Lucia, we're happy that you've found your place."

*Chapter 21*

## SANTA LUCIA

*The next day,* our guests announced a grand desire to visit the Ohio countryside. "What for?" Roseanne demanded. "In winter there's nothing but dead fields and bare trees."

"Still, we'd like to see," Elisabetta said.

"We'll have an American adventure," Paolo added. In Little Italy he found a reliable driver who spoke Italian and English and owned a touring car they could hire for a week. "It's magnificent!" he declared. "A beautiful Stoddard-Dayton, made this year, six cylinders and twenty-eight coats of red paint. The driver has tools for any repair, and there's a waxed leather roof against rain," he assured Elisabetta. "She goes twenty-five miles an hour on a good road."

"*If* you find a good road," Roseanne countered.

"I'm sure we will," said Paolo. Thrilled by the coming adventure, he spent a happy afternoon with Cesare the driver poring over maps and guidebooks. They planned an elaborate course with alternate routes for roads washed out or simply imagined by the mapmaker.

Elisabetta was flushed with excitement. "It's nothing like a train, Lucia! We go where we want with no schedule at all, we're free as birds."

At Roseanne's insistence, they packed ample provisions from Catalano's. "You can at least eat decently the first day." Her frets about the cold, rain and snow, wind, wolves, bears, wild dogs, Indians, bandits, washed-out roads, and lack of respectable inns grew so pressing that finally even Paolo lost his temper, reminding his cousin that he and Elisabetta were quite capable and Ohio no longer a wilderness.

"Maybe not a wilderness," she conceded, "but it's *country* out there. You never know what could happen."

"That's the beauty of traveling," Elisabetta said brightly. "I'm sure we'll have a wonderful time."

On a clear, windy morning, Mamma stood with me on the sidewalk, raising her hand as I did to wave them off, but she left it in a stiff salute until I levered her arm down. "Going home?"

"No, Mamma, they're driving around Ohio."

"Why?"

"Very good question," Roseanne said, stomping inside.

With my friends gone, days at Taylor's department store felt unbearably long. I shared a small office with the head bookkeeper, Mr. Hess, a slight, thin-haired man of indeterminate age. Each morning he settled into a straight-back chair, planted his feet, inked his pen, and sharpened a line of pencils. He swept the shavings into an envelope that he sealed, labeled, and discarded, opened a ledger book, and began to work. Only his hands and arms moved; the rest of his body was immobile. At the stroke of noon, he cleared his desk, unwrapped a ham sandwich, and ate silently, gazing out our dusty window. Fifteen minutes later he returned to work. Aside from the briefest exchanges regarding the day's work and a few pleasantries—"Good morning, Miss D'Angelo," "Good evening, Miss D'Angelo," and "God bless you, Miss D'Angelo" when I sneezed—nothing but the scratching of our pencils and pens and rustle of papers filled the sepulchral stillness. I longed for the friendly chaos of our union hall and even missed the insults and jabs of picket lines.

Mr. Hess had fired three bookkeepers before me, but apparently my work was acceptable. After the first week, I wondered if my predecessors had intentionally botched entries to end their tenure. But no other post offered higher pay with a day and a half free each week. So I stayed on, bolting at the stroke of six into streets full of shopgirls chattering, automobiles honking, horses snorting, and newsboys hawking the evening papers. Walking the long way to avoid Henryk's store, I unknotted muscles that ached from hours of silent, rigid work.

Mamma would be pacing the parlor, disappointed that I came alone. "The countess?" she'd demand. "Paolo?"

"I told you, Mamma, they'll be back soon." Did she miss *me* as much when I was gone?

She pulled at the wild hair I couldn't stop her from breaking strand by strand. When I asked why, she pointed to her slashed stomach, leaving me to translate: if she'd have no more children, what did beauty matter? How could I even think of taking her to Michigan? Other strange behaviors would surely emerge and nobody would believe that she had once been otherwise.

Yet she *had* softened a little with the coming of our friends. At night she sometimes dealt out chips of old memories, which I filled in like the penny postcards of her vaudeville days. "Swimming in the moon," she'd announce.

I'd say: "Yes, wasn't it beautiful that night when the moonlight made a white road in the bay? Remember lying on our rock looking up at the stars?"

"Hmm," she might say, and then: "Nannina dancing."

"You mean when you sang and clapped for us and Nannina taught me the tarantella?"

Or: "Lemons and olives."

"Yes, they were so delicious, her lemon salads with olive oil and black olives."

Not every memory was pleasant. "Dr. Galuppi!" she cried once, jerking herself upright.

"He's dead. Lie down, Mamma, and I'll tell you what happened." When she was quiet, I shared Paolo's story. It had happened during one of the doctor's "cures": having Ugo, the hulking assistant, hold a woman underwater in a copper tank until she nearly drowned. Suddenly Ugo rebelled, tired of being the doctor's henchman. He freed the woman, and together they drowned the doctor in his own tank. Then they released his caged patients, emptied his safe of a sizable fortune, seized everything of value, set fire to the laboratory, and slipped out of the city. None of the patients were ever found. Some said they had gone with Ugo and the woman to a villa in the south of France where they all lived peaceably together.

Mamma was silent. Then came a new delicious sound: a low, heaving *huh, huh, huh.* By a glimmer of moonlight, her teeth flashed in an almost-smile before she turned to the wall. Little bursts of *huh, huh, huh* led her into sleep.

On the afternoon before Elisabetta and Paolo were to return, Roseanne sent me to Lula's for beer. Isadore was there, drinking with union brothers. "Ah, Lucia, it's good to see you. I just heard from Josephine. She'll be back soon. She's arranged meetings in Kalamazoo with suffragettes and pastors and the WCTU. Everyone's ready to strike. You know what she says."

"Long pickets make short strikes."

"Exactly."

"To the corset workers!" cried one of the men, raising his mug. "Hold on tight! Keep those laces snug!"

Isadore laughed. "Don't mind them. Are you going to Michigan, Lucia?"

"She's got things on her mind besides corsets, Isadore," Lula called out.

"Well, think about it. Josephine could use the help."

"What's wrong with Henryk?" Lula asked as she filled my bucket. "If his face gets any longer, it'll hit the floor. Yours too. Did you have a fight?"

"No," I said wearily, "and he's *not* my fella. We just spent some time together."

Lula's dark eyes peered into mine. "And that time was too much for 'friends' and not enough for more than friends?"

The question untangled itself in my mind. "Yes. I guess so."

She slid the heavy bucket to me. "I'm betting you'll work it out soon. Elsewise both your faces will fall off." A regular called for whiskey. She patted my cheek and plunged into the crowd. I hauled the bucket home, pondering my problem once more. Yes, caring for Mamma in a new place would surely be difficult in ways I couldn't predict. But I might see workers win. And I wouldn't see Henryk and whatever new Miriam his father recruited. *Don't think about him.*

Mamma was knitting quietly in the parlor. In a neat row on the windowsill were strands of hair she'd broken off. I sighed. In Michigan, she'd be a crazy lady from Ohio. But if we didn't go, what would happen to *me* after more months with silent Mr. Hess? By careful saving I could eventually earn enough for college. Could I still care for Mamma? And the picture of me in a book-lined library had become troublesome, too silent when so many workers needed a voice.

At breakfast Roseanne asked if I'd be going to the Hiram House dance. That simple choice overwhelmed me. "I don't know," I said. "I can't decide."

*Elisabetta and Paolo* returned the next day, delighted by neat Amish farms and orchards, white wooden churches with steeples, forests, fields, and so much space, such endless sky. They'd seen an "enchanting" snowfall on the Cuyahoga River, slept in country inns, had pancakes with maple syrup, and watched horses race down a country road. Paolo read me a list of animals they'd seen: white-tailed deer, badger, gray and red fox, skunk, otter, porcupine, beaver, and raccoon. They'd met real Indians at a general store and been invited to a square dance. They'd eaten squirrel meat after presenting themselves at a farmhouse and offering to pay the astonished family two silver dollars for a meal. Elisabetta unfolded a quilt she'd bought at an auction. "See how perfect? It's a cloth mosaic." Both she and Paolo had modest gifts for drawing, I discovered, and had filled two notebooks with the wonders they'd seen. My mother sat quietly through the long account. She rarely listened so long to me, I thought peevishly.

"Everyone should visit Ohio. There's so much to see," Paolo concluded.

Roseanne stared as if he'd proven himself even crazier than Mamma. "Enough about Ohio. I've made you good Italian *pasta al forno*." In fact she'd made a feast, ending with espresso in delicate porcelain cups she used on special occasions. Mamma was sleepy after wine and the heavy meal. I put her to bed and came down to the parlor.

Elisabetta and Paolo were waiting. "We'd like to talk to you, Lucia," she said. Paolo closed the doors, and she began. "Paolo and I have discussed this, so I speak for him as well. You said you want to stay in America."

"Yes."

"But Teresa needs care, and giving her that care is difficult for you, is it not, especially if you want to go to college or help your union?"

"Yes, but—"

"I understand. She's your mother and you won't leave her with strangers." I shifted uncomfortably. Why repeat the obvious? Her next words stunned me: "Paolo and I want to take her back to Naples and care for her there." Elisabetta spoke casually, as if proposing some mild change to the villa, buying a new painting or acquiring a cat.

"But that's impossible! You'll never know when the bad days will come. She has to be watched all the time. Her symptoms change. She sees Toscanini everywhere. You never know when—"

"We understand. We spoke with Dr. Ricci today. We know she may never recover. We have seen a 'bad day,' and he described other behaviors and symptoms she could develop."

"She cleans, but only if she wants to. You can't give her orders."

"Teresa would *not* be returning as a servant," Paolo said firmly. "She would be part of the household."

"She won't even sing when you ask her."

Elisabetta smiled. "I haven't had headaches since we buried Filippo. Dr. Ricci thinks the villa could be a good solution, quiet as a sanitarium but familiar, with people she knows who speak her language. She can help Nannina if she chooses, when it pleases her. If not, she could knit or swim, walk in the gardens or watch Vesuvius. She may be calmer, with more good days, even if she is never again how she once was. And you could go to college or do your union work."

My mind slowed. "You take her to Naples and I stay here?" Elisabetta nodded. Strange that my first response wasn't relief, amazement, or gratitude. No, I was seized by fear of floating unconnected in America. Sick or well, Mamma was *mine*, a heavy care, but a fixed point in my world. "She'll miss me," I blurted, "she'll miss me so much."

Elisabetta nodded. "She would, I'm sure, but—"

Exactly. She'd miss me, but perhaps Vesuvius and a warm sea could do as much for her as I ever could. Yet why take on this burden? And why now, when their reward for so many difficult years had just begun? "Elisabetta, Paolo, I don't understand. You were good to us even when she was difficult. You helped us escape from the count. Wasn't that enough?"

"No," said Elisabetta. "It wasn't enough. I'll tell you why."

Paolo squeezed her hand as if giving strength and silently moved to a far corner of the parlor, pulling a random book from the shelf, unobtrusive as a shadow.

Elisabetta ran a finger along her wedding ring and raised her eyes to mine. "Lucia, you understand that I barely knew Filippo before we wed?"

"Nannina said it was a brief courtship."

Elisabetta laughed. "Yes, exceedingly 'brief.' I saw him at two balls and had one gelato with him at Caffè Gambrinus. *That* was our courtship. My father had just died, leaving me the villa, a noble title, and many debts. Filippo *seemed* elegant and gracious. He had graduated brilliantly in mathematics. His father made a fortune in shipping and wanted a title for his son. Filippo charmed my mother and promised to pay our debts. Everyone said it was a brilliant match." She glanced at Paolo.

"You must understand that all I knew of men in those years was my father. He was always a gentleman, kind and courteous to everyone. He adored my mother. I never knew him to raise his voice. He never mistreated our servants or allowed others to mistreat them. Filippo *seemed* the same, but once we married, the playacting ended. Our wedding night he spent in a brothel. I was trapped with a gambler and libertine. I thought my life was over. A month later, Paolo found me with a vial of poison. He took it away and promised to help me live with Filippo. Truly, without him I could not have endured my husband.

I moved, as you know, to another wing of the villa and had no more intimacies with him."

"And my mother?"

"She was just fourteen when she began service with us. At Carnival time we gave a masquerade ball."

I clenched my fists. *The bastard wore a mask.*

"Filippo was dressed as Louis the Fourteenth, the Sun King. As were two other men. It was the year of Sun Kings," she said ruefully. "Paolo served guests in the villa, and we had tables by the water. He sent Teresa down with more champagne. From the balcony I saw the gold of the kings' cloaks flash in lantern light. When I realized that Teresa hadn't come back, I looked again and saw two people struggling on the rocks. One wore a gold cloak."

*He pushed me in the seaweed.*

Paolo quietly returned from his corner. "I should have brought the champagne down myself," he said, "or used one of the footmen. Instead I sent a young girl alone in the dark among drunkards. I was new in service. I was an idiot. That was unforgivable." He waited until I lifted my eyes to his. "Entirely unforgivable. I am so sorry, Lucia, that I did this to your mother."

"Teresa wouldn't speak of what happened," Elisabetta continued, "but she was different after that night: silent, angry, avoiding men. She cried often. She was nearly a child herself, remember."

"I know."

"And this disgrace happened in *my* household. I know such things are common, even usual in great houses, but not in our villa, not when my father was alive. When her belly grew, I said I'd find her a place in another household. But we both knew that any new master would make her give you away."

"To be an *esposito*."

"Yes, exactly. Teresa said she'd stay with us, even with Filippo there. She seemed comforted by the water and the gardens and lemon grove. So Paolo and I promised to protect her as much as we could. We owed her that much. She began to sing, and I discovered that her voice soothed my headaches."

"The count?"

"Filippo denied that he'd touched her. What proof did I have besides shadows and a flash of gold? When you were born and cried as a babe, he wanted you given away. I said that was entirely Teresa's choice, and that's when he bought his own villa in Capri. As you grew, I hoped that if he heard you read and saw how quick you were, he'd be proud or kinder to you, even if you weren't his own. But by then his mind was weakened from syphilis. He was often in pain, more than we knew."

I couldn't rouse myself to sympathy. "He called me *bastardina*."

"I know. I cringed every time, for that and for his constant cruelty to your mother. What she suffered in my home may have led to her collapse. Lucia, we want to give her a safe and comfortable home. We can do this now with the count gone. You could be free for your work. Perhaps you'll visit us. We would be happy if you did. Please, Lucia, think what's best for Teresa, and for you."

I did think about it all that night, coming to work so bleary that Mr. Hess lifted his head to ask, "Are you quite well, Miss D'Angelo?"

That evening I walked to Lake Erie and stood on the shore, my head aching. It was true that in a large villa the cost of feeding and clothing one more counted for little. The rich, I thought bitterly, had more solutions at hand than the poor. In their walled world, Elisabetta and Paolo could easily give Mamma what I couldn't, even if I sacrificed every dream and pleasure for her sake. She might be calmer in the villa and "see" Toscanini less often. But without her, I'd be alone in America. And what if she grew worse? I might fade to a shadow in her weakened mind, a faraway daughter in a forgotten land. Still, these were *my* troubles. For Mamma, what course would be best? I watched fog roll over the pier and then walked slowly back to the boarding-house, knowing what I must do.

In our bedroom I explained Elisabetta's offer to my mother: that she could live in the villa, not as a servant but as part of the household. The count and the doctor were dead. Nobody would ever abuse her. She could sit by the water and swim in moonlight. She could knit, pick lemons, and sing to Vesuvius again. She could have familiar sights and smells and sounds around her. She could be home. My voice shook.

"You come too, Lucia?"

"No, Mamma, I'd stay here, in America. I could visit, but I need to live here." She made a swirling gesture by her head, grimacing. "Bad thoughts?" I suggested.

She nodded. "In America." Breathing heavily, as if summoning strength, she leaned her head against my shoulder and whispered, "Let me go."

"Yes, Mamma, I will, but I'll miss you so much." When she pulled away, my blouse was damp.

She touched my face. "Like vaudeville?"

"More. Then you were only a few hours away. But I hope you'll be happy in the villa, like you were at first in vaudeville."

"The countess?"

"Yes, we'll talk to Elisabetta and Paolo."

In the morning, we gave them our answer. "We'll try to make you happy, Teresa," Elisabetta said. "We'll try very hard." Mamma almost smiled, rocked a little, and then buried herself in knitting.

While Paolo arranged passage home through an agency in Little Italy, Elisabetta and I risked taking Mamma to buy traveling clothes at the May Company. The venture passed nearly without incident. She seemed to be already living in our old world, seeing the beautiful rooms fill with sunlight, hearing fishermen call, gathering lemons and plums. I was like the mother whose child was too absorbed by a coming journey to note the pain of those left behind.

I telegraphed Josephine that I'd be going with her to Kalamazoo. Mrs. Taylor at Taylor's department store grudgingly said I might be re-hired on my return, "given the good reports from Mr. Hess."

"You'll see, Lucia, there's no greater joy than winning a strike," Isadore assured me. Perhaps. Was there one last chance to claim a joy all my own? This time I didn't need Lula's reminder to take my leave of Henryk. I found him at work with his father, putting up shelves for dry goods. He said something to his father in Yiddish and stepped off the ladder when he saw me. We stood silent for a minute, facing each other.

"My mother is leaving soon for Naples. I wanted you to know," I said finally.

"Yes, that's what I heard from Lula." He ushered me into the neat office and closed the door firmly behind us.

"And I'll be going to Kalamazoo," I added. "Perhaps you know that as well?"

"From Pepe, yes, who had it from Isadore."

"He got an apple for the news?"

"Two apples." The smile flashed and faded; the dark eyes turned grave. "Lucia, I was coming tonight to talk to you."

"Do Lula and Pepe know?"

"No, nobody knows." He moved us gently away from the small window, squared his shoulders, and began. "Lucia, you said to decide what I wanted. That's what I've been doing since the night I walked you home. In fact that's *all* I've been doing. This shop is mine now. My father bought another one in Cleveland Heights. There's a flat above us, just three rooms, but it's warm and sunny. Lucia, will you live there with me? Will you marry me? Just as you are. Not changed, not converted or different, just you."

"What will your parents say?"

His smile lit the room. "That's *my* job. You win over the Kalamazoo Corset Company, and I'll win over two grocers. I've already started."

"You're on strike? You gave them a list of demands?"

The warm hands gripped mine. "Not a list. Just one: to marry the woman I love. If she wants me."

"She does," I said. "Very much."

Now his words came in a rush: "We could get married at City Hall if you like, no church, no synagogue. You could go to college. We can manage with what I make at the store. Or you could work for the union. We'll figure out the rest."

"You mean negotiate?"

"Yes. All I want is a life with you. Just—will you play Simon Says with me?" I nodded. "Simon says: Put your right hand on your heart and tell me you'll come back to Cleveland."

"Yes, I promise. Now you. Simon says: Put your right hand on your heart." He did. "And promise you'll wait for me."

"Yes, Lucia D'Angelo, I'll wait out any strike for you." Then without thought or willing any action, we wrapped ourselves in each other's arms and the face, the neck, the shoulders and chest, all that I'd dreamed of for so long were mine, our hearts beating against each other.

A sharp knock jolted us apart. Henryk opened the door. His father was standing stiffly there, wiry gray hair framing the familiar face and eyes. He pushed past his son and squared himself in front of me, filling the room. "I have question for Lucia."

"Papa, please don't—"

"What question, Mr. Weiss?"

"You love my son, Henryk?"

"Yes, sir, I do."

"Of course," he snapped. "Why not? He's a fine boy. The best in Cleveland. I mean, how—" He frowned, chewed his lip, asked something in Yiddish that Henryk couldn't answer, and stepped even closer. "When you love my son, *how* do you love him? Explain."

"What kind of—?" Henryk demanded. I held up my hand.

"Mr. Weiss, when I love him, the best in me and the best in him are like this." I folded my fingers together.

Two wrinkled hands encased mine. "Well then," said a rough voice, "from your mouth to God's ear." He slowly pulled his hands away. "So, Henryk, don't just stand there. Get her some nice apples! Even Italians like apples, no, Lucia?"

"Yes, sir, very much."

Henryk hurried away but looked back over his shoulder at us, beaming.

I floated home with my apples. Cleveland had never been so beautiful, the sky as blue as the Bay of Naples, the wintery air sweet as any lemon grove. I told nobody that night, savoring my secret alone.

The next evening I brought Mamma's finished shawl to Lula. She admired the delicate lace of pinks and purple, the softness, the design and fringe, and then hugged me tighter than any shawl could merit. The cook and her new girl hugged me too, but when several regulars lurched up, arms outstretched, Lula shooed them away.

"Lula," I demanded, "does everybody know *everything* in Cleveland?"

"What are we, girl, stone blind? That boy doesn't need to say a word. Buy an onion from him and you can see that he's happy. You don't have to be a genius to guess why. You tell your mamma this shawl is the pret-tiest thing I've worn since my wedding dress and we'll take good care girl. Give your countess this." She handed me a crock of her beer cheese. "Can't get it in Italy, I bet. And you hurry back from Michigan, Lucia D'Angelo. Don't leave a good man waiting."

*In our last* days together, my mother grew vague and easily confused, surprised at each mention of Henryk and our future together. She moved clothes from my suitcase to hers, emptied hers, and stared blankly when Paolo explained the wonders of their ship: its parlors, galleries, fine dining halls, and musicians at every meal. "They're going?" she asked, pointing to Elisabetta and Paolo.

"With *you*, Mamma. You're *all* going home to Naples."

"You?"

"No, I'm staying in America. I'm going to marry Henryk. I told you."

Her eyes widened, and she pulled away from me. "The count? The doctor?"

"They're both dead, remember?" Then she relaxed and asked how soon we'd swim in the bay.

"Oh, Mamma." The jagged speech, hesitant walk, and darting, birdlike eyes were as familiar as my own skin. How could we part? Yet how could I *not* let her go?

The days passed quickly, each one torn to bits with tasks and meetings. Dr. Ricci, Elisabetta, Paolo, and I determined laudanum doses and planned ways to manage the inevitable bad days. I pried loose time to walk with Henryk or sit in his mother's kitchen beside mounded plates of sweets as she peppered me with questions that he sometimes translated and sometimes would not. Henryk's father rarely spoke; he sat smoking his pipe, considering me.

"As if I were some new kind of potato," I said as we walked back to the boardinghouse at night.

"Well, he *is* a grocer," Henryk conceded. "But I think he's liking this new kind of potato, more and more each day. Me too. The finest, most delicious potato on earth." We stopped in dark places between street-lights, braiding our bodies together, storing up warmth against the months of separation, our joy delighting in joy.

Our wedding would be in Brookside Park when I came back from Michigan, we had determined, with Father Stephen and Rabbi Rosen presiding. To be together was happiness as warm and buoyant as a sum-mer sea. We talked and were silent, laughed at good memories and cried in remembering Enrico. I nestled into the comfort of our union, entirely at ease.

Paolo and Elisabetta hosted an engagement dinner at the Forest City Hotel. Henryk's parents came, and Lula and Roseanne. Mamma sat next to Henryk, twisting and untwisting her napkin. Yet once, furtively, she squeezed his hand. My heart thumped. When Henryk tapped his glass for attention and stood, she set her napkin down and listened qui-etly as he recited a ragged little speech in Italian: "Contessa Elisabetta, Signora D'Angelo, and Paolo, I will love and care for Lucia forever and with all my heart."

Mr. Weiss spoke to his son in Yiddish, and Henryk said something softly back that would always be their secret. Then the old smile re-turned as he raised his hand. "My father reminds me of the workers' vow before the strike: If I turn traitor to the cause I now pledge, may my hand wither from the arm I now raise." I translated for my friends.

"You deserve this woman, Henryk" was Paolo's rejoinder. "And that's our highest praise for any man."

"Do each other wrong," Lula added pleasantly, "and I'll have your heads for beer mugs."

)te to my professors, explaining that for now life was bearing me
n college. I might travel often for the union, Isadore warned. I

conveyed this to Henryk. "It's your work," he responded, "as vegetables are mine. All I want is a home with you."

At night Mamma let me lie close by her, matching my breath with hers. And then, so soon, her time in America was ending. Josephine and I were to leave Saturday morning for Michigan. Mamma, Paolo, and Elisabetta would take a later train east. When Henryk came to bring me to Union Depot, Mamma stomped upstairs. In the parlor crammed with suitcases and bundles, I felt like a child, abandoned and exposed.

Elisabetta drew me aside. "I think she *can't* say good-bye. Perhaps it's better this way. Go to the station with Henryk. Hurry, or you'll miss the train." Above us I heard Mamma's footsteps, pacing our room.

"Tell her how much I'll miss her. Tell her I'll write and we'll visit as soon as we can."

"We will, but you go now."

Henryk and Paolo carried my bags to the taxi where Josephine was waiting. Seeing my distress, she busied herself with a notebook. I looked up at our bedroom window. The curtain had been drawn aside. Was she watching? *Let her find peace without me.*

"We'll visit soon; we'll start saving right away. You can show me all around Naples," Henryk whispered. I nodded, turning my face to his jacket and the warmth of his breath.

Union Depot was packed with immigrants arriving, travelers and businessmen leaving, all of us swirling together as if mixed with a giant paddle, the air thick with voices and shouts, the rumble and squeal of trains, conductors' whistles, newsboys, and peddlers hawking provisions. Henryk hired a porter and got our tickets. I stood frozen in the swirl. Suppose this was a bad day for Mamma? Suppose they couldn't get her on the train? Suppose she bolted in the station and they lost her forever?

"I'll go ahead and get settled," Josephine announced, plunging into the crowd.

Henryk and I walked close together, constantly bumped by porters. I couldn't speak, seeing only Mamma running upstairs away from me. It was Henryk who heard voices crying "Lucia!" just as we reached my platform.

Roseanne, Paolo, Elisabetta, and Mamma were flushed and breathless just beyond a swarm of passengers. A tight group of men in fine coats and homburg hats brushed past us. "She wanted to say goodbye!" Roseanne shouted as she and Paolo helped my mother climb on a bench. Henryk put his arm around me, a prop in the buffeting tide. Now Mamma was head and shoulders above the crowd. Yet at first nobody noticed this slight woman in a burgundy coat and feathered hat. She settled her feet and lifted her arms.

"Shine on, shine on, harvest moon, up in the sky," she began, that miraculous voice rising again, clear and bold. Two passengers stopped, astonished, and then a few more. Spots of quiet grew into pools of travelers, stilled and listening. Some sang with her, but she had unhooked the words from their meanings, leaving nothing more of a boy and girl under a willow tree. No, here was the Naples Nightingale singing of our good times and struggles in America, all that we had gained and lost, all that we were together. Her arms floated, the voice arched over the crowd, stopping talk, seeming to stop even whistles and screeches and rattling wheels. A conductor stood listening. Two brakemen with grease buckets turned their heads. The last note faded and her arms floated down. A splattering, then waves of applause followed.

"Encore! Encore! Sister, sing us another!"

Mamma lifted her head. "Now," she announced in English, I will sing 'Santa Lucia,' for my Lucia." She sang the first verse, my favorite, of silver stars over waves. Here was my mother tongue, thick with love.

As her arms reached toward me, I breathed in the dark eyes, pale face, and slight shoulders that had borne so much. Tears smeared my vision; I wiped them away. She faltered in the next verse and stiffened, her eyes darting over the crowd as if searching out an enemy, then fixing on a face near me. The shoulders caved. When she seemed about to topple, caring hands helped her down.

Strangers turned to each other: "What happened? Concert's over?"

The crowd swallowed her. "Mamma," I called out, but she was gone.

A gloved hand politely tapped my shoulder. I turned toward an elegantly dressed man with a dark swoop of eyebrows. "You are Lucia?" I nodded. "My compliments, *signorina*. She sings like an angel." A slight bow and he too dissolved in the crowd.

A whistle shrieked beside me. "That's your train," Henryk said in my ear. "Hurry." He kissed me as I jumped on the train. "Remember what Simon said!" he called out as we pulled away. He kept waving, standing steady amid the platform's swirl, and he would be there when I returned in two months, three months, outwaiting any strike. Early snows sprinkled the lake as we left the station. Josephine wrote quietly in her notebook. I pressed my face against the chilly glass. Hours ahead lay the work that called forth the best of me in this land.

## Epilogue

*Near Milwaukee, 1913*

*I am standing* by the frozen fringe of Lake Michigan in early sunset. Despite the bitter cold, I close my eyes and see my mother in Naples on our rock jutting into the bay. She's dressed in a linen shift. Her hair is beautiful again, thick and rich. She has been gathering shells with Paolo and Elisabetta's little son, Luciano. On good days, she's a kindly older sister to the child. On bad days, she stays in the lemon grove or curtained in her room, knitting scarves that Paolo bundles and mails to me "for the immigrant children."

I admit that I often envy Luciano's time in the villa, free from the looming, brutal presence of the count. He has loving parents; soon he'll have tutors and all the books he'd ever want. He has the best of my mother; she sings to him and tells him stories. When we visit next year, he'll show me how sunlight fills the sitting room, how yellow plums fall in your hands and tide pools bring treasures every day.

My driver coughs discreetly. "Mrs. Weiss, are you ready? They're waiting at the union hall. The pastors are there, and the suffragettes."

"Yes, Pete, I'm ready."

Very shyly, he gives me a lemon. "I'm hoping it reminds you of home," he says. It's small and hard, but still there's the clean, sharp smell of sour mixed with sweet. "I have a blanket as well and a cushion, since I couldn't help noticing that you're . . ."

"Yes, we're expecting a child."

"Congratulations to you and your husband. I wish you joy."

"Thank you, Pete."

We drive toward the union hall, a tiny point of light across frozen fields vast as a dark sea. I feel in my pocket for Henryk's letter. Next week, or the next, depending on these meetings, I'll be home again in Cleveland. I'll see the room he's preparing for our child. We'll take our long walks and be abundantly fed by his mother. We'll lie in bed for hours talking, dreaming, and, as we like to say, "negotiating." Each morning waking together is a joy.

But first I'll speak to these pastors, suffragettes, and workers. I'll remind them of Josephine's vow: "Long picket lines make short strikes." I'll speak to the owners tomorrow; perhaps we can still avert this strike. It's been a long day. We bounce over rough country roads, but when I close my eyes, the smell of lemon takes me back to warm waters where I'm swimming again in the moonlit path to Vesuvius.

## Acknowledgments

*Writing historical fiction* is an exercise in the practice of gratitude. So many give generously of their expertise and counsel. I'll begin, historically, with the first inspiration for this project. In the fall of 2011, Dr. Serena Scaiola-Sizka, honorary vice consul of Italy in Cleveland, arranged a series of readings for my previous novel, *When We Were Strangers*. In this way, I met Pamela Dorazio Dean, associate curator for the Italian American collection of the Western Reserve Historical Society, whose subsequent help and access to the astonishing wealth of that collection proved invaluable.

Dr. John Grabowski, director of research at the Western Reserve Historical Society, was a limitless, endlessly patient source of historical background on Cleveland history, immigration patterns, and labor history. Ed Pershey, director of special projects and exhibits, assisted on issues of transportation in Cleveland. *The Encyclopedia of Cleveland History* was my constant friend. Lois Scharf's excellent article, "The Great Uprising in Cleveland: When Sisterhood Failed," addresses the early success and rapid unraveling of the Cleveland Garment Workers' Strike of 1911. In depicting Hiram College, I am indebted to the college archivist, Jennifer S. Morrow.

Leslie Woodcock Tentler's *Wage-Earning Women* is a detailed, compassionate labor history. The list of victims of the Triangle Shirtwaist Factory Fire is available online through the University of Missouri, Kansas City, School of Law. For immigration and labor history, I often interrogated my sister, Dr. Karen Schoenewaldt. In the areas of union history and organizing, I drew on Frances Ansley, J.D., of the University of Tennessee and Jobs with Justice of East Tennessee, and the Reverend Jim Sessions of Interfaith Worker Justice. Joe Uehlein directed me to sources for union songs of this era. Melissa Brenneman and Jamie Osborne, both of Knox County Public Library, were steadily helpful in a stream of varied inquiries.

I used many sources for the dating of popular songs and apologize to music historians for instances in which fancy for a particular song had me snatch fiction's privilege and slightly fudge a publication date.

An authoritative guide to classic Neapolitan cuisine is Vittorio and Lydia Gleijeses's *A Napoli Si Mangia Così*. For Teresa's sea tales I drew on *Leggende del Mare*, edited by Francesco Rocchi. My sources for opera history and technique were Karen Nickell, Vladimir Protopopescu, and *The Letters of Arturo Toscanini*, edited by Harvey Sachs. Mark Loudermilk helped with questions of historical banking and accounting practice.

For medical and birthing issues, I consulted with Leonard Bellingrath, M.D.; Elizabeth Johnson, RNC, FNP; and Corrine Rovetti, FMP-BC, specialist in women's health. Research for this novel involved diving into the gloomy topic of treatment of mental illness in the nineteenth and early twentieth centuries. For more detail on this national nightmare, I recommend Robert Whitaker's *Mad in America: Bad Science, Bad Medicine, and the Enduring Mistreatment of the Mentally Ill* and Mary de Young's *Madness: An American History of Mental Illness and Its Treatment.* In constructing Teresa's constellation of symptoms and behaviors, I was generously assisted by Dr. Laurel Goodrich, Dr. William MacGillivray, and Dr. Vance Sherwood.

For issues of Jewish-American culture, I thank Marian Jay. Judith Appleton helped with issues of Polish Jewish traditions. Readers Rosalind Andrews, Gaye Evans, Jamie Harris, Jo Ann Pantanizopolous, and Alan Sims helped me keep moving forward and prevented many infelicities. For a keen eye and listening ear, I thank Odette Shults.

My husband, Maurizio Conti, was once again wonderfully present and supportive, my own sine qua non.

Nothing tongue-ties a writer more than expressing the magnitude of appreciation appropriate for an agent and editor who create the ground, the guidance, and the critical acumen to shepherd a book from concept to production. To my agent, Courtney Miller-Callihan of Sanford J. Greenburger Associates, and editor, Amanda Bergeron of Harper-Collins, and her magnificent team I give heartfelt gratitude for their support, discernment, and skillful guiding of this project. And finally, to Miss Silvia Conti, who steadily prodded me to finish the book before her sixth birthday, I'm happy to say I did that.

## About the author

2 Meet Pamela Schoenewaldt

## About the book

3 In Conversation with
Pamela Schoenewaldt

11 Reading Group Guide

Insights,
Interviews
& More...

## Read on

14 Suggested Reading

15 Have You Read?
More by Pamela Schoenewaldt

# Meet
# Pamela Schoenewaldt

PAMELA SCHOENEWALDT lived for ten years in a small town outside Naples, Italy. Her short stories have appeared in literary magazines in England, France, Italy, and the United States. She now lives in Knoxville, Tennessee, with her husband, Maurizio Conti, a physicist, and Jesse, their dog. ❧

# In Conversation with Pamela Schoenewaldt

*Swimming in the Moon touches on many themes—the immigrant experience, workers' rights, mental illness, self-discovery—but at its heart it's the story of a complex mother/ daughter relationship. Which of these pieces came to you first as you wrote? How did this story come together?*

For days, the basic pieces of the story floated around my head like big soap bubbles. I wanted to return to the urban immigrant experience at the high tide of European immigration and to explore a mother/daughter union. One floating image was the moonlit Palazzo Donn'Anna, built out into the Bay of Naples. Masa Lamberti, my first Italian teacher, grew up in a magnificent apartment there, and when we became friends she took me through the maze of magnificent rooms with massive oil paintings, Venetian chandeliers, rosewood furniture inlaid with ivory, and an enormously tall window looking out to sea in an elegant sitting room. Had the doomed sailors been pushed to their deaths from that very window? I asked. "It's a *story*, Pamela," said Masa. But such a story that when she first told it in our Italian class I was sure I'd mistaken the vocabulary.

Now, years later in Tennessee, I imagined an immigrant with memories of lavish chambers such as these. Why ▶

would such a person leave home? Ah, a servant might, or two servants, a mother and daughter might be forced to leave. Why? Something about the mother . . . With much digital scribbling of scene fragments and story points, pop! The bubbles came together in the beginnings of a plot.

I was attracted by the idea of varying talents: a mother with a natural ear and magnificent voice utterly not understanding how someone of her own blood could have neither, and yet inspiring and instructing this daughter in how to move others with spoken language. The particular intimacy of Teresa and Lucia was an intriguing challenge: almost of age to be sisters. They are constant workmates and bedmates, yet very different in talents, interests, and character even before the terrible complication of madness.

Vaudeville seemed like a natural venue for a singer in those years, and I have my own interest in labor issues. Thinking purely as a novelist, however, I wanted this protagonist to have a set of issues beyond her own needs. In *When We Were Strangers,* Irma manages her own escape from a workhouse. I wanted Lucia to struggle, successfully or not, to bring a measure of justice to many workers.

*You've written two novels about the immigrant experience in the late nineteenth and early twentieth centuries. Did you find that conditions had changed for immigrants in the decades between* When We Were Strangers *and* Swimming in the Moon? *What had changed for women in that time?*

I'm not a historian, and volumes have been written on the massive transformation of the United States between the 1880s and the 1910s, but I can point to some changes that would have impacted immigrants such as Teresa and Lucia. The frontier had closed by Lucia's time, and most newcomers went into crowded cities to make (or not make) their fortunes. Ethnic groups were more organized, sometimes against each other, as depicted in *Swimming in the Moon.* Anti-immigrant prejudices were growing in many quarters, as Lucia experienced. Settlement houses offered useful services, but with an agenda: Immigrants must let go of their foreignness, their customs and languages. They must blend in, but also not make trouble, ask for too much, or threaten "real" Americans. Lucia constantly bumps against these expectations, in her valedictory speech, for example, and of course later in her union work.

Torrents of inventions came in the years between the novels: telephones, moving pictures, automobiles, and washing machines. Crossing the ocean was faster, even for the poor. Medicine had advanced, with widespread use of antiseptic practices still questioned in Irma's time, although antibiotics were years away. Life expectancy had improved, childbirth was less dangerous, and Margaret Sanger was broaching the idea that women could and should safely control fertility. Conveniences and pleasures available only to the rich of Irma's day were now within reach of the working class, but many like Lucia were asking why workdays were so long that little time remained to enjoy these blessings of progress.

***Lucia's reading of the names of the Triangle Shirtwaist Factory fire victims is a very moving moment. Did that historical event play into your decision to set this story when you did?***

Yes, the 1911 Triangle Shirtwaist Factory fire in New York City connects to my story in several ways. First, I began writing the novel in 2011, the widely reported anniversary of that tragedy. In my own city of Knoxville, Tennessee, I joined protests at a bridge construction site managed with flagrant disregard of worker safety. In workplaces around the country, it's questionable how far we've really come in the last century.

Getting back to the novel, Cleveland and New York were the nation's leading women's clothing producers before World War I, employing thousands of immigrants, mostly women. Many union leaders, like Josephine Carey, worked in both cities. It's possible that news of the Triangle fire pushed Cleveland garment workers to launch their own strike before establishing a support network that might have made success more likely. The names of the fallen were published widely, and it seemed likely to me that union brothers and sisters in Cleveland would have honored the dead in that way. I hope it will be clear from ▶

**In Conversation with Pamela Schoenewaldt** *(continued)*

the reading of names that the garment workers most vulnerable to unsafe conditions were Italian and Eastern European, mostly single young women like Lucia and her friends.

### How did you choose Cleveland as your setting?

I lived near Cleveland when it was a scruffy postindustrial city, before its recent renaissance. I experienced the frigid winter winds, summer heat, and spectacular autumns of northern Ohio. The Lake Erie/Bay of Naples contrast was attractive for my purposes, and of course I had done some Cleveland research for my first novel. Finally, there are many fine New York–based immigrant novels, and I wanted another setting.

As mentioned in the acknowledgments, the immediate impetus for Lucia's story came when I was visiting Cleveland for readings of *When We Were Strangers* sponsored by the Italian consulate (I'm a new-minted dual citizen of Italy and the United States) at Western Reserve Historical Society. Between readings, I was able to access archival material in the Society's Italian American collection. I began researching the 1911 Cleveland Garment Workers Strike, and, in that process, I imagined Lucia walking out to Lake Erie on a muggy summer night.

### Lula appears in your first novel, and again in Swimming in the Moon. Are there characters from this book that you'd see finding their way into future stories?

I truly didn't expect to have Lula in this book, but I enjoyed her spirit in *When We Were Strangers* and missed her when Irma left Cleveland. Early in the writing process for this novel, it occurred to me that Lula was clearly a survivor and that her success in the intervening thirty years would be credible and certainly deserved. So I put her in *Swimming in the Moon* and was glad I did: She becomes something of a mother-surrogate to Lucia after Teresa's collapse. There are fewer settings in this novel, which means more opportunities to develop layered relationships, such as the one between Lucia and Lula. However, to the question, I don't have any plans to return to the characters of *Swimming in the Moon*, but if readers have thoughts along those lines for their own amusement, my e-mail address is on my website, www.Pamela Schoenewaldt.com.

*This book also touches on the issue of mental illness and explores the attitudes and treatments of that time. Indeed, the early scene with the spinning chair is quite horrifying. What were you most surprised to learn in your research?*

Psychology was a young science a century ago, neurological research just beginning, and the only pharmaceuticals available for treating mental illness were varieties of opiates, like the laudanum Teresa uses. Sigmund Freud's brilliant, exciting explorations of the unconscious couldn't help practitioners with wards full of patients who were too poor to pay a psychotherapist or whose illness didn't permit talk therapy.

I first learned of the terrible treatment of the mentally ill in America while working on a fifth-grade social studies report grandly titled "The History of Mental Illness, by Pamela Schoenewaldt." But my school library sources had not elaborated the degree to which ignorance linked with ingenious sadism, sheer brutality, and perversion. My Dr. Galuppi is fictional, but his "treatments" were real enough in both Europe and America. Treatment worsened (if possible) when patients were lower class, poor, or female; didn't speak English; had other handicaps; or were simply inconvenient. Of course, compassionate, thoughtful professionals like Dr. Ricci did their dedicated best, and some sanitariums offered healing care to those with means, but too many public institutions were as I described or worse, closed away from public oversight, overcrowded, underfunded, understaffed, brutal, filthy, and unsafe. Lucia was right to fear them.

The forced sterilization that Teresa endured was tragically common. As immigrants poured in, newspapers, public officials, and academics began warning of "germ plasma" infecting good American stock with genetic material prone to insanity, imbecility, indigence, and promiscuity. "Scientific proof" was summoned and delivered. The solution: sterilize the ▶

undesirable "deficients." As one medical historian noted, it's easy to be shocked and scornful of this conflation of racism and pseudoscience, but it remains to be seen how a century's experience will judge our current practices.

*As you wrote, did any of the characters take the story in directions that surprised you, or did you keep them fully in line?*

Although I work out the overall plot before starting to write and begin each chapter with an outline, there are always discoveries and inventions. In successive revisions, one character begins to shape another and hence the plot. For example, Enrico's enthusiastic involvement in the strike deepens Lucia's relationship with him and hence her anguish at his death. Her friendship with Irena, her first true girlfriend, leads to Lucia's discovery that fluency in the same language isn't essential for intimacy; perhaps this experience gives her faith that a mixed marriage can be, in her word, "negotiated." I'm not sure at what point in the writing process I saw Lucia and Teresa walking to Vesuvius in Lake Erie. It wasn't in my original outline, and, yes, that direction certainly surprised me. I'm glad they returned.

The process of novel writing is a constant push and pull of the global and the local, the controlling needs of plot versus the outward push of character. Too much freedom for each character would shred the novel into a series of possibly vivid but less connected sketches, while slavish devotion to a predetermined plot strangles the very characters whose facets, evolution, and contradictions are the soul of any story.

*Your characters always feel so layered and real. Do personalities of loved ones or people you've known and met ever find their way into your writing?*

My first experience of the devastation of mental illness came when I was seventeen and my boyfriend suffered a schizophrenic collapse. One week he was himself, charming, witty, kind, brilliant, and so forth (first love, I was quite smitten). The next week he was incoherent, coarse, delusional, and grotesquely childlike. He was nobody I knew. Like Lucia, I found the shock horrific: What warnings had I missed? Was the mind truly that fragile? Who else in my life might collapse without warning? Could it happen to me? I'm sure my telling of Teresa's collapse was influenced by my own experience.

However, all the characters of *Swimming in the Moon* were inventions, even those loosely based on real people, like the union leaders Isadore Freith and Josephine Carey. It would seem logical that narrative arts are rooted in one's own experience, but in practice it seems to me that most of the layers come from looking into the scene, going over and over the material, seeing and adding more, realizing depths and limitations. My fictional Josephine, for example, probably isn't capable of Lucia's depth of intimate relationships; perhaps her organizational effectiveness comes in part from her emotional distance. Yolanda's friendship has its limits, Lula's bluntness masks a delicate compassion, and Mr. Weiss has a larger heart than his son at first realized.

**Your husband is Italian and you lived near Naples for many years. Do you ever find yourself yearning for the oversize lemons, fresh mozzarella, and sun of Naples? What about your experience, if anything, made its way into this story?**

Of course, I miss much of our life near Naples. It's hard not to. The beauty, the complex history, cuisine, language, art, and customs there are a world away from our current home of Knoxville, Tennessee. Out of nowhere come memories of sunset over the Mediterranean seen from our kitchen window, the coastline and islands, the Baroque intensity of the city, moonlight on medieval castles by the sea, hikes and city walks and long dinners with friends. Yet, in the ten years I lived outside of Naples, most of my writing had American settings. Writing about my adopted country on such short acquaintance seemed presumptuous. Time and distance have made this setting possible for me, as have the measured permissions of the historical fiction genre.

Yet, there is much in today's Naples that Lucia would recognize. The Palazzo Donn'Anna has been made into ▸

### In Conversation with Pamela Schoenewaldt
*(continued)*

apartments and noble titles are officially abolished, but the fish markets still thrive, and you can buy gelato at Caffè Gambrinus as Teresa and Lucia were sent to do. We lived for several months in a *basso* across a narrow basalt-paved street from a mattress-maker. When the power went out, as it often did, the inner room was cave-dark. You can still buy *mozzarella di bufala* made that morning, an exquisite delight like no other. On summer days in Knoxville, what I miss most are the lemon salads that we (and Nannina) made. Try one yourself if you come upon big, sweet, thick-skinned lemons. Peel off the rind, squeeze out a bit of juice, and chop the flesh in bite-size pieces. Add some good olive oil and mix in black salted olives. Enjoy and be refreshed. ∿

# Reading Group Guide

1. Lucia and Teresa's life in Naples had its advantages and challenges. In what ways would Lucia's life have been different if she and Teresa weren't forced to leave?

2. When they leave Italy, Lucia and Teresa are told: "You can be who you want to be in America." True?

3. How does the immigrant experience today compare with that described in *Swimming in the Moon*? Are there other ways in which we are "immigrants" besides the literal moving to a new country?

4. Lucia has a deep emotional connection with Irena, even though they do not share language fluency. What does this say about Lucia and, more generally, about the way that people from different cultures can connect?

5. Lucia earns money by "scribing," writing letters for fellow immigrants. In the process, she often passes on what are essentially lies about their lives. Why? Lucia also lies to the countess in her letters. Why?

6. What sets Lucia apart from the other immigrants in her neighborhood? What do you think Lula means when she says that Lucia "wants so much"? Have you ever felt that you wanted more than you were supposed to want? ▶

7. Teresa's absence while she is on the vaudeville circuit and her emotional and mental problems deprive Lucia of a sustaining maternal figure and ultimately make Lucia her mother's caretaker. How does Lucia compensate for this loss?

8. In America, Lucia's thoughts often return to her life in Naples. What various functions do you think these memories fulfill as she comes to adulthood?

9. How does Teresa's beautiful voice both divide her from and bind her to Lucia? What does the voice do—and not do—for Teresa? How does Lucia develop her own voice?

10. What challenges do workers in the novel face? How do they compare with those facing workers today?

11. What factors drive Lucia to take up the issue of workers' rights so passionately and endure so many sacrifices for the strike, even when the worker community is often bitterly divided?

12. Lucia learns that only eight in one hundred Americans in her time have high school diplomas. Far fewer, of course, went to college. Graduation has a variety of meanings for Lucia. Can you discuss some of them? Yet, toward the end of the novel, formal education becomes less crucial. Why?

13. What draws Lucia and Henryk together? What pulls them apart? Compare their evolving relationship with that of other couples in the novel: Elisabetta and Paolo, the Reillys, Yolanda and Charlie, Giovanna and Frank.

14. Lucia vividly recalls a line from John Milton's *Paradise Lost*: "The mind is its own place and in itself, can make a Heaven of Hell, a Hell of Heaven." How does this line relate to Lucia and Teresa's circumstances—and to all of our lives?

15. While the past century has brought profound changes in the treatment of mental illness, in what way is Teresa and Lucia's experience timeless?

16. What is the significance of the title, *Swimming in the Moon*? What image does it conjure for you?

17. Why did you or your group choose to read *Swimming in the Moon*? What did you take away from reading the novel? ✐

# Suggested Reading

HERE ARE SOME BOOKS I've read recently
(although not all were written recently)
in which the beauty and power of the
voice seemed wonderfully honed for
the stories they told:

*My Father's Notebook,* by Kader Abdolah
*Little Bee,* by Chris Cleave
*Peace Like a River,* by Leif Enger
*Good King Harry,* by Denise Giardina
*Plainsong,* by Kent Haruf
*The Remains of the Day,*
    by Kazuo Ishiguro
*Mister Pip,* by Lloyd Jones
*Strength in What Remains,*
    by Tracy Kidder
*Humphry Clinker,* by Tobias Smollett
*The Space Between Us,*
    by Thrity Umrigar

# Have You Read?
## More by
## Pamela Schoenewaldt

**WHEN WE WERE STRANGERS**

Too poor and too plain to marry, and unwilling to burden what family she has left, twenty-year-old Irma Vitale sees no choice but to flee her Italian mountain village. Risking rough passage across the Atlantic and the dangers facing a single woman in an unfamiliar land, Irma boldly pursues a new life sewing dresses for gentlewomen.

Swept up in the crowded streets of nineteenth-century America, Irma finds not only workshop servitude and miserable wages, but also seeds of friendship in the raw immigrant quarters. When her determination to find a place for herself leads at last to a Chicago shop, Irma blossoms under the guidance of an austere Alsatian dressmaker, sewing fabrics and patterns more beautiful than she'd ever imagined. Then tragedy strikes and her tenuous peace is shattered. From the rubble, and in the face of human cruelty and kindness, suffering and hope, Irma prevails, discovering a talent she'd never imagined and an unlikely family patched together by the common threads that unite us all.

Don't miss the next book by your favorite author. Sign up now for AuthorTracker by visiting www.AuthorTracker.com.

1/14